"The garage extended i.___
next to the garage door. The first floor had a window, which opened onto the roof of the garage. To exit the back, the gunman would either come through the garage, the door next to it or the window onto the garage rooftop.

Heeding the shouts of the onlookers Carr pressed himself against the doorjamb of the door. People in the crowd were screaming: *"He's coming out the back window! See him!"*

Carr unsnapped his holster and took out his Glock. The pistolrange instructor's words echoed in his memory: *if you have to shoot, shoot for the torso and empty your weapon.*

The advice makes sense. The belief that one can easily shoot a gun from a person's hand is a myth. The Lone Ranger Syndrome, Carr called it. Only an expert with opportunity to aim could accomplish such a feat. Otherwise, it's done by accident.

Aiming at the roof of the garage, Carr placed his finger on the trigger. There was little illumination. Only enough for a silhouette. If he saw a gun, he was going to fire.

Someone in the crowd shouted: *"There he is! He's got a gun!"* Carr started to depress the trigger...

SENSE

OF

DUTY

By

Michael P. Tremoglie

SENSE OF DUTY

By Michael P. Tremoglie
All rights reserved
Copyright 2006

ISBN 0-9777403-0-7

For information contact the author at elfegobaca@comcast.net

Chapter 1

He didn't believe he was actually going through with it. As he pulled into the parking lot, the knot in his stomach reminded him of his lingering doubts. The letter said to report to the auditorium at 8:30 a.m. It was 8:45.

Dawn had become morning since he departed his house. The humidity was rising in tandem with the sun as he walked to the main building. The stillness of the moment was disturbed only by the steady hum of air-conditioning units. The relative quiet also underscored the fact that everyone else was in class, prompting the knot in his stomach to become larger.

Once inside, he opened the nearest auditorium door. It squeaked loudly. The people seated within turned and looked. A man addressing the assembly paused to glare at him. Sheepishly, he walked to the front, his approach heralded by the sound of his own footsteps -- the only noise in the auditorium. He handed his appointment letter to an officer standing next to the podium, quickly finding a seat in the front row.

"I miss anything important?" he muttered to the person next to him.

A frown was his reply.

The speaker resumed talking. He was not dressed in the robin's-egg blue shirt of a rank-and-file police officer. Instead, his shirt was white, adorned with shoulder epaulets that featured gold bars. A gold and silver lieutenant's badge was worn over his left breast and a name tag with *Iseminger* above the right shirt pocket.

Lieutenant Iseminger looked to be in his early 50's, average height, medium build with dark hair. He spoke in a grim, sonorous tone.

"This dude sounds as dull as Al Gore," he mumbled sarcastically. His remark elicited smirks from the people next to him.

"He may sound like Al Gore, but this ain't Florida," whispered his frowning neighbor.

"Florida?" he whispered.

"The land of oranges and chads," responded the frowning classmate.

A scowl by one of the instructors next to Iseminger silenced them. They both began to listen attentively.

Iseminger informed them the Police Academy Commandant would address the audience at 10 a.m. They would then be issued badges and sworn in.

"Before the day is done," Iseminger announced, "you will be measured for your uniforms and organized into platoons. As soon as the platoons are organized, the officers and sergeants will introduce themselves."

"I am going to dismiss you now until 9:30," the lieutenant said. "A buzzer will sound and let you know when to return."

"Class, dismissed!" Iseminger called out.

The 160 men and women of the Philadelphia Police Academy's 255th class stirred from their seats and slowly drifted out of the auditorium. The latecomer moved with the flow of the crowd bound for the outside.

He leaned his 6-foot, 190-pound frame against a wall and lit a cigarette. He took long, deliberate drags, systematically puffing smoke rings while surveying his classmates.

A lot of *Jerry Springer* fans, he thought contemptuously. My old professor used to say cops are uneducated Neanderthals, recruited from the criminal classes. Some of these people seem just like that. *Damn, what am I doing here?*

During the months he had been unemployed prior to entering the police academy, the reluctant recruit was notified by his wife that she did not want to support him. Not exactly the quintessential feminist, she told him he was supposed to be the breadwinner, not her.

Although he subscribed to the Howard and Marion Cunningham marital role model, he figured it was better for them if she worked while he finished college. Then he could find a good-paying job with a future. *Then*, they could have the kids she said she wanted.

This reasoning proved unpersuasive. She was a 26-year-old woman who wanted to have kids before her biological clock struck twelve.

He was at a fork in the road. Most of his contemporaries had completed college and were progressing in their chosen careers. He felt like the kid who couldn't get a date to the prom.

Ahh, stop whining, he chided himself. You made your choice, now stick with it. Besides, it was a lot of aggravation getting here.

The hiring of a Philadelphia police officer is a protracted and laborious affair. There are several parts to the process. The first is the civil service examination.

Eleven thousand people were scheduled to take the three-hour test the same day he did. The exam consisted of three sections: Mathematics, English and Recall Skills. The scores were mailed eight months after the tests were taken. His was a 94, placing him in the top three percent -- still trailing 355 other candidates.

Many of those ranked ahead of him posted inferior scores, but enjoyed a 10-point boost denied others taking the exam. The inequity was traceable to a federal court order demanding redress for past hiring discrimination against women and minorities.

Even this couldn't obviate an excellent test score, leading to the latecomer's inclusion in the first tier of candidates selected for academy training. His invitation came by mail and read:

Michael Carr
2703 S. 8th St.
Phila., PA 19149

Dear Mr. Carr:

Congratulations on having passed the written examination for Police Officer. All applicants who pass the written examination will be required to pass a medical examination, psychiatric screening and a background investigation before they can be appointed. Accordingly, we have scheduled you for a medical examination at the time and place indicated above. Please allow a full day for processing. If you fail to report, we will place your name in the inactive file.

The physical was scheduled for the following Monday. It consisted of a doctor's examination, a psychological and vision test (including color and depth perception), plus an electrocardiogram, an X-ray of the lower back, and an audio test.

Most of the day required monotonous waiting. However, the psychological exam he found amusing. It consisted of two parts. Part one was a written questionnaire of about 350 questions of the "Do you believe you are a messenger of God?" genre.

The second was an interview by a psychologist, who, judging by his lethargic attitude, was just going through the motions. If he were interviewing the 'Son of Sam' he would not have known.

His next appointment was scheduled nine days later - for another interview - at the Police Academy, in Philadelphia's Torresdale section, about fifteen miles from his house.

He arrived a little before the 9 a.m. reporting time. As Carr drove into the Academy he passed a grove of trees that included some saplings. Each of the trees was marked with a small sign, which Carr thought identified the type of foliage for the benefit of passersby.

He drove past the main building, containing the classrooms, the auditorium, and administrative offices. Also on the grounds are the pistol range, ordnance disposal unit, K-9 kennels, an obstacle course, two trailers used for office space, and a parking lot.

His appointment led him into one of the office trailers. There he was interviewed by a police sergeant who asked a few questions based on the employment application Carr completed several months earlier.

After some small talk about what the life of a police officer was like, the interview concluded. The sergeant told Carr to go home; he would be notified when to report for a polygraph exam.

Leaving the trailer, Carr walked over to the grove. He noticed the signs didn't identify the genera of the trees, but, rather, proclaimed the names of police officers killed in the line of duty. Carr stood there for a few minutes and read the names, some of which he recalled from news reports.

Mike was pensive during the drive home. He was preoccupied with the upcoming polygraph examination. He had heard many things about lie detector tests, none of them good. Of all the parts of the hiring process, the polygraph caused him the most apprehension.

The purpose of the polygraph was to extract detrimental information an applicant might be concealing. Especially significant to the Department was any history of drug use.

The Philadelphia Police modified their hiring policy with regard to drugs. Considering contemporary mores, it had become increasingly difficult to find prospective police officers who had never experimented with marijuana. Consequently, the standards on drug use had been relaxed.

Carr had not touched grass since leaving high school. Yet, for some inexplicable reason, the idea of being questioned about the subject upset him.

He received a phone call the following Monday, telling him to report Friday morning for the polygraph test. The exam was to be administered in the trailer adjacent to the one he had recently visited.

Friday came, and Carr awaited his turn on a bench in the lobby of the academy's main building. Detective J.D. Ryan was administering the tests. This five-year veteran of the Polygraph Unit was heavy-set and pugnacious in appearance. He also liked his work.

Richard Nixon is said to have once remarked, "I don't know how accurate (polygraphs) are, but I know that they'll scare the hell out of people." Scaring the hell out of the recruits is exactly what the Philadelphia Police Department had in mind, and J.D. Ryan was the right man for the job.

The detective sat back in his chair looking through the file on the next applicant. As he did, he recalled the first thing he learned in polygraph school from his instructor, Lieutenant Leithgow: "The desire to determine if one is telling the truth is as old as mankind. Various methods have been used over the ages in an attempt to accomplish this goal."

The Chinese had a clever way of determining whether or not someone was telling the truth, Leithgow observed. Their system was the basis for modern lie-detection. Several suspects were given mouthfuls of rice. The one who had the most difficulty spitting out the rice was considered guilty. The Chinese believed, correctly, that guilt feelings would manifest themselves in bodily functions. The one lying would have a dry mouth.

The modern lie detector came into being through the efforts of three former police officers: John Larson, Leonard Keeler and August Vollmer. They recorded changes in pulse rate, respiration and blood pressure, endorsing the ancient belief that the guilt of a lie would be manifested physically.

One of the problems with this theory is that people who are introspective undergo stress merely by being interrogated -- like the 'A' student whose mind goes blank when taking a final exam. Conversely, people who are amoral will not feel guilty about any illegal or unethical act they have committed.

It is the skill of the examiner, the type of questions, and the manner in which they are asked that determine the legitimacy of polygraph results. It is for these reasons that exams are excluded as evidence in court.

"Carr, Michael," growled Ryan, as he walked quickly through the lobby.

"Over here," was Carr's meek response.

"Follow me," Ryan ordered, gruffly.

Inside of the trailer was a desk with two chairs, a row of file cabinets, and a chair perpendicular to a table on which the polygraph was placed. Carr knew it was the polygraph because he could see the paper scrolled horizontally through the machines and the pens that rested on the paper. Emanating from the machine were several wires attached to instruments such as a blood-pressure cuff and some electrodes.

"Sit down," Ryan instructed in a surly manner.

Carr realized it was going to be a long morning.

"I'm gonna begin by askin' ya the same questions that you answered on the employment application," Ryan explained. "Then I'm gonna ask ya if you answered all these questions truthfully. Then I'm gonna ask ya some more questions to which you either answer yes or no, you follow me?"

"Yeah," Carr replied stiffly.

Ryan asked him questions from the employment application. Next came a series of questions about his personal habits. Ryan began with what Carr considered the most bizarre inquiry he had ever heard.

"Have you ever done anything illegal for which you haven't been caught?" Ryan asked matter-of-factly.

The question triggered a great deal of anxiety and introspection in Carr. He recalled all the times in grammar school he pilfered chewing gum from the corner candy store. He recalled how he used to buy wine and whiskey with a fake ID card when he was in high school. He remembered how he had smoked marijuana a couple of times, and how he had once sold some uppers. In short, Michael Carr underwent a catharsis. He remembered every infraction he had ever committed, and then recited them to Ryan -- in detail.

Ryan listened patiently. With the possible exceptions of the drug use and sale, the detective thought, all the things Carr was saying were petty and irrelevant. The fact is, unless the incidents involving drug use had occurred in the previous six months, they, too, would be irrelevant.

"When did ya sell the uppers?" asked Ryan.

"When I was in high school," Carr replied.

"You haven't sold anything since?" Ryan continued -- this time with an intentional trace of skepticism in his voice.

"No," answered Carr.

"OK, I'm gonna hook you up to the machine. I'm gonna ask ya the same questions we just went through, and I want you to give me the same answers. If you want to change an answer, wait 'til we're done. Follow me?"

"Yeah."

"OK, let's go."

Ryan motioned to Carr to sit in the chair near the polygraph where he could be hooked up to the machine. The pressure cuff was applied, a coil was placed around Carr's chest and electrodes attached to his fingers. Ryan then switched on the polygraph and began the interrogation. Carr watched as Ryan repeatedly glanced from questionnaire to device while making notations on both, becoming anxious every time his interrogator spoke. He tried to ease his anxiety by looking at the file cabinets, out of the window, or closing his eyes while listening to the drone of the air conditioner.

Nothing worked. When Ryan got to the question of drug abuse, the knot in Carr's stomach grew tighter.

"Have you ever sold, distributed, used, or possessed a controlled substance?"

"Yes."

"When?"

"Nine years ago."

Ryan scribbled a note.

"Have you ever committed a crime for which you haven't been caught?" Ryan asked again.

Carr answered with a renewed recounting of his various misdeeds, expanded this time by admissions of just-remembered instances of the abuse and illicit sale of drugs.

Ryan stopped the machine and said with a degree of exasperation, "Look, I think you're reachin' a bit too much here. I don't need to know all this stuff about stealing gum and cigarettes, drinking and smoking on subways. I do need to know if you ever used drugs in the last six months."

"I told you, the last time was when I was in high school."

"Nuthin' after that?"

"No."

Ryan turned the machine on; they went through the questions again.

After a few more minutes, he shut off the machine, pushed his chair back, looked at Carr and frowned.

He then disconnected Carr from the polygraph.

Carr got up from *the chair* (as he was beginning to think of it) and sat back down next to the desk. Ryan rolled his chair behind the desk and looked at Carr.

"I still think you're reachin', and we're not gettin' anywhere," Ryan said in resignation. "I'm gonna recommend that you take this test again."

By now, Carr just wanted out of there. He didn't care if they believed him or not. He didn't care if they hired him or not. He just wanted out of that room.

"What do I have to do?" Carr asked.

"Nothing. We'll be in touch," Ryan said, tersely.

Mike nodded to Ryan as he walked out of the trailer. Walking back to his car, he glanced at his watch. It was almost noon -- three hours after he arrived. During that time, the humidity had become oppressive. Yes, it was a hot day. The temperature would continue to climb -- both meteorologically and in ways not measurable by the Fahrenheit gauge.

Driving down the expressway, Carr wondered what he would tell his wife, Stella. She was very excited about the prospect of his becoming a police officer. She would be upset if she thought his appointment to the force might be delayed.

Mike parked in front of his row house -- an uncommon opportunity in a city where convenient parking is even rarer than honest politicians. As he pulled in, he noticed that the front door and all the windows were closed. This was a sure sign that the air conditioning was on. When he entered the house, he was hit with a gratifying blast of cold air.

Stella was in the kitchen talking on the phone with her mother. When she heard him enter, she peeked over the breakfast nook.

"Ma, lemme call you back," she said just before hanging up the phone.

"Well, how was it?"she asked, excitedly.

"I have to go back," her husband replied.

"Whaddaya mean you gotta go back?" Stella's reaction was more of an accusation than a question.

"Just what I said," answered Mike, now becoming testy.

"But why?" she pleaded.

"Because they couldn't tell if I was telling the truth or not."

"Why not?"

"How the hell do I know? Ask them."

Stella said nothing. She simply turned away and walked upstairs.

He heard her use the bedroom phone to call her mother and tell her the news. Figures, Carr thought.

Two weeks passed before he returned to the polygraph trailer. Stella was miserable the entire time -- convinced that he had purposely tried to fail the test. Her doubting his integrity infuriated him.

By the day of the second polygraph, he had shed all prior anxieties. Instead of dreading the prospect, in a way, he was looking forward to the return. He saw it as an opportunity for vindication. He reported to the same trailer and was met by a small, thin man named Torres.

"C'mon in," said Torres, with a trace of an accent he took to be Puerto Rican. He once dated a Puerto Rican girl, he recalled with a smile. She taught him how to dance the Salsa and Merengue.

"We're gonna go over the exam from the last time and I'm gonna ask you a few questions. Then, I'm gonna put you on the machine. You follow me?"

"Yeah," Carr replied.

In contrast to Detective Ryan, Torres was very relaxed, friendly, and not the least bit intimidating. Torres also made Carr feel comfortable when he hooked him up to the polygraph. He could hear the rustle of paper behind him as Torres began the examination. Indeed, he was barely conscious of being questioned amid the drone of an air conditioner.

"During the past six months, have you ever used, possessed, or sold a controlled substance?" Torres asked in a calm and even tone.

"No," Mike answered calmly and evenly. He heard Torres write something down.

"Listen, I only want to know if you used, possessed, sold, or distributed a controlled substance in the last six months. Before that I don't care if you smoked it, snorted it, injected it, or handed it out for free. I don't care if you had the largest distribution network on the East Coast. I just want to know if you did it in the last six months."

"Have you ever used, distributed, sold, or possessed a controlled substance?"

"Yes."

"Have you ever used, possessed, sold, or distributed a controlled substance within the last six months?"

"No."

Torres once again shuffled paper and wrote some things down. He then leaned over and disconnected the polygraph apparatus.

"OK, you're finished."

"Well?" Mike asked.

"You passed."

Carr looked at Torres then asked: "So you think I'm telling the truth? I mean, you believe me?"

"Yeah, but it was close," smiled Torres.

"What's next?" Mike asked.

"A background investigation has to be done."

"After all this you still have to do a background check?"

"Yeah, you'd be surprised what we find," said Torres. "All you have to do is go home and wait for someone to contact you."

"Same as always," mumbled Carr.

"Good luck," added Torres.

Carr left the trailer with a feeling of exhilaration that stayed with him all the way home. As he drove down Interstate 95, he sang along to the radio.

When he arrived, he found Stella waiting for him on their front step. She was wearing a two-piece short set. She looked sexy. She had a great figure that her outfit accentuated. He thought she would be in a good mood after learning he passed the polygraph.

"Well?" she asked excitedly as he approached the porch.

"I passed," Carr replied, much more glibly than he really felt.

"Now what?" she demanded. "Whaddaya haf to do now?"

"They have to do a background check."

"Jeez, one more problem."

"What's that supposed to mean?"

"It means you'll find another way to delay starting this job."

"Don't start that again about me trying to get out of this job. If I didn't want this job, I wouldn't take it. I don't need your permission," he replied angrily and then stormed into the house. He went to the refrigerator and took out a beer, leaned against the counter and lit a cigarette.

After the background check all that remained was official notification of his admission to the academy. He received it in a letter bearing the seal of the city of Philadelphia and postmarked August 1, 2003. It read:

Dear Police Officer Applicant:
You have been selected for appointment as a police officer in the Philadelphia Police Department and will begin training at the Police Academy on Monday, August 25, 2003 at 8:30 a.m.

If disqualifying information is discovered subsequent to your appointment, you will be separated from the position of Police Officer.

Bring a valid PA driver's license when you report to the Police Academy. Female applicants should wear slacks on this date to facilitate uniform measurement. Also, know the following measurements: Shirt size (collar and sleeve), Shoe size (length and width). Please bring this letter with you and if, for any reason, you are unable to report on the above date, contact Ms. Hicks immediately by telephone at the number printed at the bottom of this page. Should you fail to report as instructed, without prior notice to us, we will assume that you are no longer interested in such employment and your name will be removed from the existing eligibility list.

The sound of the buzzer announcing the end of the break brought Carr back to the present. The recruits of Class 255 filed into the building. Slowly, Carr took one last drag from his menthol cigarette.

Iseminger greeted the returning police candidates: "All right, knock off the chatter. As you return to your seat, I want you to take your chair and find a spot near the wall."

The recruits did as they were told -- in part. The many conversations -- interspersed with the sounds of chairs being folded and dragged on the linoleum -- created a din.

"Knock it off!" Iseminger repeatedly yelled over the noise.

"Sergeant McKean here is gonna call your names out. You will respond, 'Here, sir!' He will then assign you a platoon and tell you where to sit."

"You will remain standing beside your chair until the roll call is completed. Does everybody understand?"

There was a chorus of mumbles.

"Does everybody understand?" Iseminger bellowed.

"Yes, sir!" the class replied loudly - in unison.

Sergeant McKean called out the names in alphabetical order. Carr was assigned to 'A' platoon. He took his chair and placed it near the end of the second row. In front of him was a small, heavy-set man with dark hair and glasses. To his left was a woman with blond hair, a slight build and a pretty face. On his right was an African-American woman, short and rather well-developed. Behind Carr were three guys, all of whom looked as if they could play on the Eagles' offensive line. Two were white and one black.

After completing the seating arrangements, the platoon commanders introduced themselves. Carr's platoon officer was a corporal who stood about 6-feet, 5-inches and appeared to weigh 250 pounds.

"Good morning, I am Corporal Wood," the blue giant said in a booming voice. "I am your class officer. I report to Sergeant McKean."

"In about 20 minutes, the Commandant of the Academy, Chief Inspector Igor Pulaski, will issue you your badges and swear in the class. In those 20 minutes I want to hand out some information to you regarding the clothes to be worn and the materials needed. After you receive your handout, we will discuss anything you feel needs to be clarified."

The handout also stated that recruits would need a white handkerchief, a three-ring binder, pen, pencils and a notepad.

"Are there any questions?" inquired Corporal Wood.

"Yeah, what's the handkerchief for?" shouted out someone in the last row.

"You might as well start learning this right now," Wood chided. "If you want to say something, you raise your hand. When you're acknowledged, you either start or finish everything you say with 'sir' or 'ma'am.' Understood?"

"Yes, sir," replied the recruit.

"OK, once again. Are there any questions?"

"Sir, what is the handkerchief for?"

"The handkerchief is a handy little item that all police officers should carry. In addition to the usual functions, a handkerchief is useful for administering first aid and handling evidence. Anyone else?"

"Sir, what will we need the notebook for?"

"Again, a handy little piece of equipment. While in the academy, you can use it to copy down your roster each week. The roster will be posted on the bulletin board around the side of the auditorium. In the field, the notepad is good for copying roll call instructions and for interviews. Anyone else?"

No one had any more questions.

"If that's the case, let me just say that you will have to purchase everything by next week," Wood said as he glanced to the rear of the auditorium.

"I notice the commandant is here," remarked the platoon officer. "Get ready to stand at attention when he enters."

"ATTEN-SHUN!" one of the instructors called from the front of the room. The class responded accordingly.

As recruits and instructors stood stiffly and silently, Inspector Igor Pulaski entered. The 55-year-old Commandant of the Training Bureau was tall, solidly built, with a pugnaciously square jaw and gray hair around the temples. Pulaski walked ramrod straight with a smooth, deliberate gait -- one befitting a former Marine. Conventional wisdom held that this 30-year veteran of the force was the likely successor to the incumbent police commissioner.

Pulaski welcomed the class and declared what was expected from its members. He then ordered badges to be issued, cautioning recruits against attempts to arrest anyone while heading home.

"But it's OK if you go to sleep with the badge."

The commandant's joke elicited a few laughs around the room. Pulaski swore in the recruits, delivered a short speech and dismissed the class for lunch.

After lunch, the recruits assembled for another roll call then took their seats in the auditorium to listen to a succession of lectures. The speakers were mostly departmental bureaucrats introducing their audience to health-plan options, the police pension plan, and other benefits.

Generally, the speakers were as dull as an Al Franken monologue. An exception, in Carr's view, was a captain who recounted his first few days at the academy. He spoke about how he needed a job and figured this would do for a couple of years until something better came along.

"That was 23 years ago," said the captain.

The class spent the balance of the afternoon being measured for uniforms and receiving textbooks. Once they were dismissed, a dejected Carr walked to his automobile. He tossed his badge onto the seat next to him. It bore the number 4650, a combination insignificant to Carr (save for its mandated inclusion on every official document he would file as a policeman), but one his wife was certain to play in both the state and mob-run lotteries.

When he arrived home, Stella seemed to be very excited by the return of her police officer husband. "Well, how was it?" she asked with a wide grin.

"Fine," he replied, with an edge in his voice. He walked past her on his way upstairs to get changed.

"You don't have to be so smart about it," she said, testily.

"Lighten up. I'm tired. I'm not used to waking up early in the morning."

"I was just asking," she replied.

"You want to see my badge?" Carr asked, changing the tone of the conversation.

"Yeah," she said, eagerly.

He took the badge from his pocket and handed it to her. As he predicted, she immediately noticed the number.

"4650," she said. "I wonder if I should play 465 or 650 or 405 or 605."

She took the badge to the kitchen, got a pencil and paper and wrote down the different combinations.

"Play them all," Carr shouted as he went up the stairs. "I'm gonna take a shower."

"Ya get your uniform yet?" she asked as she went to her purse.

"Not for a couple of months. Don't need it. The academy uniform is plain white shirt, navy blue pants and black shoes. I've got to go shoppin' tonight. Mebbe I'll call Tommy and Leon and ask 'em to come with me."

"OK, you call them. I want to go aroun' the corner and play your badge number."

After showering, Carr phoned Tom Marshall. Although Mike and Tom had only known each other a few years, they had become extremely close. They met while working for a local bank. Tom later finished college and was now working as an accountant.

Carr also called his cousin Leon Dover, who was a veteran police officer. He had served with distinction during his several years on the force and was now a sergeant in the 17th District.

Mike made arrangements to pick them up in an hour. He was getting dressed when Stella returned.

"You want somethin' to eat before ya go?" she asked.

"Nah, I'll just eat some cake."

"That's no good. Sit down. I'll make you somethin'."

"No, I gotta get Leon and Tom."

"I'll make you somethin' real quick. It'll take five minutes."

"OK," he replied and sat down.

Stella made him a roast beef sandwich and some mashed potatoes. Mike quickly gulped them down. He put the dishes in the sink, gave his wife a kiss and left.

"If either one of them calls, tell them I'm on my way."

About 10 minutes later Mike was knocking on Leon's front door.

"So how was your first day?" asked Leon as he got into the car. The look he received told him all he needed to know.

"I don't understand you Mike," Leon said with feigned exasperation. "Cousin Stu took the police exam twice already. He flunked both times and he's gonna try again. He's aching to get on and you're pissin' away the opportunity. You're doing something a lot of guys would love to do right now. Look how many took the exam who won't get called. "

"I am insulted that you compare me to Stu," Carr said with mock indignation. "That boy's got the IQ of house dust. Besides, being a cop is distracting me from my dream career."

"Which is?" asked Leon, taking the bait.

"Owning a national chain of adult bookstores," Mike said in as serious a tone as he could muster.

Leon moaned as Mike drove off to get Tom. The trip was brief.

"Hey, how's the newest member of Philadelphia's Finest?" asked Tom as he climbed in the back seat.

"You too?" the driver complained.

"Our baby boy here is not a happy camper right now Tom," Leon explained.

"Whatzamatter? Nobody play with you today? Nobody shared their toys?"

"Share this," Mike replied.

"So you don't like it?" Tom asked.

"I told you. I want to do what you're doing," replied Mike.

"So what's stopping you?"

"Stella! She doesn't want me to go to college. She wants to start having kids."

"You gotta do what makes you happy," said Tom.

"It's not that simple, Tom. I'm not like you. I've got responsibilities. I can't just do what I damn well please," argued Carr, irritably.

"You gotta responsibility to yourself," answered Tom.

"My responsibility to her is my responsibility to myself."

The shopping expedition took only a little more than an hour. Mike purchased everything he needed and drove his friends home. He dropped off Tom then headed for his cousin's place.

As Leon got out of the car, he urged Mike, "Try it, Mike. Give it a chance. Who knows? As our Sicilian grandfather used to say: "Camina chi pantofuli finu a quannau non hai i scarpi. Walk with your slippers until you find your shoes. "

"Okay, so what in hell does that mean? "Mike asked with a quizzical expression.

"Make the best of a bad situation."

"Now I know why our mothers married Americans," Carr replied with a laugh.

"You might like it after awhile. It might even grow on you," insisted Leon

"Yeah, like a fungus," Mike muttered as he drove off.

Chapter 2

Philadelphia Police recruits receive the state-mandated minimum hours of law-enforcement instruction. However, the city requires additional hours, yielding a rigorous aggregate of 19 weeks of training. The Academy offers a comprehensive curriculum. Before they can graduate, police cadets must evidence: competence with firearms and conversance with restrictions regarding their use; a solid grasp of governmental procedures; criminal-law precepts and courtroom proceedings; extensive knowledge regarding search-and-seizure protocol; accident-reporting guidelines; first-aid techniques; the motor-vehicle code; a high level of physical fitness, developed through vigorous exercise and classes in self-defense; sensitivity to cultural diversity, female victims of crime, the disabled and the homeless.

All in all, it is a training program designed to prepare the modern police officer for the pathologies he is likely to confront in contemporary urban America.

Michael Carr -- badge number 4650 -- began his second day as a police recruit by struggling to arrive on time. He succeeded -- no small accomplishment for someone who, during a lengthy period of joblessness, grew accustomed to sleeping until noon.

The drive to work came under an overcast sky amid cool, variable breezes. The latter represented a pleasant change from the oppressive heat and humidity of late-summer Philadelphia.

Upon arrival, Carr joined his platoon as it was forming for morning roll call -- five ranks, eight recruits each. Moments later, Corporal Wood appeared with clipboard in hand.

"Class, atten-shun," Wood growled. "First thing we're going to do this morning is learn the proper procedure for standing roll call. Your also gonna know what is expected of you in terms of appropriate appearance, and how to march."

Wood paused and glared at the platoon, "At roll call you will follow the procedure used in class. When I approach, you will stand at attention. I will call your name and you will respond, 'Here, sir!'"

With that, Wood began reading the recruit roster.

"Adams!"

"Yo!"

"Adams! Didn't you hear me? The appropriate response is, 'Here, sir.'"

"Yes sir!"

"Let's try it again. Adams!"

"Here, sir!"

"Allen!"

"Here, sir!"

After Wood ran through the names, he parked the clipboard under his arm and addressed the recruits.

"Before we begin our drill, we are going to choose a platoon leader. The platoon leader will be responsible for calling the platoon to formation before roll call. The platoon leader will, in my absence, direct the platoon on marches.

"Who has military experience?" the corporal demanded. About half-a-dozen men raised their hands. Wood pointed to the one farthest from him. "What is your name?" he asked.

"Darien, sir!" replied a short, muscular, red-haired recruit in his late 20s.

"From here on you will be platoon leader. Roll call is held twice a day -- at 8:20 a.m. and after lunch. Twice a week there will be inspections, to be conducted by Sergeant McKean. Your formation point will be to the left of the front door of the main building. Does everyone understand?"

There were random and weak replies of "yes, sir."

"I can't hear you!" barked Wood in the classic manner of a drill instructor.

"Yes, sir!" answered the platoon, this time vigorously and in unison.

"Any announcements or special instructions will also be given at roll. After that you will be dispatched to class with this command: 'Class, to your post, *harch*!'"

"Speaking of marching," Wood said with a wry smile, "we're gonna do some of that right now."

There was a general moan from the class.

"All right, knock it off! I'm gonna call the class to attention. The proper stance for this is heels together, toes apart at a forty-five degree angle. Darien will demonstrate."

"Yes, sir!" Darien said enthusiastically. The veteran marched crisply to the front of the platoon, displaying the military posture Wood had requested.

"Now when I say *right face*," Wood continued, "you will raise your right foot, place it behind your left, resting your right on the ball of the foot. Next, you will raise your left heel and pivot to the right, move the right heel to the ground, while planting the left foot next to the right -- again, with heels together, toes apart at the aforementioned forty-five degree angle."

Wood again turned to Darien. "Darien, please demonstrate this for the class."

On cue, Darien executed the maneuver with martial precision. The rest of the platoon followed. Only a few made mistakes.

Wood then had the platoon learn the command "left face."

Finally, Wood said, "I want to show you one more. Darien, demonstrate an about-face."

Darien did so. Following Wood's instructions, he directed classmates in a similar movement and then marched the unit to the first parking lot and back.

"Platoon, ABOUT-FACE!" commanded Darien. The recruits, in unison, carried out the order, as they did his successive instructions in the march to and from the rear of the grinder. The drill was executed with few errors.

Wood reassumed command with a firm voice. "Platoon, forward *harch*! Left, right left," Wood bellowed, slipping into a rhythmic form of cadence. "To your left, right, left, right, left ... goooyour left, right, left ... to yoooour left, right, left ... goyour left ... goyour left."

"Listen to him, he's singing," whispered Mildred Oxford, a former auxiliary police officer in Wildwood, N.J. Below average in height -- she was 4'10" -- and 90 pounds soaking wet, Oxford possessed a remarkably obnoxious attitude.

As the platoon passed by the main building, Wood ordered his charges to halt.

"*Right face*," he said. "*At ease*."

"Any questions?"

"No, sir!" came the chorus.

Wood responded with his closing order: "Class, to your post, HARCH!"

"A" Platoon marched into the auditorium for Intro to Government, taught by an officer who looked to be in his late 50s. The instructor, who was capping nearly 30 years as a Philadelphia officer by teaching government at a 4th-grade level, did not impress Carr.

Then again, Carr thought derisively, 4th grade was a fair estimate of the mental capacities of his classmates. His low opinion was born partly from his own vocational frustration and partly from the puerile behavior displayed by many of his fellow platoon members. The sight of a classmate throwing spitballs disgusted him. This clown and others like him would eventually be responsible for defending the weak and innocent, thought Carr. How would they deal with crises as sworn officers when they act so immaturely now? The question answered itself.

Unfortunately, there wasn't a way to screen out adolescents in adult bodies. The psychological examination seemed focused on identifying religious fanatics rather than measuring the maturity or honesty of would-be officers.

The remainder of "Week One" was comparable to the first few days at any other school. Instructors distributed syllabi, textbooks and introduced their respective subjects. Carr was adapting to the routine, though not without some inconvenience. By the close of the training week Friday afternoon, he was yawning with frequency.

However, his fatigue was forgotten once he returned home and beheld a smiling and seductive Stella. At first, Mike was puzzled. However, not for long. Today was their wedding anniversary.

Carr had been so preoccupied with his first week at the Academy that he forgot about plans for a trip to Atlantic City. The delicious sight of Stella -- her marvelous physical attributes tightly wrapped in a sultry ensemble of evening wear -- cleared away the mental fog and revived thoughts of their conjugal itinerary.

They had decided to drive to Atlantic City that evening, check into a room at one of the casinos and stay the night. He welcomed the opportunity. Carr needed the diversion from the stress and frustration of recent weeks. A night on the town would help. Even better would be a night of passion. It had been months since Stella and Mike had made love. Perhaps Atlantic City would defrost the icy gulf that separated them --- physically and otherwise.

"I gotta go to the store and get some panty hose," Stella said as he walked in the house. "You go get showered and shaved."

"Okay, how 'bout we leave in an hour," he replied, careful not to betray his lapse in memory.

"Yeah, that'll be good."

"Ya look hot, babe," said Carr.

"Oh, yeah," said Stella coyly.

"I know a place on the way down that has mirrors on the ceiling and heart-shaped tubs," continued Carr.

"How would you know about such things?" asked Stella. She was smiling as she approached him.

"A friend of mine told me," Carr deadpanned.

"Oh, yeah, what's her name?" asked Stella in mock outrage. "What did she tell you?"

"It was a *he*, and he went there with his wife. Of course, if you want me to check it out with someone else, I will. Never let it be said that I don't do what my wife tells me to do. I'm always willing to go that extra mile for you, babe."

"I'll give you an extra mile," Stella said pinching him at the waist. "You're getting fat."

"Just more for you to love."

Carr didn't take very long to get ready. Within 30 minutes, the drab attire of a police recruit had been discarded in favor of a taupe Italian shirt, chocolate brown slacks and taupe Italian loafers. The clothes were birthday gifts. This was his first opportunity to wear them.

Soon the couple was speeding to Atlantic City. After their arrival, they ate dinner and took a stroll down the Boardwalk. It was their first visit to the resort community since their honeymoon. They were to make the most of it.

They entered the Taj Mahal, a particularly glitzy casino melding the frenzy of a stock exchange with the elegance of an upscale restaurant. Stella moved under the opulent chandeliers and toward the slot machines. Mike took a pass, deeming the slots no more than glorified pinball machines.

He preferred the gambling tables. The downside there was the sheer magnitude of patronage, with people standing two and three deep awaiting their turn to wager. The only exceptions were two tables cordoned off with decorative wrought-iron railings. A sign affixed to the barrier advertised the name of the game played within: *Baccarat.* Carr had never heard of it, but moved toward the tables in search of a quiet place to sit down.

An hour later, Carr walked away $140 richer. Suddenly, he heard someone shouting his name from the gaming floor. It was Stella. She pushed her way through the crowd.

"Mike! Mike!" she screamed. When they met, she gave him a tremendous hug, nearly knocking him off his feet.

"I won! I won!" she yelled while jumping up and down. "I played this one machine for an hour and I won $200!"

"Calm down, calm down," Mike said with a smile. "Guess what?"

"What?"

"I won, too."

"You're kidding," she replied, looking at her spouse with a big, beautiful smile.

"Nope," Carr said. "I guess this is beginners' luck."

"Yeah, well maybe you can get lucky again tonight," Stella remarked seductively.

"How about we go get that room now," Carr suggested.

"Yeah, c'mon," Stella said, grabbing his hand and leading him to the registration desk.

"We're celebrating our wedding anniversary," Carr told a hotel employee. "We'd like a suite."

"Yes, sir," answered the smiling desk clerk. "I can give you 2020. It has an ocean view and is one of our better suites. We have a special tonight, so the room is at a discount rate."

"Allllll-rrright!" roared Carr. "Looks like this is our lucky night."

"Yes, sir," answered the clerk. "The bellhop will show you to your room."

The couple left, arm in arm, her head resting on his shoulder. The desk clerk took all this in and chuckled to himself. There wasn't any discount for the suite, but they looked far happier than affluent. Why not give them a break, he thought, particularly since the hotel had trouble filling the room at this time of year?

The bellhop opened the door to the room and began his recited speech: "There's cable TV, a bar, and fresh linen. Dinner is available until midnight. Enjoy your stay."

"Thanks," Mike said, handing him a tip.

He and Stella then examined the enormous and plush room. Mike let out a long whistle.

"Geez, will ya look at this place," he blurted.

"Wow," exclaimed Stella, who was awestruck -- and soon incredulous.

"Mike, look at this. There is a telephone in the bathroom."

"A sure sign of decadence," replied Mike laughingly. "Yo, hon, look at this."

As she walked into the bedroom, Mike pointed at the mirrored ceiling.

"Wow," Stella repeated.

"Hurry up and get changed," urged Mike.

Stella began to unpack.

There was a soft knock. Carr looked through the peephole and saw a room service attendant. Carr opened the door, watching as the visitor wheeled in a gift. Atop the cart was a champagne bucket containing a bottle of Dom Perignon packed in ice. The smiling attendant removed the bottle from the bucket and presented it to Carr, saying, "Compliments of the house."

"Thanks," replied the bewildered recipient.

"The desk clerk," added the attendant with a grin.

"Oh," said Carr, tipping the staffer as he quickly exited the room.

Mike undressed and slipped under the sheets. He turned on the radio, found a station that he liked, and waited for Stella. Suddenly, he remembered the champagne. He left the bed long enough to grab the bubbly and two glasses, parking them between the pillows.

The station was broadcasting a romantic ballad just as Stella entered the bedroom. She was wearing a lavender teddy. Her lovely hair cascaded over smooth shoulders. A song with a sultry sound had supplanted the ballad, more in keeping with the appetites of the moment. Stella climbed into bed, kissing her husband slowly and softly on the lips. Thus began a long and passionate bout of carnal bliss.

After its conclusion, Stella snuggled up against Mike. This had been their first intimacy in months. Mike missed this.

With morning came a call to room service for breakfast in bed. This was followed by a stroll through the hotel. Soon they were driving home via the Atlantic City Expressway. Mike and Stella agreed that this had been the best anniversary celebration in the entirety of their marriage.

Since it was Saturday, Mike suggested a walk through Independence National Historical Park. It was his favorite place in the city. Stella didn't share her spouse's enthusiasm for wandering around ancient buildings; nonetheless, she consented to go along.

As suppertime neared, Mike considered his options. He thought Stella would enjoy *Kat Man Du*, a riverfront restaurant that offered great food, a Reggae band, and a wonderful view of the Delaware River. Stella loved Jamaican music, but had other concerns.

"Where are we supposed to get the money to go out to dinner two nights in a row?" she asked, testily.

"Don't worry about it," Mike replied. "I'm gonna put it on the credit card. By the time the bill comes in, I'll have the money to pay it."

"Yeah, just like we got the money to pay our other bills."

"Look, if I'm gonna go through all this cops-and-robbers-school bullshit, the least I can do is enjoy the money I make."

Having prodded him into pursuing law enforcement work, Stella lacked a comeback. Still, her face, so beautiful the night before, all but shouted disgust. Mike didn't care. Angered by

Stella's sarcasm, he grabbed her by the arm and walked her to their car.

On the way to *Kat Man Du*, Mike tried to spark a thaw in the emotional frost that had reasserted its grip on their relationship. He reached over in an invitation to snuggle up against him. She accepted, but without enthusiasm. Whatever magic their marriage seemed to have regained in Atlantic City had dissipated the moment they crossed the Benjamin Franklin Bridge into Philadelphia.

Sunday played out as if Friday had never occurred. Stella, as usual, spent the day over at her mother's house. Mike joined Leon and Tom at a Phillies' game. Nine innings later, the trio returned to Mike's house.

"So," Tom began, "are you looking forward to your second action-packed week at the academy?"

Before Mike could answer, his cousin interjected: "Ya got everything? If you don't, I still got some stuff."

"Well, I'll tell ya what," said Mike. "If I am still there by the end of the week, I'll give you a call."

"Sounds as if you're still excited about your new career," said Tom with a smile.

"I told you to give it a try," added Leon plaintively. "I've been on the force for five years now."

"Yeah, and look at the aggravation you've been gettin'," countered Mike. "You got what ... 'bout 10 commendations for heroism? What about the big busts you made? You busted guys the FBI had been looking for for years. Whaddaya got to show for all that? Some framed 'Attaboys' on the wall and newspaper clippings in your scrapbook. So tell me why *I* should be excited?"

Leon didn't answer. He just looked down at his shoes. Tom picked up where Mike left off:

"Don't you get discouraged when that happens?"

"Nah," Leon said. "I just figure I'm going to do what I want and let them do what they want."

"Then there is all the other baloney. Hiring quotas, promotion quotas, sexual harassment suits, ethnic intimidation, use of force, somebody doesn't like the way you talked to them they make a complaint," Carr continued.

"You mean that type of thing is not justified?" asked Tom skeptically.

"Listen, there are a lot of bad cops. I know that, he knows that and you know it. Everybody does," replied Carr. "The problem is they politicize everything. So even if there is nothing legitimate, they will try to make it legitimate."

"So how do you know when it is and when it isn't?" asked Tom.

"Let the Internal Affairs people do their jobs," Dover replied.

"You can't tell me they don't hide stuff, " said Tom.

"Sometimes they do. If there is something wrong, a person can always sue. A lot of the stuff is just ambulance chasing. For example, we had one witness to a police shooting who was actually in Atlantic City when the shooting occurred."

"I guess there is fraud on both sides. Which is a shame because it prevents justice from getting done."

"True, when there is real misconduct by a cop, nobody can believe it because of all the time people cry wolf. Cops won't cooperate because they figure they are just being persecuted."

The three then sat for a moment, pondering what they had heard and said. All of them understood there was little they could do to change the status quo.

Tom glanced at his watch and began to speak.

"Well, now that we have solved the problems of God, society and man, I gotta go home."

"Yeah, I gotta boogie, too," said Leon, stretching as he rose from the chair. "I need some sleep."

"Me, too," concurred their host. "I gotta get up at four bells tomorrow. I'm a working man again."

Mike said his good-byes then headed upstairs for a shower and the sack. Soon he was prone on his bed, smoking a cigarette and thinking about what he needed to do tomorrow. He put out his cigarette and fell asleep.

During the second week, Carr began to categorize his classmates by common characteristics.

Those who took a pragmatic view of law enforcement filled the first and largest category. They saw it not as a calling, but as perhaps their best opportunity for long-term job security and decent pay.

Thrill seekers populated the next category. These recruits hungered for excitement. Many betrayed a streak of altruism.

Category 3 contained the power mongers, obnoxious people from both genders and all races who saw a badge as a permit to bully others. This group was the smallest of the three, but also the loudest and most rambunctious. Carr saw these control freaks as candidates for future front-page stories about abuse by Philadelphia police.

Mike Carr excluded himself from each of these categories. To him, police work would be a short-term arrangement to satisfy creditors. He would be a temp with a badge, that's all. He still resented those economic forces and family members -- chiefly his wife -- who prodded him into the academy.

Yet, he was becoming resigned to his situation. As Week Two wore on, he chose to become acquainted with some of his classmates. Carr feared his unhappiness might be misinterpreted as arrogance. Why compound misery by inviting enmity from other recruits?

One day at lunch, he approached a classmate sitting alone on the other side of the grinder. Something about the fellow suggested to Carr that he had discovered a kindred spirit. He decided to find out.

"Hi, howyadoin'?" Carr asked with a cheerfulness that belied his emotions. "Aren't you in my platoon?"

"No, I'm in `D' Platoon, but I seen you aroun'," replied the brooding recruit.

"My name's Mike Carr."

"Clay Watts."

"A penny for your thoughts," Carr said with a smile.

"Nah, you wouldn't pay that much for my thoughts."

"Mebbe, I don't know. You kinda look down in the mouth, Clay. How come?"

"I dunno."

"I'm not tryin' to be nosy," said Carr. "It's just that, sometimes, I wonder why I'm here. I wonder if anyone else feels the same way."

"I know how you feel," replied Watts. "Did you think about this job before you took it?"

"Yeah, quite a bit. But to be honest with you, Clay, I don't want this job."

"Why are you here then?"

"I needed work. Just about everyone in my family is in law enforcement. When I got laid off, there was nuthin' else aroun'. So when this opened up, I applied."

"You know, Mike, I agonized over this job before I took it. You're the first person I talked to that admitted to having second thoughts."

"I didn't have second thoughts. I just didn't have a choice. It was either this or divorce, and I'm to used to gettin' laid every night," Carr said jokingly.

"How do you feel about it now?"

"Pretty much the same. Nothing I've seen so far has changed my mind. How 'bout you?"

"I dunno. Since we've been here, all they've been telling us is how tough this job is. How it's the highest occupation in terms of divorce rates, alcoholism and suicide."

"Yeah," said Carr, "you work crazy hours, deal with unreasonable people in impossible situations. They ain't exactly raising our expectations, are they? I wonder why they don't put that in the job description?"

"Yeah, I wonder why," laughed Watts.

"Well, we were both stupid enough to sign on; we're both here now, so let's enjoy it. After all, they're gonna take us swimming and shooting -- just like a resort vacation."

"Yeah, a regular country club," Watts added.

The buzzer announcing the resumption of class interrupted their conversation.

"Gotta line up for roll call. See ya, Clay."

"Yep, back to the salt mines," replied Watts. "Nice meetin' ya."

Carr watched members of his platoon return from lunch. Some already had banded together in cliques. Among them were the clowns who sat behind Carr. He privately tagged them, The Three Stooges. The trio succeeded in making life miserable for nearly everyone in the platoon.

Despite their annoying presence, the second week went fairly smoothly for Carr. He conceded that the academy instructors' lessons were stamped with credibility rooted in relevant experience. To Carr's further surprise, some of his teachers were articulate and witty. Among them was Lt. Alan Wister.

Wister looked to be in his early 40s. He held a black belt in judo, a degree in sociology, and, like Carr, was a graduate of Philadelphia's storied Central High. The lieutenant presided over a class on <u>Constitutional Law and the Use of Force</u>.

Wister spoke in a rapid-fire manner. His introductory session contained recollections of some of his more vivid experiences as a street cop. Wister's class closed out the second week for recruits, to whom he posed this question: "We've been talking about the Constitution and the Bill of Rights quite a bit this afternoon. Tell me, what is a 'right'? Anyone?"

A woman in the front row raised her hand.

Wister, pacing back and forth, nodded at the student.

"It's a law saying you can do something," she said.

"I see. So if it isn't a law you can't do it, eh?" mused Wister. "Tell me where is there a law saying you can live?"

"In the Constitution," shouted another student.

"Really? Where does it say that?" the lieutenant asked.

"The part that says life, liberty and the pursuit of happiness," someone else called out.

"That's not in the Constitution," countered Wister. "That phrase is contained in the Declaration of Independence."

There was an outbreak of laughter around the room. Wister was not amused.

"That's not funny. At least she answered, and I am certain that most of you thought she was right. Now, anybody else? Do people have a right to live? If so, why?"

"If you took away somebody's life, it would be murder," said a guy a few rows behind Carr.

"So if you kill someone, it's wrong. Is that always true? After all, some of you might have to kill someone."

"It's OK in self defense," answered another recruit.

"What about defending another?" Wister asked.

"Yeah," someone shouted, "if they're in danger of getting killed."

"So why is it legal, moral, and ethical to kill in defense of one's life?" asked the instructor.

"Because people have a right to live," shouted a woman sitting in front of Carr.

Wister displayed a sly grin, then spoke: "We've come full circle haven't we? What is a *right*?"

Carr found all of this very tiresome, prompting him to violate a personal rule. He had committed himself to never volunteering to answer questions during his time at the academy. However, it was Friday. He was ready for the weekend. If he could end this discussion, perhaps Wister would dismiss the class early.

Wister acknowledged Carr's hand with a "Yes?"

"Sir, a right is a power to do something; a power with which no one can interfere."

"Good. Absolutely correct. But what kind of power?"

"What do you mean ... Sir?" asked Carr.

"What power permits me to do something free of interference from you? Is it physical power? After all, an armed robber could steal your money and you couldn't stop him. Does it follow, then, that he has a right to your money?"

"No," replied Carr.

"Is it the power of persuasion? The gift of gab?" Wister was now posing his questions to the entire class. "After all, the con artist could convince you to give him your money. What about the power of public opinion, be it reflected in law or, sometimes, in defiance of the law -- say, in the case of a lynching?"

Carr groped for an answer as Wister continued.

"What kind of power is a right, be it intellectual, physical, legal? Each of these allows me to hold what is mine and to take what is not mine. So what kind of power is a right?"

Responses from the class ranged from the plausible to the laughable. As Carr mulled over the question, he thought about his last class on the motor vehicle code. He recalled how, during the class, the concept of the code's voluntary nature had been discussed. Then it all became clear.

"The power of reason," Carr blurted.

"Perfect!" exclaimed Wister. "Now, explain what you mean."

"If you do something only because you have might behind you, then you couldn't do it if you didn't have might. But you have a right to live, regardless of whether or not you have the might to force others to let you live. Same thing goes for legal or social sanctions. But, in general, everyone must go along with the idea you are able to do something. Traffic laws, for example, are voluntary. You yield the right of way, not because you'll get a ticket, but because you know it's the best thing for everybody to do. If everyone tried to get on the road at the same time, then no one would get on it. You limit your free will in exchange for order, otherwise there would be chaos. A chaotic system isn't for the common good of everyone.

"Excellent!" said Wister. "What's your name?"

"Carr, Sir, Michael Carr."

"Well, Carr, you could go somewhere in this job. In all my years as an instructor, I have never heard such a cogent argument as yours. It still has a few holes in it, but we can deal with those next week."

"Oh, one other thing," Wister said, "I received this piece of advice as a rookie from a veteran police officer. He told me that if you think you're wearing a badge, you're wrong. What you're wearing is a ticket to the greatest show on Earth!"

"I see that we're near dismissal time. Since it's such a nice day, I'm going to give you an early start on the weekend," said a smiling Wister, who added, "That is *my* right. Class dismissed."

"Hallelujah!" muttered Carr. As he prepared to leave, he realized he had become a mini celebrity. Some of his classmates glanced at him as they left. A few nodded their approval. Even one of the Three Stooges smiled at him, giving Carr a "Way to go!" look.

The compliments were gratifying. His opinion of the Police Academy had risen over the past week. However, he was no convert to the calling of law enforcement. He was still the uniformed temp in training -- albeit a happier one.

The ride home was pleasant. As far as he knew, there were no plans for the weekend. Just a quiet two-day break with the wife. The Phillies were on TV tonight. It was a game he hoped to see.

As soon as he arrived home, Stella shared her plans; they didn't include Mike. A girlfriend was getting married, so Stella and other gal pals were honoring the future bride with a bachelorette party. Oh, and by the way, would he mind painting the kitchen while she was out carousing?

In fact, he did mind. If she wanted the kitchen painted that night, she was free to skip her party and grab a brush. Meanwhile, he'd grab a beer and watch the Phillies.

Carr said none of this to Stella, of course. What would be gained by inviting another shouting match with the spouse? Not to worry, Stella, he thought. I'll do the kitchen tomorrow.

He didn't object to her going out. She needed a night on the town with her friends. The timing was ideal, actually. She was no baseball fan, whereas he truly wanted to see this game.

After dinner, Stella dressed for the party and was picked up by one of her friends. Carr thought his wife looked terrific ---- a sure bet to draw appreciative glances from a lot of guys tonight. Not to worry, he said to himself. They had their problems, but infidelity wasn't something either of them need worry about.

Chapter 3

Saladin Christian walked into the offices of the law firm of Diamond, Norris and Pike, located on the 27th floor of the 3030 Market Street Building. He had a 9:30 a.m. appointment to see Beverly Clark -- the lone criminal attorney in a firm that specialized in estates and trusts.

He approached the receptionist, told her his name and whom he came to see. The clerk offered a perfunctory smile, picked up her phone, pressed a button on the console and announced, "Mr. Christian is here."

The receptionist listened to the party on the other end of the line and hung up. She then looked up at Christian and said, "Ms. Clark will be right with you. Please have a seat. Would you like some coffee or tea?"

"No thanks," Christian replied as he sat down on one of two Queen Anne chairs. The reception area's furnishings communicated power and prestige. In addition to the Queen Anne chairs, Christian noted tax-deductible luxuries such as a Persian carpet, a Chesterfield settee and an ornate lamp resting on an elaborately carved end table.

These lawyers really know how to live, Christian thought. He had often heard you could steal more with a briefcase than a gun. He was beginning to appreciate the truth of that adage. It made him wish he had taken school more seriously back at good ol' Central High.

Not that trafficking in controlled substances wasn't profitable; he could make much more money than most lawyers. The problem was he couldn't spend his profits as easily. Earnings had to be invested in areas outside the scope of Internal Revenue Service review -- for example, fast times and faster women.

That wasn't Christian's preferred lifestyle -- a point of contrast between Christian and other traffickers. With the latter, casinos, cars, women, and whiskey were necessities. Drug dealing was the means to satisfy their craving for instant gratification.

Christian, conversely, was a serious man with long-term goals. He was satisfied with the growth of his illicit empire, but cautiously guarded against any development that could turn his booming business into a bust.

Christian's rise in the world of narco-trafficking could only be described as meteoric -- and accidental. He began his criminal career as a car thief, using the proceeds from that endeavor to finance a speakeasy in the Germantown section of Philadelphia. One of the speakeasy's patrons had run up a large tab and chose to pay it off with narcotics. Christian had only used drugs sporadically since high school and -- for a good many years -- stood far outside the mainstream of the trafficking subculture. Thus, he was ill prepared to recycle the chemical repayment profitably -- and quietly.

Several of his other customers helped him overcome that handicap. They referred Christian to a low-level dealer who paid inflated prices for such contraband. This lucrative development piqued Christian's curiosity. He saw an opportunity to amass wealth swiftly; it was an opportunity he intended to exploit.

Christian began moving small amounts of controlled substances to test the market. A couple of easy and fruitful deals later, he decided to run the business directly out of his speakeasy. Soon, he had developed a broad and loyal client base.

More established traffickers in the city, however, viewed Christian's prosperous diversification of business interests as an intolerable intrusion. They were losing customers to this upstart. Christian became aware of his competitors' ire when his speakeasy was firebombed. The attack occurred while the speakeasy was closed. No one was hurt. In short, the arson was designed to send a message.

Christian understood the message. The fire-damaged speakeasy was repaired. His rivals responded by escalating the violence. War had been declared.

One night, guards posted outside the club's doors were gunned down in a drive-by shooting. Almost simultaneously, in the Mount Airy section of Philadelphia he called home, Christian survived an assassination attempt.

He now understood his choices: he would either have to take the offensive or leave town. Since Saladin liked Philadelphia, he opted to go on the offensive.

By spreading some money around in the right places, Christian gathered intelligence on his chief antagonists. There were two. Foremost were the Sommerville brothers, operators of a string of drug houses in the Germantown and West Oak Lane neighborhoods of Philadelphia. Next came Haines Belfield, an independent trafficker.

Christian chose to confront the smaller rival first. He hired a group of thugs and arsonists who systematically ruined Belfield's distribution network and terrorized his employees. Scratch one competitor.

The Sommervilles wouldn't fold so swiftly. Christian couldn't outmuscle or outspend them. Instead, he outsmarted them.

He manipulated the police, feeding them information that led to raids on Sommerville drug operations. Christian then targeted Sommerville suppliers and bought up their inventory of contraband or ensured its destruction. The timing was devastating to the siblings. Caught in the thumbscrews of law enforcement investigations, they needed capital to buy effective legal representation. Yet their cash flow was drained considerably by Christian's tactics.

The brothers were furious and responded predictably, crushing his speakeasy with repeated visitations of violence.

Yet, Christian enjoyed two advantages over the Sommervilles: stealth and a secure stockpile of narcotics. No one knew where to find Christian or his reserves of dope. The Sommervilles, however, were highly visible outlaws.

The challenger to the Sommerville dominance of regional drug trafficking understood he couldn't win this war by waging it from the shadows. He would have to surface eventually, though it would be on his terms.

To affect that outcome, he instructed his crew of arsonists -- he called them his "lightning bugs" -- to torch the headquarters of the Sommerville crime ring. Subsequent to that provocation, Christian called for a truce and peace conference. He would meet with the leaders of the Sommerville gang.

Christian understood the brothers would try to transform talks of reconciliation into his execution; he saw an opportunity to turn the tables. Rather than play sheep at his own slaughter, Christian set a trap for the wolves. Spies identified the route the Sommervilles would take to reach the summit. Christian's gunmen were deployed. The clan was ambushed. Four brothers perished at the scene. Two survived only to die within days at a local hospital. The carnage outraged the public. Christian's successful purge of his enemies raised his profile beyond the underworld. Investigative resources heretofore focused on the Sommervilles were now aimed at Christian, who was arrested in short order.

While prosecutors lacked sufficient evidence to convict him of slaughtering the Sommervilles, Christian was vulnerable to a guilty verdict on drug charges. Hence, his appointment with Beverly Clark, a woman he had met previously and one whose legal services he could now afford thanks to his bloody triumph in the Sommerville war.

Christian's first encounter with Clark came at a party celebrating the acquittal of one of his friends -- a member of Philadelphia's old Junior Black Mafia − the 1970's equivalent of the Crypts. Clark successfully defended Christian's crony against a charge of felonious assault. The friend urged Christian to hire Clark whenever he required outstanding courtroom representation.

That time had come.

Beverly Clark sat behind a mahogany desk in the spacious office. Her 27th floor perch offered a panoramic view of the city. To her right was City Hall, crowned with the bronze statue of William Penn. Beyond that, the Benjamin Franklin Bridge spanning the Delaware River. To her left were Fairmount Park, the Museum of Art (familiar to anyone who remembers Sylvester Stallone jogging up the museum's steps in the film "Rocky"), and Boathouse Row along the Schuylkill River. It was an impressive sight.

For someone in their late twenties to reach the stature Beverly Clark had reached meant that she was a rapidly rising star in the legal world. Beverly Clark truly believed she was doing the Lord's work − ironic for an atheist. She felt she was helping the poor, underprivileged, victims of racism and oppression. She felt that the legal system existed only to protect the unfair, ill-gotten gains of wealthy, white males. It was a curious perspective from a daughter of plenty and privilege (both supplied by a rich, white male she called *Dad*), a product of the old money, blue-blooded community of Bryn Mawr along Philadelphia's elite Main Line. Clark entered her profession with excellent academic credentials. After securing a degree in Russian Literature from Mount Holyoke College, she moved on to Yale Law School, graduating cum laude.

Vigorously courted by recruiters from many of the nation's top legal firms, Clark chose DNP. There she took advantage of the opportunity to create a criminal law division.

Her first client was far from downtrodden. She represented the live-in girlfriend of a drug trafficker. The woman, herself a drug user, was the daughter of a wealthy DNP client of long standing. She and her boyfriend were busted in a sting. Officers wanted the name of their connection. The father wanted his daughter off the hook and the scandal suppressed. Clark delivered.

She knew the presiding judge disliked handling drug cases. She compounded his distaste by bombarding him with pretrial motions. The gambit worked. Charges against the defendants were dismissed on technicalities. The rookie lawyer's success at keeping the story out of the newspapers was, in some ways, an even more impressive feat.

The girl's father and her drug-dealing boyfriend were extremely grateful to Clark. The firm showed splendid judgment in hiring this woman, the father told DNP senior partner, Percy Norris. Meanwhile, the boyfriend spread word of the attorney's shrewdness throughout the city's nether world of narco-traffickers.

Thus began Clark's rapid climb in clout and credibility within Philadelphia's power elite and, indirectly, the city's criminal subculture. The office and its view were trophies bestowed in recognition of this ascent. Saladin Christian's visit reflected the challenges, moral and legal, that accompanied her elevation in status.

Clark took a brief glance at herself in a compact mirror before punching a button on her console.

"Please ask Mr. Christian to come to my office," she told the receptionist.

As she rose from her chair to greet her guest, she glanced at her reflection in the window. She possessed a model's figure, compelling enough to have attracted the attention of Playboy scouts seeking subjects for a since published layout on female attorneys.

Yet, she chose to focus on the flab she perceived in the window glass. She blamed the alleged spread on extensive deskwork sans regular visits to the health club. That would change.

Her reverie was interrupted by Christian's arrival.

She looked him over. He was wearing a pinstriped dark blue suit -- probably a blend of silk and wool, Clark thought -- a two-tone blue and white shirt and a tie with a floral pattern. Christian did not look like a drug dealer. Clark was impressed. The business-like appearance would help Christian's case.

"Please sit down, Mr. Christian," said Clark.

"Please call me Saladin," her guest replied. " May I call you Beverly?"

"Yes, by all means." Well dressed and suave. This man intrigued Clark.

"Well, Beverly, you know why I am here."

"Yes, you've been quite the headline lately. You've even ignited a circulation war between the two dailies."

"Beverly, let me assure you that was quite unintended. Besides, there have been circulation wars in Philadelphia since the *Pennsylvania Gazette*."

"The *Pennsylvania Gazette*?"

"Yes," smiled Christian. "It was published by Ben Franklin. A real scandal sheet."

"Where did you go to school, Saladin?"

"Central High and then UNP."

"UNP?"

"University of North Philadelphia," replied Christian wryly. "School of Street Business. I graduated magna cum laude."

"It's surprising you didn't go to college."

"Surprising?" responded Christian. "What's surprising? That I would know about the *Pennsylvania Gazette* or that I went to Central High the nationally regarded, second oldest public high school in the United States, which is the academically talented high school of the school district?

"Well, I ...," Beverly Clark wasn't accustomed to having her progressive credentials challenged. Surely Christian didn't think her a racist. After all, she thought, did she not know many African Americans (in addition to those who cleaned the mansion where she grew up)? Did she not empathize deeply with black struggles against Eurocentric oppression? Did not her legal activism on behalf of minorities and women confirm her to be an ally of people of color?

"... I was just trying to assess your background for court. Sometimes judges like to know these things," continued a flustered Clark.

"Is that right?" responded Christian politely.

"I see where your original name was Joseph Jobson," the attorney continued. "Why did you change it?"

"I didn't want to keep my white slave name," Christian replied. "You see black people don't want to be reminded of their slave past."

"I can understand that and so will others," nodded a didactic Clark. "Your strong resentment of your minority status does have an impact on what you do. The court will consider that."

"Precisely," said Clark, smiling mentally.

"Now, tell me about the circumstances surrounding the arrest."

"The cops say they got some dude who said I sold drugs to him."

"Is that all?"

"Yeah, you know how it goes. They grab this dude and he tells them some story about me to get them to drop the charges on him."

"That's true, but I also know that if there is no validity to the accusation against you then the charges would be dropped."

"Miss Beverly," said Christian plaintively. "That poor boy don't know that."

The street-educated hustler was manipulating the Ivy Leaguer with the finesse of a world-class violinist playing his instrument.

While Clark explained some of the mechanics of what was to take place, Christian's thoughts drifted. The real reason he changed his name had nothing to do with slavery. It had everything to do with his father.

After his parents concluded that Christian wasn't going to lead the virtuous life, his father threw him out. The elder Jobson also told his son to change his name. The father didn't want Christian's actions to heap shame upon his brothers and sisters. His sense of irony made him choose the name of the Muslim hero Saladin and couple it with the surname Christian.

Christian was quite proud of his siblings despite the fact they had not spoken to him in years. He did not see any reason to have them associated with his criminal exploits; he kept his new name a secret from them. Indeed, until his recent brush with infamy, his brothers and sisters knew nothing about his criminal career.

"I think we have a strong case," commented Clark, bringing Saladin back to the present. "I'll talk to the D.A.'s office and see what we can do."

"Thank you, Miss Beverly. I knew I could count on you to help me."

Clark smiled at him and said, "Mr. Christian, we're not out of the woods, yet."

"Yeah," he responded, "but we sure do know which path to take."

Clark rose from her chair and walked over to Christian, who responded by rising from his chair.

"I'll call you next week," she said.

"I'll be waiting to hear from you," said Christian.

Each smiled at the other as they walked out of her office. Clark stopped at her receptionist's desk. Christian continued through the door of the suite, waving as he walked out toward the elevators.

Clark returned to her office, called her secretary and asked for the number of remaining appointments that day.

"Two more," was the answer. "The next one isn't due for an hour."

"Thanks. Let me know when he arrives. Is that a drug case as well?"

"Yes, it is," replied the receptionist.

"OK, hold all calls until I am through with both appointments."

"Fine."

Beverly hung up the phone, sat back in her chair and reviewed the Christian case in her mind. She knew there was little chance the district attorney would plea-bargain this one - too high a media profile. No, she thought, the solution would have to be political. The case could not be won in a court of law. It would have to be won in the court of public opinion.

Clark reached for the intercom button on her phone and pressed it. "Martha, find out who the firm uses at the Herald to leak a story. Also, get me the names of others in the news media who have cooperated with us in the past."

"Yes, Miss Clark."

"When you're done, come in here."

"Yes, Miss Clark."

The best way to politicize Saladin Christian's arrest was to feed a story to the press that a witness against the drug lord was coerced. The spin, as conceived in Clark's mind, would depict the police as ruthless, racist and incompetent. Attributing the charge to "unnamed sources" within the department would confer a semblance of credibility to a fable. All that she needed to do was get to the witness.

As Saladin left the building, he pondered his problems. The war was over and he had won. Now he had to win the peace. Saladin's strongpoint was that he was a firm but fair leader. He was devoid of the pretense, licentiousness, and cruelty of some of his competitors. His only foray into violence had been because he was a target. Saladin dealt with treachery within his organization by banishment or by fines. He never had anyone killed or mutilated -- unnecessarily. His underlings knew what he was capable of doing. They also knew they were more prosperous with him than without him.

By contrast, his rivals always had to deal with dissension and rivalry. Their organizations were built upon short term, hedonistic goals. Saladin was more of a businessman than a racketeer. If it weren't for stupid attempts by his competitors to eliminate him, he would be prospering today. Had they chosen diplomacy, they would all be prospering. But they didn't choose to negotiate. So he would have to rebuild. His very own Marshall Plan, he laughed to himself.

But Marshall Plans need money and he had very little. He could start by ripping off some cars. This would give him some start up capital to reopen the speakeasy. Once that was accomplished he could start dealing from his stash of drugs. He would have stiff competition. The drug world abhors a vacuum. Other dealers have already taken the place of him and his competitors.

He could sell drugs first, but then he would still need money to reopen the speakeasy. It would be better to reopen the speak, he thought, before he started back with the drugs. Once he reestablished business he could rebuild a small, but very disciplined army for protection -- and expansion. Without it, he would be vulnerable and he would be back to square one. With it, he could sustain his illegal trade and maybe move into the legitimate business world. He was growing weary of the instability and wanted something more secure.

Christian entered his leased Mercedes, started up the engine and drove down Market Street. As he motored around City Hall onto North Broad Street, he began to reconsider his game plan. By the time he reached Erie Avenue, Christian decided to pass on auto theft. Instead, he would finance the reopening of his speakeasy with drug dollars.

He turned left onto Chew Avenue to check on his secret supply of cocaine. The safe house for this contraband was located on nearby Ogontz Avenue. It was but one of a series of abandoned homes Christian purchased under the names of girlfriends. The properties were good investments and safe from searches -- so long as police did not know his girlfriends.

He parked the Mercedes around the corner from the safe house. Satisfied that he had not been followed, Christian entered the abandoned building, climbing over rubble that once served as the front steps. Next, he descended creaky stairs to the cellar and walked toward a basement wall, pushing away some fallen joists in the process.

A section of the wall was hollowed out, a fact concealed by some loose bricks. Christian removed those and reached in for his treasure. He felt it and started to retrieve it. What he extracted (and, more importantly, what no one else had discovered) were five containers holding airtight, waterproof plastic bags. When cut, the contents of the bags had a street value of $500,000 -- more than enough to revive his speakeasy. The balance of the wealth would be invested in the resupply of his stock of drugs. Other purchases would be deferred until Christian's business had reached its prewar affluence.

His austerity program would not have to last much longer.

The offices of the Philadelphia Herald are located at 502 N. Broad Street. The newspaper owned its home, one in dire need of renovation. However, the publisher of the Herald was notorious for his miserliness. Celebrated investigative reporter Neil Foster could testify to that. A decade after joining the Herald, the Pulitzer Prize winner occupied the same cramped and dirty office that he had been assigned his first day at the paper.

Foster had just graduated from Columbia University's School of Journalism, an incubator for the leaders of America's media culture. The new reporter came aboard the Herald filled with youthful idealism and driven by a modest goal: solve the world's problems.

Foster's agenda dovetailed nicely with the Herald's fondness for human-interest stories about the poor. Among Foster's early pieces: Impoverished black males driven to crime by their lack of financial resources and welfare mothers compelled to live in rat-infested tenements.

Ten years later, the problems of the world remained. Foster's labors, however, were not unrewarded. He collected a Pulitzer for a story on political corruption involving a city council member and a union boss. Many of Foster's colleagues at the Herald were baffled by the recognition. As exposes of urban graft went, Foster's was considered rather routine.

The award committee disagreed; its decision transformed Foster from just another poorly paid scribe into a media star.

As is typical of many in his profession, Neil Foster saw himself on the side of the angels.

When the call came from Beverly Clark, Foster had no difficulty believing her story. He knew all about the police practice of pressuring low-level drug dealers to provide testimony against the major suppliers. He also knew the officers were sensitive to criticism for failing to foresee and forestall the war between rival drug dealers. Foster believed police would use any pretext to arrest anyone they believed responsible for the recent carnage.

Simply put, this ally of the angels viewed law enforcement professionals with contempt, deeming most to be ethically bankrupt. In this Foster reflected the biases of one of his favorite professors at Columbia. The instructor had asserted that police were encouraged to give false testimony to achieve desired ends.

"Do you have a name you could give me to corroborate this?" Foster asked, typing Clark's information as she gave it over the phone.

"No, I can't give you the name, but it is a highly placed source. If this were ever traced back to him he would lose his job -- or worse," she explained.

"Yeah, I should know better. I'll use my own sources. Besides, if I can interview the witness, I won't need anything else."

"I have the name of the witness."

Foster sensed Clark's tip was too neatly packaged. He figured he was being used. Nothing new about that though, lawyers and politicians have played that game for a long time. However, as Foster saw it, as long as Clark's information was true, her motivations were irrelevant.

The outcome of this phone call was a front-page story published the following week. The idea of the piece was that police had hatched a conspiracy against Saladin Christian. In a later edition, Foster used his weekly column to call for the resignation of the police commissioner and an investigation of the Republican District Attorney. The publisher of the Herald, a dogmatic Democrat whose opinion of Republicans was unprintable, applauded the latter demand.

Mike Carr read the Herald's Page 1 story about Saladin Christian over a bowl of cold cereal. The accused crime lord looked familiar. Carr had a number of black friends during his high school days and Christian resembled one of his old buddies. He was sure it was not the same fellow, though.

The more Carr read the story, the more disgusted he became. The article was formulaic. It included the predictable accusation, from predictable sources that racism was rampant in Philadelphia's police force. If such a broad-brush depiction of 8,000 law enforcement professionals was not a sign of bigotry, then nothing was, Carr thought.

He wondered what the reporter -- some guy named Foster -- knew about racism. Carr knew plenty. As a white student in a mostly black elementary school, Carr learned the words 'honky' and 'redneck' before he could read *Fun with Dick and Jane*. It was not until high school that he belonged to a predominately white student body. Even there, Carr was an outsider -- a Catholic whose classmates were, in the main, Jewish. He also learned that some Jewish parents disapproved of their sons and daughters dating gentiles.

He experienced worse forms of rejection. His high school was located in a predominantly black neighborhood. He had been the victim of hate crimes by blacks; on two occasions he had to be hospitalized. He empathized with Howard Stern's reminiscences of his school days as a white kid in a predominantly black school.

Carr's education in reverse discrimination continued into his work life. One of his first jobs was as a bank clerk -- a vocation largely filled by women. He was given the worst assignments, the lowest raises and denied promotions even though he out-produced his female colleagues. Perhaps it was just a coincidence that both of his supervisors were women. Perhaps it was just a coincidence that women received the promotions and better raises. Perhaps, however, Carr did not think so.

Nonetheless, he did not let these experiences embitter him. He understood that prejudice was part of the human condition, not the exclusive property of one race, religion or gender. Though he experienced bigotry, he refused to reciprocate. He counted blacks, Asians, Jews, Latinos and -- naturally enough -- females within his circle of friends.

What did anger him was the hypocrisy he perceived in those who were quick to cry *racism*. He thought of those who demanded the forced integration of schools via busing, but who spared their kids this disruption by enrolling them in segregated private schools.

He thought of the cheerleaders for tax-subsidized public housing. Oh, they were enthusiastic about the construction of new warehouses for humanity's have-nots, provided the projects were built in someone else's neighborhood. However, propose establishing such an edifice in the environs of prosperous progressives, and these consciences of their community would defect to the Not In My Back Yard brigade.

The Herald article reinforced his low opinion of them. In it, Foster quotes a local civil rights activist about the Christian case. Richmond York, executive director of Philadelphians Against Racism Today (PART), stated that African-Americans are accustomed to abuse by the Caucasian power structure. The interview's message was plain enough: Every black convicted of a crime is a victim of a culture governed by white racists. York also reviewed atrocities perpetrated against blacks during the four centuries slavery survived on American soil. Saladin Christian, continued York, is a symbol of the persecution blacks suffer more than a century after slavery's cessation.

Carr put down the paper, finished his breakfast and washed the dishes. Stella was still sleeping, so he quietly walked up the stairs and finished dressing in one of the unused bedrooms. Before leaving, he leaned over their bed, kissed his wife lightly on the forehead, and then headed for the front door.

Distracted by the newspaper that morning, he had lost track of time. He would have to hustle down the highway to reach the Academy before roll call. He sped north on I-95 at better than 70 miles per hour.

During the drive, he continued to think about the photograph of Saladin Christian. Yes, he concluded. He knew that guy from somewhere. He was pretty sure it was from high school. So, what the hell was his name?

As Carr was trying to remember a face from the past, he was setting a poor example for a police officer of the future. He darted in and out of traffic, passing cars on the left and right. Other vehicles he tailgated, flashing his lights or beeping his horn to prod slower drivers into moving out of his way.

He turned on the radio in time for the news. Sure enough, the lead story was the alleged frame-up of Saladin Christian. By now, the newscaster had even dropped the word *alleged*.

The first class was <u>Constitutional Law and the Use of Force</u>. He knew what the topic of discussion would be -- and he was certain that it would be lively.

Carr had grabbed the Herald as he walked out the door and placed it next to him on the front seat. He again glanced at the photograph of Saladin Christian, as he drove to work, noticing for the first time the person standing next to him. The paper identified her as Beverly Clark, Christian's attorney. Cute girl. He then reconsidered his appraisal, deciding he had done an injustice to the lady.

Beverly Clark was not cute, she was drop-dead gorgeous. All that and brains, too. Whoever she hooks up with will be one lucky guy, Carr thought.

He was finally nearing the Academy. As he turned into the parking lot, he felt a sense of relief. He had reached his destination in time for roll call.

In three weeks of training, Carr had been late twice, accumulating demerits. So far, his tardiness had been rewarded with extra duty and longer workdays: mopping classroom floors after dismissal. If he continued building up his account of black marks, he faced a future of cleaning the Academy bathrooms. That prospect was enough of an incentive for Carr to prioritize punctuality.

After roll call, his platoon marched into Lieutenant Wister's class. Carr impressed the veteran officer from the first with his grasp of the concept of individual rights. Wister believed Carr would make a fine police officer who would rise rapidly through the ranks. Carr confessed to Wister that he did not intend to remain on the force. Wister said he understood Carr's current reluctance to view police work as a career, but cautioned his student not to discard opportunity regardless of where it might be found.

"Class, TEN HUT!" shouted someone in the back as the lieutenant entered the room.

"Sit down, sit down," ordered Wister in an agitated voice. "Today I want to talk about this case in the Herald. Are you all familiar with it?"

The question drew a derisive moan from students.

"This is a classic example of how politics influences the criminal justice system. Certain egalitarians insist that wealth influences the course of justice, to wit: the richer you are, the easier it is to get away with a crime. That is only true insofar as wealth influences politics. However, even in an egalitarian society, politically influential people will be treated differently from those who have no influence. "

"During the Watergate hearings in the early 1970s," Wister continued, "many people talked about wealth and power and corruption. I suggest that it was not wealth that prevented President Nixon from going to jail for he was not a particularly wealthy person. No, it wasn't wealth, but politics. It is politics that is driving what is in today's paper."

As he spoke, Wister walked back and forth across the front of the auditorium. He was becoming more animated.

"I read where a local civil rights leader has said that the arrest of this scumbag drug dealer was prompted by racism. Well, in case you haven't noticed, I am an African-American. I am not a 'Tom.' As an African-American, I want my neighborhoods to have kids playing in the streets, not drug dealers riding around in fancy cars. The idea that the African-American community doesn't want to put African-American criminals in jail is the biggest bunch of baloney I have ever heard."

The audience applauded Wister, who continued venting -- his decibel level rising. "Ladies and gentlemen, remember this as you proceed through your careers in law enforcement: Politics is the sprocket that drives the gears of the criminal justice system."

Wister spoke no more on the subject. The balance of the class was spent discussing the Second Amendment. Upon dismissal, the students prepared for physical training, usually referred to as PT.

This was one facet of academy life that Carr was eager to begin. It meant freedom from the classroom, offering him the opportunity to burn away excess pounds he had gained during his layoff.

Carr, however, found academy PT to be a disappointment: Minimal calisthenics and a few self-defense techniques taught by inept instructors. Chief among the latter was Lieutenant Franklin, the kind of guy whose chest enters the room about three minutes before he does. Though a superb physical specimen, Franklin didn't persuade Carr that he was learning martial arts from an expert.

Initially, his view was that if the Philadelphia Police Department were depending on Franklin to train its officers in self-defense, then it had better be prepared to lose many officers.

It was a view that would change.

Beverly Clark dialed the number while gazing out her office windows. Nightfall had arrived. The lights of the cityscape twinkled like stars in the sky.

Usually she was in a festive mood when making this type of call, but not this time.

"Hello."

"Mr. Christian? Beverly Clark. I just wanted to let you know that the D.A. has called me. He is not going to prosecute. Congratulations."

"I think I should be congratulatin' you, Miss Beverly. After all, it was your work that got it done."

"Not at all," she said. "That's my job."

"Your reputation is well-deserved," said Christian. "I couldn't have had a better lawyer. I'll be sure to send all my buddies to you."

"I hope you don't have that many buddies who need me."

"Ya never know Miss Beverly," laughed Saladin. "I hafta go now. You got my address to send me your bill?"

"My secretary does."

"OK. Thanks again, Miss Beverly."

"Bye."

Beverly replaced the receiver. There was something about Saladin Christian she did not like, she thought. She just could not figure out what it was.

Chapter 4

He jammed on the brakes as the guy in the candy apple red Porsche cut right in front of him as he was driving on I-95 North to the academy. Carr couldn't believe this guy did what he did. He honked the horn repeatedly.

"Sonuvabitch!" he yelled at the driver who was now a full car length in front of him. He continued honking his horn and also began flashing his high beams.

Carr noted with irony the other vehicle had a bumper sticker lecturing the world to *Practice Random Acts of Kindness*. It had two others that revealed the political leanings of its owner. One proclaiming something about saving Mother Earth and a third that heralded, *The NRA Must Go and take Charlton Heston with them*.

He was close enough now that he could see the other driver in the rearview mirror of the other car. He looked like some sort of college professor, Carr thought.

"Figures," Carr said to himself as he kept pace with him. They were both snaking along I-95.

Neil Foster looked into his rearview mirror at the driver of the car trailing him, who was honking his horn and flashing his high beams.

"Poor boy seems a little upset," Foster smiled to himself. Some slob going to his job didn't like the way I pulled in front of him, I guess.

"Sorry pal, you're going to your job, I have a career to go to," he said to himself smugly, as he stepped on the gas.

"Screw you," Foster mouthed into his mirror at the other driver. He pulled away and continued his trip to the Police Academy.

Neil Foster had convinced his editor that doing another piece about police conduct might be a good idea. Once he got the green light he called the Police Department's public relations unit. They arranged for him to interview the Commandant of the Philadelphia Police Academy about training procedures.

Because he arrived just before roll call, Foster had his choice of parking spots. He found one on the second row right near the end. He pulled in and thought it unusual that all the other cars backed into their spots.

He took his tape recorder and notepad, walked into the building, approached the police officer at the reception desk, and announced that he had an appointment with the commandant. He was directed to wait in the lobby.

Foster realized he forgot to bring some notes that he wanted to use during the interview. He had been doing some research about law enforcement training and wanted to know if the local gendarmes used similar policies.

Foster walked over to the corporal at the desk and said, "Corporal, I need to return to my car and get some things. If the commandant calls for me could you be so kind as to tell him I will be right back?"

The corporal barely acknowledged his request. Foster turned and went outside. By now the recruits were filing into the parking lot. The morning roll call was just a few minutes away.

As Foster reviewed the recruits' arrival, he noted with horror a car that just pulled into a parking spot not far from where he was parked. He looked at the driver. It was the same guy he cut off on the expressway earlier.

He watched the driver slam his car door shut, still obviously agitated from their earlier encounter. He was walking along with another recruit and was very animated describing with his hands how someone had cut right in front of him during his morning commute.

Neil Foster desperately wanted to avoid this guy he had treated so rudely this morning. He waited until the recruit walked past his car and carefully slinked into it -- less the other driver notice it and him.

He watched to see where the recruit would go to figure the best route to avoid being noticed. He waited until after they were in formation for roll call. He then skulked back to the administration building taking a circuitous route and completely avoiding the formations of recruits.

Once inside, the corporal summoned him. "Where'd you go? The commandant is waiting for you."

" I had a message waiting for me. I was talking on my cell phone. Couldn't be helped -- it was an important call," Foster replied.

"Down the hall to your right – last office."

Foster walked into the Commandant's office. It was rather austere, he noted.

"My apologies for the delay. There was an important call I needed to make."

"You cut your interview time, so there is no need for you to apologize."

"Understood. What I wanted to know, Commandant, is what are your training procedures regarding use of force?"

"This is old ground you're treading ehh ... what is your name again?"

"Neil Foster."

"This has been written about several times."

"I understand. However, I am doing something new."

"New? What could be new? The directive states certain instances when officers can use deadly force. The Herald knows this. Your paper has written about it before. All you need to do is access your archives."

"I understand that. I wanted to know how often you review this. I wanted to get a sense if this part of training is stressed."

"Mr. Foster, a Philadelphia Police Officer could potentially go to jail if he does not follow this procedure."

"Exactly my point. Do the recruits take it seriously or do they just consider this another unrealistic, bureaucratic rule to be ignored?"

"Mr. Foster, let me repeat, any one of these recruits out there could be imprisoned and sued if they violate the use of 'deadly force' rule. If you were one of them, would you take it seriously?"

"I am not one of them. So I don't know what they would do."

"Mr. Foster, I have another meeting to attend. I cannot tell you anymore than I already have. I suggest you ask a couple of the recruits. Talk to the corporal and he will arrange for you to speak to a couple – at a future, mutually convenient date."

Carr was surprised at how out of shape he was. He worked out with weights on a fairly routine basis and did a hundred jumping-jacks three times a week. He thought himself reasonably fit. Yet with every huff and puff of physical training, the exercising was a reality check.

The Department required candidates for the police force to pass the fitness test with a score of 75%. The fitness test is three parts: the bench press, 1 minute of sit-ups, and a 1.5 mile run. The standards for each are different, depending on the person's sex.

The one and a half mile run, for a male, to get a grade of 90, was 10:47, while females are allowed more time. A recruit must finish each of the phases of testing with a minimum passing grade of 75.

There was also an obstacle course to be completed within a certain time as well.

Carr hadn't jogged a mile in years. He finished his first run by walking across the finish line. His lungs weren't yet up to the challenge. He was in pain. But a grinning Lieutenant Franklin offered no sympathy.

"You'd better get in shape recruit," shouted the lieutenant. "You're going to be timed on this before long. If you can't make the time, you flunk out."

It's going to be a long 16 weeks, Carr thought.

In truth, Franklin's expectations for recruit fitness were low at this stage of training. To discourage complacency, he alternately feigned disgust and expressed ridicule. But experience told him that regular exercise would ensure the vast majority of recruits finished the mile in regulation time.

He knew that most of the cadets came from relatively sedentary occupations. A fact of modern society. Most of them spent a good amount of time playing video games, watching TV, and listening to their MP3 players. Even those who exercised regularly and were athletic did not run a timed mile and a half course.

The obstacle course was tougher, separating the can-do's from the never-wills. The course wasn't as strenuous as those confronted by military recruits. There weren't any creeks to ford, trees to climb, or ropes to slide down. Still, the academy version was sufficiently rigorous to weed out the incorrigibly weak. Franklin thought enough of the course to advocate its inclusion in annual in-service training for all Philadelphia cops. Predictably, few uniformed colleagues seconded his recommendation.

For Carr and his class, the test demanded some agility, arm and upper-body strength, a sense of balance, and speed. Among the obstacles were a chain-link fence, cargo nets, railings, a barrier made of steel pipe eight feet high, a sand pit, and a three feet wide slalom. Points were assigned or deducted based on mastery of individual obstacles and rapidity of movement.

Men who finished the course in four minutes or less earned 100 points. Women were allotted an additional 45 seconds to snag a perfect score. Mike thought this policy was nothing less than an admission that most women were ill-equipped to meet the physical rigors awaiting any street cop.

As he pondered the negatives associated with gender hiring quotas, he noticed some positives. Several of the female recruits were attractive; a couple of them were beautiful.

One of them was Sammi – short for Samantha. The other was Haverford -- Mike didn't recall her first name. Sammi was short, but built like an athlete. She had stunning legs -- muscular, but not overly so. Her hair was brown; her bright eyes blue. Haverford was tall, black, with a body of a model.

Carr rested on the grass, taking in the sights. Other men joined him as they finished the obstacle course, each sharing an observation on the two beauties.

"I can't wait for the graduation party," said one. "I bet those babes get wild when they drink."

"Dream on," said another. "Neither of them will go for any of you."

"Yeah," volunteered a third observer. "They probably got rich old men as boyfriends."

"Nah," came a response. "Why would they become cops then?"

"Ah look at 'em," another cadet remarked. "They hardly notice we're here. They gotta have a bunch of boyfriends -- old or young -- and figure they don't need any of us to show 'em a good time."

"Well, they haven't met me yet," Carr said with a grin.

His comment got a laugh from the crowd.

Franklin roused them from their locker-room talk, sans locker room, and brought them back to the lawn near the obstacle course for some calisthenics. There were the usual push-ups, sit-ups, toe-touching and other stretching exercises. He had them line up by the obstacle course and take turns trying to do pull-ups on the horizontal ladder.

This was where the boys - and girls - were separated from the men – and women. Many were unable to do pull-ups. They would have to remedy this before graduation.

They also did a walk through of the obstacle course. This was enjoyable for some and a terror for others. Like the pull-ups and the mile run, the obstacle course was a challenge for many.

The course contained several different types of obstacles to train for different functions. The course was horseshoe shaped so that the end of the course was near to the beginning. The obstacles were grouped so those that exercised similar muscle groups were in proximity to one another.

There were obstacles for jumping, like the broad jump pit, hurdles, and a rope used to swing across a sand pit. There were those for agility and balance like the pole slalom, horizontal beams and logs to be traversed. These beams and logs were arranged in either a zigzag pattern or in a straight line. There were obstacles for crawling - such as large pipe sections. There were those obstacles for upper body capability. They consisted of climbing obstacles such as ropes, a wooden wall, which was about seven feet in height, vertical parallel poles one had to climb by using one hand on each pole, and cargo nets, which led to a platform and, of course, the horizontal ladder.

Once again, when it was announced that the time was shorter for men than for women, the young men began howling and catcalls. Many of the men yelled 'sex discrimination.'

"What, you don't like the idea that men are being treated differently than the women?" Franklin responded sarcastically to the calls of sex discrimination from the guys in the class. "They are different. Look at them. Can't you tell?"

This seemed to be the standard answer from the instructors to explain the difference in the times between the genders. Carr heard it several times when someone made an issue of it.

Franklin had the platoon do some warm-up and stretching exercises. They then formed lines in pairs to start the obstacle course. There was a reason for letting them go in pairs – of which the cadets were unaware at the time. The idea was to instill some esprit de corps in the unit. Whether this did or not is another matter. However, it was the theory.

As Carr took his place at the start, he noticed his partner was Sammi. Well, he thought, this should be interesting if nothing else.

"Hi Sammi," Carr said simply.

"You are …" she replied with a vacant look.

"Carr, Mike Carr. We're in the same platoon," he said sardonically.

"Oh," was the only rejoinder she could manage. It seemed she was more concerned about the obstacle course then making new friends.

"Go," shouted Franklin and the two of them began the circuit. He let Sammi lead. She completed the first obstacle, the parallel vertical poles, with some difficulty. He was better, though not good. She then traversed the zigzag balance beams. He followed right behind her. He followed her closely during the hurdles, which were the next obstacle.

She was still in the lead, crawling through the pipes and running through the pole slalom. She was quite good at both of those, he observed.

They were almost together during the logs – four logs arranged in a straight line. Then came the cargo nets. Sammi had some difficulty climbing this. She made it, however, and moved on to the next obstacle.

Next was the horizontal ladder. She missed a few rungs and had to repeat them. This was followed by the wall. He did okay, however Sammi was not able to climb it.

There were a few more obstacles and finally the broad jump pit. She did these fairly well, though you can tell she was going to have to work at it.

Carr, for his part, realized that while he did better than he thought, he too was also going to have to work on this.

Afterwards, they did a few more stretching exercises and the class was dismissed for the day. Carr struggled to change out of his gym clothes in his car's cramped front seat. As he finished lacing his shoes, he looked toward the obstacle course and smiled. He was starting to enjoy himself. Here he was getting some needed exercise -- and being paid for it, too. Things could be worse, he thought. He could be cutting sugar cane for a living.

The cadet started up his old junker and headed home. One of the benefits of this, he thought, while negotiating the traffic on I-95 South, was that he would be able to get a new car. The credit union should be able to give him a loan, so he could scrap this car that was showing its age. It got twenty miles to the quart – and those quarts were becoming more frequent.

Stella was starting to cook dinner when he walked in the door. His wife dished out a good meal, provided it came from a short list of recipes she had mastered.

One night a week --- usually Friday -- they went out to eat. Mike looked forward to those dinners. Afterward they often saw a movie or dropped by a club for some dancing. Mike loved to dance and was very good at it. Stella was no slouch on her feet, either. The two made a handsome couple and graced any dance floor on which they stepped. Dancing was the one thing that they did well together.

Carr entered the kitchen and gave Stella a quick nibble on the back of her neck.

"Why are you cooking?" he asked. "Today's Friday. We always go out on Fridays."

"I figured we could save some money by staying home and eating tonight," she replied.

"Nah, let's go out. I enjoy it when we do. Besides, I'm working."

"Fine with me," she said.

"I'm gonna go upstairs and take a shower first."

"Please," Stella said, sarcastically.

Carr ran upstairs and got in to the shower. The warm water felt good. He let it spray for a long time.

Thirty minutes later he was showered, shaved, dressed, and hungry. He came down the stairs into to the living room where Stella was watching TV.

"C'mon, let's boogie," he said to his wife motioning her to go out the door.

The two drove to an Italian restaurant about twenty blocks north of their house, in the Bella Vista section of South Philadelphia. An area made famous by the Italian Market – 9th Street as it is known by the locals - which was prominently featured in the well-known 1976 Sylvester Stallone movie *Rocky*. The market appeared in the jogging sequence as Rocky runs down the street of an open air market and someone throws him a piece of fruit.

Given the events of earlier that day it was ironic he was going some place famous for a jogging scene in a movie.

"You know what's funny?" Carr said to Stella as he parked curbside near the front door of the restaurant.

"No," replied Stella simply.

"Part of Rocky was filmed here and he was jogging down 9th Street. I did quite a bit of jogging myself today."

"Yeah," she said disinterestedly.

"OK, so that didn't make much an impression did it," he mumbled to himself as they walked to the restaurant.

The place was one large room with a partition wall dividing it in half. The tables were arranged in columns parallel to the walls. The walls contained photographs of all the famous people who, at one time or another, had been to the nearly one hundred year old restaurant. It was like a Who's Who of singers of the 1940's and 1950's, which were the restaurant's halcyon days.

The restaurant was adjacent to a nightclub that lately only functioned as a banquet room. However, during its heyday, Sinatra, Martin, Bennett, Patti Page and all the other lounge acts of the era played there.

Stella was impressed by the memorabilia on the wall. One photograph she particularly liked was that of Frankie Avalon. He was one of the teen idols of the 1950's who used to live not too far from the restaurant. He always appeared at this nightclub where his career began no matter how successful he became.

Stella always loved the old Frankie Avalon movies she watched with her mother. She thought he was cute and occasionally would listen to his old records.

"Look Mike," she said excitedly, "we're right near Frankie Avalon's picture. He is reallllyyy cute."

"Not my type," Carr replied with a grin.

"Oh shut up," she laughed. "This must be a lucky sign. I'll have to play a number tomorrow."

"You mean you weren't going to anyway?"

"I was. Except now I will probably win."

"Mmmm – let me see if I get this. Us getting a table by Frankie Avalon's photo somehow translates into you becoming rich by winning the lottery."

"Not rich, you goof. Just win a few hundred bucks."

"You will have to explain this to me sometime."

"Forget it," she said impatiently.

"No, seriously I want to know about this. This whole number playing, lottery, gambling culture is new to me. I mean a few of my uncles wrote numbers. We didn't talk about it though. I never played numbers, except one time I played the state lottery. You play them all. You and your mother must play a thousand of them a day."

"No we don't. Stop exaggerating."

"Maybe I'm exaggerating a little. Just a little though. So tell me, I want to know."

"If you see something or if you have a dream about something there is a book you can use that will tell you what number to play."

"Now wait, you're tellin' me that somebody wrote a book about what dreams tell you to play what number. You gotta be kidding."

"No," Stella replied with a quizzical look. "I am shocked you never heard about it. You mean all these years we've known each other, you just now realize I play numbers?"

"I'm not saying that. I'm saying that I never was very familiar with the whole system of how much you play, how much you bet, how you bet – and I sure as hell ain't familiar with dream books."

"Well, you play football pools. Playing numbers is the same."

"No, in football pools I choose 'X' number of teams, pay a dollar or whatever, and get a certain amount times that money bet in return if I win."

"Now I'm confused."

"Okay, I bet a dollar and choose ten teams. Each team has a point spread. Say the Eagles are playing the Rams here in Philly. The Eagles are favored to win by 6 points. I choose the Rams and the score is Eagles ten, Rams six, then I win. If all my teams win I get fifty bucks."

"So playing numbers is the same thing. I bet a dollar and play the number 546. If 546 comes out, I win five hundred dollars. I can play all the combinations of 546 and I'll get two hundred. Understand now?"

"That's easy to understand. I still can't figure the dream book though."

"Let's say I dream about getting married. The next morning I look in the dream book for married or wedding or husband or wife and it will tell me to play a number like 546."

"I am completely clueless about this. So who writes these books?"

"I don't know."

"Well, how do they determine what means what number?"

"I don't know. What difference does it make who wrote it," Stella started laughing.

It was that cute little laugh she always got when she thought he was acting like a little boy. She would look at him and smile, and her eyes would twinkle. He loved when she laughed like that. She was so sweet and so innocent.

Except this time he wasn't getting the warm and fuzzies about her laugh. He didn't think she looked sweet and innocent this time. This time he felt like she thought he was a fool.

"I guess you're right. It doesn't make a difference, does it? Funny though, after all these years of you running out to play numbers, I never gave it much thought how or why you played them. I knew you would see a number sometimes and play it. I never knew you consulted a book."

"Why is that so bad?" she asked suspiciously.

" No."

"Sounds like you're saying I'm stupid or something."

"No, forget about it. I'm sorry I asked," he said. " Let's look at the menu."

"Why do you think I'm so stupid?"

"Will you knock it off. I just want to order. Look, our waiter is coming to the table now."

"I'm not stupid. I may not be as smart as you -- doesn't mean I'm stupid," Stella said bitterly.

"I didn't say anything. I just said let's look at the menu. Can't we look at the menu together?"

Stella opened the menu and started reading. The waiter arrived. "Can I get you something to drink? "

"I'll have a Scotch and soda," Mike replied. "Stella do you want a glass of wine?"

"I can order myself, thank you very much," was her response. She looked at the waiter and smiled, " I'll have a Scotch too."

"Are you ready to order?" asked the waiter.

"I am. I don't know about my wife," replied Carr.

"No, I'm gonna need some more time. My husband is smarter than me and can read faster."

"Okay, I'll be back in a few minutes then."

Mike looked at Stella quizzically. Stella didn't notice him at all.

"Ahem," he said jokingly. "You want to tell me what's going on? 'Cause I must have missed something."

"You treat me like I don't know what I am talking about."

"I asked you how to play numbers. I'm the one who is the student here."

"Yeah, but you make it sound like it is stupid."

"Honey, I told you half the people in my family do it. About the same for yours. I don't like it. So what? I think dream books are bizarre. Gamblers always have bizarre habits. People always make fun of those habits. Don't take it seriously."

"Okay, I guess that's true."

"So what do you want for dinner? The waiter is returning."

Stella ordered and they were served relatively soon.

All through dinner she didn't say a word to him unless he said something to her first. It was a very quiet evening.

Chapter 5

Beverly Clark entered that morning's staff meeting amid a shower of compliments. News that charges against Saladin Christian were dropped had circulated through the firm. Clark accepted the praise with a perfunctory smile.

Usually she felt good about getting clients off. Even the slimiest among them had one or two redeeming qualities. But Christian was different. In his presence, she sensed that she was being manipulated. This was a new and distasteful experience.

Beverly Clark was accustomed to being in control. Growing up, she almost always got her way with her parents. This was particularly true with her father, who was an absolute fool when it came to his little girl.

At the exclusive Agnes Irwin School in Rosemont, Clark enjoyed a degree of latitude not accorded classmates. In college, she steered people and orchestrated circumstances to her advantage.

It was no different at Diamond, Norris and Pike, where fellow attorneys either coddled or deferred to her. That isn't to say she was universally popular. She wasn't. More than a few colleagues detested her. She knew that, but dismissed them as an expression of male jealousy toward a woman outpacing them on the success track.

Nonetheless, such foes knew better than to openly vilify a favorite of the firm's partners. It was far more politic to join in the cheers over Clark's latest legal triumph.

Saladin Christian was no less skilled than her in-house enemies at exhibiting an artificial cordiality. But unlike them, he neither feared nor felt inferior to her. Clark knew that and was disconcerted by it. After the staff meeting, all she wanted to do was get out of the office for a while and try to forget Saladin Christian.

Clark reached for the speakerphone and hailed her secretary.
"Yes, Ms. Clark?"
"When is my next appointment?"

"10:30."

"10:30?" Clark repeated, sounding more than a little irritated.

"Yes, Ms. Clark."

"I thought I told you yesterday to keep this morning open."

"No, Ms. Clark."

"Yes I did. Before you left yesterday, I distinctly reminded you."

"The appointment was made three weeks ago, Ms. Clark."

"Well, then you should have canceled it!" shouted the boss. "Cancel it now!"

"Yes, Ms. Clark."

Martha Yocum rose from her chair and walked to the restroom where she began to weep. She had worked at Diamond, Norris and Pike for 15 years. Never in all that time had she been treated so shabbily.

Until she became Clark's secretary a few months ago, Yocum had received excellent performance evaluations. Her reassignment to Clark reflected Lester Diamond's interest in the promising lawyer's success. Yocum had the experience and competence to navigate Clark through the bureaucracies of both the firm and Philadelphia's courts.

Yet, Clark showed little appreciation for Yocum's talents and increasing impatience with Yocum's perceived deficiencies.

Today Martha Yocum would resign.

At that moment, nothing would have pleased Clark more.

"Damnit, why is it impossible to find competent people?" she grumbled.

Clark stepped away from her desk, glanced at the digital time display on her phone, then looked out her window. It was time to go to the spa. She could relax there. The spa was the reason she cleared her schedule. The 10:30 appointment could wait.

Clark checked to see who would be made to wait. Her personal planner showed the time open. *It couldn't have been that important of a meeting.*

But even if it were, she could do no wrong today. Should the client complain, the firm's bright young star would smooth things over.

Clark grabbed a coat, opened her office door and walked past an unoccupied desk out into the reception area. She paused to tell her receptionist to please inform Ms.Yocum that she would be back about 2 p.m. *It is so like Martha not to be at her desk when I need her*, Clark thought bitterly, as she boarded the elevator. *I don't know what Lester Diamond saw in her. He gave her such great praise when he assigned her to me. How this firm ever prospered with people like that is beyond me.*

Just then her mind switched subjects.

Clark wanted to attend an American Bar Association conference in Chicago the coming month. She would need a week off. Lester would whine at first, but eventually relent. After all, Clark could make some good contacts for Diamond, Norris and Pike during a Midwestern junket.

The elevator door opened, drawing in cool air from the lobby. Clark exited the building and walked to JFK Boulevard. There she would catch a cab for a cross-town ride to the spa.

"Hello, Ms. Beverly."

From behind her Clark heard the deep and now familiar voice of Saladin Christian. She stopped and turned to greet him with a well-rehearsed smile.

"Mr. Christian."

Standing with him was a comely young woman in a tight-fitting leather skirt. A very short, tight-fitting, leather skirt, Clark noted. She wore her hair in cornrows. Her pretty face was thick with make-up. She looked a decade younger than Christian.

Just his type, Clark thought with disdain.

"So nice to see you this morning, Ms. Beverly," Christian said smoothly. "What a pleasant surprise."

"Yes it is," replied Clark. "What brings you here today?"

"I came to pay my bill. I thought you might want to be paid."

"Well, it wasn't necessary for you to come in person. You could have placed your check in the mail."

Christian grinned and suppressed laughter at the artlessness of this Ivy League attorney.

"Ms. Beverly, I always deal in cash. I am paid in cash and I pay my bills in cash. It simplifies matters a great deal, don't ya know."

"Oh well, I guess nobody will complain about that. Cash is best," she said, trying to remain pleasant.

"Exactly so. By the way, this is Tyesha. Tyesha, Ms. Beverly."

"So nice to meet you, Tyesha."

Tyesha barely acknowledged the greeting.

"Don't mind her, Ms. Beverly. Tyesha is a little surly this morning."

"That's okay."

"Yes, I tell Tyesha she should be a lawyer. She always likes to argue. Isn't that right, honey?"

"Hummph!" spouted Tyesha.

Christian smiled, "Like I said, don't mind her."

"I do have to go," said Clark.

"Can I take you somewhere?"offered Christian.

"That's okay, I was just going to hail a cab."

"Maybe I can drive you."

"No, I can take a cab. Thanks anyway."

"Okay, it was nice seein' you."

"Same here, bye."

Clark turned and quickly walked toward a taxi that was just discharging a passenger. She had just run into the last person in the world she wanted to meet.

It was possible that she acquitted a murderer -- or more precisely – a murderer who was not accused of murder. She made sure he was not even tried for the crime for which he was arrested let alone the crimes for which he wasn't arrested – which probably included murder.

Saladin may be a victim of a white racist society, but he was probably a murderer nonetheless.

Clark was glad he was not arrested for murder. She did not like murder cases. Clients may have to be executed if they are convicted. Beverly did not believe in capital punishment. There were too many inequities in it for her. Too much racism involved.

Yet, she thought, Saladin is so contrarian that he even tells me capital punishment is not racist. Imagine someone like Saladin who believes in capital punishment.

"Why would you be in favor of capital punishment?"she recalled asking him.

He smirked with his patronizing, yet seductive grin.

"Ms Beverly, capital punishment is not racist. I know myself that many who are convicted of murder were convicted once before for murder. I think the exact figure is one in ten or something close to that. I also know that while blacks are disproportionately convicted of murder -- murder victims are also disproportionately black."

She recalled how smoothly Saladin smiled as he continued, "I have siblings and elderly parents. I want them safe too. Just as safe as if they lived in a rich, white neighborhood."

Saladin Christian at times seemed to be Belial incarnate, she thought with a shiver.

"He makes me feel stupid," bristled the lawyer to no one in particular. "Imagine him lecturing me about being black. I know all about what it is like to be black in white America."

Christian is a typical man. He is an oppressive egotist who patronizes women and sees them as playthings.

Suddenly, the memories flashed in her mind. The cold table. The even colder doctor. Clark began to shudder as she sat in the back of the cab. The recollections became more vivid.

"Bourse Building," she told the driver.

Beverly Clark was 17 years old when she met Cameron Webb. She had just begun her senior year at Agnes Irwin. The school hosted a Welcome Home Dance for alumni. Webb was the date of her cousin, an Irwin alum.

A sophomore at Princeton, Webb had blonde hair and blue eyes. He was intelligent and, she thought, sensitive. In fact, Cameron Webb was nothing less than the boy of her dreams. They talked and danced together. Several weeks later he called her.

They dated a few times. She fell in love. It was the second time in her life she was in love with a boy. The first was the first boy she ever dated, when she was a high school sophomore. However, that was not like this. A high school sophomore cannot be in love like a high school senior can.

He kept asking her to sleep with him. She refused. She kept refusing his advances the remainder of the time she was in high school.

She noticed he was spending less and less time with her. He told her it was because of his studies. Yet, when his semester ended in May, he was still not around that much. She suspected he was seeing someone else. She was worried she might lose him to another woman.

The night of her graduation, Beverly's parents had a party for her. They invited a lot of people. She did not know many of them and felt rather bored. Later in the evening Cameron arrived. He stayed even after the guests departed and her parents retired to bed.

They went to the pool house and made love for the first time.

Two weeks after she moved into her dorm room at college, Beverly Clark learned she was pregnant.

She shared the news with Webb at a party during fall break. He was sympathetic, but denied the baby was his. He then asked her how many other boys she had slept with. She was shocked and hurt. She started to cry.

Eventually Webb conceded paternity and talked of doing the honorable thing. However, his parents opposed a marriage. They were concerned for his future. After all, his father said, he was in his junior year at Princeton. He was supposed to finish college and go to graduate business school – get an MBA.

The elder Clarks also rejected a shotgun wedding. Beverly was going to college. She was supposed to go to law school. She was a bright student who simply made a mistake, her parents reasoned. Mistakes can be rectified.

She and Cameron listened to them talk about this from the Dining Room. Actually 'talk' was not the appropriate word to use. Shouting was more like it.

Her father shouted at his father, his mother shouted at her mother, her mother shouted at her father and his father shouted at his mother.

" I think they should get married," her mother said, " They can live here while Cameron finishes Princeton. Beverly can take a year off from college and stay home with the baby. She can return afterwards."

"Absolutely not," yelled Cameron's father. "I will not have him burdened with the responsibility of fatherhood while he is in college. It is a distraction."

" Well then, she can either have the baby adopted or abort it," her father said finally.

"I think an abortion would be best," chimed in Cameron's mother.

After some more arguing, the solution everybody agreed on was an abortion. Everybody except Cameron and Beverly that is.

"Nobody seemed to want our opinion," she muttered to herself. "No one asked us."

Cameron was swayed by his parents and eventually favored the abortion solution. He told her so.

She wanted the baby. She figured she could work as a waitress while living at home. Her mother could take care of the baby while she was working. If not, they could hire a nanny.

She figured this was a good plan. The best plan for her. But her parents wouldn't have it any other way. They harangued her. They did everything they could to get her to change her mind.

Eventually, they succeeded. They took her to an abortion clinic in Center City Philadelphia. Cameron's mother was on the local Planned Parenthood board. She knew the director of the abortion clinic there.

Beverly walked through a phalanx of protesters to get to the office. She was frightened. Not so much by the protesters, all they said to her was that she should consider keeping her baby or adoption.

No, she was scared about the procedure itself. She never thought of abortion as something one does unless one absolutely has to do so. This was not the case for her.

However, she had already made one mistake by sleeping with Cameron with whom she was still in love. She would listen to her elders because they knew what was best for her.

Beverly Clark had the abortion. Years later she was still having nightmares about the operation.

Cameron was relatively unaffected by the whole thing. He stopped by her house a couple of times to make sure she was doing well. They didn't date anymore. Although she thought that was just a temporary thing. It would be like this just until people forgot about her pregnancy. Then they would get back together.

After his junior year at Princeton, Cameron transferred to Stanford. He came by to tell her he was transferring just a few weeks before his semester began. It was August, she had just returned from a vacation with her parents in Europe. She did not think much of it. She was a little shocked that he never said anything about it before.

She was upset about him transferring. She thought she would never see him again. He reassured her he would.

Clark never saw Cameron Webb again. The last she heard he was practicing law in Los Angeles.

She often wondered what would have happened if she had the baby. If she would have listened to the advice of the old Madonna song. How did it go, "Papa don't preach ...cause I've made up my mind I'm keeping my baby."

I wonder what my father would have said then.

"Men are completely worthless," Clark muttered.

"Whawas that?"asked the cab driver.

"Men are worthless!"she barked.

"If you say so lady."

The cabby looked in his rearview mirror. *What a goofball*, he thought.

Chapter 6

Richmond York, Executive Director of Philadelphians Against Racism Today (PART), was watching the old portable TV he kept in his office in the ramshackle building at 4th and Susquehanna. The reporter was excitedly telling the Channel 6 News viewers about the dropping of charges against Saladin Christian. The backdrop for the report was the Police Administration Building (known to Philadelphians as the Roundhouse because it was shaped like a pair of binoculars standing on end). He rambled on excitedly about the allegation that police illegally coerced a statement out of a witness.

Cops doing it again to a brother, York thought to himself bitterly. They're always doing that.They don't go after the white boys like that. Those dagoes are running around all the time shooting up each other, and they don't go after them like that, he thought angrily.

"I should call a news conference and ask how come the cops are trying to frame a brother while they ain't coming down on those Mafia boys," Richmond muttered to himself. He dialed the number of a TV reporter to whom he always fed stories. Before he finished, he changed his mind and hung up. No sense in doing that, he thought. It's old news now.

I should have contacted the defense attorney, that Beverly Clark woman early on, Richmond scolded himself. That's one reason donations are down, he continued deriding himself. I haven't been out there shining the light on these injustices.

For over fifty years, Richmond York had been in the forefront of the civil rights struggle. He had marched in Alabama, raised money for the Black Panthers, helped organize the Zulu Democratic Movement and the African People's Democratic Workers Party. Richmond York marched, protested, was arrested and jailed, tear-gassed, and shot. He had been in the thick of the civil rights struggle going back to the 1950's.

Despite his years devoted to the cause, York was not considered a major figure in the civil rights community. He had long felt that he should be included in the pantheon of Civil Rights leaders. In fact, he should have been in there before the rest.

Richmond considered Jesse Jackson, Benjamin Davis, and the rest, Johnny-come-latelies. They were just cashing in on the work he did.

Richmond York was a deeply embittered man. He felt that his former companions had slighted him. Forget about traveling to Libya to speak to Khaddafy or being invited to the White House, he was not even invited to the Mayor's office, Richmond reflected sourly.

Richmond York was not just a foot soldier in the civil rights war – he was a leader. However, unlike some, he wasn't in it for personal gain. Richmond York became a civil rights activist because he wanted to help people.

Yet, altruism does not translate into fame and fortune. Now York wanted both fame and fortune. Albeit he wanted to obtain the accolades because of his good works, not because he attended the right dinners.

His ignominy was his own fault. He knew that all too well. At one time, he was one of the 'A' team. But he let that opportunity slip away. As he made the rubberchicken circuit giving speeches, he started drinking. The drinking started slowly. At first, he only drank during the many dinners and cocktail parties he was required to attend. Next, he started to drink at lunch. Just a few beers in the beginning, but this quickly changed to a few mixed drinks. Then he was drinking after work, then at home before and after dinner. Pretty soon he was consumed by drinking and began to neglect everything else.

When his colleagues noticed his problem they tried to help, but he rebuffed them. They warned him that he was providing a convenient excuse for his enemies to ruin his career. But he disregarded their warnings. It would not have mattered had he heeded them -- it was too late. His enemies had already documented his misdeeds and they brought his transgressions to the leaders of the movement. Richmond York was banished to his native Philadelphia and given the responsibility of a local chapter for a fledgling organization. It could have been worse, but his long faithful service to the cause was considered.

Richmond had dedicated his efforts since then to regaining his position. However, his results were not encouraging. The local chapter was going broke. Donations were down. Membership was declining and active membership was almost nonexistent. It was a downward spiral that, if not turned around quickly, would lead to bankruptcy for the organization. If that happened, Richmond York would never be able to work in the social-welfare industry again. National would not help either, Richmond raged to himself. They want me to go bankrupt. They would like nothing better to take over this chapter. Well that ain't going to happen, he thought. He knew how to raise funds. He was successful at it once and he would be again. Just have to get on the phone and start contacting people, he told himself. Got to meet the people. Shake that money tree, see what falls out.

"I am going to start with Salmon Clearwater. Son of a bitch owes me big time," he said to no one in particular. He picked up the phone and dialed.

"Hello," said a sweet sounding female voice

"Where's Salmon?"

"Who's this?"

"It's Richmond, Latifa."

"Richmond? Richmond who?"

"You know damn right well Richmond who."

"I know, I know, I was just teasing you," laughed Latifa, "I'll get him."

"Okay."

There was the sound of the receiver being placed on a table. A few seconds later the high-pitched voice of Salmon Clearwater was on the line.

"Richmond, my brother, what's goin' on?"

"I need your kind assistance, Brother Salmon."

"What can I do for you? Anything you want. If I can give it, I will."

If I put a gun to your head, thought Richmond.

"As you know," Richmond said, "PART has been very active in promoting civil rights for our people. We have also been engaged in helping the poor. We have done more to help the needy than any other organization."

"That's true," concurred Salmon.

"In order for us to keep on giving, to keep on fulfilling our duties, to keep on keepin' on, we need money."

"Richmond, you don't have to sell me. I know PART is a worthy cause. I know you need funding. Hell, we all need that. Trouble is, I don't have it. Nobody I know has it. Only the white people got it. And only some of them."

"My problem, Salmon, is I don't have any more contacts in the white community. *My friends* saw to that."

"You got to get some *new* friends."

"Can you help me with that?"

"Yeah, some, but not enough to do you any good."

"Salmon, we have known each other for a long time now. If you don't want to help me, just say so, brother."

"Brother, believe me I want to help, but I can't. But I think I know how you can help yourself."

"How is that?"

"You need to get on the news more."

"What do you mean?"

"You need to be more visible."

"How?"

"You had a perfect opportunity with this Saladin thing. But I didn't notice you anywhere."

"I was going to call a reporter this morning about that; I figured it was too late."

"Hell no, it ain't too late. Get on the phone. Call the media. Get some of your people together and go stand outside of the Roundhouse. Make sure the TV cameras are there. That's what you need to do. Calling me on the phone ain't going to help you get money."

"True," acknowledged Richmond.

"Hell I know I'm right. They ain't going to give money to somebody they ain't never heard of. Would you?"

"No, I wouldn't. You're correct. I'm going to go down to WKYZ-TV right now and get a hold of my buddy down there and get him to get me some publicity," said Richmond.

"That's the way to do it brother."

"Salmon, as always, I appreciate your help."

"No charge, brother."

"Later."

"Bye."

"After all I done for him, he brushes me off and tells me how to raise money. He wouldn't be where he is today without me," Richmond muttered, as he placed the receiver back into the cradle. "What goes around comes around, my brother."

Richmond dialed a reporter he knew.

"Jesse, I need to talk to you. When can we get together?"

"What can I do you for you Richmond?"

"I am going to call a press conference about this Saladin Christian arrest. I think this is just another outrage perpetrated against the African-American community."

"Richmond, what do you really want?"

"I need to get some press for my organization. What's hot right now? Is that Saladin story any good?"

"Yeah, you can make something from that. What you got in mind?"

"I was hoping you could help me."

"I can't advise you Richmond. I can do an interview with you. I can always do a side story on the disparity between the arrest records between blacks and whites. That's a pretty routine one. I can do a lot of things, but I can't be your PR guy."

"Good, I'll call some of my people. We'll march to the Police Administration Building."

"How many people you figure to get?"

"I don't know, why?"

" 'Cause if I bring a TV crew down, they are going to want to see a big crowd. They usually don't come out for a couple of dozen people."

"I can get more people than that."

"If you can do it before the end of the week that'll be good."

"I'll do better than that. I'll have them by tomorrow."

"I'll see you tomorrow then."

"Good!"

Richmond returned the phone to the cradle. The next call to make, he calculated, was to the Mayor's office. He would ask the mayor for an appointment to discuss the conduct of his police department. Getting his picture taken with the mayor would raise his status in the African-American community. Of course, hizzoner has got a whole lot of people on his case already, so he might not meet, Richmond thought.

York figured the rally would increase pressure on the mayor. By calling the U.S. Attorney, Richmond could almost guarantee the mayor will meet. York calculated that the prospect of PART demanding a federal investigation into his police department would make the mayor's schedule more flexible.

However, in order to get cooperation from the US Attorney, York needed to get to his congressmen and senators. He knew he would get action from someone. But he needed to get action within a timeframe. The Saladin case wasn't going to be on the front-page forever.

This was how it was done, Richmond thought smugly. Who knows, if I am able to pull this off, I might be able to start getting some big donations in here. The mother's milk of politics is money. If you can demonstrate that you can affect public opinion, then you can get money. That's how we did it in the old days. First, we created a spectacle to get media coverage. That got us more members. More members got us more money. More money got us more publicity.

"It's time for a little old fashion hell raising," Richmond York said to himself.

Chapter 7

In the eight weeks he had been in the Academy, the weather had changed from the heat and humidity of late summer to the more temperate weather of autumn. With the changes in the weather came a change in the Academy uniform. The white, short sleeve shirt was replaced with a white, long sleeve shirt, and black necktie.

Mike Carr looked at himself in the full-length mirror in the hallway outside of the auditorium. The mirror, which had been placed there specifically to enable the recruits to check their appearance, had a sign next to it detailing the acceptable uniform clothing and cosmetic appearance for both male and female. Since Carr had been "gigged" several times for failing to pass uniform inspection, he made it a habit to check his appearance each morning before roll call.

Police Department guidelines called for clothes to be neatly pressed and shoes to be shined. The hair could not be longer than the top of the earlobe, and not below the collar line of the shirt in the back (rules for females were different). Facial hair was not permitted except for a mustache, which could not be wider than the upper lip, or lower than the corner of the mouth. The platelet of the shirt had to be even with the belt buckle. The belt buckle had to be centered on the waistband of the trousers. The tie had to rest along the platelet of the shirt. The tip of the tie had to rest at the top of the belt buckle.

In the morning, before roll call, the lavatories were usually a hubbub of activity. The recruits would frantically adjust ties, shine shoes, or fix shirts. Some recruits, whose hair was not quite regulation length, tried to comb their hair behind their earlobes so as not to look too long. The male recruits rarely got away with it. The female recruits usually did. The platoon officers were apparently sympathetic to the dilemma of women' s appearances on and off duty. Most of the men griped that it was just another example of the double standard that was being used.

Carr checked his look in the mirror. He was satisfied that his appearance would pass. He just got a haircut last night and trimmed his mustache. His shoes were shined -- to a mirror like quality. His pants and shirt were neatly pressed. He adjusted his tie once more.

The academy uniform was not particularly pleasing to Carr. He thought the uniform was more appropriate for a prep school. The tie was especially loathsome.

Mike reviewed his appearance one last time and went outside for roll call.

He took his place in line and responded with an enthusiastic, "Here, sir" when his name was called. He had become increasingly comfortable over the past couple of weeks. He even made a few friends. He still felt that he was different than the rest of them, but there was some commonality.

He was also starting to appreciate some of the training he was getting. There were some positives to all of this, he reminded himself. Over the past eight weeks, Carr had been fascinated by some of the lessons he received. His class on ordnance taught him how to make a shotgun out of some metal tubing, how to make a handgun out of some rubber bands and some metal, and different ways to construct a bomb and other esoterica.

Other than the stories told by his family and his friends who were cops, Mike's knowledge of police work came from the same source as everyone else -- television and movies. These sources varied in accuracy and realism because their primary purpose was to entertain. Joseph Wambaugh novels, and similar novels written by ex-police officers were, Carr figured, accurate enough. However, by the time these books made it to the movies or TV they were distorted.

The first time Carr fully realized just how bogus police shows were, had been during a class on vehicle investigations -- car stops -- as they are known in the parlance of the department. The lesson given to his class that day demonstrated what actually happens during a car stop. What instructors taught only remotely resembled anything on TV.

The class was taken outside on the grinder that morning. There were two cars parked in the drive path. One was the private vehicle of an instructor, the other was an Emergency Patrol Wagon (EPW) - a Chevy van with benches in the back bolted to the sides.

They were going to role-play a car stop. Two recruits were selected from the class. One was a woman named Megargee and the other a man named Robinson. They were to play the role of cops. Two instructors, Corporals Hasbrook and Aubrey, were to play the role of car thieves.

The scenario the 'cops' were given was that they had just stopped a car for a traffic violation. Police radio had told them that the car was stolen. They were supposed to arrest the individuals in the car.

Megargee and Robinson climbed into the van with Megargee taking the driver seat. Hasbrook and Aubrey got into the car. Another instructor told them to begin. Although he could not hear them, Carr could see Megargee gesturing to Robinson what he should do. Robinson approached the passenger side of the vehicle and stopped at the end of the passenger rear fender. Megargee approached the driver, taking care to stay behind him at about a forty-five degree angle. So far, they were both doing exactly what they had been taught.

"You'll have to get out of the car," Megargee told the driver, Corporal Hasbrook.

"What's the matter?" Corporal Hasbrook replied.

"This car has been reported stolen. You and your friend will both have to get out of the car," Megargee said, clearly.

"Stolen? This car ain't stolen," protested Hasbrook. "There's got to be a mistake."

"Maybe, but you still have to get out of the car."

"If you say so," Hasbrook said, as he opened the door and got out.

"Your friend too," said Megargee.

Hasbrook leaned back into the car, as if to tell Aubrey to get out and then bolted away from Megargee. Megargee, surprised by Hasbrook, hesitated at first and then yelled at Hasbrook to stop. Robinson, who had been watching Megargee and Hasbrook, started to circle around to help Megargee pursue Hasbrook, when Aubrey burst out of the car from his side and ran in the opposite direction.

Robinson, like Megargee, yelled for Aubrey to stop and started to chase after him. Megargee stopped her pursuit of Hasbrook and started to go after Aubrey. Then totally baffled, she stopped, and didn't do anything. Robinson made a futile attempt to run after Aubrey. In the confusion, both Hasbrook and Aubrey got away.

"Okay, stop now," yelled the third instructor, who was unknown to Carr.

"Believe it or not, this is what normally happens when you stop a car that has been stolen or involved in a crime."

"That's if they stop at all," added Hasbrook.

"Yeah," chimed in Aubrey, "most time they won't. But if they do, they're gonna take off on you. One thing you won't get is for some car thief to get out of the car, walk up to you with his hands held out, and help you put the 'cuffs on."

The class chuckled at Aubrey's remark.

"Don't laugh," continued Aubrey, "Phil Donahue thinks that is exactly what happens."

This got another laugh from the group.

"In the real world, however, they're going to run, as fast they can, in as many different directions as possible."

"Now you see what happened to Robinson and Megargee. This will happen to even veteran cops," Aubrey lectured. "This is why we have developed procedures on the proper way to have the occupants exit the vehicle."

"The first thing you do is just what Megargee and Robinson did. The investigating officer goes to the drivers side - STAYING BEHIND THE LAST PERSON IN THE CAR," Aubrey shouted for effect.

"The backup stays to the rear of the passenger side. The investigating officer will now be somewhat protected in the event an occupant of the car would try to shoot him. The backup will be in a position to watch the occupants of the vehicle and respond in case something does happen."

"You will hear us tell you that over and over and over again," emphasized Hasbrook. "Too many cops do not follow the procedures. That's why they get hurt."

"Later on you will see films, actual videos, of police officers getting into gun battles after they have stopped a car. In one case, you will see an officer actually shot and killed while making a car stop."

The instructors stopped talking a moment to let that sink in.

"We cannot emphasize enough how important this is," said the third instructor.

"So what do you do once you have stopped them, and you need them to get out of the car, but you don't want them scattering?" asked Aubrey, rhetorically.

"It's very simple, you tell everybody to get out of the same side of the car.This way you can keep a watch on all of them. It's also more difficult for the guys on the other side to climb over to get out of the car."

"What happens if one guy jumps out and runs anyway?" someone called out.

"Let 'em go," replied Hasbrook. "As long as you got one of 'em, he'll give you the others."

"Besides, it's more important to back up the other officer. If you start chasing after one of them, the other might try something. The important thing is that you get one."

"Are there any other questions?" Hasbrook asked.

No one raised their hands.

" By the way," asked Aubrey, "do you know the proper way to position your vehicle behind the stopped vehicle?"

There was some muttering but nothing that indicated anyone knew the answer.

"Okay, this is also important. If you already know, it won't hurt to hear it again. If you were asleep in class that day, this might save your life."

"When you have pulled over a vehicle, your are to place your vehicle behind the other one but to the right or the left -- so that your headlight is fully exposed. This is done so that when you are standing near the stopped car, you will be protected from oncoming traffic. At night, make sure you shine the spotlight into the rearview mirror."

"Every so often an officer gets clipped by a passing car while doing a car stop."

Now that is something you never see on TV, Carr thought.

"How many times do you see a cop get run over while writing a ticket? "Aubrey asked. " It happens more than you think."

Carr recalled this was the first time the seriousness of the duties of being a police officer really resonated with the class. The gravity of their duties were driven home that day.

Carr's thoughts were interrupted as the platoon was called to attention. Sergeant McKean, and Corporal Wood began inspecting their people.

McKean walked ahead of Wood as they inspected everyone's appearance. Soon McKean stood directly in front of him. Wood was to McKean's right holding a clipboard with the roll sheet on it. If there were an infraction, McKean would tell Wood, who would make a notation.

McKean looked Carr up and down -- checking the length of his mustache and sides of his hair. He also looked at the crease in his pants and the shine of his shoes. After he was finished, McKean then made an about-face and inspected the back of the recruit standing in front of Carr. When he completed this task, McKean executed a perfect right face, walked to the end of the line, made a right face, and repeated the process with Wood walking in perfect tandem.

So far so good, Carr thought, as McKean inspected the back of his uniform and haircut. No demerits today. He continued to stand at attention as McKean reviewed his appearance.

"Demerit," McKean said, simply.

He heard Wood take the clipboard from underneath his arm and make a notation. *Demerit*, Carr thought in disbelief, *how in the hell did I get a demerit?* For what? McKean was looking at the back of my neck when he said it. I got a haircut last night, why would I get demerit? It couldn't have been for the pants, they just came from the dry cleaner. Maybe the coat? Maybe I got a stain on my coat or something. But McKean was looking at the back of my neck when he said it.

McKean continued to go down the line of recruits. After he was done, he stood in front of the platoon with Wood still trailing him.

"You did fairly well today," McKean said. "There were only a few infractions and most were minor."

Minor or completely fucking fabricated, Carr thought, indignantly.

"By next week you should be issued your batons, Sam Browne belts, blouse jackets and your leather coats. The next inspection we have after you receive them will be with the batons. There is a certain way to hold your baton during inspection and roll call."

"Corporal Wood, take over," McKean said turning to Wood. Wood performed a smart salute, which was returned by McKean, who then strode towards the building.

"You people are shaping up. That's good. You're ahead of some of the other platoons. Like Sergeant McKean said, there weren't any major infractions. If anybody has any questions, see me before your next class."

Wood stood at attention,"Class, *atten--shun*. To your post, *harch*."

Carr marched with the platoon to the auditorium for his class. There were a couple of minutes before it started. He turned around and found Wood.

"Corporal Wood, sir," Carr called out as Wood was headed back to his office.

Wood stopped and nodded his head to Carr, "What's the matter Carr? "

"I can't figure out why I got gigged. I got my hair cut last night, my pants just came out of the cleaners, and my shoes were shined this morning," Carr said, in an exasperated tone.

Wood smiled knowingly and nodded his head.

"Turn around. Do you feel this?"he asked Carr, as he ran his finger up and down the nape of Carr's neck.

"Yeah," replied Carr.

"That's why you got the demerit. Technically, that is considered having the hair beneath the collar line."

"You're kidding me?" replied Carr, forgetting to add the 'sir' to his question.

"You' re kidding me, sir," Wood corrected him, with a smile.

"Sorry, sir"

"No problem," said Wood, "and no, I 'm not kidding. I got the same problem, see." Wood ran his hand up and down the nape of his own neck.

"The best thing to do Carr," Wood advised, "is to make sure you shave the back of your neck from now on."

"Okay, thanks sir."

"No problem," replied Wood.

He is not such a bad guy, Carr thought. Some of the guys had taken to calling him "Woodendick," but Carr felt that was unjustified. He really seems like a nice guy. You're never going to please everybody, Carr thought to himself, especially when you are the boss. There is always something, somebody is going to say about you.

Carr walked to his next class, <u>Search and Seizure</u> and took his seat. The instructor, Corporal Hayden walked in and the class started to rise to attention.

"Remain seated," Hayden commanded.

"Today's class is on the rules regarding searches of people and property and seizures of same."

"There is a lot to cover in this area. It is very controversial, as you probably already know. So, try to keep your mind on your work. Under the heading of *Search* in your text there are a couple of different subheadings," Hayden said. "One is *Frisking*, there is another called *Consent Search*, and another called *Search Warrant*. All of which will be explained in more detail."

Hayden was standing perfectly still at the desk in the front of the room as he spoke. He was a good speaker, Carr noted. He rarely referred to his papers, but he was stiff.

"The first thing I want to deal with is the frisk," Hayden continued. "A *frisk* is a little different from a *search*. As you know, or should know, the Fourth Amendment guarantees against unreasonable searches. The courts, in their questionable wisdom, have defined over the years what unreasonable searches are. The one area where they have been prudent, and granted great latitutde to law enforcement, is the area of searching for weapons.This is what is known as a *frisk*."

"I need two people to come up here and demonstrate."

When no one volunteered, Hayden chose one person from the front of the class and one from the back.

"You are gonna be the bad guy," Hayden said to the one recruit. As he spoke to him, Hayden slipped something in the recruit's back pocket out of view of the other recruit.

"You are gonna be the good guy and have to search him," Hayden said turning to the other subject.

The *bad guy* stood facing the blackboard, the *good guy* instructed him to raise his hands and place them against the blackboard.

"Okay now," Hayden said to the class, "this guy has just been stopped and the police officer has him up against the wall. Officer, what do you do now?"

The *police officer* started patting down the sides of the *bad guy* from his armpits to his ankles. He also went through his pockets taking out everything that was in them.

In the process, the *good guy* found a knife, a couple of plastic bags presumably containing controlled substances, and some cash.

"Now, as you can see, the police officer has removed from the bad guy's pockets -- a weapon, some narcotics, and some cash. Now, what do you think is going to happen to the bad guy?" asked Hayden.

"Jail!"

"He's history!"

"Bye, Bye!"

"Maybe!"said Hayden. "Unless the officer can claim reasonable suspicion as to why he searched for a weapon and found the narcotics, they cannot be used as evidence, so the bad guy will never be charged for possession."

"How come the drugs won't be used?" asked the *good guy*.

"I didn't say they wouldn't. They may or may not. Depends if the officer had probable cause to search for drugs. Remember he found them in a search for weapons -- AND EVEN THE SEARCH FOR WEAPONS was not done properly. Let me deal with that after we talk about the drugs."

The class was now giving Hayden their full attention.

"Okay, you two can sit down now," Hayden told the recruits.

"Except in certain circumstances, if a search is illegal, then the evidence obtained in that search is tainted and cannot be used in court. This is called the *exclusionary rule.*"

"Wait a minute," said one of the class, "if you stop somebody without probable cause, and the severed hand of a recently murdered person is in his pocket, you're telling me that the hand cannot be used as evidence against him and he will be let go?"

"Not unless it was in plain view – or you can come up with, as the courts would say, a 'reasonable suspicion' as to why you found the hand. It is a very gray area."

"That's ridiculous!"

"That's the law!"

"Let me give you some examples of case law that I can recall. A 1993 Supreme Court case, Minnesota v. Dickerson, stated that when an officer found crack while frisking a suspect the officer exceeded his authority. Meanwhile a 1983 Supreme Court case, Michigan v. Long, said the opposite because an officer found a pouch containing marijuana in a car they were searching for weapons. So it is confusing."

There was a grumble of disbelief and outrage in the classroom. Carr himself was not shocked at all. He heard about the exclusionary rule and how abhorrent it is.

There were many stories his family told him of how they would arrive at the scene of a crime and ask someone a simple question that later would be used as evidence. This evidence would be thrown out because a judge would rule that the question and the answer were essentially an interrogation without advising the suspect of his right to an attorney.

The end result is that an undeniably guilty person, who has committed a heinous crime, is set free because of a totally absurd line of reasoning. Carr always held the opinion that if the public ever really knew what went on in a courtroom they would probably follow Shakespeare's advice about lawyers.

"Now let me talk about the frisk. The way it was just demonstrated was a very superficial frisk. There are about a dozen potential hiding places for weapons that were not checked."

"Come up here," said Hayden pointing to someone in the front row. "Stand against the wall like I'm going to search you."

"This is what your classmate did."

Hayden then patted the recruit along the side.

"Now that was a typical TV frisk. What was neglected was the waistband, the collar, the wrists, arms, ankles, and crotch."

There were some giggles and catcalls at the mention of the crotch.

"Laugh now, it won't be so funny when somebody sticks a knife in your throat that they had hidden between their legs," commented Hayden wryly. "Don't be shy about searching there. The bad guys know you don't like to and that's exactly where they'll hide something."

Hayden then demonstrated the proper way to frisk a person. He patted nearly every square inch of the person, while the person was nearly perpendicular to the wall. The legs were kept spread as far apart as possible.

"The reason you keep the person in this position," said Hayden, "is so he will be off balance. While you're concentrating on the frisk he could try to assault you. This way as soon as he moves you can shove him to the ground."

"The other thing you want to do is divide the body in half left and right. Search the one part first then the other. This will also allow you some more defense against an assault."

"Are there any questions?"

"What about the cash?"

"Oh yeah, the reason I said that the cash will be used to file a complaint," laughed Hayden, "is that if you didn't come by the cash through a technically legal search, the defense attorney is going to advise his client to say you stole it. You weren't suppose to have it anyway, so the bad guy will say that you took some of it."

"Really?" called out someone.

"It does happen some times," replied Hayden.

"Okay, your next class is about to start, so I think you better get going. Don't worry if you didn't understand something, we'll go over this again."

"Class dismissed," Hayden said.

The class got up and milled around a bit. Carr went outside for a cigarette. He usually did this between classes. If nothing else, being in the Academy has restricted his chain smoking. He was only allowed to smoke in the morning, at lunch, and between classes -- never in the building.

After Carr finished his cigarette, he went back into the classroom and sat down. He was curious about his next class – Radio Procedures. They were scheduled for just one class on this subject.

The instructor was a Sergeant Barnett. Carr's cousin knew Barnett and asked him to pass on his regards. Leon said Barnett was injured several months ago handling a domestic dispute. The irate wife of a drunken husband threw a pot of boiling water at her spouse. She missed her spouse and hit Barnett instead. Barnett was not badly injured, but it was enough to get him restricted duty for a while. Usually an officer on restricted duty is assigned to the Radio Room. However, Leon told him, Barnett has a college degree and requested a temporary Academy assignment. Since the Training Bureau needed extra instructors and valued those with college degrees, Barnett got the assignment. According to Leon, Barnett was a down-to-earth guy.

The buzzer sounded the beginning of the next class. The recruits took their seats and waited for Barnett to enter. The door opened and Barnett entered. A recruit in the back stood up and started to announce Barnett's arrival.

"Remain seated," commanded Barnett. He proceeded quickly to the front of the classroom. He seemed a little nervous, Carr thought.

"My name is Sergeant Barnett," he informed the class, "and this class is in the proper use of the radio."

"What we're gonna do is have a little exercise in the use of the radio. This is more important than you might think. Knowing what to say on the radio could help you in a tight spot or, at the very least, save you some embarrassment."

"AND YOU WILL KNOW," Barnett said loudly, "when you have said something stupid over the radio because you will get 'clicked.'"

"'Clicking' is what your fellow squad members, or anybody else listening in, will do when you say something dumb. To 'click' somebody you keep pressing the talk button on your radio. The sound over the airwaves is more like the rustling of cloth. Maybe at one time it sounded like clicking. Anyway, 'clicking' is what it's called."

"As soon as I find out if we're set up, we're gonna go outside. We have about ten handheld radios. What I want to do is get ten people, assign them a car or foot beat number and you will get assignments from Police Radio. In this case, the radio room is the one here at the Academy. Lieutenant Stenton is in there right now trying to get us a frequency to use."

"Before we begin the exercise I want to give you some basics. First thing is the radio alphabet. In the Philadelphia Police Department the radio alphabet is based on first names. For example A=Andy, B=Barney, C=Charlie and so on. Here is a sheet with them all listed."

"There will be no Alpha, Beta, India, Hotel, Zulu,"said Barnett as he passed out the sheet. "If you use the military one you'll get clicked."

"The next thing I want you to learn is how to make a call and respond. When you make a call, you state your assignment and wait for radio to acknowledge."

"For example, if your vehicle number is 42, you'll say, 'forty-two' and radio will acknowledge by responding 'forty-two.' If you're called and given an assignment, you do the same thing. After getting your assignment you reply – 'okay.' That's all, no Roger Wilco, or over and out, or 10-4, or any of that stuff."

The class chortled.

"Which brings me to another point," Barnett continued. "There are no codes in the Philadelphia Police Department - with two exceptions."

"We don't refer to a robbery in progress as a 1045, or 1492, or 1776. If there is a robbery in progress then Radio will say there is a robbery in progress. It's really simple."

Again, the remark got a little bit of a laugh. Barnett looked as if he were loosening up a little bit.

Somebody opened the door and signaled Barnett that everything was ready to go. He opened a box that was under the desk and took out some handheld radios. They looked to be brand new.

If these are new radios, Leon will go bananas when I tell him, Carr thought. He is always saying how they have substandard equipment in his district. Yet, here in the Academy, they have brand new gear. They got it backwards. However, that was the City of Philadelphia's logic for you.

"Okay, I need ten people to use the radios," Barnett asked when he was finished taking out everything.

This time there wasn't a lack of volunteers. Carr himself raised his hand and was immediately selected by Barnett. He chose nine more people and gave each a radio and a call sign. Carr's call sign was Four-Foot Beat-Two. This meant that he was assigned the second foot beat in the Fourth District, which just happened to be his home district. The others were assigned vehicle call signs.

Vehicles are designated by their district number and then a sequential number that did not exceed two digits - except for EPW's that were in the hundred series. So, for example, the second car in the Fourth District would be Four-Two or Forty-two. The second van in the Fourth District would be Four-Zero-Two.

When he went to get the radio, Carr introduced himself to Barnett.

"Yeah, I know who you are," said Barnett. "Leon called me the other day and described you."

"Oh, I didn't know that. Does this mean I can cut your class?" Carr said with a grin.

"If you want, that's up to you," replied Barnett, flatly. "Okay, everybody with a radio outside with me. The rest of you report to the Radio Room."

The class did as instructed and split up. Carr went outside. Barnett handed him a map of the Fourth District. What do I need this for, he thought resentfully, I live in the Fourth. When he looked at the map, Carr reconsidered, there were a couple of streets listed that were unknown to him.

"I want you to take different positions around the grounds," Barnett directed. "Stay far enough away from one another, so you won't hear each other except through the radio."

The recruits walked in different directions and took positions that were fairly spread out. Carr took a long walk all the way down to the fence near the pistol range. He was as far away as one could be and still be in the Academy. He considered walking to his car and taking a nap but changed his mind.

After this he would go to lunch, and after lunch, there were two classes he could pretty much sleep through -- <u>Motor Vehicle Code</u> and <u>Intro to Government</u>. After that, he would go home and tomorrow he would be off for Thanksgiving. Not a bad deal, Carr figured, and with any luck at all, they'll let us go early.

Carr familiarized himself with the handheld unit. There wasn't much to it. An on/off/volume switch, the speak button, and a frequency dial. He turned on the unit, adjusted the volume, and raised the antenna. Within a few seconds, Carr heard a voice calling someone.

"Forty-nine!" the voice announced.

"Forty-nine!" another voice replied.

"Forty-nine, 2340 South Tenth, Disturbance House."

"Forty-nine, Okay."

"Forty-nine repeat the address!" commanded the Dispatcher, who was being played by Lt. Stenton.

"Huh, what?" replied Forty-Nine. Carr now recognized the voice as belonging to a guy named Woodward, who was a real clown.

"Huh, what -- is not a standard reply, Forty-nine," said Stenton sternly.

"Huh-- I mean Yessir, I mean OK," said Woodward becoming more flabbergasted.

"The proper response is: Forty-nine OK," said Stenton. In the background, you could hear some laughing.

"Forty-nine, OK!"

"Forty-nine repeat the address!" said Stenton.

"Repeat what address?"

"The address of the assignment you received less than two minutes ago Forty-nine."

"Oh, Huuuh."

"Forty-Nine, I told you 'Huh' is not a standard reply."

There was more laughing in the background when Stenton was on the air. This was followed by several swooshing noises that sounded like the 'clicking' Barnett mentioned.

"Okay, knock it off!" Stenton said. "Forty-Nine, I'll repeat the assignment. When you acknowledge, I want you to state your call sign, repeat the address, and then say okay."

"Forty-nine, 2340 South Tenth, Disturbance House."

"Forty-nine, 2340 South Tenth, Okay."

"Forty-four, back up Forty-Nine on a Disturbance House, 2340 South Tenth."

"Forty-four, Okay"

"Four, Three," came a voice that sounded like Barnett.

"Four, Three," responded Stenton.

"Four,Three, hold me out with a car stop at Weccacoe and Oregon."

"Forty-three, Okay," responded Stenton. "A car to back up Forty-three at Weccacoe and Oregon with a car stop?"

"Forty-eight, I'll back him."

"Good, that 's exactly how you respond," Barnett chimed in on the radio.

For the next ten minutes, the exercise continued with assignments being dispatched and the assignees responding. Carr didn't have much to do. Stenton seemed to have forgotten about him. He spent most of his time trying to peek into the pistol range. The chain link fence that separated the range from the rest of the grounds ran the width of the parking lot. There was so much foliage that he really couldn't see anything. He was standing there daydreaming when he heard the Dispatcher/ Stenton call him.

"Four Beat Two."

"Four Beat Two."

"Four Beat Two, report."

"Four Beat Two, OK," Carr responded. Report, what does he want me to report? Carr wondered. Does he want me to go to the radio room?

"Did I miss something?" Carr muttered to himself.

Whatever he meant by it, Carr figured the best thing to do was head up to the radio room. Better to do that than to have him call me again, Carr reasoned. He started to walk up the path to the main building when he was called again.

"Four Beat Two."

"Four Beat Two."

"Four Beat Two, meet a complainant - Snyder and Moyamensing."

"Four Beat Two, Snyder and Moyamensing, Okay."

"There's a vehicle occupied by four males parked around the corner. The occupants are acting suspicious."

"Okay," replied Carr forgetting to say his call sign.

"Four Beat Two, do you want a description of the vehicle?"

"Four Beat Two, Okay."

"Say, *That's Correct*, Four Beat Two."

"That's correct."

"A blue Chevy, license Pennsylvania, A-Andy, B-Barney, C-Charley ,1-2-3."

"Four Beat Two, blue Chevy, Pennsylvania, A-Andy,B-Barney,C-Charley, 1-2-3."

"That's Correct."

"Four Beat Two Okay."

So I guess I don't have to walk up there now, Carr thought. As he started to walk back to the pistol range Stenton came over the radio, "All units report to headquarters."

That must mean we're through playing CB radio, Carr thought. He reversed direction and headed to the main building again.

Carr was correct. Ten more recruits were sent out and they did the exercise all over again. This continued until lunch. By the time the third group went out, there were a lot of crank calls on the radio. The exercise became a farce.

After everyone had a turn, they were dismissed for lunch.

His class after lunch was a snoozer. The teacher was dry and the subject dryer. Carr's biggest challenge was not to snore too loudly.

"Don't get up," the instructor, Sergeant Whitby said, as he entered.

"We're gonna go through this next chapter and then, I have just been told, I can let you go home."

There was a resounding cheer from the class.

"Okay let's get started, chapter four," said Whitby. Carr opened his book up, placed one hand in the crease and with the other hand supported his head. Within a couple of minutes, he was asleep.

He was awakened by Whitby saying, "Class dismissed, have a good turkey day."

Carr quickly gathered up his books and, without a word to anyone, headed out the door to his car.

On the ride home, Carr went over what he would be doing that night and Thanksgiving Day. Stella was cooking dinner, as usual, for her parents. He always looked forward to their stimulating conversation, he thought acerbically.

They would come late and leave later. There are a couple of football games on TV. He could tolerate their presence by ignoring them and watching the games.

They would probably have to do some shopping tonight, Carr thought. Knowing Stella, he doubted she did any during the week. Probably spent most of the time over her mother's house.

Sure enough, Stella had a laundry list of things to do. In fact, they had everything to do. Apparently, Stella had not bothered to buy anything for tomorrow's feast.

Since he had started the Academy, she was only working part time. They had arranged that she would do most of the household chores while he worked full time. Predictably, Stella approached her household duties less than enthusiastically. More often than not he wound up doing many of the same tasks as before.

Stella had made a big issue of how she should be staying home and being a housewife. This is why he joined the PD – so she could be a housewife. *If she wanted to be a housewife so damn bad then she should do it,* he thought angrily.

"C'mon, let's get going," Stella commanded, almost immediately after he arrived.

"Wait a second, I just got home."

"The stores are gonna get crowded," said Stella.

"You mean everybody waited until the day before Thanksgiving to go shopping like you did," Mike said testily.

"Don't get smart," replied Stella.

"C'mon let's go," said Mike, in a low angry tone.

"What are you gettin' so mad about?" Stella demanded.

"Nothing," replied Mike curtly.

"No, tell me, I want to hear this," Stella asked, belligerently.

"I said nuthin'," Mike said evenly. "C'mon let's go."

"I'm not going anywhere," Stella bellowed. It was obvious now that she was more inclined to argue than to shop.

Mike stopped in front of the door. He was approaching his
limit now. It was beginning to wear on him. Stella kept up her
badgering.

"Answer me. What are you gittin' mad about?"

"Didn't you have all week to do this?" Mike said clipping his
words. He still faced the doorway.

"No, I didn't have the car," Stella replied, her voice dripping
with spite.

"Couldn't you have borrowed your mother's?" asked Mike.

"No. Why should I?"

"Because we're feeding them, aren't we?"

"Yeah, so what?"

"So why can't they help out? What does your mother do all day
anyway? She sits around drinking coffee and watching TV."

"Don't worry about what my mother does or doesn't do."

"I don't care what she does. But I do care about what you do. If
you can't do what you're suppose to do, then go back to work full
time," Mike bellowed. "You're the one who said you wanted to
stay home and be a housewife and mother. So act like it."

"I am acting like it. Until we have kids, I work part time and
take care of the house."

"So how come you couldn't go shopping."

"Because I didn't have the car," Stella snapped.

"You didn't need the car," Mike thundered. He turned around
and walked out of the house slamming the door.

"Where you going, come back here," Stella shouted after him.
"I gotta go shopping."

"Go yourself, "Mike replied as he hopped into the car. He
shoved the keys into the ignition, started the car, and drove off.

"Now where the hell am I going to go," Carr muttered to
himself. "It's four in the afternoon on Thanksgiving Eve."

Maybe I'll stop at the bar, Carr thought. Better yet, maybe I'll
go to one of the new topless joints on Columbus Boulevard. Nah,
why pay all that money just to drink. What's the sense in looking
at the girls. I can't fool around with them. Maybe I'll just go to the
corner taproom, shoot some darts, watch ESPN. It'll kill an
afternoon, he reasoned.

Carr turned onto Ninth Street and drove two blocks to the bar. He planned to stay there for about two hours, just until dinnertime, and then he would go home. If Stella weren't calm by then, he would grab a shower, change clothes, then go back out. This time, though, he would stay out the whole night. He would stay over a friend's house or, if necessary, check into a motel. Tomorrow he would go to the Central-Northeast High Thanksgiving game as planned. After that, he would improvise.

He parked near the tavern and walked inside. The place was crowded. He recognized some of the people. However, he was shocked to see, sitting at the far end of the bar, a foxy little blonde. It was Leon's wife, Sheila.

She saw him as he walked in and began to shift uncomfortably in her seat. She had a frown. He walked over and took the empty seat next to her. The bartender cleared the leftover drink in front of Carr.

"Cutty and Club," ordered Mike. He gestured to Sheila, "Get her whatever she's drinking."

The bartender looked at Sheila waiting for her consent. She nodded her approval.

" White Zinfandel?" asked the bartender.

"Yeah," Sheila replied.

"So what's a nice girl like you doing in a place like this?" Mike asked with a smile.

"I needed a drink. I come here all the time," Sheila said

"C'mon, I know you better than that," replied Carr.

"I could ask you the same question," Sheila said. She reached in her handbag and pulled out a pack of cigarettes. She took one and returned the pack to her handbag. She then took out a lighter and lit it.

"No secret. I got in a little difference of opinion with the love of my life," Mike said.

Sheila smiled at his remark, "The love of your life, huh."

"Of course, isn't Leon yours?"

"I'd rather not say right now."

"What's going on Sheila? I have known you for too long and have too much regard for you not to know that something is going on and not want to help, if I can."

"Nuthin's wrong," protested Sheila.

"Bullshit," Mike replied.

"I am serious. Nothing's wrong," Sheila said as she took a long drag on her cigarette and slowly exhaled the smoke through her pursed lips.

"Sheila, first of all, you normally don't go to bars. Secondly, even if you did, you sure as hell wouldn't be here on Thanksgiving Eve. Normally you're cooking and taking care of your kids. Now if you don't want to say what the problem is -- that's fine. It's none of my business."

She is sharp, Mike thought as he looked at her. Her blonde hair was straight and was a little longer than shoulder length. It was parted in the middle with the right side draping straight down and the left side had a curl in the front. She reminded Carr of the old 1930's movie star Veronica Lake. He always liked that look.

"Well, I really don't know if I should tell you this or not," Sheila said. Of all her in-laws, she liked him the best, from the time she first met Mike, when she and Leon started dating back in high school. They use to double date quite a bit with Mike and Stella in those days, she recalled.

"Listen, Sheila if you think I'm gonna go back and tell Leon anything you say – don't. I'm not asking you just so I can go back and tell him. I know Leon has some shortcomings. All I'm saying is, if you want to talk, I'm here."

Sheila looked at Mike. She felt she could trust him. Even if he betrayed her it wouldn't matter, she rationalized. If he told Leon everything she said -- it might do some good. If Leon knew that she found out, maybe he would stop. The rest of their family and friends were going to find out eventually anyway. Besides, what she really needed was someone to talk to right now.

"Leon's got a girlfriend," she blurted out.

Mike at first couldn't believe what he had just heard. Leon's fooling around on Sheila, he asked himself in disbelief.

"How do you know this?" asked Mike evenly, sipping on his drink.

"Because he's staying out late at night when he is not on duty. He is supposed to be working as a bartender at the FOP. That's what he told me. But I found out that's not true."

"You don't know about this?"accused Sheila. She looked at him with the cigarette dangling out of the side of her mouth.

"No, Sheila, I don't," Mike said earnestly.

"Would you tell me if you did know?"

"What do you mean, would I tell you now or would I have told you before?"

"Both."

"I probably wouldn't have told you before. I probably would tell you now."

"I guess that's the best I can expect."

"Are you absolutely sure?" Mike asked. "You know sometimes people suspect things..."

"No I'm sure," Sheila cut him off. "I even know her name. It's one of those bimbos at the FOP."

Leon has got to be out of his mind, Mike thought. Fooling around on Sheila. Not only was she hot looking, but she was a good mother and a genuinely good person. Unless she is a raging bitch when nobody is around, or frigid, Leon should have his head examined, Mike thought indignantly.

"I have heard about the bar at the FOP, but that's one pleasure I've denied myself," Mike said. "If you're absolutely sure why don't you confront him about it? Why don't you get a divorce?"

"I did confront him about it, that's why I'm here. We got into a big one tonight. So I took the kids to my mother's and came here. I didn't tell her why we argued, just that we argued. We were supposed to have them over for dinner tomorrow. I'm gonna stay over there instead."

"What about a divorce?"

"We'll see," Sheila said. "But first I want to know why."

"Well, I hope you know what you're doing Sheila," Mike said. "I feel for you. Stella and I are having are own problems -- not like yours -- but it's getting to be pretty bad."

Mike figured to change the subject back to himself. He didn't want to hear any more than he already had. He also figured hearing about his problems might take Sheila's mind off her own.

"We don't seem to have much in common with one another anymore," Mike said. "The things she thinks are important are not important to me and vice versa."

"That's how it starts, Mike," Sheila said softly.

Mike finished his drink and ordered another one. He pulled a cigarette out of his pocket and lit it. Sheila also got out another one. He lit hers.

"I gotta go to the Ladies Room," Sheila said getting up from her stool. " Order me another drink will you."

"Sure."

Mike signaled the bartender to get another drink for Sheila. The bar was becoming more crowded as more people were done work. For the most part the crowd was mostly young, single guys in their early twenties. Guys whose idea of Thanksgiving was beer, football and Mom's turkey dinner. There were several women in the place also in their early twenties. They too wanted to drink the night away.

Carr figured if he weren't married he would be doing the same thing. As it is, he is married and he is still here, sitting next to a married woman. Maybe this was an augury of what was happening in his marriage.

No way he would cheat on his wife though. There was no way he would ever cheat on Stella - no matter how bad things got. He made a commitment and he intended on sticking with it. If things got too bad, he would get a divorce.

He watched Sheila walk back from the Ladies Room, getting a couple of smiles from guys as she walked by. She is gorgeous, Mike thought. He recalled when Leon first started dating her. They were all in high school then. It seems like a thousand years ago now, Mike thought regretfully.

Sheila returned to her seat. She grabbed her drink and held it up to Mike as in a toast.

"Happy Thanksgiving," she said with a sour tone.

"Things'll work out, Sheila. It might not be what you think," Mike consoled her.

"Leon is no fool. He knows what he's got with you. He'd be stupid to throw it away. Besides, he loves the kids. If he is cheating on you, and I still can't believe he would be stupid enough to do that, there must be something wrong with him. It has nothing to do with you."

"What do you mean?"

"In the Academy they always talk about how cops are among the highest occupations in terms of divorce rates," Mike said. "They are always telling us how the stresses and the strains of the job are such that people who are married have problems."

"He has been drinking a lot lately," Sheila interjected.

"There you go," Mike said. "Maybe he should go to counseling or something. Maybe he just needs to talk to somebody he doesn't know."

"I don't know," said Sheila as she finished her drink. "I gotta go back to my mother's. I don't want the kids to suspect something."

"How'dya get here?" asked Mike.

"I walked over."

"I'll drive you back."

"No, you don't have to."

"Nah, it's about time for me to be getting back anyway," Mike said finishing his drink. He calculated how much he spent and placed a couple of dollars on the bar for what he thought was an appropriate tip. The bartender looked at him from the other end.

"Thanks, you have a good holiday," said the bartender.

"Yeah, you too," replied Carr as he took Sheila by the hand and escorted her out of the bar.

Once outside, Carr buttoned up his jacket. The weather had turned cold and damp. There was a frosty mist in the air.

"It got cold out," Sheila said as she turned up her coat collar.

"Yeah, they're predicting rain for tomorrow," Mike said as he opened the car door for Sheila.

It was only a short drive to her mother's. They were both quiet. Mike pulled up in front of the house and unlocked the car door so Sheila could get out.

"Well, Happy Thanksgiving, I guess," Mike said.

"Yeah, same to you," Sheila said opening the door.

"Thanks for the ride," She said leaning over and giving him a kiss on the cheek.

"No problem," replied Mike

She ran to the front door without bothering to look back. Mike waited for her to enter before driving home.

Leon has got to be out of his mind, Mike thought. Stepping out on a woman like that. He always was a little goofy, even when we were younger. He always thought the grass was greener on the other side.

When he arrived home, he found grocery bags on the floor in the kitchen. There were some other bags on the dining room table. The oven was on. He could hear Stella walking around on the second floor.

"You done all the food shopping?" he asked, not really sure what was happening. He had expected an argument when he returned.

"Yes. I borrowed my mother's car," Stella said simply. She was hanging some of her clothes in the closet as she spoke to him.

"Oh," Mike replied.

"I'm sorry. You were right," Stella said. She came over to him and gave him a hug. They kissed and walked upstairs to their bedroom.

Chapter 8

The Monday following Thanksgiving was always a strange
workday. The mood at work was a mixture of the usual Monday
dreariness and the anticipation of the Christmas season.

In the Police Academy, it was no different. There was a certain
sluggishness among his classmates that Monday – a sort of
mindnumbed robot-like quality one finds in an audience for a
Michael Moore movie.

But there was also the electricity and warmth of the Christmas
season. This electricity was compounded by the fact that the
remaining six weeks in the Academy for Carr's class was going to
be action packed.

The class was scheduled for one week at Temple University
for *cultural sensitivity* training, and two weeks at the Pistol Range
for weapons training. They would spend one day at the Fire
Academy, and one week of Red Cross Water Survival training.
There was a lot to do between now and graduation, Carr thought,
and he wasn't looking forward to it. He was just starting to get
used to being a recruit and soon he would have to leave cops and
robbers school and play for real.

Before roll call, Monday morning, Carr checked the week's
roster. His platoon was scheduled for the Fire Academy on
Friday. Of all the things Carr did not like about recruit training, the
Fire Academy was at the top of the list. He had dreaded that day
from the beginning.

In the Fire Academy, the recruits were required to climb a
thirty-five foot extension ladder and a fifty-foot hook and ladder.
Any recruit that didn't do it was dismissed.

Michael Carr never climbed up ladders -- ever. It didn't matter
if the ladder was six feet or sixty feet, he did not like climbing
ladders. Carr tried to think how he could avoid the class. He
figured he could call in sick Friday, but they would probably
schedule him to go with another platoon later on. He could fake an
injury, but that probably wouldn't work either. He wasn't sure what
he was going to do, but he knew he there was no way in hell he
could go up the ladders.

His brothers and cousins had told him stories about the ladders. They told him the extension ladder was straight up in the air. Recruits climbed to the top and held onto the ladder using only their legs. This was called the *Steeplejack* test.

He asked Corporal Wood about it. Wood told him that the *Steeplejack* was a test in the Fire Academy, but one given only to firemen, not to police recruits. However, Wood only smiled when Carr asked him to describe what was in store for Friday.

The week leading up to the Fire Academy went quickly. Carr was carrying an 'A' average. The classes were just a rehash of things they had learned. Most of his time in class was spent daydreaming. The only exception to this was Wister's class, which was still his favorite. This week they had a discussion on the use of deadly force and hot pursuits.

"Currently there is a movement to discourage police officers from engaging in pursuits," Wister began his lecture. "What is the rationale behind this? Does anyone know?"

"There have been too many innocent people killed in car accidents as a result of police pursuits," replied Mildred Oxford.

"Do you think that's true?" challenged Wister.

"Yeah, there have been a lot of people killed unnecessarily."

"How many people?"

"I don't know, a lot."

"If you don't know, why did you say a lot?"

"Because I hear about it a lot."

"So you really don't know. It is only because the issue has received a lot of media attention that you have formed your opinion. Is that fair to say?"

"Yes."

"So we have learned a tangential lesson here," Wister said as he began pacing.

"What we have learned is the power of propaganda. The media exposure of a certain subject can skew the relative significance of that subject. This tactic is used by so called *activist groups* very effectively. When Mildred says that she thinks it happens a lot, it is because the subject has been played up a lot. The idea is to exaggerate it, so that more people will listen to you," Wister lectured. "But I digress. Let's return to the main issue. Should police engage in pursuits?"

"I don't think anybody says they shouldn't, but you have to use judgment," replied Jay Emerson.

"Define what you mean by judgment."

"If it's for a robbery or a murder then we should pursue, but if it's for a traffic violation then I think we should let them go."

"Okay, but that raises two issues. First, how do you know the routine traffic violator has not just committed a murder?"

"You don't."

"The second is what will the average person do when he commits a traffic violation, either by going through a stop sign, or a red light, knowing that the police will not pursue?"

"After all, why should John Q. Public pullover and pay a fine knowing that if he doesn't pullover, the police can't stop him?"

"Most people will, because the average person is law abiding," replied Emerson.

"So what you're saying is that since most people are law abiding, they will voluntarily obey police. Sort of an honor system - is that it?"

"Sort of."

"Like people obey the income tax laws," Wister said smiling.

"OOPS," said Emerson. The class laughed.

"Most people will. For those who don't, we'll have to use other means to get them," chimed in Art Darien, the platoon leader.

"So you're saying that about ninety percent of the public will voluntarily comply with the police and pull over when signaled. The small percentage who don't can be brought to justice some other way."

"Let's say you're correct, and human beings are inherently altruistic," Wister continued. "For the small percentage who do not obey, don't you think that will lead to increased recklessness on the roads and higher traffic fatalities? After all, traffic laws, in part, were enacted to curb traffic accidents. If laws are enacted, but not enforced, then that is the same as not enacting the law."

"I think that's true," said Carr. "What's gonna wind up happening is that most people won't obey the law. The unintended consequences are that traffic accidents will increase because more people will disregard the laws."

"Do you think people are gonna run away from the cops and risk their lives just to avoid getting a traffic ticket?" asked Emerson

"People ain't gonna speed away from a cop just because they don't want to get a ticket for running a stop sign."

"They will, if they know the cops aren't gonna chase 'em."

"But how are they gonna know? The police ain't gonna make an announcement sayin' it's okay if you run from us," said Darien caustically.

"You're gonna have these young jitterbugs runnin' around thinking -- what the hell, the cops ain't gonna do nuthin' if I push it a little," insisted Carr. "You'll probably have more cars running from the police than less."

"There's gotta be away to get them later on. You know like helicopters, gettin' their tags and finding 'em later," said Emerson.

Wister listened to the discussion. This was good he thought, divergent opinions and a lively discussion. It's not enough just to teach them what the laws are. You have to teach them why the laws are made this way.

"That sounds good, but the fact is, if some people, who aren't inclined to follow the rules, figure they can get away without following them, then they won't. The more they get away with, the more other people won't follow the rules, and you get a downward spiral from there," Carr said.

"Well, everyone has made good points," Wister interjected. "You can see how even among police officers, who are supposed to be strong law and order advocates, there will be differences in opinion. We are not monolithic."

"I personally would lean towards Carr," Wister said, "but that doesn't mean the rest of you haven't brought up good points."

"In the end, the best law or policy will be what is best for the most people. That has yet to be determined," Wister said.

"Okay, the period will be over in a minute. You're dismissed," He then abruptly walked out of the room.

The platoon milled around inside the auditorium. It was raining and everyone opted to remain inside - everyone except Carr. He went outside despite the downpour and smoked a cigarette. Mike was worried about the upcoming class at the Fire school

Carr leaned inside the door jam to minimize the effects of the rain. No sense in worrying about it now, he argued with himself. If you don't climb that ladder, he told himself, you're going to be fired - in which case Stella will go ballistic. So it's going to have to get done.

He died out the cigarette against the door jam. He tossed the butt in the ashcan near the door and returned to the auditorium.

The only noteworthy thing he learned the rest of the day was in his Motor Vehicle Code class. He was told there were four people that they should never give traffic tickets: Police Officers, Firefighters, Nurses, and Doctors.

"Ya never know," cautioned the instructor, "you might be wheeled into the ER one day, and the person you just gave a ticket might be operating on you."

He went to bed right after dinner that night. He didn't bother to tell Stella his misgivings about the Fire Academy. It would just give her another reason to complain. He wasn't going to talk to Leon or Tom about it either. They would just bust his chops. Leon had already told him stories of how people froze on the ladder and how they had to be carried down by the Fire instructors. The hell with it, I'll cross that bridge when I come to it.

The morning of the big day was cloudy and cold. The platoon reported directly to the Fire Academy which consisted of a main building, another edifice that resembled a burned out building, and a square, windowless, concrete structure that appeared unoccupied.

The platoon assembled in the classroom of the main building. Here they received about two hours of instruction on the different types of fires, the types of fire fighting equipment, and some departmental procedures. Carr found the lecture fascinating and the instructors quite good.

After the lecture, the platoon was led to the windowless building.

"One of the things we try to accomplish in training here," said the Fire Lieutenant, "is that we want to make sure the trainees are able to handle themselves in a crisis."

"One of the methods we use is *The Maze*," continued the instructor. "The Maze simulates a burning building. In such an environment, there will be black smoke throughout the structure. There will be little or no light. A person becomes disoriented very easily."

"What you will do is enter the maze and try to find your way out. There are no lights and no pathmarks. You will have to rely on your own capability to adjust to unfamiliar surroundings."

"Corporal, start sending them through in groups of three."

"Don't worry," the Fire Lt. said, with a grin, "we've only lost one person in the ten years we've done this."

"Line up by threes," Wood ordered.

The platoon lined up as instructed. Carr partnered with Mildred Oxford and Jay Emerson. The three entered through the right-hand door, which was closed immediately behind them. The air inside was cool. The concrete walls and floor were damp.

It was pitch black inside - reminiscent of an amusement park haunted house. He half expected a fireman, wearing a fright mask, to come at him with an ax, screaming at the top of his lungs. Carr could hear the distant giggling of the preceding recruits as they stumbled around trying to find their way out of the building.

Oxford and Emerson were ahead of him. He could smell Oxford's perfume. He could also hear her advising Emerson what to do. Just like Mildred, Carr laughed to himself.

"Carr," Oxford whispered.

Uh Oh, Carr thought, now I am going to be the object of her pedantry.

"Yeah," Carr replied in a low voice.

"How you doin'?" Mildred said in a hushed tone.

"I'm doin' fine,"said Carr.

"Mildred?"Carr called out.

"Yeah?"replied Mildred softly.

"Why are you whispering?" Carr asked quizzically.

In the background, there was laughter.

"I don't know," replied Mildred angrily. "What's the difference? I know how to get out of here. You want to follow me or not?"

"Actually, I kinda like it in here," replied Carr. "No standing inspection, no Wood, no cleaning restrooms. I was actually thinking of staying."

"Suit yerself," Mildred said tersely.

Carr frowned to himself. The best thing to do, he calculated, was to go the opposite way of Mildred. Let Emerson cast his lot with her.

Mike Carr rarely got lost. He usually knew how to get somewhere or how to backtrack. His sense of direction told him to go left. He did and then felt a wall to his right. There was a path directly in front of him and one to his left. His sense told him to take the left. He did this and followed this corridor to a 'Y'; he took the right branch and soon he felt the fresh outside air. In a few moments, he saw the sunlight of the exit door opening.

Once outside Carr looked for Oxford and Emerson. Just as he suspected, they were still inside. When they did exit, a full two minutes later, Carr greeted them with a smile.

"Mildred, Jay," Carr smiled and nodded to them.

Jay returned his smile. Mildred ignored him.

After the platoon finished the maze, they were led over to the burned out building. On one side of the building were two extension ladders leaning against two windows. The other side had a hook and ladder truck parked with the ladder extended to the roof of the building.

"Okay folks, this is the moment you've all been waiting for," announced Corporal Wood in his best game show host voice.

"Everybody line up. It's time to go up the ladder to the roof!"

Carr noticed that there were several Fire Academy instructors around now. Three were inside the building standing near the windows. There were two more instructors standing near the base of the extension ladders.

"Okay, I want you to line up here," said a Fire instructor motioning to an area near the base of the 30-foot ladder.

"You will each climb up the ladder," the instructor continued, "enter the window and then climb down the other ladder."

A wave of excited talk swept over the class. Carr overheard Darien mumble, "I hate these fucking things."

ı

"About midway up the ladder I want you to circle one leg around the rung. Secure yourself to the ladder with that leg and then let your hands go and simulate drawing your weapon as if somebody were in the window shooting at you," announced the instructor.

Carr couldn't believe what he just heard.

"Sir," Carr called out to the instructor, "I just want to make sure I got this right. You want us to, halfway up the ladder, hook one leg onto the ladder, lean back, and act as if we're returning fire at somebody in the window?"

"That's correct," replied the instructor.

There was another bubble of talk from the class.

"They gotta be kidding me," Carr muttered to nobody in particular. "The ladder is the last damn place in the world I'm gonna be if somebody is shootin' at me from the window."

Darien and Emerson, who were both standing next to Carr, laughed.

"Let's get started," Corporal Wood commanded.

The platoon gathered near the ladder. One by one, the recruits started the ascent. There weren't any problems. Nobody froze; nobody seemed to be concerned, except for Darien who was in the back of the group pacing back and forth muttering to himself.

Art Darien was the dominant personality of the platoon. He had a pugnacious appearance, accentuated by a scar on his cheek. Despite his machismo he was obviously out of his element in this drill. However, to his credit, he was handling it with style. He did not try to conceal his reluctance. Instead, he engaged in self-deprecation. Up until now, Carr was one of the few in the platoon who did not like Darien. However, his opinion of him was changing as he saw how gracefully Darien was handling this uncomfortable situation.

As the exercise progressed, Carr noticed how the recruits who had completed the climb formed a crowd around the ladder used for the return. Apparently, Wood was not keeping track of who had completed the exercise and who had not.

Carr came up with the idea of drifting over to the group who had already made the climb. By doing so, he figured Wood would not notice him and he would not have to go up the ladder. He had kept a low profile all day, he thought to himself. Chances are he would not be missed.

Carr started to slowly meander to the group that had completed the climb. They were only about ten feet away from where he was standing. Once he reached the crowd, he talked to a few and drifted towards the back of them.

"Boy I wouldn't want to do that for a living," one of his classmates remarked to him.

"Yeah, ya got that right," Carr replied, loudly. "I don't want to have to do that again."

"Yeah, I don't either," replied the classmate

Carr could feel somebody looking at him. He turned around and saw Corporal Wood looking right at him with a smile on his face. Wood was standing at the foot of the ascending ladder supervising the climb. He was now holding up the line as he looked at Carr. Wood pointed at Carr and motioned Carr to come to him. Carr innocently looked behind him as if he were trying to find whom Wood was calling. Wood just smiled.

"Carr, get over here!" Wood boomed.

"Sir?" Carr replied quizzically.

"Get over here!"

"Yes sir," replied Carr. He slowly walked over to Wood.

"You're going up next," Wood commanded as Carr stood in front of him.

"I already went up sir," Carr replied innocently. Catcalls and hoots came from his classmates.

"Bullshit, get up there."

With a sense of foreboding, Carr approached the ladder, put his foot on the bottom rung, and began his climb. At the top of the ladder was a Fire instructor looking at Carr from out of the window.

"Good morning, sir," Carr called up to him. "Howyadoin' today?"

"Keep coming up," said the instructor ignoring Carr's greeting.

"That's what I'm doing," Carr said keeping focused on the instructor.

"Okay, now put your leg around a rung, lean back, and pretend you're drawing your weapon and firing it at me."

"Yes sir, put my leg around a rung, lean back, and pretend to draw my weapon and fire at you, yes sir, I got it," Carr echoed.

"You know sir," Carr said as he let go of the ladder and leaned back, "if somebody really was up there shooting at me I sure as hell wouldn't be here."

"You know, if you'd shut your mouth, we could get this done faster," said the instructor sharply.

"Sir, if I stop talking to you," Carr replied calmly, "we ain't gonna get this done at all."

The instructor made no reply. He just watched as Carr completed the maneuver and continued the ascent.

"How long you been on the department?" Carr asked, as he neared the window.

"About ten years," replied the instructor.

"You ever lose anybody doin' this?"

"Nope. Everybody gets up okay."

As he neared the top Carr cautiously climbed off the ladder into the window by putting one leg on the windowsill, pushing off the rung and jumping into the room.

"Okay, go back down now," said the instructor pointing to the other window. Another instructor was directing the recruits out of the window.

Carr walked over and started to climb on the ladder.

"Don't look down as you get on, " coached the instructor, "and don't worry about missing the ladder. You won't. Just look at the ladder not the ground."

Carr quickly looked at the ladder and then looked up to stare at the ceiling. His foot found the rung and he slowly made his descent. That wasn't so bad, Carr thought, as his foot found terra firma. As a matter of fact it was enjoyable, he smiled to himself.

"OHHH DAMN!" Carr heard someone bellow. He looked up to find Darien standing on the windowsill staring down at the ground. The sight of Art Darien, class leader and all around tough guy, clinging to the ladder brought laughter to the platoon. They all cheered when Darien reached the ground and, in an exaggerated fashion, knelt down and kissed it.

Within a few minutes, the last member of the platoon finished the climb. There was a lot of horseplay and insult trading, as the recruits discussed their impressions of the climb. Ninety-nine percent of the platoon had no problem at all with the climb.

"Okay, follow me over here," Wood instructed as he motioned to the Hook and Ladder.

The class walked over to the vehicle in small groups. As he turned the corner, he looked at the long expanse of the Hook and Ladder. For the first time he really appreciated the size of the equipment. Also, for the first time he noticed a net underneath the ladder.

"We're gittin' serious now," Carr muttered to nobody in particular.

The platoon stopped in their tracks as they neared the Hook and Ladder. The ladder rose to the top of the structure, which Carr estimated to be about fifty feet high.

"This here is a fifty-foot Hook and Ladder," the Fire instructor announced to the platoon. "This is the next, and the last piece of equipment, you'll climb today."

"Once you're done climbing up," continued the instructor, "you will come down by the staircase in the rear of the building. You won't have to climb back down -- unless of course you want to."

"Excuse me, sir," Darien raised his hand, "What's the net for?"

"In case you fall off the ladder," deadpanned the instructor.

There was laughter from the platoon. Carr noticed one of the platoon, a woman named Charette Devon, had a look of horror on her face when the instructor mentioned falling. Carr remembered that she was one of the people that had climbed the extension ladder reluctantly.

"Okay, line up," shouted Wood. The platoon formed a line near the apparatus. One by one, the recruits went up the ladder. There were nervous jokes and teasing by the platoon as each waited their turn.

Charette Devon was in front of Carr. Most of the platoon looked a little nervous, but Devon looked horrified. When her turn came, she balked a little, but when Wood shouted at her, she began to climb.

About midway up the ladder, Devon looked down at the net and stopped climbing. At first, some of the platoon laughed and shouted at her to continue. After several seconds, everybody realized this was more than just hesitation. One of the Fire instructors shouted up to her, but Devon did not budge. Finally, an instructor climbed up after her. Carr watched as the instructor talked to her and made some gestures with his hands. Meanwhile at the top of the ladder, another instructor called down to Devon and gestured for her to climb up. After several minutes, Devon finally moved and continued her ascent - the Fire instructor following her every step.

Carr was next. He gingerly stepped on the bottom rung and began climbing. This ladder had rails that were perpendicular to the rungs. Because of this Carr did not get the feeling that he was suspended in mid-air like he did on the 30 foot ladder.

As he climbed the ladder he looked only at the wall in front of him. Once he glanced up at the roof and immediately regretted his action. He made another mistake when he glimpsed down at the safety net. If I keep doing this I am going to end up like Devon, Carr reminded himself. He returned to glancing at the wall and continued his climb.

When he arrived on the roof, he found Darien and Mildred Oxford standing there.

"You okay Carr?" asked Darien, genuinely concerned.

"Yeah, I'm fine," responded Carr with much more composure then he really felt.

After everyone finished climbing they were dismissed for the day. Carr was in a good mood. He could not believe that for the second time in his life he actually climbed a ladder. Funny how this place makes you do things you could not – or would not – do, he thought. He wanted to celebrate. He got in his car and started to go home. Before he got on the expressway, he found a phone booth and pulled over.

He made three phone calls. The first call was to Stella to see if she could join him for a drink. The second was to Tom for the same reason; the third to Leon.

"Hey Babe," Carr said lightheartedly.

"Where are you?" asked Stella.

"At a phone booth, wanna go get a drink," said Mike.

"Nah, I'm was just going to stop over my mother's. I didn't make dinner. I figured we could order pizza instead. But if you're gonna go get a drink, I'll eat over there."

"Yeah, that might not be a bad idea," Carr said.

"Okay, I'll see you when you get home," Stella said.

"Okay," Carr replied and hung up.

Both Leon and Tom said they would meet him at a nightclub near Independence Hall called Bank Street 5. It had a small intimate crowd, good beer, good music that did not drown out the conversation, and it was a favorite of office workers.

Mike arrived first and found a seat at the far corner of the bar facing the entrance. He laughed at himself. At the Academy, the instructors had told the class that they would start behaving differently after awhile. The instructors said they would look at people differently. Be suspicious of certain things. In general, acquire a set of new habits. Always sitting in a public place facing the entrance was one several instructors mentioned.

Leon and Tom arrived a few minutes later.

"So how'd it go today?" Leon asked, as he and Tom took seats next to him. "You look happy."

"Fantastic," Mike replied enthusiastically.

"Wow, you are happy," Tom said with a chuckle.

"Yeah, I gotta admit today is the best I've felt about being in the Academy," Mike said. "I actually feel like I accomplished something. You know what I mean?"

"Yeah," said Leon, "there are a lotta days you feel like that on this job."

"Yeah, well, today is one of them for me."

"Well, don't keep us in suspense St George, what dragons hath thee slayed today," said Tom.

"I," Carr announced proudly, "who never, ever have been more than two feet off the ground, climbed fifty feet into the atmosphere."

"Ohhh," said Leon, "you were at Fire school today."

"You got it!" said Carr.

"What are you guys talking about?" asked Tom.

"Every recruit has to spend a day training at the Fire Academy," explained Leon. "They want to teach you some basics, and they want to get you used to climbing ladders. Cops are always called when there is a fire, so they want to make sure you have an idea of what's happening."

"Oh," replied Tom, "so you are a regular Edmund Hillary."

"Edmund Hillary? Isn't that the guy Hillary Clinton said she was named after?"Leon quipped.

"Yeah right," Tom replied dourly not realizing Leon was joking.

"Two ladders," Carr continued, ignoring them, "a 30 foot extension ladder, and a 50 foot hook and ladder."

"Damn," exclaimed Tom with a laugh, "I don't think I've even been on one that high."

"Yeah," chortled Carr, "you know it's high because they got a net beneath it."

"Yeah, and that net don't look to comfortable to land on," Leon chimed in.

They ordered another round of beers and some sandwiches as Carr regaled them with the day's events, starting with the maze and building to a crescendo with the 50 foot ladder climb.

When Mike was finished the conversation he turned towards the more mundane issues of work and marriage. Tom, the only unmarried one of the trio, was keeping a watch on all the unescorted young women who were entering the bar.

"So Leon how's the wife and kids?" Tom asked.

Carr was anxious to hear the reply.

Leon did not reply quickly. He took a long sip of beer and turned slowly to look at Tom. His face was furrowed.

"Not so good. Or maybe very good depending on how you want to look at it," Leon replied.

"Whaddaya mean?" asked Tom

"I think Sheila and I are gonna split up," Leon said, flatly.

"Really?" replied Tom, in a shocked voice. "How come? What's wrong?"

"Is she runnin' around on you?" Mike said, not wanting to let on that he already knew. He wondered if Leon already found out about his conversation with Sheila and that was the reason for the catharsis.

"No, not her -- me," Leon said, with a hint of remorse.

"You? How come?" asked Tom in a concerned voice. "You two been havin' problems?"

"Yes and no. I mean I love Sheila and the kids. But she wants to live one way and I want to live another."

"I don't get it," said Tom.

"I'm not sure I do either except that while I want to go places and do things, Sheila just wants to stay home and take care of the kids, visit her mother, and go to church on Sunday."

"Yeah so, what's your point?" asked Tom.

"I want to go out. I want to go to nightclubs and dancing. I want to go on vacation to someplace other than the Jersey shore or the Pocono's every year. I don't want to have to drag along her mother either."

"Sounds to me like you're growin' apart," said Tom.

"So Oprah, you just get in town?" Carr asked Tom sharply.

"Listen to yourself, Leon," Carr continued. "You're complaining about a woman that cooks, cleans, takes care of the kids, goes to church, and takes care of her widowed mother. Wow, what a lousy bimbo. You oughta dump her tomorra."

"Yeah, I know. That's why it's tough to do," said Leon forlornly.

"Who's the girl?" asked Tom

"I met her at the F.O.P." Leon said.

"Christ, Leon," Carr shook his head in disbelief. "How in the hell you could you dump Sheila for somebody ya met at the Fraternal Order of Police hall? Everybody knows those girls are just uniform chasers."

"I know."

Carr started to realize that he was not helping matters by being so judgmental.

"Listen, Leon," counseled Carr, trying to be detached. "Everybody feels like this. It's no big deal. I feel this way myself sometimes. There are times I feel like walking out on Stella. But ya know Sheila's a good woman. There ain't many like her."

"Yeah," Tom declared, "I'm single, I know. There ain't much out there."

"Well, I found another good woman. She and I have fun together and that's more than I can say for Sheila."

"Yeah," reasoned Mike, "that may be true. How long have you and Sheila been together? What happens when the novelty of this relationship wears off?"

"I dunno," said Leon. "I know what you mean. But right now, I'm havin' fun."

"There's another saying, 'a moment of pleasure can lead to a lifetime of pain,'" cautioned Tom.

"What the hell, look, you're over twenty one. If you don't know what you're doin' then shame on ya," said Mike as he finished up his sandwich.

"You got that right," said Leon, taking the last few bites from his sandwich.

"I don't know about you guys, but I gotta go," said Tom. He finished his beer and placed the bottle on the bar. He threw some dollar bills next to the empty bottle.

"Me too," said Leon.

"I might as well, too," said Mike.

The trio walked outside together. Tom and Leon went one way and Mike the other.

Mike thought about Leon and Sheila on the way home. His own marital problems were different from Leon's. Leon and Sheila were a classic case of one spouse being tired of being married.

The problem between he and Stella, Carr reflected, was their relationship was totally based on sex. Of all the girls he slept with Stella was by far the best. That was important when he was twenty, but it did not seem so important now. If sex was all there was to it, well…

Chapter 9

The following Monday, Carr's platoon and 'B' platoon reported directly to Temple University in North Philadelphia instead of to the Academy. The recruits would spend this week at Temple to receive cultural sensitivity training. Unlike some recruits, Carr did not have any real objections to sensitivity training. He always got along quite well with everyone. In high school, one of his closest friends was black.

There were four two-hour lectures scheduled. The first two lectures were on African-American culture. The second two were on Hispanic-American culture.

The platoon was seated in an amphitheater. Carr sat in the last seat, in the last row, as he usually did when given the choice.

The first instructor was an African-American History Professor. She taught the history of slavery in America.

"Good morning," the instructor said mechanically as she entered the amphitheater.

She was a tall, dignified woman. Carr guessed her age to be late thirties or early forties. Her stride was very long and she had a haughty air about her.

"I would like to begin with the origins of slavery in Africa and the transatlantic slave trade. This will take the first hour. In the second hour, we will discuss the effects of that slave trade on the African-American mentality."

"Tomorrow," the instructor continued, "we will talk about segregation and the customs and culture of African-Americans."

"The objective of this lecture is to make you aware of the differences between the behavior encountered in white neighborhoods and in African -American neighborhoods."

"Are there any questions?"

A member of 'B' platoon raised his hand.

"Yes?" the instructor acknowledged.

"What is your name?" the recruit asked simply.

"Mizzz *Besoto*," she replied emphasizing the Ms part. "It is an African name."

"Oh!" said the recruit.

|

"Unfortunately, some people mistake my name for Italian or Spanish," Ms. Besoto said rather testily. "While those countries did colonize Africa, my name is not of that origin."

Carr was a little surprised my Besoto's belligerence.

"She's got an attitude ain't she?" Carr overheard Mildred Oxford say.

"Yeah, acts like she's a queen," muttered Art Darien.

As the lecture continued, things became progressively worse. As a rule, Carr never asked questions in class. In fact, with the exception of Wister's class, he rarely participated at all. However, what he heard this day was more than he could bear.

At one point during her lecture, Ms. Besoto asked, rhetorically, "What do we know about the men, women, and children that were captured by the Europeans and taken to work on the plantations in America?".

"Well, we know that they were ill fed. We know that they were shackled and had to walk long distances. We know that they had to endure crowded, unsanitary conditions, voyaging across the ocean."

"So what does that tell us that about the Africans who were enslaved by the Europeans and brought here to America?" Ms. Besoto asked once again rhetorically.

"It means that they were survivors. It means they were robust. It means they were strong."

"What is she implying, a superrace?" asked Emerson – also rhetorically.

"She's a little *Miss Kizzyish*," Darien said.

"More like Nurse Ratched," Emerson replied.

Besoto heard Emerson's remark which echoed in the amphitheater. So did the rest of the class. There was a rumble of chuckles.

Besoto stood silent, scowling at her audience. It was at this point that Carr raised his hand.

"Ms. Besoto?" Carr called out as the laughter subsided.

"Yes."

"You have made several references to the Europeans capturing the Africans, and to long marches to the boats, and the cruel treatment they received during the voyage," Carr said testily.

"Yes."

"Well, I'm not a historian, but I watched The History Channel and they had a show about slavery. They said the slave trade in Africa was well established long before the Europeans came along. Not only that, but the Europeans did not have to go inland to capture slaves. The slaves were already waiting for them in the coastal trading cities. They had been enslaved by other Africans," said Carr, innocently.

" I'm not a historian – I did stay at a Holiday Inn," Emerson whispered sarcastically, mimicking the TV commercial.

" You watched the *History Channel?* " Darien whispered in mock astonishment. "Next you're gonna tell me you subscribe to PBS."

"There are differing opinions to that," Besoto replied. "Some historians believe what you say is true, others do not."

Carr tried to rebut Besoto, but she ignored him and continued.

After the lecture Carr spoke with Oscar McClellan, an African-American recruit who was one of the few people he talked to on a regular basis. He thought about what he said and how it might have sounded to Oscar.

"Oscar, I hope you weren't angry about what I said. I wasn' t trying to put down blacks, but I felt that she was trying to put down whites."

"That's okay," replied Oscar.

"Yeah, I mean I'm not a racist. I think everybody is the same. There is good and bad with all people. Hell, my best friend in high school was a black kid named Joe Jobson."

"Yeah, I know what you mean," replied Oscar. "Listen, I'm meetin' somebody for lunch. I'll talk to you later."

"Yeah, sure," said Carr. He got the impression that McClellan did not believe him.

So what? I know who I am, Mike Carr thought to himself angrily, I do not have to convince somebody that I am not a racist. I never have been and never will be.

Carr recalled an incident that happened a few years ago when some female black high school students beat a white woman. The woman was picking up her daughter from a daycare. She tried to make a turn but the students coming home from school blocked her path. She told them to move and words were exchanged and then the woman was beaten. The black girls apparently had shouted racial epithets at the white woman during the incident.

However, when the local paper reported the story, Carr remembered bitterly, they immediately reported it as whites assaulting blacks because they were walking through a white neighborhood. It turned out to be the exact opposite and the newspaper later retracted the story.

Yet the first instinct of the journalist was to automatically assign racism to the whites. They talk about bigotry? They should look at themselves in the mirror.

When the lecture reconvened, Carr reluctantly took his seat. He had thought about cutting the class.

Ms. Besoto was joined by two other professors. Together the professors discussed the effects of slavery on the modern African-American. Their approach to this subject was similar to Ms. Besoto.

The class on Hispanic culture was somewhat similar. Although the instructor at least made a bona fide attempt to teach the recruits about Hispanic culture. Carr liked the Hispanic culture he learned from watching old western movies and television shows. He learned a few Spanish phrases from them.

The day ended with no great revelations from this class – although he learned a few more Spanish phrases to add to his repertoire.

The next morning's lecture dealt with women's issues. Two actors reenacted a typical domestic dispute involving a husband, wife, and baby. The actors took two recruits and had them role-play the officers given the assignment to handle the dispute. The whole thing was actually quite entertaining Carr thought, although he did not know how realistic it was.

After the morning lecture the class was dismissed for lunch. The recruits ate in the cafeteria and went to the student lounge to avail themselves of the games there. With their white shirts and black ties, the recruits were conspicuous to say the least. The average student wore jeans and a sweatshirt.

Some of the Temple students knew the identity of these strangely attired people walking among them. Being the open minded, educated young people they were, the students would occasionally call out " oink, oink " or "souee" as the recruits passed by. The recruits, being brutal, ignorant, uneducated, police officers in training, usually ignored the students--usually.

Jay Emerson and Art Darien had been playing air hockey in the lounge during lunch. Air hockey was a favorite of Carr's. After they ate, the three of them, along with Mildred Oxford and Harry Denison, went to the lounge.

As Emerson and Darien walked to the air hockey table two students cut in front of them and occupied the table. Jay and Art looked at one another in disbelief. Mildred who was a couple of steps behind Art yelled out.

"What are you two doing?" she shrieked at the students.

"Yeah," protested Emerson, "we were going to play."

"Too bad," said a blonde haired boy of about twenty, "you snooze, you loose."

"Yeah, you gotta move fast here," joined in the other student. He was short with long, dark, black hair.

Jay Emerson was a laid back type of guy. For all of his teasing, Carr found that Jay was not mean-spirited, just playful. Jay understood what these students were doing and was willing to pass it off as just two kids having fun. So, as Mildred was about ready to scream at them, Jay picked her up and carried her away from the table. As he did so, the blonde student started making sounds like a pig.

"Oink, snort, Oink," he mimicked. His partner started laughing.

Art Darien, who up until now had not said a word, walked up behind the blonde headed kid.

"You know you do a pretty good imitation of a pig," he said.

"Thanks," replied the student sarcastically. "I guess I got the potential to be one of Philadelphia's finest."

His partner laughed.

"Yeah, could be," said Darien coolly.

"If you really want to I could enter your name in for a candidate," Darien said, gritting his teeth. Darien was still standing directly behind the student. The student continued playing not even acknowledging Darien.

"No, I have more important things to take care of. I stopped playing cops and robbers a long time ago," the student said with a grin.

"Yeah, but you got so much to learn yet," said Darien. He grabbed the student by his belt in the middle of the back. He then lifted the student off the floor and onto the air hockey table.

"For instance let me show you how to frisk a person," Darien said, as he pressed the students head against the table.

The dark haired student went to assist his friend, however Emerson stood in his path. The student took one look at Emerson's bulk and backed up.

"A frisk is to make sure that the police officer is not in danger," Darien growled.

The student tried to get up but Darien's firm grip dictated otherwise.

"Darien! Let him go," came a loud deep voice from the entrance to the lounge. The voice belonged to Corporal Wood.

"Sure Corporal," replied Darien. "I was just demonstrating a police procedure to this gentleman."

"Okay, knock it off," said Wood. "Darien, you and your friends clear outta here."

"You," said Wood sternly to the student, "go back to your game."

"I' m gonna sue you bastards. You wait," said the blonde kid.

"Fine. I'm gonna sue you too," replied Darien.

"Yeah, me too," yelled Oxford. "You called me a pig. That's sexual harassment."

"I didn't harass you," said the student excitedly. He was obviously concerned about an accusation of harassing a woman even if she was a cop. In the politically correct world of the university, sexual harassment was a capital offense.

"Knock it off, all of you or I' m gonna lock everybody up and then sue all of you. You're all causin' me emotional distress," said Wood impatiently.

Grumbling, the students returned to their game. Carr, Darien, and the rest left the lounge with Wood.

"Sorry, Corporal," said Darien. "I didn't mean to cause you any grief, but those dudes were asking for it."

"Yeah, I know," said Wood. "It's a problem every time we come here. There's usually a wiseguy who thinks he can push the recruits around and get away with it. Nobody has ever let it get to them before."

"You think the school will complain to the Department?" asked Darien.

"Nah, I think the wiseass is more worried about Mildred filing sexual harassment charges against him than anything else."

"Yeah, I figured that would shut him up," said Oxford with a smile.

When class resumed, the platoon was treated to several sociologists and psychologists presenting their take on domestic violence. Carr was mindful because he knew that these disputes made up a lot of what a cop does. He also knew how volatile they could be. He wanted to be able to know how to handle them properly. The reenactment in the morning's class had given him a few clues but Carr still consider the morning class entertainment. This class would be the real thing with the experts in psychology and sociology presenting their theories.

As eager as Carr was to learn -- that is how little he learned. The entire lecture was nothing more than a dissertation about the oppression of women by men.

As he rode the subway home, he reflected on his experiences at Temple. It had been quite a revelation. However, what he had learned was not quite what the Police Department of the City of Philadelphia had sent him there to learn.

When he got to street level, he opted to walk home rather than take the bus.

It took about ten minutes for him to walk the six blocks to his house. He opened the door and smelled the aroma of spaghetti and meatballs. Stella was in the kitchen stirring a pot.

"Hi," she said simply.

"Hi, whatcha doin'?" Mike said. He walked over and gave her a quick kiss on the cheek.

"Just makin' some gravy," Stella replied, not bothering to return the kiss.

i

"Now, I thought we were told that it wasn't gravy but sauce," Mike said jokingly.

"Who said?" replied Stella.

"Remember?" Mike replied, "we looked up the definition in the dictionary. It's not spaghetti gravy, it's spaghetti sauce."

"Well, you say sauce, I'll say gravy," replied Stella with a silly grin.

Mike came up behind her put his arms around her and started nibbling her ear and neck. Stella closed her eyes but continued to stir the pot.

"Not now!" Stella protested softly, "the gravy will burn."

"Sauce," Mike said as he kissed her.

"Gravy," Stella insisted as she returned his kiss.

"Whatever," Mike said as he reached behind her and turned off the burner. She turned it back on. "Not now," she said emphatically. He smiled and walked into the living room.

After dinner, he helped her wash the dishes. Stella finished wiping off the table. After she was done, she got her coat from the closet.

"I'm goin' to the store. Then I'm gonna stop over my mother's," Stella said.

"Can't you stay home tonight," he asked plaintively.

"No, I need to do some errands."

"Okay," Mike said, "I'm going to bed."

He locked the door after Stella left and walked upstairs and went to bed.

He was asleep by the time she came home.

The remainder of the Temple classes was more of the same. He was glad it was their last day.

When he arrived home, he found that Stella was over her mother's house. She had a left a note telling him to fend for himself for dinner. She was going to eat over there. If he wanted, he was welcome to go join them.

Screw that, Carr thought angrily. Maybe I'll go out for a beer.

Carr changed his clothes, called Tom, and arranged to meet him at a restaurant that Mike liked for its roast beef sandwiches.

125

As he got into his car Mike shivered a little bit. The weather was turning colder. It was colder now than it was when he walked home from the subway.

Tom was sitting in a booth near the door looking at the songs on the jukebox when Mike came in. Mike sat down facing the door. He was developing the habit of doing that every time he was in a public place.

"What's happenin'?" said Tom as Carr sat down.

"Nuthin' much, how' bout yerself?" replied Carr.

"Same ole, same ole."

"How's the Academy?"

"We were at Temple University all week."

"Temple? How come?"

"Cultural sensitivity training."

"HHmmph!"

"Yeah," Mike said, "I was actually looking forward to it at first because I didn't have to report to the Academy. But I'll tell, you the professors were just trying to brainwash us."

"So what else is new. How's the wife?" asked Tom, changing the subject.

"Drivin' me insane."

"Don't they all," said Tom with a grin.

"Boy, you are the perceptive one, aintcha," Mike said smiling.

"What can I say. I always told you I'm good," said Tom still grinning.

"That's not what your girlfriend said."

"Which one? I've got four or five."

"Yeah, you can't afford the one you got."

"You got that right," said Tom. "Girlfriends are expensive."

"Yeah, that's why I got married," laughed Mike.

"You mean it wasn't love or lust? Just finances?"

"Yeah," said Mike, "That's what I thought, but I've found out since that it was cheaper just dating them."

"How's Leon doin'? Does he still got that girlfriend or did he do the OJ thing with her – or the Robert Blake thing - with his wife?" asked Tom.

"Don't know. Nothing's been in the papers so I guess he hasn't been indicted," responded Mike. "Who knows? Maybe his wife did the Blake thing in reverse."

"What's good for the gander is good for the goose," affirmed Tom.

"But I'll let you in on this," Mike continued. "I knew about it before then."

"How?" asked Tom quizzically.

"I saw Sheila at the bar around the corner from me the night before Thanksgiving," said Mike. "She was sittin' by herself when I walked in."

"Yeah, what did she say?"

"She told me about Leon's girlfriend. Obviously, she was upset. She acted like she was fed up with him. If he wanted to go off with someone she didn't give a damn."

"Why didn't you mention it to Leon?"

"I don't want to get in the middle. It's their problem. They gotta work it out for themselves," said Mike.

"I think he's goofy myself," said Tom. "Sheila's a good woman and a hot looking one at that. Guy's got someone like that, he ought to appreciate it."

"I was thinkin' the same thing," said Mike. "That night I got in an argument with Stella. That's why I was at the bar. Talkin' to Sheila is a lot different than talkin' to Stella."

"Waddaya mean?"

"I dunno, it just seems like Sheila's got her head screwed on straight. Like she wants to take care of her responsibilities. I don't always feel that way with Stella."

"So you figger that Leon's to blame."

"Ah, there ain't no blame in these things. Everybody's right and everybody's wrong. Just like me and Stella. We have our problems. It's not always her fault," Mike explained.

"Yeah, somebody once told me it takes two to get married and two to get a divorce."

"Well, if me and Stella ever get a divorce, it'll be a mutual type of thing. It won't be because one of us is steppin' out on the other."

"You wouldn't cheat on her?"

127

"Nah, if I want to cheat on her I'll get a divorce," said Mike finishing off his sandwich.

"You can look can't you?"

"Whaddaya mean?" asked Mike

"I mean it's OK if you look at another woman. Right?" replied Tom. "That ain't cheatin' is it?"

"No, that's being comatose," replied Mike wondering what this was leading up to.

"Good then let's go to that new topless bar on Columbus Blvd."

"Nah, whaddayawant to do that for. Them broads won't go for you," Mike said.

"You don't think so? Guess what? One already has."

"Yeah?" replied Mike

"Yeah!"

"Well then, lead the way," Mike said as he finished his beer.

Tom grabbed the check and Mike left the tip. The two of them went in their separate cars and met again in the parking lot of The Den. The bar was euphemistically called a "gentlemen's club." It was basically a high rent version of a Go-Go bar. Mike used to go to these places when he was dating Stella. He remembered being 18 years old and going into clip joints. The scantily clad girls would sit down and ask customers to buy them drinks. Meanwhile one of them would be dancing on stage. The idea was to keep the customer buying drinks at outrageous prices.

Now the dancers come off stage, after they are done, and talk to the customers and get tips. The customers aren't allowed to touch them any place in an intimate way. The girls just teased them enough so the customers would place dollar bills in their G-strings.

Mike and Tom spent a few dollars in that manner. Actually, Tom spent a few dollars, Mike just laughed at Tom's antics. He had a couple of drinks and left. Tom stayed behind engaged in a conversation with one of the girls.

It was eleven o'clock and Mike was getting sleepy. He drove home and found that Stella still wasn't there. He became a little concerned because Stella didn't usually stay over her mother's so

ǀ

late. He debated with himself for a few minutes about calling. Finally, he dialed the phone.

On the second ring, his mother-in-law answered.

"Hello!" she said. Her tone of voice was always surly.

"Yeah, Mom, it's Mike," Mike said sheepishly. "Is Stella there?"

"Hold on," his mother-in-law replied abruptly.

"Hello!" Stella shouted.

"Yeah, It's me," Mike said softly. "I just wanted to make sure you were still there."

"Why? You checkin' up on me?"

"No, I was just worried because you weren't home by now. You usually ain't out this late."

"Well, I'm okay."

"Fine."

"Bye!" she said abruptly and hung up the phone.

Chapter 10

The mid-December morning sun pierced the night's veil, diminishing the effect of the oncoming headlights. Mike turned on the heat in the car turning the dial all the way. He had to report directly to the Pistol Range today. The platoon was scheduled to be there until the end of the calendar year. They were to be joined by 'B' platoon.

Carr looked forward to the pistol range for a couple of reasons. He wanted to learn how to shoot. Second, he didn't have to wear the academy uniform. The pistol range let the recruits dress anyway they wanted. The only requirement was that they had to wear a baseball cap. Carr wore a short down jacket, blue jeans, sneakers and a Phillies cap. When he arrived at the range, he entered the gate and was directed to a bungalow. As Carr walked to the bungalow, he examined the grounds.

The range resembled a country club. Concrete walkways, which were flanked by shrubs and flowers, connected the buildings. The lawn was well maintained. Carr could see on the far end of the range itself targets in front of a berm. Above the targets were numbers. On top of the berm were some trees. In the middle of the grounds was a tower with an enclosed booth. From the top of the booth protruded two speakers. There were two light poles on either side of the tower. Approximately twenty feet in front of the tower was a row of red fence posts. Each post had a number corresponding to the targets. Carr also noticed some numbers on one of the walkways that traversed the grounds near the entrance. These numbers also corresponded to the target numbers.

Carr entered the bungalow to find most of the platoon had already arrived. They were sitting on folding chairs arranged in rows. One of the instructors motioned to the wall where more chairs were stacked. Carr walked over, grabbed a chair, opened it and sat down. The remainder of the platoon wandered in a few minutes later.

Promptly at eight o'clock, an instructor strode into the room from an office outside. The platoon started to rise but he motioned them to remain seated. He was dressed not in the uniform of a police officer, but with dark blue combat fatigues and a dark blue baseball cap, with the departmental emblem on the front.

"My name is Sergeant Pentridge, I'll be the CO for your stay here," he announced.

"During that time," Pentridge continued, "you'll learn how to maintain your weapon and how to use it properly. We'll give you certain strategic scenarios based on actual incidents and test your reaction to them. You will be tear-gassed. Finally, you will be tested for qualification and for badges."

Carr listened and wondered how he would do handling a pistol. He had not been around firearms since he was a kid.

"What we will do today is issue you a weapon. This will be your permanent issue weapon. The one that you will be issued upon graduation."

"Officer Gaul will handle the issue," said Pentridge. He walked into another room as Officer Gaul stood in front of the platoon.

"Good Morning," said Officer Gaul. "I am going to call your name. You will go to the front of the room, an instructor will issue you a gun. You will read the serial number from that gun to the instructor."

"If there are no questions let's get started," said Gaul.

"Adams."

As Gaul called out the names, the recruits went to Pentridge who handed each a weapon, and a holster. The recruits had to repeat their names and the serial numbers of the guns to a third instructor who recorded it on a list. The weapons were the standard issue, 9 mm Glock, Model 17, semi-automatic pistol.

One of the recruits, after getting his weapon, started pretending he was a gunfighter. He holstered the gun and pulled it out aiming at his friend. Both of them started to laugh. This drew an immediate, very loud, and very sharp rebuke from Gaul.

"Put that damn weapon away," boomed Gaul. His voice reverberated off the walls of the room. Immediately the recruits fell silent.

"Gimme that," Gaul said angrily. He reached over and snatched the gun out of the recruits' hand. "What in the hell do you think you're doin'. This ain't no toy."

"What's your name?" shouted Gaul.

"Baker, sir," the recruit replied evenly.

"Baker, I'm gonna bounce you the hell outta here so fast you ain't gonna know what happened," shrieked Gaul. "Is that what you want?"

"No sir."

" Then you better make sure that the entire time you're here you don't take your weapon outta your holster *unless you are told to do so by an instructor.* You don't point the weapon at anything other than a target," said Gaul loudly.

" The same goes for the rest of you," shouted Gaul, as he turned to the rest of the class. "You have been warned. Whoever does somethin' like this again is getting fired. On the spot."

"Does everyone understand?" asked Gaul loudly.

"Yes sir," the class answered in unison.

With that, Gaul resumed calling the role. The recruits very quietly went up took the equipment issued and returned to their seats. There were no repetitions of any horseplay. It took about twenty minutes for the entire platoon to be outfitted. Once the issuing of the weapons was completed, Gaul stood at the head of the classroom.

"I want to give you some basic information about the training here. First thing," he said holding up the gun, "this is a Glock, Model 17, 9mm semi-automatic pistol. During the next two weeks, you will be trained to qualify to shoot as a police officer, and you will also shoot for a badge."

Gaul went on to provide a great many details about procedures and policies. Carr's mind started to wander and only came back when Gaul dismissed the platoon for lunch.

Carr filed out of the room and walked to the lunch truck that was parked just outside the gate. Most of the platoon did the same. Carr turned up the collar of his coat. He stuck his hands in his pocket and waited in line to order his food. The steam from the lunch truck helped warm him.

"Gimme a tuna salad and a coke. Wait, make that a hot chocolate," said Carr.

"Yeah, it's gittin' cold out. Get that hot chocolate," said Darien, who was standing behind him.

¡

"Yeah, it seems like it got colder than it was this mornin' even," replied Carr.

"Makes you wonder how we're gonna hit the targets because we're shivering so much," said Darien.

"It's supposed to get colder later this week," chimed in Oxford who was warming her hands over the steam.

"Just what we need," replied Carr.

"Where's Baker?" asked Emerson, joining the group. "Do you believe that dumb fuck? Playing cowboy."

"He's always been a shithead," said Darien.

"Yeah, I remember when we were at the Fire Academy, he was playing around acting like he was in the movie *Towering Inferno*," said Mildred.

"Yeah, well, he probably won't be fooling around like that anymore. George Jefferson there got the message to him," quipped Darien.

"He does look like George Jefferson, doesn't he?" mused Mildred.

"Yeah, a little. Hey, I gotta go out to my car, I'll be right back," said Mike as he walked towards the gate. He threw out the wrapper from his sandwich and the Styrofoam cup from the hot chocolate as he walked out.

"You going to the Starsky and Hutch mobile?" asked Mildred.

"Huh, Starsky and Hutch?" Mike replied quizzically.

"Yeah that's what we call it. It's the same color."

"First George Jefferson, now Starsky and Hutch. You guys are really into '70's TV shows. You're really watching too much Nick at Nite," Mike replied smiling, as he walked towards his car.

By the time he returned, lunch was over and the platoon was back in the building. Pentridge and Gaul were standing at the front of the class flanked by two instructors.

"All right, settle down," said Gaul as the class filed in. "We got a lot of work to get done."

"I want to introduce Officers Waverly and Anderson. They will be your range instructors along with Sergeant Pentridge, and myself," Gaul continued.

"We're gonna go out on the range now. I want to familiarize you with it. Officer Waverly will call out your name and you will be assigned a number. The number will be the position on the range that you occupy. This position will be yours for the entire time you're here."

"Call out the role Bill," Gaul said turning to Waverly.

"The number Officer Gaul referred to will be painted on the walkways," Waverly added. "I want you to go to the walkway closest to the hut. That is the fifty-yard firing line."

"You will also find walkways at twenty-five yards, fifteen yards, seven yards, five and three yards."

"For now I want you to stay at the fifty," Waverly said. "So when I call your name, find your spot on the fifty-yard line."

"Adams..." barked Waverly.

Carr was assigned number nine. He awkwardly attached the holster to his belt and walked out to the fifty-yard firing line.

"Listen up," came an amplified voice from the speakers on the tower. "This is Sergeant Pentridge. I want you to walk forward to the three-yard line."

"DO NOT TOUCH YOUR FIREARMS!" Pentridge boomed. "Anyone who touches their weapon without authorization will be immediately dismissed."

Pentridge's admonishment was unnecessary. The incident with Baker was still fresh in the platoon's collective memory.

The class began walking forward. When they reached the three-yard line, they stopped. Ahead of each of them, just in front of the berm, was a frame to which the targets are attached.

"Each morning, as soon as you arrive, you will get a target from the supply hut. You will place the target on the frame. You will then report back to the building for roll call," said Pentridge.

"You will be given instructions for the day. You will receive ammunition and we will go over what will be taught that day. In the beginning, every thing will be done without ammunition. In a short time you will be given ammo, but for now, we just want you to get accustomed to handling a gun. We anticipate you to do live firing by tomorrow."

"Okay, let's get started," Pentridge said. "On the command: Ready on the right, ready on the left, all ready on the firing line, everybody will face the target. Have your knees slightly bent."

"When I give the command to aim, draw your weapon, spread your feet shoulder width apart and point your weapon at the target." The edge of the target is facing you now, when it is time to begin firing the target will turn automatically to full view. When firing is completed the target returns perpendicular to you."

"At the three-yard firing line, you will be doing hip shooting. Meaning that you do not use your sights. You will repeat this from the five and seven-yard lines. Later, from the fifteen-yard line you will do point shooting, which means you use the sights. At the twenty-five, you will do barricade and kneeling, there will be prone at the fifty when we shoot for badges only – not to qualify."

Carr looked at the berm in front of him and turned to look at the fifty-yard line. It seemed like a mile away.

"Ready on the right, ready on the left, all ready on the firing line! At the sound of the horn you will draw your weapon and simulate firing. When the horn blows again you will cease firing."

Pentridge paused and looked up and down the line to make sure everyone was ready. When he was satisfied, he sounded the horn.

Carr drew his weapon slowly, spread his legs shoulder width apart and slightly bent. He held the gun at about chest level aimed at the berm..

"You're holding your weapon the wrong way," a voice from behind said. It was Officer Waverly.

"You right-handed?" asked Waverly

"Yeah."

"Okay, you hold the gun with your right-hand and rest the grip in the palm of your left hand. Keep the gun at lower chest or upper abdomen level. Keep your right arm out straight and your knees bent," said Waverly. "Got it?"

"Yes sir," replied Carr.

Waverly moved on down the line correcting the recruits next to Carr. The other instructor was doing the same thing for the recruits on the other side of the tower.

"Keep repeating this drill, until I tell you to stop," Pentridge ordered. "Number twenty-five keep the weapon lower."

Carr repeated the motion each time remembering to pull the gun from the holster slowly. For some reason he was having difficulty with this. It felt awkward.

135

Michael P. Tremoglie

A stiff breeze blew steadily from behind the berm. It swirled around the range much like the wind would in a stadium. This was a problem on a cold winter day. The whistle sounded. "Cease Fire!" Pentridge bellowed form his perch. "You will repeat this same drill. This time however you will simulate firing your weapon five times. Ready on the right, ready on the left, all ready on the firing line," instructed Pentridge, followed by the whistle.

The sound of fifty metallic clicks reverberated throughout the range. The class repeated this motion several times.

"We will do the same thing," Pentridge ordered. "Except now you will pull the slide open and simulate ejecting the magazine and reloading another magazine. Then you will simulate firing the weapon with your OTHER hand. Does everyone understand?"

"Line instructors, demonstrate please!" commanded Pentridge, not waiting for a response. Gaul and Waverly, one on each side of the tower, stepped in front of the firing line and demonstrated the procedure.

"You will need to learn to handle your weapon with ease from both left and right sides," said Pentridge. After Gaul and Waverly demonstrated the drill again, they assumed their positions behind the recruits.

"Ready on the left," barked Pentridge, "ready on the right, all ready on the firing line."

Pentridge blew the whistle.

Once again, Carr pulled the gun from the holster and pulled the trigger five times. Pentridge made the class repeat the drill until the line instructors had a chance to examine each recruit. Once he felt comfortable that everyone could handle this Pentridge ordered everyone to the five-yard line. Then again at the seven, then finally to the fifteen.

"Okay, from here we do point shooting," Pentridge said. "Officers Waverly and Gaul will demonstrate."

"Nuthin' to this," said Waverly. "Same as before 'cept you use your sights," said Waverly. "Any questions?"

When there weren't any, Waverly signaled Pentridge and they drilled this until the instructors were comfortable that everyone knew what to do.

136

"Okay, back to the twenty-five for barricade and kneeling," Pentridge ordered.

Once again, Waverly and Gaul demonstrated the positions.

"In barricade position," Waverly said, "you place one hand on the barricade, spread your thumb out, and rest the wrist of your gun hand on your thumb."

"When you switch to your other hand you do the same thing," Waverly continued. "Simple, right? Any questions?"

Once again, no one had a question. Once again, the class practiced until the instructors felt comfortable with the execution.

"We'll now go to kneeling. In this position, you will get down on one knee, the knee of your shooting side. You will rest your elbow opposite your shooting side on your bent knee resting your weapon in the palm of that hand," Pentridge said.

Carr had a problem with this at first; he had a tendency to kneel upright like he was genuflecting.

"You need to sit back when you do that," Waverly instructed him.

"Okay, we'll stop here. It will take too long to go into the next drill, so we'll save that for tomorrow. Class dismissed," said Pentridge. "Bright and early kiddies."

Mike turned in his gun and holster and walked out to his car. He got behind the wheel and drove off. By the time he arrived home night had fallen. He found Stella on the phone with her mother. He went upstairs without even saying hello to his wife. He changed and washed for dinner.

When he came down Stella was watching TV in the living room. She had a cup of coffee on the floor next to her feet. She was in her housecoat watching a game show that they both liked.

"What's for dinner?" he asked.

"I made a roast, it'll be done in about ten minutes," she replied. "Aintcha gonna say hello first?"

"You were on the phone when I came in."

"Yeah, I was talking to my mother."

"What a surprise," he muttered to himself.

"What?" Stella said.

"Nothing. How's she doing?" Mike replied quickly changing the subject.

"She's OK. What did you say?" Stella demanded.

"Nothing. If I was talking to you, you woulda heard me," Mike replied becoming a bit irritated.

"You're always mumbling," said Stella, angrily.

Carr walked into the dining room and grabbed the newspaper on the table. The headline was about a lack of African-Americans on the Police Department. Carr skimmed through the story. A local civil rights leader, Richmond York, wants more blacks on the PD.

"The only people who lose their job to racial quotas will be the little guys--not the CEO's," Carr muttered to himself.

"Set the table," Stella ordered interrupting his thoughts.

"Sure," Mike said softly.

Mike placed the dishes and silverware on the table and Stella served the food. They ate without talking to one another. After he was done, Mike took his plate into the kitchen.

"The roast was great," Mike said to Stella leaning over to kiss her on the cheek

"I'm thinkin' of goin' back to work full time," Stella blurted out without acknowledging Mike's compliment.

"Full time?" Mike replied incredulously. "The whole idea of me becoming a cop was to make enough money so you could stay home, be a full time housewife, and we can start working on a family."

"Yeah, I know. However, we ain't working on a family and I'm getting' bored doin' house work. There is only so much cleaning I can do. Besides we can always use the extra money."

"That makes sense. But then again it always made sense to me that you should work anyway. But I want to go to school while you're working, instead of being a cop."

"No, because if you do that then I gotta work, and we'll never save any money."

"Yeah, but I'll make a better living in the future."

"Maybe, maybe not. There's a lotta college graduates that are outta work."

"Yeah, name one."

"I don't know, but you hear it on the news all the time."

ı

Mike stood silent and cursed himself. We've been in this arena before, he thought. We're not going to settle anything. She does not want me to go to college and that is all there is to it. The only way I can do it is if I get some money from either a tuition assistance program or taking out a loan through the credit union, Mike thought.

"Yeah, I guess that's true. Besides we would probably be better off with two incomes instead of one," Mike said finally. "You got any ideas of where you're gonna work ?"

"Yeah, I was thinkin' of doin' nails at my hairdresser down the street," Stella said.

"At Rosie's?" Mike asked.

"Yeah. We've talked about it. She figured it might attract more customers. Even men are getting their nails done nowadays."

"What is she gonna pay?"

" We haven't talked about that yet."

"When you gonna know?"

"Next week."

"Fine," said Mike not wishing to pursue the subject any more. "Listen, I want to go to the store. I need to buy some thermal underwear. It's real cold standin' outside at the pistol range. The cold goes right through you."

"Okay," replied Stella, "could you drop me off over my mother's?"

"Yeah sure," replied Mike.

They got their coats and walked outside to the car. Mike noticed, for the first time, the Christmas decorations on the houses in the neighborhood. Nearly all the houses on the block were decorated - - some very elaborately. There were houses with illuminated figures of Santa Claus in his sleigh. Others were decorated with lighted snowflakes or stars. Still others had the frame of the houses outlined in flashing or steady burning lights. Some were of many colors; some all white.

It was a beautiful scene. One that Mike always enjoyed and always helped put him in the Christmas spirit.

"You know we haven't decorated for Christmas yet and it's next week," Mike said to Stella.

"Yeah, I guess without any kids it's tough getting into the Christmas spirit," Stella sighed gloomily.

"Ya know that's the second time tonight you brought up kids. Are you giving me a hint?" Mike asked.

"I don't know. My mother told me yesterday that Nancy is pregnant again," Stella said, referring to her younger sister. "This is her second kid. I don't even have one yet."

"So what is this, a race?" asked Mike.

"No, but I would like to start having kids before we get too old."

"I want kids too. But I know that we better have our finances together first. Your brother-in-law, at least, has got a good job with the union. I don't have that," Mike continued. "That's why I want to go to college, so I can get and keep a good job, so we can start a family."

"Yeah, but it cost money to go to college and a lot of college graduates are out of work."

"Yeah, and a lot are making tremendous money."

"I don't know."

"Well think about it. I still say it's a good investment," Mike said as he pulled up in front of his in-law's house. "Maybe in a coupla years we can start having kids and we won't hafta worry about whether or not the union boss likes me. Maybe I can get a job with the FBI or DEA. Who knows?"

"I don't know," Stella repeated, "I'll see ya later. My mother will drive me home."

"Okay."

They gave each other a quick kiss and Mike drove off to the store. There was a hardware store next to a clothing store around the corner. He made up his mind not only to buy thermal underwear, but also to buy some Christmas lights at the hardware store. He was tired of the set that they had.

He thought about what Stella had said. It seems that she is getting uneasy about things. Whether it was impatience or something else, he couldn't say. It was a new development that's for sure. But then again, it was consistent with Stella's inconsistent nature. No matter what he did, she was never going to be satisfied.

He found the thermals, grabbed two pair, and then went to buy the Christmas decorations. They were nearly sold out. He grabbed three strings of alternating lights that played Christmas carols. After paying for the merchandise he went home. After trying on his thermals, he placed one pair on a chair ready for tomorrow, refolded the other and put it in his armoire.

He then went downstairs and unpacked the lights. Mike found some tape in the kitchen and began putting them up.

After about two hours, all the lights were up. "I'll do the Christmas tree tomorrow night after dinner," he said to himself while putting everything away. After he straightened up he took a shower and went to bed.

Stella came home around midnight and muttered something under her breath about the Christmas lights. Mike had purposely left them on so she would see them when she arrived home. He heard the sounds of them being unplugged. As she came up the steps, he rolled over and pretended to be asleep.

The next morning Mike arrived at the pistol range early. He drew his weapon and a target from supply. After placing his target on the frame of his spot on the firing line, he returned to the hut.

After roll call, the class went to the firing line. They spent the entire day simulating. The class was getting bored with the dry runs.

At the end of the day Pentridge told everyone the news they had been wanting to hear. "Tomorrow we go to live firing," he announced.

There was a cheer from the class - followed by a lot of chattering.

"Be here on time tomorrow. We have a lot of work to do. Class dismissed," said Pentridge.

The next morning Carr made roll call just in time. He had to hustle to hang his target and get back in time to get his weapon and ammunition. This time they were issued a gray set of ear protectors.

"Each time you're issued ammunition, you will be given enough for the day's course," said Pentridge.

"Today we are doing a 48 round course. You will take the rounds out of the boxes and place them in your right front pants pocket, or if you prefer your right front jacket pocket," Pentridge continued. "Okay, let's go to the firing line."

Pentridge went to the tower. From his perch he addressed the platoon.

"I want you to take two rounds from your pocket. Place those rounds in the magazine and HOLSTER YOUR WEAPON!"

The platoon did as instructed. Carr nervously opened the slide of the automatic. He pressed, with his right thumb, the release button and caught the magazine. After inserting the cartridges into the magazine, as he had practiced the past two days, he inserted the magazine into the gun and then holstered the weapon.

"We're going to do hip shooting from the three-yard line. As I have told you before, most shootouts will occur from this distance OR LESS!"

"Okay, live fire exercise. Hip shooting, from the three-yard line," Pentridge Announced. "Ready on the right, ready on the left. All ready on the firing line."

On the sound of the whistle the target turned and Carr reached for his weapon. Just as he had done in the drills, he shifted his feet to shoulder width and bent his knees slightly. He brought the weapon up, resting the grip in the palm of his left hand, found the trigger with the crook of his right index finger and squeezed the trigger. The firing pin on the hammer struck the cap in the cartridge, which exploded and in turn ignited the powder in the cartridge. The expanding gas expelled the lead bullet through the muzzle at a speed of about 1400 feet per second.

The force caused the weapon to recoil in his hand. The sound of the shot hurt his ears.

It was then he realized, he did not have on his ear protectors. He apparently had not heard Waverly's admonition to place them on. Carr hesitated pulling the trigger again. He wasn't sure whether he should stop and put his protectors on or continue. He pulled the trigger again, and the sound made him jump. This time he started to holster his weapon and put on the protectors.

"You're not done firing!" growled Waverly.

"Yes sir, but I want to put these ear protectors on," Carr replied meekly.

"Aw the sound of the pop scare the wittle baby," Waverly said mockingly.

"No sir," replied Carr tersely. He aimed at the target and quickly got off the remaining rounds not caring whether he hit the target or a boat in the river.

"Reload!" ordered Pentridge after the platoon was finished.

This time Carr put on the protectors. He took some rounds from his pocket, loaded his gun, holstered it, and awaited the command to begin firing.

"Ready on the right," Pentridge announced, "ready on the left, all ready on the firing line."

Pentridge blew the whistle.

Carr drew his gun and emptied the rounds into the target. From what he could tell, he didn't get close to a bull's-eye. However, that was to be expected, he consoled himself, after all he was still a neophyte. Nobody else seemed to be doing much better. Carr ejected the magazine.

"Reload!" bellowed Pentridge.

Carr reloaded the remaining cartridges from his pocket into the clip, closed it, and holstered. On the horn, Carr drew his weapon and emptied the rounds into the target.

"Reload! Repeat firing."

Carr did as instructed.

"Bend those knees," Waverly yelled, kicking Carr behind his right knee.

"Keep that arm straight," Waverly yelled, this time yanking Carr's shooting arm nearly out of its socket. Carr immediately straightened his arm and made a conscious effort to keep it straight.

"Make sure you clean up that brass!" Waverly shouted to everyone near him. "Place the brass in the brass box. If I find any brass near you, I will personally take a brass box and hit you across the knee with it."

This time after they were done the platoon was instructed to tear down the target and return to the building. There was a lot of chatter among the recruits. Carr met Darien and Oxford on the walk back.

"How'd ya do?" asked Mildred, as she walked next to Carr.

"I am definitely not ready for the Olympic team," replied Carr with a grin.

"Me neither," said Darien, joining the conversation.

The platoon settled inside the room. They were joined in a few minutes by the instructors who reviewed some common errors they saw on the line. After the instructors had finished, they were dismissed for lunch.

After lunch, the platoon was issued more ammunition. This time they were instructed to line up on the five-yard line. They practiced more hip shooting from the five and seven before moving to the fifteen where they practiced point shooting.

On the whistle, Carr drew his gun and raised it to shoulder level, fired all six rounds and holstered his weapon.

After the first series, Carr assessed his effort. Not good, he thought. Two off the target completely, the remainder were outside of the torso. He seemed to be pulling his shots up and to the right.

The next two series improved somewhat, but not well enough. By the sixth series, Carr still was shooting up and to the right.

"You're jerking the trigger," Waverly counseled him as they walked back to the hut for more ammunition and review.

"Okay," Carr replied simply.

They repeated the fifteen-yard line drills for the balance of the afternoon. Carr followed Waverly's advice but still was not straightening out his shots.

The next day, day four of the range, they practiced shooting from the kneeling and barricade positions. The barricade shooting was easy when they practiced without live rounds. However, when using live rounds the gun jumped all over the place. His shots were all over the target, that is, the rounds that did not wind up in the river. Of course, Waverly was all over him because of it.

"Number nine, what the hell is the matter with you?" Waverly didn't call anybody by their name just their position number on the line.

Waverly stood behind him to the right when Carr fired his next series. Carr tried securing his shooting hand with his opposite one to prevent it from moving. This corrected the problem. All the rounds were on the target paper. It was progress.

"You're getting better," Waverly said. "Just keep practicing. You'll do fine. By the end of the week you should be able to group them in the torso."

"Yes sir, thanks," Carr replied.

By the end of the day, there was a marked improvement in Carr's shooting. It'll be better tomorrow, he thought, as he drove home. Nothing to worry about. We don't have to qualify until next week, he consoled himself.

What was starting to affect him-- and everyone else - was the weather. The temperature had been in the teens all day with a wind chill below zero. Since they were prohibited from wearing gloves on the firing line, just pulling the trigger was becoming a major effort. The only remedy one had was to keep one's hand in one's pocket between firing. It wasn't much help.

Later that evening after dinner, he went into the bedroom and practiced in front of the mirror. Stella walked in on him as he was in the middle of a drill. She giggled at the sight of him.

"I was just practicing," Carr said evenly.

"Oh well, at least you look like you're enjoying it," she said.

Chapter 11

The next two days of range training were more of the same. Carr was improving rapidly though. He had been complimented by Waverly on his progress. This made him feel good. It had been a long time since someone had complimented him on doing a good job.

That Friday afternoon the platoon reviewed the week's lessons before dismissal. They would report Tuesday since Monday was Christmas. The day off would have to be made up, as would New Year's Day.

When they were done everybody wished each other a Merry Christmas. On their way out of the range Pentridge, Gaul, and Waverly serenaded the platoon with Silent Night.

"Yo, isn't that against the separation of church and state?" Darien yelled to them with a smile.

By week's end Carr had become one of the better marksman in the platoon. He had surprised himself with his facility in shooting. The whole experience was fulfilling, and it was fun. If he could arrange it, Carr would spend the remaining time in the academy at the range. Even the instructors seemed to be better. He was in a very upbeat mood when he arrived home that evening.

His upbeat mood was ruined after dinner when Stella gave him the news about her new job.

"I'm gonna be a barmaid," Stella blurted out as she was washing the dishes.

"A barmaid?" Mike repeated raising his voice.

"Yeah, they make good money," Stella said. "Natalie makes a couple of hundred bucks a week in tips."

"Yeah, but you also work at night in places that are occasionally held up."

"Oh, that won't happen."

"Really? You know this for a fact?"

"That's not what's bothering you. What you're really worried about is guys flirting with me."

"That crossed my mind," Mike admitted.

"Yeah, Natalie's husband had the same problem. She said you would too."

146

"Very perceptive that Natalie."

"What's that mean?" Stella said.

"Nuthin'," Mike replied.

"Tell me."

"Nuthin', it just means she's smart."

"Well, aren't you jealous?"

"I wouldn't say jealous. Just concerned that something might happen," Mike replied. "But if you want to do it go ahead. I trust you."

"I thought you would say that. So I went ahead and told her yeah. I'm gonna start after Christmas."

"Where you gonna work?"

"At Ollie's on Second and Wolf."

"You're not gonna work New Year's Eve are you?"

"If we're not doing anything I might."

"By the way, what are we doing for Christmas?"

"The usual. Over my parents for dinner Christmas Day. If you're not working."

"Why would I be working Christmas Day?"

"Cops work Christmas."

"I'm a recruit," Mike corrected her. "What about my parents?"

"We can go over there Christmas night. They're eating over your brother Jake's during the day. Christmas Eve they're going over your sister's. We're gonna go over Leon's Christmas Eve."

"Fine. We got any shopping left to do?"

"No, I did all of it."

"Well there's a coupla things I gotta get, so I'm gonna go now."

"The stores are gonna be crowded."

"They're gonna be crowded all weekend. But whaddaya gonna do. I didn't have the advantage of being home," smiled Mike.

"Yeah, right," replied Stella. "Get outta here."

Mike drove to Strawbridge's department store and parked in the multilevel lot behind the store. He walked across the connecting bridge, which was convenient to the Women's Apparel Department.

Mike saw a dress that he liked and bought it for Stella. Next, he walked to Women's Coats and bought Stella a parka with a fox fur hood. Stella always wanted one. He couldn't afford it last

147

Christmas. After paying for the coat he went to the Gift Wrap department and had both presents wrapped.

He was lucky. He got both presents in one night. He could relax this weekend. He stopped over Leon's house before he went home. He wanted to find out anything he could about shooting. When he resumed classes he was scheduled for night firing, qualification, the badge course, and tear-gassing. Any advance information Leon could give him would be helpful.

"Yo, come on in," Leon greeted him at the door. "What's up?"

"Stella and I were gonna stop over Christmas Eve," Mike said, "I wanted to know what we could bring."

"Nothing,"Leon said, "we got everything."

"You sure?"

"Yeah. We don't need nuthin'. We got food, soda, cakes."

"That's cool. Where's Sheila?"

"She's upstairs," Leon said, motioning towards the stairway. "How's the Academy?" he asked.

"I wanted to ask you about some of the things that we're doin' next week," Mike said. "We're going night-firing, then tear gas training, the badge course and qualifying."

"Whaddaya want to know?"

"What's tear gas training like?"

"You go in a shed, you get some masks, they set off some tear gas and you put your mask on as quickly as you can. Then you take your mask off stay there for a while and then you walk out."

"Don't sound so bad."

"It's not," said Leon. "The gas burns a little. But when you get outside you wash off with a hose and you're OK."

"What about night firing?" Carr asked.

"You go to a range down from the one you're on now," replied Leon. "There is a sled with a target on it that moves toward you and you fire at it."

"How about badge and qualification?"

"I forget exactly what it is, but the qualification means you pass and the badge is you get a ribbon for being an expert and some other ones," said Leon. "How ya doin' with it?"

"Not too bad."

⌐

Sheila came down the stairway followed by their youngest daughter, Katie, who was four years old.

"Hi Katie," Mike said in a little girl like voice.

"Hi Uncle Mike," Katie replied shyly.

"Hi Sheila," Mike said, cheerfully.

"Hi Mike," Sheila replied evenly. "How's Stella doing?"

"Okay, I just went out and bought her Christmas presents."

"You mean you talked to Santa," Sheila said nodding towards Katie.

"Huh, oh yeah," Mike said. "Actually, I talked to one of the elves because Santa was busy with the kids."

Sheila smiled at him. What a gorgeous woman, Mike thought.

"Where's Janine?" Mike asked.

"She's upstairs taking a bath," Katie replied softly.

"Oh, a bath huh," said Mike. "Did you take a bath?"

"Yeah, Mommy gave me one."

"Mommy did. What about Daddy? Can't he give you a bath?"

"He gave me one last night. Tonight was Mommy's turn."

"Is that right?" Mike said with a grin. "They take turns."

"Yeah."

"That's good. Maybe one day I can give you a bath. Would you like that?"

"Nooo!" replied Katie.

"Only Mommy and Daddy huh," said Mike.

Katie nodded her head yes. Mike mimicked her.

"Yeah, I was the same way when I was your age," said Mike.

"I thought you still had Mommy and Daddy give you a bath?" Leon said sarcastically.

"Shh, don't tell anybody," said Mike.

"C'mon Katie let's go downstairs and play with your toys," Sheila said, ushering Katie downstairs.

"Bye Katie."

"Bye Uncle Mike."

"She's cute," Mike said, as Sheila and Katie left the room.

"Hows things goin' at the Academy?" Leon asked, quickly.

"I told you we're at the range."

"Nah, I mean with the people. You still don't like 'em?"

"I'm getting use to them. Generally, I think most of 'em are a bunch of assholes. But I don't let anybody know what I'm thinking. I just do my work."

"That's the best way. Especially when you get in a district," said Leon. "That's gonna be soon now, huh."

"Yeah, in a coupla weeks."

"Hows everything going with you?" Mike said nodding towards the basement door.

"The same," Leon said simply.

There was a long pause. Neither knew what to say.

"Well, I gotta go," Mike said, quickly. "We'll see you Christmas Eve."

"Yeah, about nine."

"See ya then," Mike said as he left. There were snow flurries as he drove home. He turned on the news radio station to get a current weather report.The report was just ending as he turned on the radio. There was no major snow expected. That was good Mike thought. White Christmas was very pretty, but if you had to drive that day ...

On Christmas Eve, Mike and Stella visited with Leon and Sheila. Tom stopped over as well. Together the guys watched a couple of football games on TV while Sheila and Stella talked to Tom's latest girlfriend, Nancy.

She was an accountant. They met at work. She was attractive with a very good sense of humor. They were apparently getting serious.

"How long you two been dating?"Mike asked Tom as he sipped on a beer.

"A couple of months."

"How come you never said anything before?"

"There was nuthin' to say."

"Oh, Oh," chimed in Leon, "sounds like he's in love."

"Yeah, sure does,"said Mike.

There was a noticeable absence of a sarcastic response from Tom. He would have to talk to Stella about it later on, Mike thought. She usually could tell if there was matrimony in the air.

They all went to midnight mass with the exception of Sheila who stayed home with the kids. After Mass they went back to Leon's had a couple of drinks then left.

Christmas morning, Mike and Stella exchanged presents.
"I always said you had good taste in presents," Stella said as she modeled her gift. She bought him a new suit from Boyd's-- the city's best men's store. Of course, it was one of the more moderately priced suits, but Mike was thrilled by it.
"Let's get over to Leon's. Give the kids their presents," Mike told Stella as they finished breakfast.
"Be right there," replied Stella with a smile. "I can't wait to see them open the gifts we got them."
They stayed for an hour, then went to Stella's parents for dinner.
"Merry Christmas," Stella's father greeted them with a smile as they walked in the door.
"Merry Christmas," replied Mike as Stella kissed her mother.
Stella's parents, Zachary and Lily were a strange couple. Lily was a tall woman with long blonde hair. She was still attractive despite the fact that she was a grandmother. Zachary was a little man albeit a powerfully built one. He reminded one of a bowling ball. Stella had elements of both in her so he could never say for sure which one she took after. It was also the same with Stella's personality. Her father was a laid-back sort. Her mother on the other hand was a domineering type.
"How's boot camp coming along?" asked Zach. He was an ex-Marine who referred to the Academy as 'boot camp.'
"Pretty good. We're down the range now. I'll be outta there by mid-January."
"That's good. Still hate it?"asked Zach.
"I can honestly say that there are some things I like, but I'm never gonna like bein' a cop, Dad."
"Still a hard head."
"You sound like my father."
"Maybe your father's right."
"About what? About becoming a cop?"
"What else you gonna do?"

"Finish college, get a good job in a company, work my way up and become a CFO, or COO, or CEO."

"What are they?"

"Chief Financial, Chief Operations, or Chief Executive, Officers. Basically the people that run the show."

"Well you can do the same thing in the police."

"Yeah, but they don't pay as much and it's more political. Besides when you get right down to it I just ain't interested."

"Yeah, but you tried doing the business routine and you couldn't make it. You been laid off or quit how many times in the past few years? There comes a time when you gotta realize you're not gonna be the Wall Street wonder boy. You need to settle down. Plan for the future. Start a family."

"Well, that was good for you," Mike continued motioning to his father-in-law not to interrupt, "and it was good for my father, and brothers and everybody else. But it's not what I want. I figure I can earn more. If I can't, well, that's my problem. If I do, then I get what I want."

"Yeah, but most people don't make it. What are you gonna do? Go broke chasin' a dream?"

"No, if I were doing that I wouldn't be a cop right now," Mike said, "I know not to get carried away. All I'm saying is I'm not condemning you because you took the easy way. Don't condemn me because I'm taking a risk."

With that, Mike got up and walked away from his father-in-law who was shaking his head and muttering to himself. Lily called them to dinner.

After dinner, Mike and Stella left to visit his parents. The conversation with his father being very similar to the one he just had with his father-in-law. Only this time with his brothers chiming in to berate him. He was happy to leave after only an hour.

The next morning, Mike got to the range early. The weather was becoming extremely cold. The forecast had predicted snow on Thursday, which was when the platoon was expected to qualify. This wouldn't change the schedule at all.

Cold as it was Carr had a good day shooting. Maybe being aggravated had something to do with it. Whatever the reason, Carr was shooting accurately and rapidly.

"Good, good," Waverly commented. "That's a nice tight grouping. You see all those rounds in the throat area? That's good shooting."

Carr was pleased with himself. He kept shooting that way consistently even from the fifty yard line. He wondered if he could possibly get a Distinguished award next Tuesday.

The next day was split between being tear-gassed and shooting. They spent the morning shooting. In the afternoon, they were led inside a shed about fifty yards from the range. Inside the shed, Gaul and Waverly distributed gas masks to everyone. Everyone babbled nervously as they waited for the canister to be discharged.

Gaul set off the canister and the shed filled up with the gas. The platoon was instructed to put on their masks. They walked in a circle for a while. They took off their masks walked around a little more, then went outside where Waverly was waiting with a hose, which was used to wash themselves off.

Carr didn't mind it at all. It burned a little and made him cough, but not unbearably so. Just about everybody else felt the same way.

Actually, Carr was more concerned about how the snow was going to affect his shooting the next day for qualification. So far, the cold had been bad. The instructors had made it a point, especially when they were night firing, to bring them inside frequently to warm up as much as possible. Keeping them outside, in the cold, was negative training, Pentridge said. If a recruit were too cold on the firing line then he would develop bad habits. It was better to have them spend less time on the line than develop bad habits.

The morning of qualification was cloudy. The forecast was for a storm front to move through in the afternoon, and dump eight to ten inches of snow before midnight. The temperatures would dip into the teens, then into single digits by evening.

"No way we're gonna shoot today," Carr muttered to himself as he walked to his car. It was bitterly cold with a biting wind.

The engine took several minutes to get warm. The steering wheel was like ice. The defrost took a while to work.

By the time he got to the Range, there were flurries. When he went out to the firing line it was snowing heavily--big wet flakes. The wind was swirling. The wind chill had dipped to below zero. Despite all this, they began the qualification.

"Three-yard line. Live firing for qualification," Pentridge announced from the tower. "Six rounds right hand, six rounds left hand. On the horn. Good luck. You got perfect weather for this."

"Ready on the right! Ready on the left! All ready on the firing line."

The horn sounded and Carr drew his firearm to the hip position, squeezing off six rounds with his right hand. He emptied his casings, reloaded, squeezed off six more with his left, and holstered his weapon. He quickly put his hands in his front jacket pockets.

By the time he was at the twenty-five yard line, Carr's hands and feet were numb. His face felt like the surface of a popsicle and was beginning to hurt. It was snowing so heavily the targets were becoming obscured. No matter how much he stamped his feet, or flapped his arms, or rubbed his face and hands he was still cold.

"Now I know how the guys at Valley Forge felt," Carr said aloud to no one in particular. He stood with his hands tucked inside his jacket, under his armpits or in his pockets – all futile attempts to keep them warm.

At the twenty-five yard line they used the barricade, which were cold and slushy. When Carr placed his hand on the barricade, it became slippery. He had to wipe his hand off on his pant leg before reloading. They also had to shoot from the kneeling position at this distance. Now his knees were wet and cold.

The horn sounded and qualification was done. The platoon went immediately back into the hut and waited for their scores while they warmed up. It took about thirty minutes for the instructors to tally up the scores. Carr got an eighty-five. Not bad, he thought, better than he figured.

There was a lot of chatter in the room as everyone discussed their scores. Pentridge walked to the front of the classroom.

"Listen up," he shouted above the din. The conversations quickly halted.

"You have performed brilliantly," Pentridge proclaimed. "Given the weather conditions you people had to train in you should all be proud of yourselves."

"IN FACT," Pentridge continued, "given this weather you qualified in, you could easily add ten points to your score."

The classroom glowed with delight.

"Tomorrow we're gonna go to the Torresdale Gun Club. We'll spend the whole day there doing scenarios," Pentridge said.

"We'll give you a set of circumstances and you'll have to make a 'shoot, don't shoot' judgment."

There was some laughter.

"This is no joke," Waverly said sternly. "These scenarios we give you are from real life incidents. In some cases fatal incidents or incidents where a police officer wound up in jail."

"After we're done that we're gonna show you some films about the same things. Some are reenactments. Some are videos from camcorders installed in police cars. In one film, you will actually see a police officer being killed. The video was taken from the officer's camcorder as he made a car stop."

Pentridge let that sink in before he continued.

"OK, see you tomorrow. Once again, congratulations."

The next day the cold lingered. The storm, which had ended at midnight, had dumped six inches of snow in the city. Driving wasn't too bad. A little slippery on the side streets, but the highways and main drags were plowed and salted. Traffic was heavy, though, and Carr missed roll call. So did some others.

They drove over to the Gun Club and spent the day going through the scenarios and watching the films. The program was thought provoking to say the least. In some ways, it was downright chilling. Especially the videotape of the officer who was killed making a car stop. The three occupants of the car assaulted him, took his weapon, and shot him, as he lay unconscious on the ground. The platoon was told that to date the men had never been found.

155

Afterwards they were dismissed for the weekend and the New Year's holiday. Carr arrived home just as Stella was getting off the phone.

"I'm workin' New Year's," she told him.

"Why?" he replied.

"Why not? We're not doing anything. It's gonna be another dull New Year's Eve."

"Oh, you want to go out and boogie?"

"No, I just figgered to make some money since we ain't doin' nuthin'."

Carr just turned his back on her and went to change.

He was asleep on New Year's Eve when Stella got home about three in the morning. He didn't speak to her the next day. He went to a bar instead.

He stayed at the bar for about an hour and then left. At home, the lights were out and Stella was gone. When she came home later that evening he saw that she had her waitress clothes on.

The next morning, they began practice for the badge course which meant shooting prone from fifty yards. The snow began early the day they shot for awards or the "badge course." The temperature was a relatively balmy twenty degrees. It snowed lightly at first.

By the time Carr arrived at the range it was heavy. One inch had accumulated by 8 o'clock. By 9 o'clock, when they lined up to begin shooting, there were three inches. By the time they were ready to shoot from the fifty-yard line, six inches had fallen on the ground.

Carr had worn sneakers because the weather forecast had not called for this much snow. His feet were numb. He was not going to shoot Distinguished this day. He did make Marksman, which was the lowest of the three awards. Still, it was quite an accomplishment, since only four of seventy-five recruits were awarded anything.

At the end of the day, Pentridge once again addressed them and formally awarded the badges. After the presentations, he gave a speech to the platoon.

"I want to tell you that as a group we the instructors feel that you are probably the finest group of recruits we have ever had here."

There were shouts and clapping.

"So, on behalf of the instructors, I just want to say we're proud of you and wish you good luck in your careers."

There was another round of clapping, hooting, and hollering from the platoon.

"Class dismissed!" barked Pentridge for the final time.

When he left, the snow had stopped and the temperature had climbed to above freezing. The snow was slushy. The snowplows slowed the ride home. Parking was also a mess. Carr finally found one two blocks from his house.

After dinner he reflected on the two weeks, he had spent at the range. He examined his Marksman badge. He had accomplished something and he had been recognized for his accomplishment.

Not a bad week, he thought.

Chapter 12

The last few weeks of training revolved around reviewing work, making up any tests that were missed, and preparing for finals. The class also received their uniforms and their firearms. All four platoons were now on site for the last few weeks and met everyday in the auditorium.

There was a great deal of speculation about assignments. Some recruits spoke with conviction that they knew where they were going to be assigned. They claimed to have friends in the Central Planning Unit, the department tasked with determining district assignments, which were based on deployment needs and departmental policy. The recruits were not given their assignments until graduation day.

The policy was to station recruits at districts in the division adjacent to the division in which they resided. Divisions are roughly coextensive with geographical sections of the city. So Central Division was the Center City area, North Division was the northern part of the city, etc.

The districts are components of the divisions. Carr lived in the 4th district, which was in South division in South Philadelphia. He figured to be assigned either to Southwest, West, or Central Division.

Many officers came from the Frankford, Port Richmond, Kensington, Tacony, and Holmesburg sections of the city, which were all located in the department's East and Northeast Divisions. These neighborhoods were ethnically Irish, English, Polish and German and they had a long history of furnishing police officers.

Since the majority of recruits came from one section of the city, determining assignments of a new class became a complex operation. This was further complicated by another, unofficial policy, that a police officer was punished for minor infractions by transferring him to the district farthest away from his residence. Since most officers lived in the city's Greater Northeast section, the Southwest division was a punishment division and was usually fully staffed. All in all, the likelihood of a recruit knowing his assignment before graduation was slim – albeit not impossible.

ⅼ

At lunch one day, Carr was joined by Millie and Art, who by now were an item. The gossip was that love, or lust, had bloomed. They were seeing each other outside of the Academy.

"Mike, didja hear I'm getting the 14th District," Millie said to Carr, as they walked out the door. "It's all arranged."

"Oh, you and the Commissioner been friends long Millie?" Carr asked, straight-faced.

He pushed open the door, walked outside, reached into his breast pocket and pulled out his cigarettes. He shook the pack until one came up. He offered it to Millie who pulled it out and placed it between her lips. He shook up another one and did the same. He lit both and leaned against the phone booth.

"So what makes you so sure you got the 14th? Besides why would you want the 14th? I hear it sucks."

"Nuh-uh. The 14th covers Germantown, Mount Airy, and Chestnut Hill. Germantown sucks but Mt. Airy's OK, and Chestnut Hill is great," Millie said enthusiastically. "They got a little bit of everything in the 14th. You can get a lot of good experience there."

"Bullshit,"snapped Darien. "If you want some good experience, you got to go to East division."

Carr watched with amusement as they argued the various merits of the two districts. He had talked to Leon two nights earlier. He said he could request that Mike be assigned to the 17th with him.

Mike mulled it over. The 17th was in South Division about thirty blocks from where he lived. He could basically roll out of bed into work. The 17th was a high crime district. It was busy. Leon could show him the ropes. The downside was what if he and Leon couldn't work together it could carry over to their personal lives. After thinking about it, Mike told him to go ahead.

"It doesn't matter. Nobody knows for sure where they're going -- except for Millie," Carr quickly corrected himself in a mocking tone.

Darien and Emerson snickered at Carr's gibe. Millie playfully smacked him on the arm. Carr finished his cigarette and the group went back inside.

As he took his seat, Lt. Wister began the class. Wister came bouncing in with his usual mercurial style -- anxious to begin his next to last class. He was going to review next week's final -- then give them his usual farewell. As he walked to the head of the class, he told everyone to be seated.

"Take your seats, take your seats," said Wister. "Okay, I want to go over the work for the final exam next week. Before I do, are there any questions?"

Wister glanced around and quickly went on to review for the final. Carr was comfortable with the subject so he used the opportunity to take a nap. Something he had never done before in Wister's class. It was also something Wister made a point to tell him after class.

"My class too dull for you, Mike?" Wister asked, as he walked out of the room.

"No sir," Mike replied sheepishly. "You know I always find your classes stimulating. I heard every word."

"Every word, huh?" Wister sneered. "Still thinking of quitting?"

"As soon as I can get another job!"

"Too bad," Wister replied. He continued walking down the corridor. " Well, if I don't see you, good luck."

After the final exams were completed, the platoon began practicing for commencement. The day before graduation, they had a full dress rehearsal.

A woman by the name of Mona Belgrade walked into Lt. Iseminger's office immediately after rehearsal and handed in her resignation. Gossip was that she had used her appointment just to get a paycheck and never intended to become a police officer. She learned how to swim and how to shoot, and was paid for it. Carr could not imagine what his wife would say if he pulled a stunt like that.

The morning of graduation Carr dressed in his full uniform: coat, tie, hat, Sam Browne belt, and pistol. Stella watched as he dressed.

"I don't know why you don't want me to go to your graduation," she said with some exasperation.

"I told you, it's no big deal," he replied with a surly tone. "Besides the ceremony is in Center City. You know what a hassle it is to park in town."

"What's the difference? It's your graduation."

"Yeah, right, my graduation," Carr grumbled as he finished dressing and walked out the door. "I don't know how long this will be. I will probably come straight home after though."

The recruits assembled in an anteroom of the Pennsylvania Convention Center. They received their assignments as they lined up for the procession into the auditorium.

"Carr, 17th District," Iseminger called out.

"You got the 17th, Carr?" Art Darien called to him from down the line. "You live near the 17th, dontchya?"

"Not too far," Mike replied.

"You can roll outta bed into work," Mildred teased.

"Nuthin' wrong with that," Mike replied.

I wonder if this were coincidence or Leon's request, Carr chuckled to himself. He would give him a call after the ceremony.

Carr peaked through the curtain outside. The hall was filling up with guests. There were wives, mothers, girlfriends, fathers, kids, and even grandparents. Maybe he should have told Stella to come, he thought. No sooner did he think that then he noticed Stella, her parents, and his parents walk into the hall. Figures, they haven't done a damn thing I wanted them to do yet. When I asked them not to come, they do it anyway.

When the class paraded in Carr looked over as Stella called out his name. His parents and his in-laws waved and smiled as well. Carr just frowned and shook his head as he walked by. They laughed at his displeasure.

Commissioner Billy Wills, the first African-American to hold the position, stood at the podium and gave a speech with the predictable platitudes and well-worn phrases.

"You represent the citizens of the great city of Philadelphia," Wills said earnestly. "Never forget that you are there to serve them."

161

There were the usual rounds of applause at the appropriate times. After his speech, Wills stepped back from the podium, and Igor Pulaski addressed the audience.

"Each recruit will be called in alphabetical order and will come up to the stage to receive their diploma. This will be the first time they will be addressed as Police Officer," Pulaski said in a staid tone. "Lieutenant Iseminger, call the roll."

Iseminger walked up to the podium and began the roll call. Both the Commissioner and Inspector Pulaski were behind him to his left.

"Police Officer Wilbur Adams," Iseminger announced.

As the recruit walked to the stage, he saluted the Commissioner and accepted his congratulations. He then walked to Pulaski, saluted him, received his diploma, saluted Iseminger and continued to salute three more of the Police Department brass, before returning to his seat.

Shortly thereafter Iseminger called, "Police Officer Michael Carr."

Carr marched to the podium executed a very proper and stylish salute to everyone along the reception line then returned to his seat.

Finally Iseminger called the last name, "And concluding class number 255, Clay Watts."

As Watts arose from the rear of the class and walked to the stage, the 255th class of the Philadelphia Police Academy rose and applauded.

After Watts returned to his seat, Pulaski approached the podium and announced, "Class 255 you are dismissed."

Once again, the class cheered and filed out of the hall looking for their guests. Carr found his. He was talking to his father-in-law when a TV reporter approached him.

"What would you like to say to the people of Philadelphia Officer, eh, Carr is it?"

"Yeah, it's Carr, and I don't want to say anything. So shut that light and go bother somebody else," Carr said testily.

The reporter had a puzzled look on his face. He finally smiled and went to find another, more cooperative graduate.

⸻

"That's no way to build relations with the media Mike," his father said.

"I don't want to build relations with the media," Mike replied. "Besides, I owe too many people money. Someone might recognize me and know where to find me."

His father laughed.

"Who do you owe money to?" Stella asked.

"It's a joke dear," Carr replied. His father-in-law laughed at the gullibility of his daughter. Mike's parents called him over and introduced him to a Deputy Commissioner that his father knew.

"Congratulations Mike," said the Deputy Commissioner. "If you're half as good as your old man here, you'll be a great officer."

"Thanks sir, but I don't think that will be possible," Mike said stiffly. The real meaning of his words was quite apparent to his father.

"I'll just do the best I can," Mike said, smiling. His father spoke to his friend a few moments then the Deputy Commissioner excused himself and went to speak with someone else.

"Hey, let's go get something to eat," Stella said after they completed taking pictures.

"Where do you want to go?" asked his mother. There was some discussion before they settled for a restaurant nearby. Mike wasn't too talkative through lunch.

"So where are you assigned?" Stella asked him.

"17th District," Mike replied, "Leon's district."

"You're lucky," Stella said with a tone of surprise.

"Yeah," Mike said simply, not letting on how he possibly got the assignment.

After lunch, everybody wished him luck and left. Mike and Stella drove home in their car. Once home, Mike quickly changed out of his uniform. He sat down in the living room and flipped on the TV.

"When do you start?" Stella asked. She sat down next to him.

"Monday. I report at 8 a.m. Which reminds me, I gotta call the Captain's office and make an appointment. All new personnel are required to make an appointment to see the Captain," he explained as he dialed.

After he was done, he walked to the kitchen and took a beer out of the refrigerator.

"Where's the notebook computer?" he asked Stella.

"Upstairs why?" Stella replied.

"I want to redo my resume. This way I can go through the paper Sunday, see what jobs are around, and send it out."

Stella scowled at him.

"You'll never change," she muttered, in disapproval.

"I don't want to change," Mike said quietly. "I take care of my responsibilities."

Chapter 13

Police Officer Michael Carr reported to the 17th district after a very sleepless night. The district was only ten minutes from his house. But it took another five to find a place to park. The neighborhood around 20th and Federal streets was not the best in the world. Here even cops have their cars stolen. In fact, in this district, cop cars were occasionally stolen. He found a spot about two blocks away, pulled in, locked it up and walked to the station.

It was a cold day, so he wore his departmental patrol jacket. It had a reinforcement for his nametag and two holes for his badge. He had his clip-on tie, blue shirt, blue serge wool pants, with light blue seam stripe in brocade, and uniform hat with badge in front.

He reported to the operations office. The corporal checked off his name and said: "You're in three squad."

"Roll call's in five minutes -- in there," he said, nodding his head to a darkened room next to the office.

"The locker room is downstairs in the basement. Your locker is 242. Put your own lock on it."

"Yes sir," Carr said. He walked to the roll call room. There were benches throughout the room and they faced a desk at the head of the room.

"You don't have to call me sir," replied the Corporal.

"Okay," Carr replied simply. The Corporal just smiled and returned to his paperwork.

Carr walked into the room and was joined by a sergeant followed by some other officers. They milled around waiting for roll to begin. He took a seat on one of the benches. The sergeant flipped the lights on and walked to the desk. Officers filed into the room. He checked his watch. Roll call was about to start – 8 a.m., right on time, Carr thought.

He got up to take a place in line. Carr noticed some other officers coming from an anteroom near the office and walk through the main room to the lockers. The sergeant noticed them too. He walked over and closed the door so they couldn't enter.

"Okay lineup!" the sergeant shouted. "Anderson!"

"Here!"

"1710."

"Barnes!"

"Here!"

"1714."

"Carr!"

"Here, sir," Carr replied reflexively.

"1704."

A wagon. Not too bad, Carr thought. He had expected as much. It was common police department procedure to assign a rookie officer to a van with an experienced partner. It didn't always work out that way, but if given the choice a sergeant would prefer to put a rookie with an experienced person.

In Philadelphia, police officers worked alone in cars. The only way to have a rookie work with a veteran was to assign the rookie to a van.

He now listened to find out who his partner was. Carr's partner was a black guy named Walton.

After roll, the sergeant motioned for Carr and two others to go with him. One was Clay Green; the other was Betsy Chester.

"Good morning, I'm Sergeant Beck. I'm the late end supervisor. For this tour you'll all work the late end but when we go to 4 to 12, one of you is going on the early end."

Beck noticed the puzzled looks on their faces and said, "Didn't anybody teach you what that means?"

The three shook their heads no.

"Each squad, or platoon if you prefer, is divided into early and late end. The early end starts at, for instance, 7:30 a.m. on day work and reports off at 3:30p.m. The late end works 8 to 4. This way there is always coverage out on the street. Generally, the early cars are odd numbers and late end are even numbers. The lower numbers work the lower or east end. The higher numbers work the upper, or west end, of the district. Do you understand me?"

They all nodded in unison.

"Okay. Sometime during the day you will be called in for your talk with the captain," Beck continued. "Any questions? No. Go to your posts."

Carr found 1704 parked in the street. Walton was standing next to it waiting for him patiently.

"Hi, Darnell Walton," smiled Walton. "Go ahead, get in. I'll drive."

Walton was in his mid-thirties and had been on the force for ten years. He lived in the Nicetown section of the city. He was over six foot and slightly overweight. He liked being a cop, though, he no longer had the zeal he had when he first joined. In the beginning, he thought that he, as a black man, was going to correct all the racial injustices that existed in the police department. He long since realized that he had many misperceptions about racial prejudice and the police department. He also realized he wasn't going to change the system.

Darnell Walton did his job -- and he did it well. He protected the people who lived in the 17th district -- and he went home after his tour. That's all he wanted to do. He didn't want to be a supervisor. He didn't want to be a detective. He didn't want to work a special unit. All these opportunities had presented themselves over the years, but he didn't want them. Beck always chose Walton to break in rookies because he was a good cop and Beck knew it.

Beck watched Carr get in the wagon with Walton.

"What's the deal with him?" Corporal Porter asked Beck.

"He's Leo Dover's cousin. Leo told me he really isn't crazy about being a cop. Just doing it until he gets something else," Beck replied.

"Walton's a good choice for his partner," remarked Porter.

"That's why I put them together," Beck said. "From what Dover told me he would make a great cop, if he changes his attitude."

"He might. Ya never know," said Porter.

"If nothing else, we know he's not a plant by Internal Affairs," Beck muttered.

"The rumor mill always says one graduates with every class," replied Porter.

"So, what do you know about the 17th?" Walton asked cheerfully.

"A lot, I live over in the 4th. I got some relatives that live here and Leon Dover is my cousin."

"Ole Leon's your cousin huh," Walton said. "He's a pretty good cop. The guys in his squad like him. I'm not sure if the Captain does. You know Captain Hazzard?"

"No," replied Carr. "Except Leon doesn't seem to like him much."

"Yeah, the Captain can be a dickhead sometimes. Leon could probably run the place better. Whaddaya know about Beck?"

"Nothing. I didn't get a chance to talk to Leon. We'll probably talk tonight."

"Beck's okay. Real easygoing. The other supervisor Sergeant Long is also pretty easy. So's Corporal Porter. They don't fuck with you. The Lieutenant however is a different story. He just wants to fuck with people."

"What's his name?"

"Winton. Just came in from the Academy a coupla months ago. Maybe you know 'im."

"Winton!" Carr repeated with surprise. "That shithead reamed me out the first day I was in the Academy."

"That sounds like him," Walton laughed. "We try to avoid him when possible. He usually doesn't do much anyway. Especially on last out. Then he is usually sleeping. He nods out right after roll call and wakes up just before the early end reports off."

"Figures," Carr said repugnantly. Last out in police jargon is the midnight to eight shift. The term is a misnomer. Last out is actually the first shift of the day since it starts at midnight.

"The shifts themselves will take some getting' used to," Walton said. "They're against the clock. It's 8 to 4, midnight to eight, and 4 to 12. We work six on, two off. So like on this shift we'll get done Saturday at four. Then we come in Monday night at eleven-thirty, if you're on the early end; otherwise midnight."

" Sounds like it could be confusing," said Carr.

"Yeah, the union's been tryin' to get it changed. There's also something known as group days. You know what they are?"

"Not exactly."

"The concept behind the group days was to compensate for the six day work week. So I think it's once every eight weeks you get your regular days off, or RDO'S for short, and a group day. We also get compensated for working holidays by receiving compensating days at the end of the calendar year. You can take them as vacation or pay."

"Good to know," said Carr.

"You ready to book?" asked Walton.

" Whenever you are," replied Carr.

" You completed the routine check of the equipment. Looked for body damage, checked the lights, wipers, sirens and various other equipment? You reported any malfunctions or damage to the Corporal?" asked Walton.

"Yeah," Carr responded.

"If everything is in order, contact the radio room and make us available for assignment," instructed Walton. "The mileage is 59226.5."

Carr recorded the figure on the log sheet. Walton put the van in gear and pulled out of the parking spot. Most of the vehicles were parked on the street since the 17th, like most districts, did not have a parking lot.

"1704," Carr said after depressing the transmission button. There was no reply.

"1704," Carr repeated. There was still no reply.

Great, Carr thought to himself, the first time he tries to transmit over the radio he looks like a smacked ass. He was about to try it a third time when a female voice came on the air.

"1704," the voice said. She sounded as if she were attempting to stifle a laugh.

"1704 in service."

"1704 OK," the voice responded. The transmission kept cutting off as the dispatcher was trying not to laugh over the airwaves.

"1704 take a school crossing at 32nd and Reed."

"School crossing 32nd and Reed. 1704 OK," Carr responded. From the textbook nature of his response, the dispatcher could tell he was a rookie.

"Welcome to the 17th, 1704," she said light-heartedly.

"Thanks," said Carr simply. He had a more clever response, but he didn't want to get too cute -- especially on his first day.

Walton drove to the school crossing. "Put us on location," he instructed Carr.

Carr got the radio and announced, "1704."

"1704," acknowledged the dispatcher.

"1704, on location," said Carr.

"1704, OK."

"You get out on the intersection and cross the kids. I'll standby here. If you were in a car then you would put the outside speaker on and listen for a call. Technically when you're on school crossing you're still in service," lectured Walton. He reached behind him for the newspaper lying on the floor. "If we get anything I'll beep the horn."

Carr exited the van and walked across the street to wait for a group of students. He held traffic up for them as they crossed the intersection to get to school. Carr then repeated this for another group coming in the opposite direction. When he was finished, he heard Walton beeping the horn. He trotted over to the van.

"We gotta call, get in," said Walton, evenly. *"Man with a gun."*

"Man with a gun?" Carr said in an astonished tone, as he entered. "It's eight fucking o'clock in the morning."

"Yeah, so. You figure crime only operates at certain hours?" said Walton. He started the van put it in gear and drove off. "We gotta go to 2415 Ellsworth. Tell radio were en route."

"1704."

"1704," acknowledged the dispatcher.

"1704, 2415 Ellsworth en route."

"1704 OK."

The house was only a couple of minutes away from the school crossing. Carr notified radio of their arrival. Walton seemed awfully relaxed about getting this call, Carr thought. He would have figured a man with a gun would have created more of a stir than it has.

Carr got out of the van and followed Walton to the doorway. Carr unbuttoned his holster and placed his hand on his gun. Following what he learned in the Academy, he stood to the side of the doorway, away from any windows.

Walton, however, walked up to the door as if he were visiting his sister. He knocked on the door and was greeted by a woman in a robe. She looked to be in her fifties.

"You call the police?" Walton asked politely.

"Yes, my husband is upstairs and he's got a gun," the woman declared, angrily.

"What's your husband's name?" Walton asked walking towards the stairs. Carr watched him and moved over to be in a position that if the husband fired at Walton he could return fire. Carr was amazed that Walton made no effort to conceal himself.

"Jesse," the woman replied spitting out the name.

"Jesse!" Walton yelled up the steps. "Jesse, this is the police. I want you to come down here. Now!"

"Yassuh, I'm comin," Carr heard a soft voice in the hallway upstairs. Down came a frail looking, ederly man in his pajamas.

"Where's your gun Jesse?"

"Upstairs, officuh. I got a rifle. I didn't point it at her."

"Did he threaten you with it?" Walton asked the woman.

"No, but I know he's got it up there."

"I just keep it for self-defense officuh."

"He didn't threaten you with it?" Walton asked the woman a second time.

"No, we got in an argument and he said he was going to hit me."

"I did not."

"Wait a minute, Jesse. Let your wife finish."

"He said he was going to hit me. So I called the police and I told them that he had a gun upstairs."

"Okay, do you want to file a complaint against your husband?"

"No, I just don't want him to say he gonna hit me."

"Jesse you gonna hit her?"

"Nuh suh officuh. She da one dat try to hit me."

"Jesse, I don't want to have to come back here because you hit your wife.You hear me?"

"Yassuh."

"And I don't want to hear about no rifle."

"Yassuh, my gun is just for self-defense."

"Okay," Walton said. He turned slowly and walked out the door. Carr was amazed by Walton's attitude. He thought Walton was being careless. He told him so when they returned to the van.

"Nah, you get to know after a while if you come into a dangerous scene," Walton said. "Most times the calls for a man with a gun are just like this. People just make that call so the police will get there faster. But that doesn't mean you shouldn't be prepared. If I'm a rookie, I would do exactly what you did. You know even the bad guys know the rookies 'cause they always got their hands on their guns."

Carr just sat back and took it all in. Walton was a good teacher. He was a good honest cop. They didn't bother to return to the school crossing as school had already started. Instead, Walton drove to a corner store and bought some coffee. Carr bought some cigarettes. They drove around while Walton acquainted Carr with the streets of the district. There were only a few Mike didn't know. Walton also acquainted him with the demography as well as the geography. He told him about certain gambling houses, prostitution houses, drug houses and street corners. He basically filled him in on the who's who of the 17th District.

They stopped for lunch at one o'clock. Police officers were only allotted thirty minutes for lunch. They ate at a fast food place at 26th and Snyder, which was outside of the district. This was against policy. However, Walton wanted to teach Carr which rules could be bent.

When Carr went to pay for the meals he was waved off by the cashier. Puzzled he walked back to the table and told Walton.

"They don't let us pay for the meals," Walton told him. "This way we eat here more often and that guards against holdups. They figure it's worth it to them."

"Do all of them do that?"

"As far as I know."

"Isn't that against the rules?"

"Nuthin' wrong with it. If you don't want to do it just pay him."

After their meal, Walton continued to tell Carr the nuances of the job, when he noticed a car with six young men in it.

"C'mon we're gonna pull this car over, get them all out of the car and frisk them. They'll bitch and moan, but don't let that bother you," Walton said. He positioned the van behind the car and flipped the siren on.

"Notify radio of the plate number, make and model. Ask them for an NCIC and BMV. Also, tell them our location. You know about the National Crime Information Center and Bureau of Motor Vehicles data bases, don't you?"

Carr frowned as Walton grinned.

Slowly the car pulled over onto the curb.

"1704."

"1704," acknowledged the dispatcher.

"1704, Need an NCIC and BMV for a car stop, 2-1 and Washington Avenue. Chevy Cavalier, Pennsylvania A-Andy, C=Charlie, Z-Zebra 5-4-1. Hold us out."

"1704 OK."

Before Carr was done, Walton had jumped out of the van and was talking to the driver. Carr jumped out and took a position on the passenger side just behind the taillight. He had his holster unbuttoned and his hand on his gun. When the driver of the car leaned over to get something from the glove compartment Carr pulled his gun from the holster. He replaced it when he saw the driver handing Walton his owner's card.

Walton walked back to the van and signaled Carr to join him.

"Run these," he said as he handed Carr the driver's license and owner's card. Before Carr could call the dispatcher, she was calling him.

"1704 no wants or warrants on your vehicle."

"1704 OK. Could you run the driver?"

"OK."

Carr then spelled the name of the driver and gave the address. In a few minutes, the dispatcher replied that there was no record. Meanwhile Walton had everybody out of the car and was frisking them. When Carr walked up he gave Walton the license and registration. Walton then handed them to the driver.

"Have a nice day," Walton said, smiling.

"Yeah, you too Darnell," replied the driver, also with a smile.

"You two old friends?" asked Carr as they got back in the van.

"Oh yeah, I hassle him all the time. He's a drug dealer. I know it and he knows I know it. He don't worry 'bout it. I'm like a mosquito to him," said Walton. "He ain't worried about gettin' locked up. He ain't worried 'bout gettin' killed. He ain't worried ' bout nuthin'. Thing is, he gonna end up face down in the river one day soon. I always tell him I'm the one who is gonna take him to the ER."

During the remainder of the afternoon, Walton continued explaining various procedures. Most of the time, he went straight by the book. Sometimes he did not. Whatever he did, he always explained the difference between the theory of police work as taught in the Academy and the actual practice. As Carr was starting to learn, there was a dramatic difference between them. No matter how realistic they tried to make the Academy training, it still does not totally prepare one for the realities of the street.

At 3 o'clock Carr, along with Clay Green and Betsy Chester, reported to Captain Hazzard's office. They waited in the anteroom of his office for about ten minutes.

Hazzard received them just before he was ready to leave. He was a friendly, middle-aged man, with a portly physique.

"How was your first day?" Hazzard asked in an avuncular manner. He was placing various items in his briefcase as he spoke. "It's different from the Academy isn't it?" He looked up and smiled at the three of them.

"Yes sir," they mumbled.

He continued organizing his briefcase as he spoke, "You're all with good people. You'll learn. In the meantime, I expect you to conduct yourselves properly and give your fullest cooperation to your supervisors. Any questions?"

"No sir," came the reply.

"Okay, you're dismissed for the day. If you think of anything, I have an open door policy. You can feel free to come in here any time you'd like."

"Yes sir," the three mumbled in partial unison. They rose from their chairs, saluted Hazzard, then left the office. On the way out, the three didn't speak to one another. They just headed for their lockers.

"At least we get done early. That's good," said Carr. Neither Green nor Chester responded to him. Surly bastards, Carr thought. He opened his locker and placed his holster, baton, hat, slapjack, nametag, and briefcase into it. He took off his badge and put it in the badge holder his father had given him as a graduation present. He put his gun in the hip holster his oldest brother bought him. He tucked the holster inside his waistband in a crossdraw position. He put his patrol jacket back on and left.

He arrived home twenty minutes later. Stella had dinner ready early. He went over Leon's after dinner to go over some things he had learned. He had a few questions to ask him.

Leon wasn't home, so he drove to the store got some new razors and went home. Stella had ironed his uniform shirt for him. He lined up everything he needed for the next day and went to sleep.

The next morning Walton and Carr worked together again. The day was uneventful. Working the 8 to 4 tour normally was slow, but during the winter, it was slower. That didn't mean that things couldn't happen. They did. Carr heard plenty of calls over the radio, but, generally speaking, it was quiet. According to Walton this was largely the result of the cold weather, and because it was daytime.

"During the day," Walton posited, "the jitterbugs are sleeping it off. So there ain't the disorderly crowds, vandalism, and assaults. Also, the domestic disputes are down because usually somebody is out of the house or sleeping it off. Most of the daytime problems happen in the schools and when the schools let out. When the kids are out on the street and unsupervised, that's when you get your problems."

As if to underscore the point, the radio crackled with a call for a robbery.

"17th district. Robbery point of gun. 2-9 and Grays Ferry Avenue. One black male, wearing overcoat, and sneakers. Last seen entering into a yellow station wagon, heading east on Grays Ferry Avenue," the electronic voice of the radio related calmly.

"Let's go," said Walton putting on the lights and sirens. As they did, they passed 1703 wagon.

"Shouldn't those guys be in on this too?" asked Carr.

"Hah," smirked Walton, "that's Slocum and Yewdall, they don't like to do anything unless they're assigned to it."

"I thought everybody gets this call."

"Yeah right," Walton sneered.

By the time they arrived on the scene, the radio issued another call for the same thing at Broad and Carpenter.

"Must be the same dudes," Walton said. They got back in the van and headed for the area around Broad and Carpenter. As they drove to the assignment, they again passed 1703 wagon parked.

"Those guys aren't too ambitious are they?" said Carr.

"You'll see," Walton replied. Once again, they arrived on location, drove around the area and couldn't find anyone.

"No sense in looking anymore. They probably long gone. You try your best to find them. Sometimes you'll stumble right across them by accident. Once, I was answering a call for a shooting and I went to the wrong location. I went to the next block up. Well, who is running down the street but the shooter. I snagged him just I as I was getting out of my car," Walton recounted.

"Dumb luck, huh," Carr smiled to himself.

"Yeah," replied Walton. "It's near four. We might as well report off."

They drove back to the district. Walton parked the van and went straight to the locker room. Carr turned in the log and the 48's to the inside crew -- police officers performing clerical functions. It was the last day of the tour. Carr would have Sunday and Monday off and report to work Tuesday morning at midnight. After he reported off, he wondered again how he would function with the time change.

Later that evening Mike got a call from Leon.

"How is it?" Leon asked him.

"Not too bad," replied Mike. "I tell you working with Walton is a real education."

"He's good people," Leon responded. "If more cops were like him the crime rate would be cut in half."

"You ain't kiddin'!" replied Carr emphatically.

"Yeah, you'll learn a lot from him."

"There's one thing I learned today."

"What's that?"

"We got a couple of shitheads in the squad. This afternoon we were running around answering a robbery in progress call and twice we passed these guys in 1703 wagon, sitting there not even bothering to answer up."

"Were they out of service?" Leon asked.

"Does it matter?" Mike snapped. "They were just parked there not doing nothing?"

"You'll see a lot of that. Guys are gonna hold themselves out on jobs and not put themselves back in service. Some are not gonna answer up their calls and you're gonna get bagged with the job. Especially, since you are a rookie. It goes on all the time."

"Why doesn't the Sergeant do something about it?" Mike asked.

" He should, but he can't keep track of everybody."

"I don't know. It just seems to be exactly what we were talking about before. I told you I can't deal with people like that."

"Don't let it get to you. Don't let them bag you with their jobs all the time either."

"You're probably right," said Carr, "Look I gotta go now. Any ideas for how to deal with the shift change?"

"Yeah, stay awake until about four. Things will slow down then. Try to nap for a little bit your first couple of nights. You won't fall completely to sleep. You'll hear the radio. Besides, if you're working with Walton one of you will hear it. You don't want to be sound asleep driving around. Guys get in accidents that way."

"Okay. Well, I'll let Walton drive. If I do nod off, it won't matter."

"Walton will probably want you to drive to get used to it. Or maybe he still wants to show you the ropes. Let him do what he wants. Right now he's the boss."

"Okay, thanks."

"Gimme a call if you need anything. I'm finishing up four to twelve so I'll probably see you Tuesday morning."

"Adios," Carr said as he hung up the phone. What to do now. It was Saturday night, though it really didn't feel like it. The thought of going to work at midnight on Tuesday morning was abhorrent to Carr. Stella was working, so there wasn't much he could do with her. The best thing he could do was make dinner and watch some TV.

He reflected on his first week as a real live police officer. There were some exciting things and some dull ones. Walton seemed nice. His rookie colleagues and those guys in 1703 wagon seemed like dregs. The ringing of the telephone interrupted his thoughts.

"Hello," Mike answered.

"Mike, Leon."

"Yeah."

"I forgot to ask you. You want to work as a security guard and pick up some extra bucks?"

"Yeah, sure," replied Mike eagerly. He was always looking out for some extra jobs.

"Toy City needs security guards. They hire off duty police because we're allowed to have guns. It's against policy. If you get caught, you would get fired. Although, the department kinda overlooks it. I been doin' it for years. So have a lot of other guys. It pays 20 bucks an hour under the table."

"Sounds good to me."

"Yeah, all you do is chase away the kids that come in the store. As funny as that sounds for a toy store, it's the kids who don't have parents with them that are doing all the stealing. So they don't let kids under sixteen in without a parent."

"Why do they need cops then?" asked Mike.

"Stops holdups. The bad guys know there are off duty cops in there. They see guys standing around the cash register in plainclothes with bulges under their shirts. They know they're cops."

"They get any holdups?"

"No. But their competitors do."

"Okay, when do I start?"

"How about tomorrow? I was suppose to go in but I gotta go somewhere."

A tryst with your girlfriend no doubt, Mike thought.

"Okay. Where do I go?"

"24th and Passyunk. Just check in with the manager. Get there at one o'clock. You leave at nine when they close but you gotta stay for them to close up. You know count up the money and everything."

"Sounds good," said Mike.

"Seeya," Leon replied.

Mike hung up the phone and went back to planning his evening. Didn't seem like much to do except watch TV. He turned on the set and watched a movie. His thoughts turned back to the security guard job. This could be a good deal because the extra money could be used for many things.

The next morning Carr arrived at the store at twelve-thirty. He had forgotten about it, so he was late. When he checked in with the store manager, he was told that they already had a guard. The manager nodded to an older man with graying hair sitting on a stool by the front door. Carr walked over and introduced himself.

"I was suppose to work here today," Carr said.

"Yeah? Well, I was told to be here by Langdon," replied the man, in a hostile tone.

"Who's Langdon?" asked Carr

"He's the guy that runs this."

"Oh, well, if he told you, he told you. There must have been a mix-up," said Carr innocently.

"Yeah, mustabeen," replied the man tersely.

Carr went home and left a message for Leon. He got a call from him later that night.

"Sorry. That happens sometimes. This guy Langdon isn't the most efficient person in the world," said Leon apologetically.

"The guy that was there was a surly bastard," said Carr

"What's he look like?" asked Leon. Carr described him.

"Nobody I know," said Leon. "Next time I'll give you a slot. In fact, I'll call Langdon and tell him to put you on the list."

"Okay," replied Mike.

Monday night began the midnight to eight or *last out* tour. Carr arrived at eleven-forty, changed into uniform and stood roll call. He once again was assigned to 1704 but without Walton, who was using his group-day off. His partner this evening was named Gillespie.

After roll call, he saw Leon in the room.

"Hey, how you doin'?" asked Leon. "Who you working with?"

"Some dude name Gillespie. You know him?"

"Not really."

"Well, I gotta go."

"Later."

179

Mike found 1704 wagon and got in the drivers seat. He was going to start the car and begin the check when he realized he didn't have a key. Since he didn't know where to get one, he waited for Gillespie.

After waiting several minutes he went looking for him. He found him in the operations office with a cup of coffee in his hand reading the paper.

"Gillespie?" Carr asked.

"Mike Carr," he said quickly before Gillespie responded.

"Oh, hi. I was waitin' for ya," said Gillespie slyly. "You ready to go?"

"Yeah," said Carr. This guy is a bullshit artist, he thought. Waiting for me hell. He knew where to go. He wants to screw around. Who does he think he is kidding? This is going to be a great night, I can see that now, he thought to himself.

"How do I get a key for the vehicles?" Carr asked as they walked to the van.

"See the corporal or ask Walton. That's who ya been workin' with, ain't it?"

"Yeah. He can give me a key?"

"You get a copy," Gillespie said.

They got in the van, went through the routine, then Gillespie drove off. Carr was the recorder -- so called because he keeps the log. Gillespie didn't say much to Mike as they drove around. Before they even went into service, Gillespie drove to a convenience store and bought a coffee and newspaper.

"You want anything?" asked Gillespie, as he entered the store.

"Nah," replied Carr.

After he returned they drove to a side street, where Gillespie parked and read the paper. Carr sat silently. He lit up a cigarette and listened to the calls on the radio.

"17th District. Broad and Federal, report of shots fired. All units responding please identify."

"1710 in."

"173 in."

"1702 in."

Carr reached to pick up the radio.

"Don't answer that," ordered Gillespie. "They already got enough units."

"Yeah, but we're three blocks away," protested Carr.

"Yeah, but 1703 should get that. I don't want to get their jobs. They won't take ours."

Carr leaned back into the seat. What the hell is this? They were police officers. There was an emergency. What's all this petty bullshit?

As the evening developed, Carr noticed that Gillespie was selective about what calls he answered. Carr could not figure out what the criteria were for answering a call. When it came to assigned calls Gillespie had a routine.

"1704, 1617 Wharton Disturbance House."

"1704 OK," Carr replied.

"You should not have answered that," Gillespie said. "That's on 07's sector."

"Oh!" replied Carr. Big fucking deal, he thought. When they arrived, Carr went to inform radio they had arrived. Gillespie stopped him.

"Wait! Don't tell them yet," Gillespie instructed as he walked out of the van. Carr followed him to the doorstep. Gillespie knocked on the door and a woman answered.

"You call," Gillespie asked, in an irritated manner.

"Yes, I did. But you're too late. My husband already left," said the woman indignantly.

"Fine. If you have any more problems, just give us a call," said Gillespie with a smile. He turned and walked back to the van.

"If you take as long as you did tonight, what good is it gonna do," yelled the woman.

Gillespie turned around and looked at the woman.

"Hey, look lady, we're very busy. You ain't the only one in this city you know," Gillespie said sharply.

The woman quickly shut her door.

At 3am, Sergeant Beck called for a meet. They met with him at 17th and Catherine Streets.

"He wants the log," Gillespie said.

Carr took the clipboard, got out of the van, walked to Beck's vehicle and saluted.

"How's it goin'?" Beck said as he returned Carr's salute.

"OK Sarge," replied Carr, handing Beck the clipboard. Beck signed the log and returned it to Carr who gave him a salute.

"Get back to work," Beck grinned, returned the salute, and then left.

Carr got back in the van and Gillespie drove off without a word. Gillespie went to a driveway behind a warehouse. He placed the gearshift in park, propped his head up against the window and started to nap.

"We'll sit here for a while. Try to get some sleep," Gillespie mumbled.

This was one instance when Carr willingly took Gillespie's advice. Leon had said it was a good idea to do so. He slumped in the seat propping his head on his elbow and his elbow on the door. Gillespie kept the engine running and the heat on. Carr cracked his window open slightly to let some air in.

"Why you leaving the headlights on?" Carr asked.

"Lieutenant doesn't want anybody sitting with the lights off. He said it's a bad image," Gillespie said.

Carr tried to fall asleep. Initially it was difficult, but eventually he drifted off. He noticed however that he could still hear the radio dispatching calls.

They only received two calls between 3 A.M. and dawn. Gillespie woke up with sunrise and drove to a donut shop. "C'mon, let's go to lunch. Tell radio."

"1704 lunch, 34th and Grays Ferry," Carr called in.

"1704, OK."

Carr was not particularly hungry, so he just ordered some tea. Gillespie got a full breakfast.

"First time on last out?" Gillespie asked him.

"Yeah."

"Nuthin' to it. You just need to stay awake until about two. Except during the warm weather. During the warm weather it stays busy until about four," said Gillespie.

"Sometimes you get called to pick up prisoners and bring them down to the district for hearings or transport them to the Detention Center. Another thing, there is a restaurant that closes at two on Reed Street. The owner will slip you a few bucks if you sit there until he closes up, counts his cash and goes home. It 's a clean note, so everybody does it."

It was the most Gillespie had said to him.

"That's good to know," Carr replied.

"The only reason I'm telling you this is because I know you're Leon's cousin. I don't say that to rookies. Ya never know who is a plant by Internal Affairs."

"I hear ya," Carr said. He really did not feel like talking at this point. He wanted to report off, go home, and get some sleep. He was stiff and sleepy. It was going to take some time before he could get use to this shift. It was also going to take some time to get used to working with some of his colleagues.

The next night, he worked with Walton again. Once again, Walton was in his teaching mode. After lunch, however, the two switched places. Walton promptly went to sleep. He stayed asleep until it was time to report off.

So this is the guy who, if all cops emulated, the city would be safer, Carr laughed to himself.

Carr was wide awake and drove around in circles all night. Since the district was a small densely populated place there were not many places to drive.

Despite this Carr managed to drive sixty miles that evening.

Chapter 14

Saladin finished dressing in the bathroom. He tightened the knot in his tie, reexamined its length in the mirror, splashed on some cologne, and walked back into the bedroom.

Tyesha was sitting up in the bed now. She was trying to find a radio station she liked. She had not put her nightgown on and Saladin toyed with the idea of climbing back into bed with her. Business before pleasure, he reminded himself.

"I'll see you tonight," he said to her.

"Do you have to go now, honey?" she purred.

"Gotta tend to business. I'll be back."

"I'll be waiting."

Saladin walked out the door to his car and drove to his new speakeasy at 15th and Bainbridge streets in South Philadelphia. The one in Germantown was doing so well he opened another one two months ago. Both speakeasies were outlets for his drug trafficking, which was booming. The competitors were not a problem. Everybody was content with their own business. Nobody was getting greedy. The only potential problems would be with the Cosa Nostra, but so far, they only hassled their own.

Saladin parked his car around the corner from the entrance. It was a three-story building he owned. The speakeasy was in the basement. The first floor was a delicatessen. He used the top floors as a warehouse and office.

"Hey Pearl," Saladin greeted the barmaid. She was tall, slinky, and scantily dressed. She looked a little like Vanessa Williams. Saladin never approached her though. He had always heard that you never dip your pen in the company ink well. He figured it was sound advice.

"The video poker machines in yet?"

"Pretty soon, sugar," said Pearl, in a husky voice.

Saladin always had a latent desire to have a casino. He ordered two video poker machines to enhance the atmosphere in the speak. He figured to expand the number later.

He walked up the steps past the bar to his office on the second floor. He wanted to check his account book. Saladin insisted on keeping accurate books. It was a dangerous thing to do. There were advantages and disadvantages. On the one hand, the books could be used as evidence against him -- especially if his bookkeeper became an informant. On the other hand, it gave him a good idea of his financial position. This was important to him. All things considered, Saladin would rather keep a record of his money.

He was not comfortable just spending it. He wanted to know how much he had, where it came from, and where it was going. As he examined the books, he smiled to himself, eventually he would leverage these earnings into a legitimate business.

After he finished counting the cash in the safe, he separated the money into three piles and recorded each disbursement. One pile was placed in an envelope with the amount marked on the front. This was for the bartender to use. Another pile was returned to the safe. The third pile Saladin rolled up and bound with a rubber band. He put the wad in his pocket. He walked out of his office into the bar.

"Here you go, Pearl," Saladin said, as he tossed the envelope to her and walked briskly to the door. "I'll be back in an hour."

He got in his car and drove back to the Germantown speakeasy. There he met with one of his suppliers, Jules Duncannon, who had a shipment ready for delivery and wanted payment.

Saladin wanted to talk Jules into giving him some more on consignment – a risky proposition for a drug dealer. Duncannon had been dealing with Christian for a while and knew him to be as good as his word. Saladin did not think he would have a problem. Duncannon sat at the bar sipping a bourbon and water. Saladin joined him.

"Here's the money," Saladin said. He placed the envelope on the bar in front of Duncannon. "Where's the stuff?"

"Here you go," Jules said pushing a satchel over to Saladin's chair. "It's good stuff."

"Yeah, I know. I want some more but I can't pay you until after I sell. Can we deal?"

"You want credit?" asked Jules, incredulously. He was going to give it to him, but he did not want Saladin to think he was going to get it easily.

"Yeah," replied Saladin, bluntly.

"Credit costs, brother," Jules said smoothly.

"How much?"

"How much product you want?"

"100 bags."

"Okay. I give you 98 bags and charge you for a hundred."

"Say what? I get 98 and pay you for 100."

"Only if you pay me within 90 days. After that you get charged more."

Saladin pretended to ponder a little then replied, "Okay."

"One more thing. Don't fuck with me brother. I better get my money or you're gonna get offed," Duncannon said, unnecessarily. Saladin knew what Duncannon was capable of doing. He had no intention of betraying him. He could not afford it.

"Just make sure you get me the real deal. You'll get your money," replied Saladin, evenly.

Duncannon finished his drink and pushed away from the bar. "I'll give you a call tomorrow to set something up," he said as he left.

Saladin grabbed the satchel and took it in his office. He took several bags and put them in his safe. He made some calls to his customers and arranged to meet them back at the Bainbridge speak. It was a more central location relative to his buyers. He was thinking of moving his headquarters there from Germantown.

He did not know the politicians and the cops in the district the way he knew the politicians and the cops in Germantown. However, that could be arranged quickly. Philadelphia had its own hierarchy of corruption.

The politicians and the police in Philadelphia had a long history of corruption, as did other cities. The corrupt cops represented a minority, a sizable minority, who made it easy for people like Saladin to prosper. As long as the residents voted the way the ward leaders told them, things would not change. It was only when the shooting started that the politicians and the cops got nervous and started cracking down. When the bad people got out of control, the politicians, judges, and police would not help them. Public outrage was the only thing that could control the hoods. As long as people were silent, crime would flourish.

Saladin waited at his Bainbridge office for the first customer who arrived shortly after he did. Saladin exchanged the bags for money. This act repeated itself for the next two hours. Before each appointment ended, Saladin got a commitment from each to move more of his product and to return in two days to get a new supply. A couple protested, but most were anxious to get more.

After his customers were done, a local ward leader came in and Saladin gave him a "donation" for his party. The ward leader would distribute the money to the election campaigns of certain corrupt judges. Next Saladin gave some money to one of his lieutenants to distribute to some corrupt local vice squad cops. Saladin assiduously recorded every transaction in his books. As long as the public tolerated the corruption, crime will flourish, he reminded himself.

All power to the people – isn't that what my revolutionary buddies used to say. Now they are all working for me.

Afterwards, he walked into the speakeasy. It was now two in the morning. The place was starting to fill up. Speakeasies in Philadelphia were nothing more than nightclubs that stayed open and served liquor past the legal closing time. They were a nuisance to the neighbors; that's about it. They were considered victimless crimes.

Saladin spoke to some of his customers. He then went behind the bar and counted the receipts. He also checked the stock of liquor.

He got a bottle of Jack Daniels, found an empty table in the back, and sat down. He was joined by one of his lieutenants. They drank and talked for a while. At various intervals, several people joined him in conversation. After two hours he rose from his chair, played some darts, and then left. By the time he got home, it was near dawn.

Beverly Clark awoke at sunrise. She opened the drapes and let the sunlight into the bedroom. She had one appointment this afternoon that piqued her curiosity.

Saladin wanted to start a corporation. What a thing for him to want to do, she thought. Saladin obviously wants to go legitimate.

Ordinarily, she would have turned this over to the appropriate section of the firm, but she wanted to handle this herself. It was not anything complicated. However, she did want to know what kind of business he was starting. She poured her coffee, took it into the bathroom with her and turned on the shower.

Saladin woke at noon. Not much sleep, he thought as he turned off the alarm on the clock radio. He climbed out of bed and into the shower. Afterwards he made breakfast and left for Beverly's office.

This business he was starting was something he had been thinking about for a while. He was going to call the nightclub Midnight Magic. He had a good location for it right on the riverfront. With all the new nightclubs down there, it should get a lot of traffic. He was going to put the club in his brother's name. They had a long conversation several weeks ago. He told his brother he wanted to go straight. It was the truth. The nightclub would be his first real foray into legitimate business.

If successful, there would be more. If not, he would try something else. He would use the money he got from the crack sales to make the down payment. Saladin had been operating on a shoestring budget since the war with his rivals. Now that all the legal bills have been paid, the speakeasies were up and running, and his crack business was back, he should be able to see his way clear.

There were some hurdles to overcome. The liquor license was a major one, which is why he needed his brother. With his brother fronting for him and some money crossing hands, he should land the license.

The property had some title problems, but he would get that taken care of as well. Beverly drawing up the paperwork and using her firm's political pull was a major asset. Beverly was more than willing to do anything she could to help him. He was her social project. She was going to turn him into an honest businessman. He knew what she was trying to do. This was why she wanted to handle the case herself. She was playing the missionary - helping the poor natives see the light.

ı

Saladin laughed to himself as the image came into his mind of Beverly Clark, the white missionary goddess, saving the natives. He could just picture Beverly in a pith helmet.

Once the club was opened, he could start moving some of his money into a smaller legitimate business. He was not sure what he wanted to do. A clothing store maybe, or an appliance store -- something that was not heavily regulated by the government. However, he really wanted to open a nightclub. It was an old dream of his.

The nightclub he pictured was like those in the old Hollywood movies. It would have round dinner tables instead of banquet tables. The waiters and waitresses would all be dressed like wizards and witches. The dance floor would be enormous -- big enough for everybody in the place to be on it at the same time. There would be a stage with a live band. A big name entertainer would appear every month. They would do two shows a night. At midnight, every night, there would be a magic act. Saladin wanted David Copperfield to open the place. He had made some inquiries about him appearing.

Before driving to Beverly's office he stopped at the spot where his club would be. Right now, it was the site of an abandoned warehouse and factory. They would be cleared as soon as he bought the land. He would smooth it over and make a parking lot. He would rent the lot to the other clubs and restaurants temporarily. The club would be unique in Philadelphia.

He got back into his car. He had one more stop to make. He went to the Bainbridge speakeasy to count the night's receipts. He opened the door and went to the safe.

He actually had two safes. One his lieutenants knew about, one they did not. They would put the cash in his office safe on the nights he left early. When he returned the next day, he would move the money from the one safe to the other one located on the top floor.

It was not that he did not trust his employees, but if one of them left, they would know where the safe was and the combination. He felt that if he left cash in there and he was ripped off, it was his own fault. This way, he did not have to stick around every night to count the take. He could get some sleep and go in the next day.

If he caught somebody skimming from him, he would take care of him. His employees knew that. They knew what could happen. They had good jobs. They were well paid. Why get greedy and killed? This was basically the way he posed it to his lieutenants. So far it worked. He never had a problem with skimming.

He placed the money in the secret safe. Next, he pulled out a wad of bills before he closed the door. He went back to the car and drove to Beverly Clark's office; just a few blocks away. The drive took only a few minutes even with the lunchtime traffic. He parked in the lot of the building and took the elevator to Beverly's office.

Clark reviewed Saladin's proposal. There were two rental properties, one in Germantown and one in Fishtown, which was actually a vacant lot on the riverfront.

A pretty clever fellow this Saladin, she thought. When she first met him, she thought him to be the stereotypical young black man- - a lot of talent, but no opportunity except through crime. Just a poor boy trying to make good in a white, racist society. However, in the six months or so they had known one another, she was no longer so sure. Beverly did not know what to make of him.

None of his brothers and sisters became criminials. He did not appear to be a weak-minded person. Saladin Christian did not fit her idea of what a black man is. She was confused by his attitude. She was confused by her feelings.

The phone rang.

"Yes," answered Beverly depressing the speaker button.

"Mr. Christian is here."

"Send him in."

The door opened and in entered Saladin.

"Hi Miss Beverly," he smiled.

"Saladin, good seeing you," greeted Beverly.

She sat down behind her desk as he took a seat.

"So tell me what are your business plans? What is the nature of your corporation?"

Saladin told her about the nightclub.

"So you're going to be a nightclub owner. How nice. With the tourist business increasing, this town needs a new night club."

"Yeah, it's been a dream of mine for a long time," Saladin replied.

"Sounds impressive. I have already drawn up the paperwork. There shouldn't be any problem with the license for your brother."

"Thanks, I appreciate your efficiency."

"Would you like to put the rest of the properties and businesses under the corporation?"

"Yeah, put everything under there. This way my liability is limited. You'll handle all the details about stock and all that won't you? I don't know much about those things."

"Not a problem. By the way who are the officers of the corporation? We'll need to have them come in."

"Well, there's Tyesha and myself. Wait, my brother will be too – and at least one of my sisters."

"Okay, have them make an appointment and we can have everything signed, sealed, and delivered within a couple of months."

"Fantastic! I'll get in touch with them and we'll all get together next week. Monday okay?"

"Check with my assistant."

Beverly got up to escort Saladin to the door.

"Bye, Miss Beverly," Saladin smiled as he walked out of the office.

"Bye, Saladin," Beverly replied perfunctorly as she closed the door.

She shuddered as she returned to her desk -- well how about that, Saladin Christian in the entertainment field. Then again, he has been in the entertainment field for a long time, she thought.

Saladin drove back to the Bainbridge speakeasy. This is a lot better than stealing cars, he thought. It's a good thing that he chose to go back into trafficking rather than start back from the beginning.

Or was it? How much devastation was he responsible for by selling his poison? How many crack babies did he bring into the world? Gotta get out of this business, he thought.

191

There was a message waiting for him from Duncannon. He wanted to meet at nine that evening. The shipment must be in, Saladin thought. He wanted to move it all quickly. No sense in having a large inventory.

Saladin called Hannibal Stevens. Hannibal was in charge of Saladin's expanding numbers business. Diversity was an important component of Saladin's plans -- not only in the legal business, but the illegal as well. The numbers racket was an old reliable standby. He wanted to get into prostitution next and he wanted Hannibal to explore the possibility.

"Hannibal, whatsup?"

"Nuthin' bossman," Hannibal always addressed Saladin that way. "I got in touch with some friends and they're gonna see what they can do about gittin' us some ladies we can manage."

"Good. How's the take on business?"

"Okay, but it seems to be slowin'. This past month is not as much as it's been. It seems to have dropped off a little."

"By about how much?"

"I don't know. I ain't too good with numbers," Hannibal said laughingly.

"Yo, if I want a comedian I'll go get tickets for Eddie Murphy. Now, I want to know how much?"

Hannibal frowned into the phone. That was a stupid move. Kidding around about the bosses' business ain't smart Hannibal chided himself.

" 'Bout twenty," Hannibal replied in a more businesslike manner.

"Twenty per cent!" Saladin bellowed. "What's causing it?"

"I don't know yet, but I am working on finding out," Hannibal replied cautiously.

"You better find out," warned Saladin. He was furious. Hannibal had been one of his most trusted employees. The idea that Hannibal may be ripping him off was not only maddening but discouraging as well. This bullshit about 'he doesn't know' is just a ruse. There ain't no way in hell he doesn't know.

"I'll get right on it boss."

"You do that," Saladin said sternly. He quickly hung up on Hannibal just to emphasize the gravity of the circumstances.

Saladin sat back in his chair. Now I know what small business owners go through. No wonder they hate paying taxes.

"Enough with the daydreaming," Saladin said outloud bringing himself back to work. Time to meet with Jules. He walked out to the bar. He was joined by Duncannon in a half an hour.

"Everything arranged?" Saladin said, as he poured Duncannon a drink.

"Yeah, no problem," Jules replied evenly. He tossed the drink back and held out the glass for a refill.

"When?"

"Tomorrow. How quickly will I get my money?"

"No more than a week."

"Good."

Jules was satisfied that he would be able to get paid on time. He placed the shot glass on the table and pushed it to Saladin.

"Later," Duncannon said simply. He got up and walked out.

Saladin leaned back and calculated how quickly he could move it and how much he could get for it. Deducting what he would have to pay Duncannon, he should make enough to pay for the nightclub.

Good, he thought, that's where he wanted to be. Enough money to fund all of his operations and his investments. It's been a long time since he could say that.

Saladin went home and took a nap. He would have to close out both speaks and drop in on Hannibal to see what he was up to tonight.

Too much driving around. I need somebody to drive me so I can get work done. Somebody I can trust, Saladin thought.

"I know just the person to call," Saladin said to himself. When he arrived home he called Malcolm Hadfield. Malcolm had been a long time associate -- back to the car thievery days. He was in semi-retirement, but now Saladin needed him as a counselor and as an assistant.

"Malcolm? Saladin," Saladin said. "I need your help."

"What do you need?"

"Pick up a car and meet me at my house tonight. I want you to be my driver. I'll explain. Also, if you know somebody who can be trusted and be a driver for me full time I would appreciate it."

"Yeah, I got somebody. I'll be over. What time?"

"About nine."

"Okay," Saladin responded, then hung up the phone.

This will be good, he thought. If he can help me out it would take a lot of pressure off. It's necessary that I have a trusted lieutenant. Obviously, Hannibal wasn't it. Of course, when Hannibal sees Malcolm he's going to realize something's wrong, Saladin calculated.

The best way to get around that was to act like Malcolm was just an old friend trying to get back into the business. Hannibal knew Malcolm was retired. He could fool Hannibal for a little while with that story, at least long enough to figure out what Hannibal was doing. He didn't want to frighten Hannibal off. The new driver would also be good for Saladin. Some minor reorganization was due. The addition of Malcolm and a driver wouldn't raise suspicions, he reassured himself.

Saladin Christian was satisfied with himself. In a little more then a twelve month span Saladin had been to the top of his trade, engaged in a protracted struggle against powerful competitors , been involved in potentially disastrous legal procedures, rebuilt his business, and was now poised to be back at the top of the trade as well as begin a legitimate business venture.

Not bad for someone who just started as a small time car thief. Who knows, maybe one day he would be up there with the other icons of criminal history. Saladin laughed as he thought about the prospect of him being the subject of a television biography.

Later that evening, Malcolm came around with the car and a young guy named Washington Paxon. He looked to be in his mid-twenties. A tough looking kid that seemed to be smart. Malcolm filled him in on some of Wash's background as they rode together in the back seat of the Lincoln Towncar that Malcolm had obtained for Saladin.

"Ridin' in style," Saladin said as he climbed in. Malcolm laughed at Saladin's remark.

" We used to ride in these before," replied Malcolm.

"Yeah but we own this one. We didn't own those," laughed Saladin.

The two reminisced about the old days for a few minutes, then Saladin got down to business. He got Malcolm caught up on some things and filled him in on some of his plans. He didn't go into all the details. Malcolm didn't need to know them and Saladin learned a long time ago to never let anybody know everything.

"Those are pretty impressive plans," Malcolm remarked.

"Now you know why I need somebody with experience to help me out. Somebody who is smart and who I can trust."

"Saladin, we come a long way since we started stealing and selling cars," Malcolm said. "In those days I was your mentor, so to speak. Now you passed me. There ain't nothin' I can help you with. I don't know all these things that you getting' into."

"Yeah, but you know how to get things done. You know if somebody is settin' you up for something. The rest of this stuff is just details. I can hire people to take care of them," Saladin said.

"These dudes," he continued, "they been raised on music videos and greed. They only look out for themselves and in the end nobody wins, everybody loses. Besides, you were always better at organizing things than I was."

"That's true. You never could figure out which end was which. Course you seem to have learned," Malcolm responded.

"Just from the master," Saladin smiled. "Another thing I need is to bring in some more new blood. You always seemed to be better at recruiting new people. The first guy I trusted is Hannibal and I think he's bad."

"You don't know that for a fact. Remember, you got a lot of things on your mind. Could be you jumping to conclusions with this boy Hannibal."

"Could be. You gonna meet him yourself. You tell me what you think," Saladin said.

"OK, I'll let you know."

"So you gonna join up?" Saladin asked.

"Yeah, why not," replied Malcolm. "I been gettin' edgy lately anyway in semi-retirement. Sounds like a good reason to get back into it full time."

"You won't regret it Malcolm. It'll be a good move for you. Besides I got lotsa good lookin' mamas down at the speaks. Who knows, one of them might go for an old man like you," Saladin laughed.

The two of them drove down to the speakeasies to orient Malcolm with the operations. Saladin just introduced Malcolm as an old friend. They closed up the speaks and counted the receipts. Saladin showed Malcolm how he handled the books.

"Sure is impressive. But I got some ideas that might help you," Malcolm said.

"Good. I want to hear them. That's why I aksed you to come in with me."

"Yeah. I think you do need to go to school," Malcolm said, smugly.

Chapter 15

Sunday daywork in late winter was just about as slow a day as one could get in the 17th district. There weren't going to be many jobs coming out on a day like today. Even a rookie knows that, Carr thought.

In the forty-eight days he had been a police officer Carr had worked each tour twice. The biggest challenge thus far had been to adjust to the shift rotation. The rotation disoriented him. On occasion, Mike would wake up and not be sure whether it was day or night; Saturday or Tuesday. He would just get used to eating dinner at a normal hour, only to change from daywork to midnight to eight. Then he would have to get used to eating cereal for *dinner*.

The rotating shift wreaked havoc on his social life. There were Saturday nights when he was off, and Saturday nights when he worked. Some weeks his 'weekends' were on Tuesdays and Wednesdays. There were nights when he had missed parties, and there were days when he missed ballgames. Sometimes he would make it to a party only to have to leave early and have his wife remain. Other times she would be at a party and he would arrive after midnight and pick her up.

Compounding the problem was his security guard job. On two occasions he had worked from midnight to eight, gone home, ate breakfast, and went right back out again to the security guard job. The extra money was appreciated. He was making up for the money he lost being out of work. But in many ways it didn't seem worth it. He and Stella rarely saw one another. When they did, they were too tired to do anything but sleep.

Besides becoming acclimated to the shift, he had learned much in the past seven weeks. Carr learned that police were called for varied reasons. Some people called simply because they were lonely. Some because they didn't know who else to call. Police are usually the first governmental service that people consider.

Walton taught Carr as much as he could. He took advantage of the relative tranquility of the winter months to ease Carr into the district. Mike got to know the characteristics of the 17th district. He also got to know the character of the squad. He found out that, despite the reputation police officers have for esprit de corps, most of the squad really disliked one another.

Carr learned who in the squad was conscientious and who was indolent. At times it seemed that most of the squad fell into the latter category. In fact, there were only two squad members, other than Walton, who Mike considered to be conscientious.

One was Gil Walker, a wily old veteran, assigned to 1714. The other was Max Grant who worked 1716. The rest of the squad possessed an attitude of - *we don't have to do our job and nobody can make us.*

Once, on last out, he learned how the dispatchers were complicit in this game of do nothing. Carr listened with fascination to a call assigned to 1701--arguably the laziest duo in the squad.

"1701," called the dispatcher.

1701 did not reply.

"1701!" repeated the dispatcher. Still no reply.

"1714 and 1715, take a Disturbance House-- 2322 Watkins Street."

"1714 OK," replied Walker.

"1715?" called the dispatcher. "1715, back up 1714."

"1716!" interrupted Max Grant.

"1716," echoed the dispatcher.

"I'll back up 1714."

Walton started to laugh as the sequence ended.

Carr looked at him. He was disgusted by the whole thing.

"When 1701 didn't respond, radio doesn't want to send down numbers so she called the other two."

"Send down numbers?"

"Report an infraction like not answering an assignment. So when 1715 wasn't gonna back up Walker, Grant in 1716 did."

"Yeah, but, it's like whoever feels like working works, and whoever don't doesn't."

"That's about it."

"Fucking ridiculous," muttered Carr.

"Get used to it. Get used to it, and get smart about it," lectured Walton.

ǀ

"How come the Sarge doesn't say anything? Doesn't he realize that the more this kind of shit goes on, the more people are gonna do it?"

"You got it all figured out dontchya? You been here all of seven weeks, not even and you know how to fix everything that's wrong?" Walton chided him.

Carr didn't bother to reply. He just kept his mouth shut.

On this particularly placid day he was partnered with Walton once again. They had been given the assignment of surveying abandoned cars. It was a relatively mindless duty. They drove around to various locations to see if the abandoned cars were still there. Carr took the driver's seat and Walton was the recorder.

"Darnell, you see that guy go through the light?" Mike said.

"No, I wasn't paying attention," replied Walton.

"It was right in front of us."

"Yeah, so you want to stop him, go stop him," Walton replied.

Carr thought about it. Up to this point Walton had always done the driving. He had made many car stops with Walton but he never initiated one. He was past due.

"Yeah, let's go get him," Carr replied. He flipped on the beacons and the siren.

"Call it in!" he told Walton. Walton informed radio of what they were doing and the plate number of the vehicle.

Surprisingly, the car didn't stop. He followed the vehicle, which neither increased nor decreased its speed.

"No record. Nothing in NCIC," responded radio moments later.

"If it's stolen, it hasn't been reported yet," Carr said. He was baffled. If the car were stolen, he would have expected that the driver would have increased speed. On the other hand, the driver obviously was not going to cooperate. He appeared to be a middle-aged man dressed in a suit. Not what he expected a car thief to look like. A murderer maybe, but not a car thief.

The car continued traveling a few more blocks then turned into a lot on Washington Avenue. The driver blew his horn and a garage door opened. Now Carr was really mystified.

"What the fuck is going on?" Carr muttered outloud. The car drove into the garage and Carr followed. He got out of the van and approached the car as the driver opened the door. Out of the car came two crutches and the driver swung both of his obviously dysfunctional legs out of the car.

Immediately, Carr felt embarrassed. My first car stop, and I get into a pursuit with a paraplegic, he thought to himself in disgust.

"What are you doing?" demanded the driver

"Sir, you went through a red light at 20th and Carpenter. I signaled for you to pull over. Why didn't you?" Carr said evenly. He was becoming a little indignant at the attitude of the driver.

"I did not go through a light. What do you mean by following me?" the driver asked inignantly. "Why don't you find some criminals?"

"I want your license, registration, and insurance card," Carr said in measured tones.

"Here," said the driver, tossing Carr a wallet. Carr got the wallet and tossed it back.

"Take the cards out and hand them to me," Carr said growing angrier.

After he got the cards, he gave them to Walton to check out. Judging from the company name and the name on the license this guy was obviously the owner of the company. Some rich dude who thinks he doesn't have to obey the law, Carr thought.

Carr returned the cards to the driver with a ticket for going through the light and another ticket for disobeying a police order. Predictably, the driver was angry. "I'll see you in court!" he yelled at Carr.

"It'll be my pleasure," Carr said with a smile.

"What an asshole," Carr said to Walton, as they drove away.

"Him or you?" Walton said.

"What!" Carr said indignantly.

"Never follow a car into a garage like that, number one. Number two, don't get out of the van and walk towards the car without checking out the place. You coulda been walking into an ambush," admonished Walton.

"It was my first car stop," protested Carr.

"It mighta been your last," Walton replied.

Carr had to admit that Walton knew his business. He was glad he was partnered with him. He obviously had a lot to learn. What

Carr really wanted was a busy tour. He wanted to get a feel for police work.

On the next 4 to 12 tour Carr got his wish. His last two nights of the tour were on a Friday and Saturday. They were also the first two warm nights of the year. A warm front had moved into the area. The temperature rose, unusually, into the 80's during the day and dropped into the 50's at night. After twelve weeks of snow, sleet, rain, and single digit temperatures, this warm spell felt like summer. The excitement in the air was palpable.

As soon as Carr and Walton got into the van they got an assignment. Walton was driving. He dropped the lever into gear and drove rapidly to the call. It wasn't anything dire, just a domestic dispute. However, Walton drove like a man on a mission.

As soon as they were done with that assignment, they received another assignment for a theft at a local discount store. The security guard was holding a prisoner caught shoplifting. Carr and Walton arrived and took the prisoner to the district jail cell.

No sooner did they go back into service than they received another assignment. They were to investigate a person who was allegedly stripping a car parked in a vacant lot. They arrived to find a man repairing his own car. Walton verified the ownership via police radio.

"Wow, three jobs and it's not even five o'clock yet," Carr remarked as he loosened his tie. It wasn't so much a loosening as a disconnecting. The tie was a snap on.

"First warm night of the year and a weekend at that," Walton said as he reached for the radio. "It's gonna be rockin' tonight."

Walton was right, Carr thought. He could feel the electricity in the air. There was someone on every street corner. Traffic was heavy. Music from car radios floated through the air. Barroom doors were open – the music and laughter from them adding to the cacophony. People were out and about, no question about it.

Walton handed the radio to Carr.

"Call this tag in," he said nodding to the car directly in front of them. Carr informed radio of the tag while Walton pulled the car over. Walton approached the vehicle while Carr waited for the response from radio.

"That tag comes up on an '92 Chevy. Is that what you got in front of you?"

"Nope. We got an '01 Caddy," replied Carr. He got out of the van and walked to Walton who was getting the cards from the driver--the lone occupant of the vehicle.

"Check these out. I'll get the VIN," said Walton. Carr ran the name and then the Vehicle Identification Number.

Walton stood by the driver. As car returned to the radio.

"That VIN comes up stolen, 1704," replied the dispatcher.

Carr laughed to himself.

"Okay hold us out. We'll be taking one into West Detectives," Carr replied. He told Walton radio's response.

"Step out of the car please," Walton ordered the driver. Carr backed up enough to let the driver out of the car.

"What's wrong?" the driver asked, innocently.

"Turn around, place your hands on the car and spread your legs," Carr commanded. Walton just stood there allowing Carr to take the lead.

"The car has been reported stolen," Carr said after he frisked and handcuffed the driver.

"Stolen? This is my car," protested the driver.

"That's not what police radio said. You'll have to straighten it out. All I know is what I've been told. I can't let you drive off with what is supposed to be a stolen car can I?"

"No."

"Fine, then don't bust my chops," Carr said tersely. He led the driver back to the van and placed him inside the back. They took him to West Detectives for processing.

"How did you know it was stolen?" a fascinated Carr asked Walton.

"I didn't. He made an illegal left turn. That's why I was stoppin' him," Walton said simply. "You never know what you got with a car stop. That's why you gotta be careful."

After they finished the paperwork on the stolen car and notified the owner, they transported their prisoner to the detective division. By the time they returned it was dusk. So far they had been busy. It was going to get busier.

A call came out for a man with a gun inside a house. Walton turned on the lights and sirens and sped towards the location. He didn't have to say anything to Carr.

"1704 en route," Carr advised radio.

"1704 Okay," acknowledged police radio.

They were the first ones on the scene. The house was on the end of a row. A crowd had gathered outside the rowhouse, the first floor of which was elevated from street level by the front lawn and steps leading to the front door. The back of the house had a narrow driveway leading to a small garage which was street level.

Walton instructed Carr to secure the rear of the house. He was going in the front.

As Carr started walking to the back of the house he heard shouts of *"He's coming out through the window! He's got a gun! He's got a gun!"*

The garage extended from the basement and had an entry door next to the garage door. The first floor had a window, which opened onto the roof of the garage. To exit the back, the gunman would either come through the garage, the door next to it or the window onto the garage rooftop.

Heeding the shouts of the onlookers Carr pressed himself against the doorjamb of the door. People in the crowd were screaming: *"He's coming out the back window! See him!"*

Carr unsnapped his holster and took out his Glock. The pistol-range instructor's words echoed in his memory: *if you have to shoot, shoot for the torso and empty your weapon.*

The advice makes sense. The belief that one can easily shoot a gun from a person's hand is a myth. The Lone Ranger Syndrome, Carr called it. Only an expert with opportunity to aim could accomplish such a feat. Otherwise, it's done by accident.

Aiming at the roof of the garage, Carr placed his finger on the trigger. There was little illumination. Only enough for a silhouette. If he saw a gun, he was going to fire.

Someone in the crowd shouted: *"There he is! He's got a gun!"* Carr started to depress the trigger. Suddenly, through his gun sight was the horrified expression of a ten-year-old boy. He lowered the 9mm Glock.

"Jesus Christ," Carr gasped.

"Get the hell outta there," he yelled. As quickly as the head appeared, it disappeared.

"Carr," Walton called.

"Over here Darnell," Carr said, as he holstered his gun.

"He's not here, he left a little bit before we got here. Let's get the flash over the radio."

"Darnell, I almost shot a little kid," Carr blurted.

"Don't worry about it," Walton responded, impassively. "Get the flash out."

Carr went to the van and gave the description over the radio.

"1716," Grant cut into the transmission to ask a question. "Was that a baseball cap or a hat he was wearing?"

"Baseball cap."

"Okay, I see him," Grant said calmly. "He just passed me on 25th street. I'm gonna get him now."

"Backup for 1716 at ...what's your location 1716?" asked the dispatcher.

"2-3 and Pierce," responded Grant.

"Back up for ..."

"1714, I got him. I'm on location now," interjected Walker.

"1704, we're going over," Carr said.

Sergeant Beck drove up, "Darnell, who is the complainant?"

"The wife, Sarge. They got in an argument. He pulled out a gun. The gun is on the table."

"Okay, bring the wife over and the gun. I'm gonna go over with 1716."

"17B. I'm going over to '16s location," Beck notified radio.

"17B, okay," the dispatcher replied.

"Wait, I'm gonna transport the complainant over,"said Beck. "Darnell, put her in my car and you guys come on over. No sense in her riding in the back of a van."

A few minutes later, the woman identified her husband. Grant turned him over to Walton and Carr who transported him to detective headquarters. Grant, as the arresting officer, followed.

After placing the prisoner in a cell, Walton and Carr returned to their van.

"1704 available," Carr notified the dispatcher.

The frenetic pace of the evening continued.

i

"1704," called radio.

"*1704,*" Carr responded with a trace of impatience.

"Disorderly crowd at 29th and Reed."

"Anything else you want us to do on the way there?" Carr responded.

"Welcome to the 17th rookie," sneered the dispatcher. This was followed by clicking.

Carr smiled.

"I can barely keep up with the paperwork," Carr said fumbling with the log. He was on his second page - -and they still had two hours remaining.

Darnell laughed, "Get used to it rookie. Wait until summer. You ain't gonna get a chance to catch up. You gonna haf to do the paperwork at the end of the night."

"Good. I guess you're gonna be doin' the driving this summer," Carr shot back with a grin.

They pulled up to the intersection. Standing on the corner was one of the largest people Carr had ever seen. He was hitting a Stop sign and leaving dents in it. The man was standing with a crowd of about six other people outside of a tavern. Walton double-parked the van. Both he and Carr walked over to the crowd.

"Y'all are gonna have to move," Walton said calmly.

"Yeah says who?" a small man standing on the steps of the tavern shouted belligerently.

Walton ignored him. "Come on fellas. We got a complaint. Either go back in the bar or go home."

The big man kept hitting the sign. Carr imagined his head substituted for the sign. He put his hand on his nightstick, but didn't draw it from his belt.

The man hitting the sign looked at Walton.

"What makes you think you and your honky friend gonna make us do anything?"

Carr kept quiet. Walton glowered at the man. "'Cause if you don't, you gonna be spendin' the rest of the night behind bars. And if you give me any shit, you gonna be spendin' longer than that. Now whatchyou wanna do bro'?"

"I ain't your brother," the man replied spitting out the words.

"I know dat homie," Walton replied in a street patois. "Ain't no way you and me got the same Momma."

The others in the crowd howled in laughter.

"Come on Stan," said one of the crowd grabbing the giant and leading him back into the bar.

Carr looked on with a mixture of relief and amusement. Just as the crowd filed back into the bar, an elderly man came up to Carr. He had noticed him when they drove up. He was sitting, on his front step, barely discernible in the dark.

"Thank you so much officer," the frail old man said to Carr. "They been out here for a half an hour carryin' on, pissin', yellin', breakin' bottles and cursin' everybody up the street."

"No problem sir," replied Carr. He could see that the man was visibly shaken and upset.

"I told 'em to stop, but they laughed at me. Dey pushed me and spit at me."

"Many times a rowdy crowd walks past my house late at night. Of course, they're just passing by – not planted in front of the house like this crowd was. Nobody should have to live like this," said Carr empathetically. "You want to file charges against anybody?"

"No, I just want them away."

"If they cause you any more problems just call us. That's what we're here for."

All night long the assignments rattled off from the radio. One after another they came out like an assembly line. At eleven o' clock they received another *Disturbance House* assignment. When they arrived at the house a woman with three kids was standing on the sidewalk.

"Did you call the police?" Walton asked.

"Yes, I did. He threw me out and he won't let me back in," the woman snapped.

"These your kids?" asked Carr.

"Yeah," she replied.

Carr walked over to them. The oldest seemed to be about seven.

"How old are they?"

"Eight, six, and two."

"So what happened?" Carr asked.

"We got in a argument and he threw me out," she answered.

"What's your husband's name?"

"Norbert."

"Okay. Let me go talk to Norbert," Carr said. He walked to the front door and knocked on it with his baton. Norbert came to the door.

"Your wife called and said you threw her out. Is that true?" Carr asked.

"Damn straight. She come home after being at the bar down the street all night. What am I supposed to do?" Norbert replied, indignantly.

Carr looked at him. He could sympathize with him, but at the same time he knew it was the wife's house just as much as his. More importantly it was the kids' house.

"Were the kid's out at the bar too?"

"No."

"Then how come they're not in the house?" Carr asked simply.

Norbert look stunned by the question.

"I didn't throw them out. She took them to go with her," he replied.

"I tell you what Norbert," Carr said, "I don't care what goes on between you and your wife.You two are adults and can work out your problems. But I do care about those kids. There ain't no way I'm gonna see them sleepin' out in the streets tonight. So I'm gonna tell your wife that she and the kids can come back in and if she wants to stay the night then she stays. If I get a call tonight that something happens to her and the kids I'm throwing you in jail. You got that?" Carr barked.

"Yes, sir, but what about if she threatens me? You gonna throw her in jail? What about if her boyfriend comes over here and tries to beat me up. You gonna throw him in jail?"

"Absolutely! In fact, I'll tell your wife right now."

Carr called to the wife, "Ma'am come over here."

The woman and the kids came over to the step where Carr was standing.

"I told your husband that all of you can go back into the house. You can stay or leave. He can stay or leave. But the kids stay no matter what -- and one of you stays with them. Anybody causes trouble, you or him, I'm gonna come back and lock them up. Now you both understand?"

They both nodded their heads.

"Okay, you can go back inside now," Carr ordered.

The woman went in the house followed by the kids. Norbert went back upstairs and the woman sat in the living room.

"Like I said, any problems and somebody gets locked up," Carr said and left.

"You handled that like a pro,"Darnell said as they got back in the wagon. "You act as if you were Dr. Laura.."

"Really, maybe I'll get a radio show."

"All kidding aside, you did a good job. Those kids mighta been wanderin' around all night or wind up in the bar until closin'."

"Yeah, you know, tonight I helped somebody get their stolen car back, I stopped a woman from being shot by her husband, I helped some kids get a place to stay. That ain't a bad days work," Carr said.

"You tell me one social worker that handles as many problems in a day as we do," said Darnell. "We do more to help people than any of those so called welfare workers do. And you ain't seen nuthin' yet. The longer you're on this job, the more you gonna clean up the messes people make for themselves and the messes the social workers can't handle."

On the next four to twelve Mike was assigned his own car, 1724. He was excited about it. Now he had a chance to see if he could do the job on his own. The shift began in mid-week so it wasn't a particularly busy but it was diverse. It was also the first time he made an arrest by himself.

His first call was interesting. It was a *Disturbance House* call in which the husband and wife were playing tug of war with their one year old.

Car 1740, assigned to a surly fellow named Johnston, responded as well. Few people in the squad talked to him and he spoke to even fewer.

ו

As the couple stood there tugging on the baby, Johnston intervened and immediately awarded the baby to the mother. Outraged, the father tried to hit Johnston. Carr intervened and calmed the father down.

"He can't take my baby like that," the father shouted.

"Listen, calm down. Nobody's taking your baby. But it's nine o'clock at night. The kid's got to get to sleep.You gotta place for him to sleep?"

"I was going to take him around the corner to my store."

"You got a crib there for him? You got food and milk for him?"

"No," realized the father.

"Well that's what the other officer is doing. He is just making sure that your kid is cared for," Carr said soothingly

"Okay, then. Listen, I want to thank you for treatin' me like a man. But that other dude…" he headed for Johnston. Carr got into his path and gently escorted him to the corner.

"Just take it easy and if she won't let you in tomorrow you call us. You have rights too."

"Thanks," the man replied.

When they finished Carr asked Johnston why he took the baby away from the father.

"Because the mother always gets the kids," Johnston answered testily.

"How do you know she ain't an ax murderer?" Carr insisted.

"THE MOTHER ALWAYS GETS THE KIDS!" Johnston repeated loudly. "In court the mother always gets custody. I just did what the court is going to do."

"Really? The mother always gets custody?"

"Ninety-nine percent of the time."

"Doesn't seem fair."

"It isn't. But I ain't got no control over that," replied Johnston, testily. He abruptly got into his car and drove away.

"One more instance of injustice. Every law professor in the world should be a cop for about a year before they are allowed to teach," Carr said to himself.

Later that evening he made his first solo arrest.

"1724 meet a complainant, 2-4 and Wharton, regarding a robbery," the static voice of police radio commanded Carr.

"1724 OK. When did the robbery occur?"

"About eleven o'clock."

"Any flash?"

"We didn't get any. The complainant is a female. She'll be standing on the corner."

"1724, OK."

This was dumb, Mike thought. How the hell do you take a call about a robbery and don't ask for a description? He drove quickly over to the location but not with lights and sirens. He didn't get the sense that this was an urgent development. As he pulled up to the location, he saw a woman standing alone dressed as if she were going out to dinner or a nightclub.

"1724 on location," Carr notified radio.

"1724 OK."

Carr walked up to a very well dressed woman standing near a bus stop. She was chewing some gum and had a cigarette dangling from her lip.

"Did you call the police?"

"Yes, I did. I was robbed. Some man came down here while I was waitin' for the bus. He grabbed me and tried to kiss me. When I fought him off, he took my handbag and ran."

"What did he look like?"

"All I remember is that he had on dungarees, sneakers, and a jacket."

"What color jacket?"

"Like white."

"Tall or short? White, black, brown? Fat, skinny?"

"Mistuh aroun' here we all be black."

"Okay, a black male, wearing dungarees, sneakers and a white jacket."

"He wasn't fat or skinny, and he was about your height," the woman added.

"OK. Wait one minute. I want to get this over the radio."

"1724."

"1724."

"Yeah, I got a founded robbery and sexual assault. Committed by a black male, wearing dungarees, sneakers, and a light color jacket. About five foot ten inches, medium build. Last seen heading east on Wharton by foot from twenty-fourth about twenty minutes ago."

"Okay, stand by."

"All units, flash information on a sexual assault and robbery twenty minutes ago at 2-4 and Wharton. Committed by a black male, five ten, medium build, wearing dungarees, sneakers, and a light colored jacket. Last seen heading east on Wharton by foot from Twenty-Fourth."

"1724, hold me out while I take the complainant to detective division," Carr informed radio.

"24 OK," the dispatcher acknowledged.

"Miss, I'm gonna take you to talk to the detectives," Carr said sensitively.

"Okay."

"1724!"

"1724!" Mike acknowledged. He wasn't sure who was calling. It sounded like Grant.

"Yeah, 1716, I got a ped stop here at 2-9 and Reed who matches the description. Can you bring the complainant over?"

"1724 en route," Carr said. He drove the woman to Grant's location. Grant had a man handcuffed standing next to his car. Mike pulled up and told the woman to see if she could identify the man. He shined his spotlight to illuminate the man's face.

"No, that's not him," said the woman.

"You sure."

"Yeah, I'm sure."

Carr leaned his head out the window and yelled over to Grant, "Let him go. He's not the one."

"Okay," Grant acknowledged.

"1724, turn me back around to detectives with the complainant. My mileage is 23 point 4 at nine thirty," Carr informed the dispatcher. Police were required to furnish time and mileage to the dispatcher whenever a male was transporting a female. It helped if there were allegations of sexual misconduct later by the female.

As he turned onto Dickinson Street, Mike noticed a man standing on a porch looking like he was sticking a key in the door. He would have given anyone the impression of someone just coming home for the evening. However, he matched the description of the perpetrator. The jacket was a beige color and a pullover. Carr slowed down.

"Ma'am, did this guy have on a zipper jacket or a pullover?" Carr asked.

"It was a pullover type."

Mike stopped in the middle of the street turned on his spotlight and shined it at the person on the porch.

"Did it look like that?" Mike asked her as he trained on the man on the porch.

"THAT'S HIM!" shrieked the woman.

Mike dashed out of the car and jumped onto the porch in almost a single motion. He had drawn his gun and aimed it at the head of the man.

"FREEZE!" he bellowed at the top of his lungs. The man stood perfectly still. Peripherally, Mike noticed an opened handbag on the porch. He shoved the man against the storm door with his hand, then cuffed him and led him to the car.

"Get out of the car," Mike ordered the woman. He shoved the prisoner into the back seat and locked the doors. He leaned into the car through the driver's side window and grabbed the radio.

"1724, I need a wagon at my location," shouted Carr into the transmitter.

"What have you got there?" asked the dispatcher, calmly.

Mike suddenly realized that he never notified radio. "I got the guy. I got a positive ID from the complainant and I grabbed him."

"What's your location 24?"

"27th and Dickinson, middle of the block."

"A car to back up 1724 until a wagon gets there."

"1716, I got 'em."

Grant pulled up in a few seconds later.

"You got here fast," Carr said.

"I was just around the corner. How 'bout giving me the complainant while you follow the van into detectives?" Grant asked.

"Sounds good," Carr said as he directed the complainant into 1716 as the van pulled up.

After placing the prisoner in the van, Carr followed it to the Detective Division, where he spent the rest of the shift being interviewed by the detective and filling out paperwork.

After roll call the next day Sergeant Beck complimented him. "You made a collar a lot of veterans wouldn't have made Carr."

Later, Leon said to him that Beck had told him, "Your cousin learns fast. He's sharp. He's gonna do well."

During the next tour he was partnered with Walton. Walton had a group-day the night he made his arrest. This was the first chance he had to talk to Carr about it.

"You made that arrest on Dickinson Street last week, the one where the guy was pretending to go in the house?" Walton asked.

"Yeah," replied Carr.

"Well the house he was going into belongs to the girlfriend of a guy in three squad. Her daughters were sitting on the step when the guy ran up. He musta saw you coming down the street and figured to fool you," Walton told him.

"As soon as the kids saw that they got scared and ran inside. They called their mother and told her what was going on. She figured the guy was trying to break into the house. So she grabbed a shotgun and was ready to shoot through the door when she saw your spotlight on. When she saw that she stopped."

"You mean if I didn't turn on my spotlight, I woulda got shot too."

"Yup."

It would not be the last time a Mike Carr arrest would be so ironic.

Chapter 16

"Here you go Jules," Malcolm said as he handed over the wad of cash to Duncannon, "All the money Saladin owes you, plus interest."

"Thanks, Malcolm," Duncannon smiled. He counted the money. "What's the matter, Saladin getting too big to pay off hisself?"

"No, he's just busy with *ek-zec-u-tive* things," Malcolm laughed.

"It's a good thing he's got you around to assist him," replied Jules.

"You think he's gonna need some more any time soon?"

"As a matter a fact he does. But he's gonna have to tell you how much and when. In the meantime, I want to know if you want to buy some armament."

"Armament? You mean like guns?" Jules said raising his tone.

"Yup. We been doin' some shoppin' and we got everything from street sweepers to grenades," said Malcolm, sounding like a car salesman.

"What are street sweepers?"

"Kinda automatic shotguns. You can clear a corner real fast with one of 'em."

"I sure can use them. Lately I been gettin' some heat from the wops. They been wantin' me to pay them a street tax. Last week they tuned up one of my associates and they warned me I was next."

"Surprised to hear that. They usually stay with their own," said Malcolm.

"Yeah, well they usin' some brothers to help them out," said Jules bitterly. "I don't know who, but I'd like to find out."

"Yeah, it would be nice to know what brother is goin' in business with the Mafia."

"When can I see your merchandise?" Jules asked.

"Day after tomorrow. We been gettin' a lot of stuff in lately."

"That's pretty good. You call me and we'll arrange a meet," said Duncannon. He finished his drink and left the bar.

Good, that's two prospective customers in one week, Malcolm thought. He was pleased with himself. Malcolm always felt he probably would have been a good salesman.

"If we knew then what we know now," Malcolm sighed remorsefully.

In the time that had passed since Malcolm had been assisting Saladin, the organization began to enter into the prostitution and gambling fields. Malcolm had given Paxon some responsibility in handling those ventures. He could tell that this was deeply resented by Hannibal Stevens.

Hannibal knew that the decline in income from the Bainbridge speakeasy had hurt his standing with Saladin. When Saladin announced Malcolm was going to be his lieutenant, Hannibal didn't think much of it. Malcolm was, after all, an old friend of Saladin's. But when Hadfield was given the responsibility of handling the new forays into gambling and prostitution, Hannibal knew he was on the outside. He figured Saladin no longer trusted him.

Even though he considered himself fortunate not to be in a shallow grave in New Jersey, Hannibal was still embittered. He wanted money.

He had made some contacts in Saladin's old auto theft ring and managed to convince a garage owner that he could supply him with cars for replating and would cut him in on the profits. He did not tell the garage owner that Saladin was not involved. The name of Saladin would keep the garage owner in line. Up until now it had worked very well.

Malcolm knew about Hannibal's sideline. He wasn't worried. In fact, he was glad, because it would be easier to phase Hannibal out if he had something else. Besides Malcolm had his hands full with the gambling and prostitution ventures, and the new one into gun dealing. Saladin's business was expanding. He was getting larger pieces of the drug trade. He was even acquiring the business of others. Just like they do on Wall Street, Malcolm thought.

Saladin also began to get involved in politics. He met Richmond York at a fund raising function and made an appointment to see him the following week. It was this appointment that kept Saladin from meeting with Duncannon.

"Saladin, so glad you were able to make it," Richmond greeted him.

"Thanks for inviting me Richmond. I have been wanting to meet you."

"That's good to hear."

"As a minority business owner who enjoys some success, I think it important to be able to plow some benefit back into the community."

"Of course. I want...."

Saladin waved him off. He did not want to endure one of Richmond York's famous soliloquies.

"What I would like, Richmond, is to meet some people, community leaders, who I can work with to meet your goals," Saladin said.

"Saladin, I would be more than happy to introduce you to people that are willing to help PART and the African-American community."

"That will be fine," said Saladin. He took an envelope out of his jacket pocket. "I know the organization will really help our brothers and sisters."

Saladin placed the envelope on Richmond's desk. "Here's a little something to kick off the campaign."

"Why, thanks Saladin. I didn't expect this so soon," said Richmond taking the envelope and slipping it in his desk.

"Yes, well, no time like the present," Saladin said rising from his chair. "You'll have to excuse me, Richmond. I have another appointment I have to keep."

"Of course, here, let me help you with your coat."

Richmond helped Saladin on with his coat and escorted him to the door. When Saladin was gone Richmond opened the envelope. Twenty thousand dollars in various denominations, Richmond was stunned.

Never had he received a contribution of this magnitude. He knew what he could do with it. There was much that PART needed and Saladin was a tremendous asset. No question about it. This was Manna from heaven.

"That is one hot looking lawyer!"

Carr heard the anonymous comment as he was standing outside of a courtroom in City Hall. A whistle punctuated the remark. He saw the object of the lust was Beverly Clark.

Mike was milling around with other police officers, waiting to testify in the robbery arrest he made. Clark walked right past him as she entered the courtroom.

No question about it, Mike thought, she is one sexy woman. A guy could be real happy with her. Pretty and smart, a can't miss combination.

"I wouldn't mind being cross examined by her," Mike said to no one in particular.

"I think you're gonna get your wish," Max Grant said to him. "She's the defense attorney in your case."

Sure enough when Carr was called to the stand to testify Beverly Clark was the defense attorney.

"So, you did not actually see the accused commit the crime?" Beverly asked softly.

"No ma'am," confirmed Carr.This was his first experience in court. He was excited, apprehensive, and curious. He was concerned that he would be duped into saying something that would impugn his credibility. He was carefully calculating his responses waiting for Clark to twist his words and to create the impression that he wasn't telling the truth.

"AND you arrested him, based on an identification done in the dark of night at a distance," asked Beverly in a crescendo.

"No, I held him for investigation," replied Mike simply.

"Did it ever occur to you that this might have been a mistake?"

"Objection. The officer simply reacted to what the complainant said," said the Assistant District Attorney.

Good, thought Beverly, he is stepping right into the trap. His protestation just enhances the image of wrongdoing.

"That's not true your honor," Beverly averred. 'The officer first shined a spotlight on my client, which put the complainant in a frame of mind."

"Sustained," said the judge, wearily.

Beverly continued her interrogation. It didn't matter that her question was disallowed. The jury got to hear it. That's all that mattered.

"Why did you shine the light on my client?"

Although Carr was making a conscious effort to say only what happened and not to editorialize he was beginning to lose his patience.

"Because the *victim* had given me a description that could be applied to the man I saw on the porch," Carr hissed.

"But the description was rather indistinct - was it not?" said Beverly haughtily, "By that I mean..."

Carr cut her off in mid-sentence, "I am well aware of what indistinct means counselor. I may not have been educated at a fancy college, but I do have a vocabulary."

The judge chuckled at Carr's remark.

"Could you instruct the witness to confine himself to answering the question, your honor," Beverly bristled.

"I think he responded in a very concise manner. But please continue officer, and answer the whole question."

"It is true the description could have been applied to many people, but many times that is all you have to work with. That's why you grab as many people as possible," Carr sounded like a veteran police officer. "You play percentages. One person you grab may be the one."

"But you had no proof that my client had committed a crime."

"I had an identification. That's enough to investigate him."

"The complainant could have been mistaken."

"Possibly. But the fact that the victim's handbag was on the porch next to *your client* wasn't a mistake was it?" seethed Carr.

Beverly Clark realized that she now had lost her advantage. The inclusion of the handbag in the officer's testimony was going to negate anything she could do. She knew the handbag was going to be presented. Finding it on the porch was the most incriminating part of the case. But if she avoided the mentioning of it, until such time as she had planted the seeds of doubt about the conduct of the police officers then she would have a chance for an acquittal.

Well, she comforted herself, even great lawyers make mistakes. This was a tough case to win. He had been all but caught ꞁ

red-handed. Since both accused and victim were African-American the racism ploy wasn't available.

"I have no further questions," Beverly said, resignedly.

"No questions," said the DA.

"You can step down," said the judge to Carr. He immediately left the witness stand and walked by Beverly Clark. As he did he smiled and winked at her. Beverly --to his surprise-- returned his smile.

This year the annual PART banquet was held at the Society Hill Sheraton hotel. This was only possible through Saladin's munificence. Without his money, the affair would have been at some caterers in Germantown. They would not have attracted the quantity and the quality of the people there they had by having the banquet at the Sheraton Society Hill.

"Judge Ruby Parrish, I would like you to meet Saladin Christian," Richmond said gesturing with his drink. "Saladin, Judge Ruby Parrish."

"My pleasure Judge Parrish," said Saladin. A very pretty judge, thought Saladin. Not only was she pretty, but she was educated. This is the kind of woman I need. I am tired of the Tyesha types, he thought bitterly.

Richmond certainly came through. Not only were there judges and politicians at the banquet, but a pretty judge.

"Are you Common Pleas court?" Saladin asked.

"Yes I am. Are you familiar with the court system?"

"Somewhat," replied Saladin stifling a laugh. "I find the judiciary to be very fascinating."

"Oh my, that is so good to hear," Judge Parrish said, in a lusty tone.

Saladin sensed her mood.

"Maybe we can go outside for a bit and discuss the finer points of law. It is getting stuffy and crowded in here," Saladin proposed.

"I would be happy to," smiled Judge Parrish.

There are political connections and there are political connections, Saladin smiled to himself.

219

Chapter 17

Barnett inspected the photograph on the desk in front of him. He had been transferred to the Organized Crime Unit from the Police Academy two months earlier. The transfer was a consequence of his promotion to Lieutenant. He was assigned to assist in the investigation of Saladin Christian. Barnett reread the history on Saladin and was quite impressed. In a short time he had risen from a smalltime car thief to run one of the biggest crime networks in the city.

Every indication was that Saladin was diversifying into prostitution and gambling. Ironically, Barnett thought, Saladin's career was in contravention to the normal organized crime boss career track. Most of these hoodlums started out gambling and gravitated into trafficking in controlled substances.

Saladin displayed a real talent for organization and tactics, Barnett noted. He was positively brilliant in eliminating the Sommervilles. Barnett remembered the Sommervilles from his days as a cop in the 22nd District. They were major bad guys -- ruthless as they come. Saladin handled them rather adroitly. He also managed to dodge the legal bullet too. Of course, having Beverly Clark as your attorney didn't hurt.

Barnett's job was to build a case against Saladin so strong that even Clarence Darrow would not be able to have him acquitted. The feasibility of such a task was contingent upon the quantity and the quality of the informants available. Informants were the only avenue available because the law enforcement officers - federal, state, and local - to date had been unable to infiltrate Saladin's organization. They were not able to cultivate anyone in the Saladin organization who would introduce one of their 'narcs' into the group.

The only lead to Saladin available so far was an oblique one. Oddly enough it did not come from DEA, FBI, the State Drug Task Force, Philadelphia Narcotics or Barnett's own unit, but from a 22nd District Burglary Detail team.

Burglary Details or BD's are plainclothes officers who report directly to the captain of a district. The name itself was one of those archaic terms that permeate the Philadelphia Police

Department. The BD's responsibilities are defined by the captain and sometimes did include burglaries, but generally, they operate as a plainclothes investigative unit for the captain.

BD teams are deployed at the discretion of the captain to whatever he felt was necessary. This meant gambling investigations, robberies, homicides, auto thefts, or anything else considered urgent.

It was by way of an auto theft investigation that enough evidence was acquired to obtain an arrest warrant for Saladin. The 22nd BD team had been trying to find who was operating a stolen car ring out of the district-- which encompasses part of North Philadelphia. They had staked out an area where a few stolen cars had been recovered. They arrested a young kid, already on probation, who led them to a garage owner who was involved in a *replating* operation.

Replating is the method used by car thieves whereby a car is stolen and the thieves buy a similar make and model wreck. They use the wreck's vehicle identification number (VIN). The VIN of the wreck is removed and placed on the stolen car. Many of these cars are shipped to foreign countries for sale. A variation on this is buying a new car, shipping it overseas to a friend who sends back the VIN and title, which are used to replate a similar make and model stolen vehicle. It is a multibillion-dollar racket.

The garage owner said that he dealt with a man by the name of Hannibal Stevens, who said he represented Saladin Christian. He said that he had seen Saladin once with Hannibal as the two came to collect some money.

This was sufficient for him to get the arrest warrant for Saladin, for auto theft and receiving stolen property, that he was going to serve today. While not quite the same thing as drug trafficking, it would still be enough to place him in prison for a while. All of these wiseguys have an Achilles heal, Barnett thought as he left the office, it was just a question of finding it.

Barnett and Detective Justin Wood drove to the 17th District. He wanted to get a couple of uniform police officers to help him serve the warrant. He chose the 17th because that is where Saladin's new speakeasy was. Once in the district he contacted police radio.

"This is William 24, could I get a 17th District wagon to meet me at 15th and Bainbridge? I am serving a warrant," Barnett said.

"Is there a 17th district supervisor available," called the dispatcher.

"17 Barney," the sound of the smooth electronic voice of Sergeant Archie Beck answered, "have 1704 meet him."

"1704 OK," responded Walton even before the dispatcher had a chance to call. A few minutes later Walton pulled up next to Barnett's sedan. He was partnered with Henry "Hammerin' Hank" Hoffman instead of Carr this day.

Walton did not like Hoffman. He thought Hoffman was mean and lazy. He also knew that Hoffman was afraid of him.

"Good afternoon gentlemen," Barnett said to Walton and his partner. "We gotta warrant for Saladin Christian."

Walton let out a long whistle, "You don't go after the small ones do you? You gonna make the pinch at the speak?"

"Yeah, Walton I want you to go to the front door with me. The other two can seal off the back alley, " said Barnett motioning to Wood and Hoffman.

"C'mon Hoffman. You get to earn your pay today," Walton said as he exited the van. Hoffman grumbled as he moved his large girth out of the van. Walton walked to the front of the building, while Wood walked down the block to 16th Street and turned the corner to the alley entrance. Hoffman did the same on the 15th Street side. As soon as everyone was in position, Walton banged on the door of the speakeasy.

Malcolm Hadfield had spotted the police van from a second floor window and alerted Saladin, who was in the basement. Saladin hurriedly walked to the third floor of the tenement to a dark storage room.

Inside the room was a trap door cut into the ceiling. The room was dark. Empty cartons stacked to the ceiling concealed the door. Saladin opened the door and climbed onto the roof. He crouched down and walked on the tar of the flat rooftops to the 16th Street end of the row of homes. He peeked over the side to see Wood at the entrance to the alley.

It didn't matter. As long as they did not see him up on the roof, they would not think to look for him up there. Even if they did, they would not find the trap door. By the time they got a hook and ladder, Saladin would be long gone.

Washington Paxon opened the door when he estimated Saladin was on the roof.

"What can I do for Philadelphia's finest today?" Paxon greeted Barnett and Walton with a smile.

"We got a warrant for the arrest of Saladin Christian," Barnett said, brusquely. He walked past Paxon, flashing the paper in front of him as he proceeded down the hallway. Coming out of a room near the end of the hallway was Malcolm Hadfield.

"Where's Saladin?" Barnett growled at Hadfield.

"Hasn't been here all day. In fact, he wasn't here yesterday or the day before that," Malcolm replied, pleasantly.

"We're gonna look around," Barnett said. He walked through the office and opened all the doors. He went through all the rooms on the first floor while Walton did the same on the second floor. They searched the third floor together.

Barnett knew they weren't going find Saladin. But what he did want was to get an idea of the inside of the building and map it out. He could tell what part of the building the speakeasy was in. He saw where the files were kept. He also noted the storage rooms where the liquor stock and possibly any stolen property would be. There was also a dark storage room on the third floor. If they ever raided the place they would be able to quickly go to the places where contraband or documents could be found.

"Tell Mr. Christian that we're anxious to have him as our guest, *if* you happen to see him," Barnett said to Hadfield as he and Walton left.

"You know he might be out in the back. Maybe in the yard of another house," Walton said to Barnett.

"He's long gone Darnell. Otherwise they wouldn't have opened the door," Barnett said evenly. "I got the information I wanted though. Besides he might even turn himself in now that he knows we got a warrant for him."

Once outside Barnett signaled Wood to return to the car. Walton did the same with Hoffman.

Barnett waved to Walton as he got behind the wheel and drove away, "Thanks Darnell. If you see him, grab him, or at least give me a call."

The vehicles drove off in different directions. Saladin watched as the cars left and returned to his office.

"Did they say what they had?" he asked Hadfield and Paxon.

"No. Just that they had a warrant," Paxon replied. Hadfield shook his head in confirmation.

"Well, maybe I'll contact my lawyer," Saladin said pensively. "I'd like to know what they got."

"Why don't we go back to work," Hadfield nodded to Paxon. "You let us know if you need anything."

"Well, rookie, how do you like being a police officer so far?" Max Grant asked Carr.

Grant, Walton, and Carr had gone, after work, to an outdoor, waterfront nightclub located on a pier in the Delaware River.

Darnell and Max had taken Carr under their wings. They both felt Carr could be a good cop. They also understood his reluctance to be one of the "thin blue line." Much of what he felt, they also felt at various times. However, not everything was measured in dollars and cents. They figured Carr would learn this eventually – if he didn't resign first.

Grant was in his early thirties. A conscientious and industrious police officer, he was also intelligent and courteous. Grant had been on the force for eight years. He was going to college at night with plans of getting a degree. His ultimate goal was to work for the DEA.

His education had been interrupted by his divorce, but he recently resumed classes and expected to graduate next year. A tall, athletic looking, handsome man with dark hair, and mustache he looked remarkably similar to Carr. Indeed, the two could pass for relatives.

"Well, in the words of Lieutenant Alan Wister of the Philadelphia Police Academy: this isn't a badge -- it is a ticket to the greatest show on earth," Carr laughed.

"Yeah, you do get to see some pretty unusual things."

i

"Hey rookie, you're buyin'," Walton said, taking a seat next to Max.

"You tellin' him about all of his mistakes Max?"

"What mistakes?"Carr said.

"Just kidding,"said Walton. "He's nervous ain't he?"

"What is this, an FOP convention?" Leon said to Tom, as the two of them joined the others at the bar. Carr had invited them earlier to meet there.

"We were just asking the rookie here how he likes being a cop," Darnell said to Leon.

"You were a real surly son of a bitch when you started. You still feel that way?" asked Leon.

"In all honesty, I'll say this much, I have gotten a feeling of relevance that I never got from any job before. The things you see and do on this job are amazing sometimes. It's been a real education."

"Whaddaya mean?" asked Tom being the only civilian in the group.

"For one thing I always thought spouse abuse involved husbands beating up their wives. Every Disturbance House I've had so far where there's been violence, it's been the wife assaulting the husband."

"Yeah, but you won't hear that on the nightly news," said Grant.

"Whaddaya drinkin' Leon?" asked Walton.

"Coors, and get one for Tom here.You guys met?" Leon asked, pointing to Tom, Darnell, Max. "Tom, this is Darnell Walton and Max Grant. Meet Tom Marshall."

"Hi," said Tom

"Pleasure," said Grant .

"Yeah, same here," said Walton.

"Okay, two Coors comin' up," Walton continued signaling the bartender.

"I had a job the other day," Carr related, "where I walk in the house and this dude had been slashed from head to toe. They were like razor cuts up and down his whole body. When I asked him who did this he says he don't know."

225

"Then down the steps comes his wife yellin' and screamin'," Carr said sipping his beer. "I said to him, she do this to you? He sez yeah, but he don't want to press charges 'cause he loves his wife."

"Yeah, I had a guy one time," Walton chimed in, "where his clothes were scattered all over the front lawn. He's got bumps and bruises all over him. And the wife is standing in the doorway yellin' at him."

"Git out da house and stay out!" Walton mimicked. "Ya ain't nuthin' but a no good bum. You come back in here and I'm gonna hit you with mah hammer again."

"And another thing," Walton said, trying to contain his laughter, "you ain't no damn good in bed."

"Then she slams the door," Walton said between guffaws. "I mean the whole neighborhood heard her. It was all I can do to stop from fallin' over in laughter. But when I asked him if he wanted to press charges he said no."

"Some of these things are hilarious," said Grant. "You see so much of them. That's why when police officers treat things callously it's not always because they don't want to do it. It's just that we see it all the time and we become jaded."

"I can understand how you get that way," said Carr earnestly.

"If you let this shit get to you it'll drive you crazy," said Leon woefully. "This is an emotional roller coaster. One minute you're trying to keep someone's brains from spilling out into the street, and then an hour later you're sittin' down havin' dinner with your family. Or you just get finished subduing an armed felon whose trying to shoot you and a half hour later you're going shopping with your wife."

"Yeah, you got that right," Max said. "A guy I know, who was in 'Nam and later became a cop in the 26th, told me the biggest difference between the two, was that in Nam he was in shit all the time. He behaved like a wild animal to cope with the insanity that was always around him. But as a cop, he only had insanity on duty. He became mean and nasty like he did in Nam while on duty. But when he went off duty, he was supposed to somehow turn off the nastiness."

"That's true," said Leon. "It ain't easy. When you come home you can't be like you are at work."

"I thought you weren't suppose to be brutal as a cop," said Tom innocently. "I mean isn't that why a lot of cops get in trouble? Look at the Rodney King case."

"Let me ask you something," said Walton peevishly. "You got some dude that has just ripped off an old lady. Took her social security or welfare check. He not only took the money but kicks her in the head. No good reason to do so. He is just mean. Now you're chasin' him down an alley. He turns around and tries to kick you. What are you gonna do - give him a kiss?"

"No, that's not what I mean," said Tom defensively. "But you don't have to beat him to death."

"I'm not sayin' you do. But you can't walk up to him very sweet and kind, and ask him to let you put the handcuffs on. I guarantee he ain't gonna do it," said Walton sharply.

"*And* as far as Rodney King is concerned," sneered Leon, "a lot of people believe the cops did what they were suppose to do. Remember this was a guy who had beaten and robbed a storeowner. He was driving in a way that endangered the lives of innocent people and then he resisted arrest. You know there were two other guys in the car and nothing happened to them."

"Tom, listen. Nobody calls the police when things are going fine," explained Carr. "The only time the cops are called is when there is a problem. Police officers make judgments in a fraction of a second - a judgment that will have serious consequences. A judgment that will be criticized by people who have the luxury of deliberation."

"Yeah, twenty-twenty hindsight," said Leon. "Listen, I'm not saying cops are without sin. There are enough jerk-offs out there with a badge. We know that better than you do. I always said we need more guys like Mike and Max and Darnell. In fact, I've said many times if we had more guys like Max and Darnell the crime rate would be cut in half."

"Yeah, but that doesn't justify the criticism we get in the press," Max said. "It's amazing how groups like the ACLU talk about safeguarding rights of criminals, but let a cop be accused of something and they want to hang him without a trial."

227

"Yeah, they're the worst hypocrites. However, no matter what, we're gonna get criticized. It's a tough job," said Leon. "Let's face it, the type of personality that makes a good cop makes a lousy waiter. So we're never gonna get the benefit of good public relations."

"Like the guy said, one minute you're in the middle of a savage predicament and the next minute you're in the serenity of your home," Max added.

"Peaks and valleys," affirmed Darnell. "It is an emotional roller coaster for sure. Periods of absolute monotony, punctuated by intervals of bedlam."

"It's enough to change anyone," Leon lamented. He placed his drink on the bar and ordered another round.

"That doesn't excuse brutality or rudeness," Tom insisted.

"Nobody's excusing anything. All we're saying is that sometimes we get accused of being that way even though we acted properly. There is a perception - among some - that police are cold and cruel. If anything, the opposite is true. We do more to help the unfortunate and the defenseless than any million social workers and civil rights workers," Max responded.

"We do more to help poor people than all those poverty pimps and racehustlers out there," Walton said, emphatically.

"You guys notice this place is getting crowded?" Leon said, abruptly changing the subject he felt was becoming way too serious. The nightclub crowd had wandered in as they had been talking. The bar was crowded about two deep.

"I am starting to feel out of my comfort zone," said Darnell. He nodded to the girls seated at the other end of the bar.

"Yeah right, I can understand that," laughed Max. "These girls can put two coherent sentences together. They're too smart for you."

"I doubt if those ladies know what a sentence is," Walton chortled. "I think I'm gonna leave. I don't want those women to molest me."

"Yeah, me too, I don't want to see those women molesting you. I would puke," Max said finishing his drink. "Well rookie, I guess I'll see you at work."

"OK, Max take it easy."

ⁱ

"Later Mike," said Darnell.

"Take it easy," he said to Tom and Leon.

As they walked out Leon turned to Tom. "You gonna stick around or you gonna go over your girl's house?"

"Over her house."

"Yeah. How about you Mike? You leaving?" he asked Mike.

"No, I'm gonna stick around for a while," Mike said.

"I think I will too, Can you drop me off Mike? I drove here with Tom," said Leon

"No problem."

"Adios then," said Tom, "Don't go flirting with these girls – you're married."

"Yeah, right" Mike replied.

After everybody left, Leon went to the bar to get a drink. Mike got up and walked over to the end of the pier. He looked out over the water. The river mirrored the lights of the various ships and boats, as well as those from the Ben Franklin Bridge.

He thought about what Tom had said. Six months ago he would have thought Tom was absolutely correct. Now it was different.

"Whaddaya doin'?"Leon said as he approached. "Thinking of jumping?"

"No, just noticing how peaceful it is. Real different from work."

The water was calm. The scene was tranquil. It was almost as if one were someplace else -- away from the noise only a few feet away.

He noticed some of the after work crowd still lingering past happy hour. Men in dark suits, stockbrokers it seemed from the parts of the conversations he could hear, acting like fools trying to impress pretty young secretaries with their material wealth. The young ladies were trying to impress them with their sophistication.

"Look at those nitwits," Mike said to Leon. "Acting like they are millionaires trying to impress the girls."

"Yeah, I can only imagine the lies they're telling," Leon smiled. "I knew a guy once who fooled this girl into thinking that he was the CEO of PNB Bank. Good looking girl too. Smart as a fencepost though. She actually believed him."

"Buncha phonies," Mike spat out the words.

Carr finished his beer and flicked his cigarette into the water. "C'mon let's get out of here," he said to Leon.

He walked out of the nightclub and got his car from the valet.

"Here ya go buddy," said the valet,a young kid in his late teens.

"I'm not your buddy," Carr said, harshly. His glance matched his tone. The valet stood there with his mouth open.

"Shut your mouth, wouldaya tryin' to do catch flies," Carr said sarcastically. The valet was dumbfounded as Carr drove off.

"Whatever happened to manners," Carr muttered.

Leon raised his eyebrows looking at him. "Wow, that was a mood swing if I ever saw one," he said in disbelief. "Bipolar?'

"Maybe," Mike replied, "Maybe it was the alcohol talking. Maybe it was the last three assignments. All of them involved young punks terrorizing the locals. All these kids that I either chased or locked up, called me buddy. I'm tired of punks calling me buddy. I am tired of a lot of things."

Leon said nothing.

Carr was still in a surly mood when he walked in the door of his house. He was later than he told Stella he would be. She started in on him.

"Couldn't you tell me when you were coming home?" Stella complained.

"I told you I was goin' out," Mike said piercingly. "I left a message on the answering machine."

"I'm not talking about that. I'm talking about what time," She yelled.

"Lower your voice. Who the hell do you think you're talking to?" he said menacingly. He moved so that he was standing with his nose about a half an inch from hers - like the manager of baseball team arguing with an umpire.

"Get away from me," She said and tried to shove him. He instinctively reacted by pushing her arms away and grabbing her blouse and shoving her against the wall. He turned her so she was facing with the wall. She bumped her head in the process.

"Ouch!" she screamed and grabbed her forehead. He just stood there and watched her. He didn't bother to offer her any aid.

"Get away from me," she said as she walked away from him and upstairs. "I don't know what got into you but I'm not going to put up with this shit. Who the hell do you think you are -- not telling me what time you're coming home."

She was still fuming as she got ready for work. She looked at herself in her dresser mirror. There was no bruise from the bump. She then examined her figure. Not bad, she thought, I drive all those hunks at the bar crazy. I must have been propositioned a dozen times since I've been working there. Even the owner said business has increased since I have been there. He should know how lucky he is to be married to me.

She finished dressing and left the house without saying anything.

Mike watched his wife drive away. He then lit a cigarette flopped on the sofa and turned on the TV.

"I'm sick of this," he said shutting off the TV. "The hell with it. I'm going to get a drink."

Since Stella had the car his destination was limited to whatever was within walking distance. He walked to the taproom around the corner from his house.

When Stella arrived at work she told Nancy what had transpired between her and her husband.

"Wow, that doesn't sound like Mike," Nancy said. "I mean he's never done anything like that before has he?"

"No," replied Stella as she took a tray of drinks from the bar.

"Are you sure you didn't do anything to start this?" said Nancy skeptically.

"Nothing more than usual," Stella replied coyly. She took the drinks to the table. Nancy just shook her head.

The waitress uniform was a modest outfit. Just an ordinary pants suit. But Stella always had one extra button undone on her blouse. The blouse had also shrunk a little which enhanced her figure even more. She was the most popular waitress in Ollie's.

Stella placed the drinks on the table and collected the money.

"Hon, if I were married to you I'd never let you outta bed," the tall, blonde, handsome man, in his late twenties said to her. Stella just smiled and gave him the change. He took a dollar bill and gave it to her as a tip, stuffing it in her blouse.

"Thanks," Stella said with a smile. She hurried back to the bar. On one hand she was embarrassed and angry. On the other, she was flattered.

Carr walked in recalling the last time he was at the tavern was on Thanksgiving when he met Sheila. He had not been back since. The bar was relatively empty. During the summer months people are away and business falls off a bit. He took a seat facing the door. He wanted to be able to watch people as they entered.

"Scotch and soda," he ordered. The bartender cleaned off the bar and placed a cocktail napkin in front of him.

"Okay," said the bartender.

He watched the big screen TV. A baseball game was on. He finished his first drink and ordered another when he was stunned by who walked in next.

Leon entered the bar looking very agitated. Mike almost fell out of his chair laughing. Every time I come in here I meet the Dover family, he laughed to himself. Who knows, maybe next time the kids will be here. Leon spotted him sitting there with a grin on his face.

"What are you laughing about?"Leon said rudely.

Mike didn't want to let on about his conversation with Sheila. "I thought you were going home?"

"So were you. So what?"

"So I got into an argument with my wife. Why are you here?"

"Same thing," he said testily.

"C'mon I'll buy you a drink,"said Mike."You're argument is obviously worse than mine."

"Yeah,"sneered Leon."You know I think she found out about my girlfriend."

"So what if she did?"said Mike."You didn't think you could keep this up forever did you?"

"I thought I could."

"Nahh, you're better getting' it out in the open."

"Yeah."

"Look, Sheila's a good woman. Whatever is wrong between you two can probably be worked out. You two ain't like those

screwballs we see on the job," said Mike. "You had to see this job
I had the other day. These two guys are having a knock down drag
out and I get in there to separate them. Then they go after me.
Turns out it was two brothers."

He figured if he talked shop that would ease the tension.

"Haven't you learned yet that when you get a call like that you
take your time getting there. You try to arrive after it's over. Then
you take the winner to jail and the loser to the hospital," lectured
Leon.

"Yeah, I've heard that," said Mike. "The other one I've heard
is that it's better to be tried by twelve than carried by six."

"It's true. You pull up on a job and you hear there were shots
fired, or somebody has something in their hand. If you think
you're gonna get hurt, then you shoot. Let a jury sort it out later."

"Yeah, you wind up with your picture on the front page of the
Herald and the subject of a federal investigation," said Mike
trenchantly.

"Better to be on the front page for being investigated than for
being dead," Leon said.

"Listen, your first obligation in this job is to yourself. After you
been on as many years as I have, you learn that the city don't care
about you, most of the public don't give a shit about you, and the
news media is lookin' to hang you," Leon continued. "You only
got yourself and the guys you work with and that's it."

"Some of the guys I work with I don't trust," said Mike.

"Yo, in an organization of 8,000 you're gonna have more than
a few crumbs. Some squads have a lot of guys that are assholes.
But most will stick by you in a tight spot."

"Yeah, circle the wagons."

"Don't laugh. The public doesn't understand what goes on. The
public either thinks you're a hero or a bum. They put you on a
pedestal or they put you in the toilet. There's no happy medium.
Your friends and family look at you the same way. Let me ask you
this, don't you think Stella has been treating you differently?
Don't you think she was excited about the idea you were gonna be
a cop? Lemme tell you, she was. Because she was gonna be the
wife of a cop. In her mind and the mind of most people she knows,
you're a hero. This way she's gonna expect more out of you.

When you came back from the Academy down in the mouth about bein' a cop, she was disappointed. You were going against her values. You were dismissing as unimportant what she finds important. She changed her mind about her husband then."

"How do you know all this?" Mike asked. He was absolutely dumbfounded that Leon knew about the inner feelings of his wife, "What did she tell you?"

"She didn't tell me anything. She didn't have to. I've seen this before. Only it's after a guy's been on the job for a while and he develops a drinking problem or something else goes wrong. The wife goes from being real proud of her husband to detesting him."

Mike just sat on the stool not really knowing what to say. He never really thought about this before. Stella was treating him differently. She went from disappointment at his initial resistance, to anger because of his gloom at starting the Academy, to pride when he graduated, and now lately she has been indifferent.

"Because when she realizes that he isn't Superman, once she realizes that sometimes he takes the job home with him, then he isn't so happy with him anymore. Then the marriage starts to go south," Leon said quietly. His words trailed off as he raised his glass.

"I'm outta here," Leon said abruptly placing the glass down and shoving it across the bar. He threw some dollars bills down next to it.

"Where ya headed?" asked Mike.

"I don't know. FOP maybe. You want to come along?"

"Yeah, but you gotta drive. Stella's got the car."

"Okay, c'mon," Leon said. "You been to the FOP club before?"

"No," responded Mike.

"It's an experience. Plenty of women around. They got a thing about screwing cops."

"Yeah, well that ain't my thing," Mike replied, distastefully.

Chapter 18

Washington Paxon and Hannibal Stevens sat in Stevens' car reviewing their plans. The two new allies were outside of Paxon's house on 75th Avenue. During the time they worked for Saladin they discovered that they shared some characteristics. Both were ambitious young men who wanted what Saladin had. Both concluded that Saladin's current legal problems could help them rise to power.

"The way I figure it," Hannibal said, in his low gravely voice, "we can let the cops take care of Saladin. Once he's locked up, we'll convince Malcolm to either follow us or retire."

Paxon smiled, "Yeah, either that, or we'll retire him."

"Now what I want to do is drop a dime on Saladin. I figure to let the cops know where they can find him. Then I'm gonna make sure he stays there until they come and get him."

"I'll keep the old man away," said Paxon, referring to Malcolm Hadfield. "That way you'll be Saladin's only guard."

"I'll let you know when Saladin's gone. You take Hadfield back to the speak and we'll explain to him the facts of life."

"Cool!"said Paxon.

The two parted. Paxon went into his house to call Hadfield. Hannibal drove off to a phone booth at the corner of Broad and South Streets near the speakeasy. He dialed the number for the 17th District.

"17th District, Officer Smith."

"What's the number for the Organized Crime Unit."

"Organized Crime? 215-686-1111!"

Hannibal hung up and redialed the number for the Organized Crime Unit.

"Organized Crime, Officer Black."

"Yeah, Officer Black, I got some information about Saladin Christian. I hear you're looking for him."

"Hold on."

Stevens could hear the receiver being placed on a table. The silence was interrupted by Barnett's smooth voice.

"Lt. Barnett, Can I help you?"

"No. I can help you," replied Hannibal testily. He didn't like cops, especially white cops.

"Okay, then help," Barnett responded, dourly.

"If you want Saladin Christian he'll be at 1503 Bainbridge this afternoon. If you want him, go get him. Make sure you watch the room that leads to the roof, " Hannibal abruptly hung up. He walked to his car, got behind the wheel and drove off.

In a few moments he was at the Bainbridge speakeasy. He found Saladin in his office.

Hannibal walked in the office.

"Saladin, anything you want me to do."

"No, I'm waiting for Malcolm. You seen him?"asked Saladin, not bothering to look up from his account books.

"No, you want me to call him?" he asked innocently.

"I did that already."

"Okay, I'm going to check the stock."

"Fine."

Hannibal went up to the third floor stockroom and waited. He figured the police would be arriving in about fifteen minutes. The plan was for the police to capture Saladin. Hannibal was going to make a major change to that plan.

He would leave the front door unlocked and lock the back. Stevens would try to get Saladin up to the roof after the police arrived. It was up on the roof that Hannibal's plan would come to fruition. Hannibal planned to hit Saladin on the head and bust his skull. He would then push Saladin's body off the roof.

He would climb off the roof by going into the window of a neighboring house. He already arranged for the window to be open and a rope to hang from the roof leading to the window.

As long he was planning to oust Saladin, Hannibal felt, it was better to dislodge him permanently. Why leave his plans to the erratic criminal justice system? If his plans worked out perfectly, Saladin would be killed and the police charged with the murder.

He did not make these plans known to Paxon. He wasn't sure how Paxon would react. If he were reluctant, Stevens thought, he could not be sure that Paxon wouldn't turn against him later. Stevens determined that he would handle this himself and tell no one.

Barnett hung up the phone. So we finally got ourselves a malcontent in Saladin's organization, Barnett thought smugly. I wonder how that happened.

"Justin," Barnett yelled across the office, "let's go."

Barnett took out Saladin's file and headed for the door. Detective Justin Wood knew better than to ask questions. He just grabbed his gun and left.

A few minutes later they were in Barnett's unmarked car driving to the speakeasy to arrest Saladin. Barnett told Wood to get a 17th District van to meet them.

"William 24. Could I have a 17th District van meet me at 15th and South?" Wood asked the South Division band radio dispatcher. Barnett filled him in about the Stevens' call as they drove.

"1704?"queried the dispatcher.

"1704," responded Walton, "we got it."

Walton turned to Carr who was driving, " Probably serving a warrant. That's near Saladin's speakeasy. They missed him once. They're probably trying again."

Within ten minutes Carr arrived at the intersection. Barnett approached the van as Carr pulled over.

"This is the guy we're looking for,"Barnett said handing the photo to Carr.

"You probably heard of him. He's armed and dangerous."

Carr looked at the photo and was stunned. There on the card was the name of his old high school friend Joe Jobson a/k/a Saladin Christian.

"Yo, I know this guy," exclaimed Carr. " We use to go to high school together. Matter of fact, we were pretty good friends."

Walton laughed, "Well you kept some real good friends."

Barnett looked at Carr suspiciously, "You have a problem locking him up?"

"No,"Carr replied, defensively.

"Let me know now," Barnett said, skeptically.

"If I do, I'll let you know,"Carr said, contemptuously.

"Okay. The information we got is that he is inside the building at 1503 Bainbridge. We were also warned to watch the room leading to the roof. So he must have a way to get up there from inside. I want two guys to cover the entrances to the alleys. I need a uniform with me at the door. Once we're inside I'll look for him downstairs. The other guy goes to the top floor to see if he can find an exit up there. Everybody understand? " Barnett said.

Everybody acknowledged they understood their assignment.

"You go inside with the Lieutenant," Walton instructed Carr. "I want to get him coming down the roof."

"What makes you think he'll be coming down the roof?" asked Carr.

Walton did not respond.

Barnett returned to his car and drove to the 1500 block of Bainbridge Street. Carr followed him in the van.

Barnett parked at one end of the block near a fire hydrant. Carr parked at the opposite end of the block. Barnett and Wood exited their car. Wood went to the alley. Barnett waited for Carr to join him.

Walton notified radio they were on location and then he and Carr exited the van. Walton walked to the alley opposite the end Wood was on while Carr joined Barnett.

Barnett and Carr went to the front door. Barnett knocked on the door. Carr stood on the other side of the doorway. The door swayed open mysteriously when Barnett rapped on it. The motion of the door reminded Carr of a horror picture.

"Police!" shouted Barnett into the house. Barnett quickly moved inside followed by Carr. They both drew their weapons. They were in a darkened hallway. A lone light bulb provided poor illumination. There was a window at the far end through which sunlight entered but did nothing to brighten the hallway.

The hallway was dank and dusty. Barnett led the way down the corridor. Carr followed a few steps behind him. He was far enough behind that Barnett could not be surprised from the back. Suddenly at the end of the dusky corridor a silhouette of a man appeared. It reminded Carr of the target silhouettes at the Pistol Range. Just as suddenly as it appeared it vanished.

"Police! Hold it!" Barnett yelled futilely.

238

Carr couldn't tell where the man had come from much less where he went. Another silhouette appeared, almost mystically, as if created by the shadows.

"Police! Freeze!" Barnett yelled again to no avail. Once again the silhouette disappeared. This time Barnett ran down the corridor.

"Find the steps and get up to the roof," he shouted to Carr.

Carr became confused. He thought he should back up Barnett. Then he thought he should get more help from outside. Finally, he did what Barnett had told him.

Carr found the stairwell about midway down the corridor. Barnett was searching the offices at the end of the hallway.

"I found the steps. I'm going up," he called to Barnett. There was no response.

Carr bounded up the steps two at a time. As he approached the third floor, he heard a movement. The third floor was also dimly lit -- only a naked light bulb at the top of the stairwell. Not even sunlight came through a window. There was a faint sound from behind him.

"Carr where are you?" Barnett called out.

Carr heard him but did not respond. He did not want to give away his position until he determined the source of the noises. Carr noticed a ray of sunlight emanating from the ceiling. He thought he noticed a ladder.

The sunlight disappeared as he heard the slam of a door. The sound came from the direction of the sunlight. He trained his gun in that direction.

"Police! Freeze!"

Suddenly someone pulled the collar of Carr's shirt and yank him backwards. Someone reached out of the shadows, grabbed his gunhand, and squeezed. This caused Carr to inadvertently pull the trigger. A shot rang out.

There was a scream from above him near the ceiling and a thud of someone falling on cartons. The person who grabbed Carr ran up the ladder. A door opened letting the sunlight in again. Carr could now see his old friend Joe Jobson lying on a pile of boxes blood flowing from a gunshot wound in his back--- from his gun. There was the sound of footsteps from behind.

"Carr! Where the fuck are you!"

It was Barnett.

"Somebody help me," Saladin groaned.

"Carr!"Barnett shouted again. He pulled out a flashlight and trained the beam in the direction of the call for help.

"I'm over here Lieutenant," Carr said. He was confused and shaken. Barnett flashed his light on Carr then on Saladin.

"What the hell happened, Carr?"Barnett demanded.

"He shot me! What the fuck does it look like?" Saladin yelled.

Barnett walked over to him and examined the wound. He took out his handheld radio.

"Wood, Walton get in here -- fast. We're on the third floor. Bring a first aid kit if you got one and some flashlights. Start Rescue in. We got a shooting and a hospital case," Barnett barked. He put his radio on the floor, took out a handkerchief and placed it on the wound.

"Don't look too bad Saladin," Barnett said, calmly.

"Bad enough!" Saladin said, angrily.

"Joe, It wasn't me. I mean, somebody grabbed me," Carr said defensively.

"Joe? Who the fuck are you, calling me Joe?" Saladin demanded.

"It's me Mike. Mike Carr," said Carr, still sounding confused.

"Mike Carr. Mike Carr from Central?"

"Yeah, from Central."

"You no good fuckin' sonuvabitch," yelled Saladin. He was lying on his stomach. He propped himself up on his arms to face Carr in the darkness.

"Shine that light on him," Saladin ordered Barnett. Barnett turned the flashlight on Carr's face. "You knew it was me and you still shot me. Helluva way to treat your ole high school buddy."

"I'm tellin' you somebody grabbed me from behind," said Carr. "Grabbed my gunhand. It jerked. I squeezed the trigger. That's what happened."

"That's enough Carr," cautioned Barnett. "You two want to conduct a high school reunion that's fine. But keep your mouth shut about the shooting, rookie."

"Oh, so's you a rookie," Saladin said, mockingly.

Just then Wood and Walton came up the steps, preceded by the beams of their flashlights.

"Damn it's dark up here," Wood exclaimed.

"We got Rescue coming in now. They shouldn't be long," Walton said. "Who's been shot?"

Barnett gestured towards Saladin. Wood and Walton opened the First Aid kit and began attending to Saladin.

Barnett grabbed Carr and took him into the hallway. "You know I gotta take your gun and we gotta go to IAD."

"Wait," said Carr. "There's a door up in the ceiling. It must lead to the roof. Somebody went out that way. Maybe we can find him. I'll open it."

Carr climbed up the ladder and shoved open the door. Light and fresh air, both welcome additions, entered the room. Carr and Barnett climbed up on the roof. They searched the roof but couldn't find anything.

"Nobody up here," Barnett said.

"I am telling you somebody came up here," Carr insisted. "I told you I came up. I heard a noise from the ceiling. I had my gun out. It was too dark to see anything. I called out "Police Freeze" or something like that. The next thing I know somebody grabs my gunhand and the collar of my shirt, yanks me back, and the gun goes off. Whoever grabbed me ran for the ladder and the ceiling trap door."

"Did you get a look at who grabbed you?" asked Barnett.

"How!" shrieked Carr. "It was dark and he grabbed me from behind."

"Carr, you sure you just didn't lose it and shoot as soon as you heard a noise? Let's face it, you're a rookie. It's dark. The guy's a dangerous criminal, you hear a noise. It's understandable."

"No!" said Carr emphatically. "Somebody grabbed my gun."

"OK. Why don't you go outside and show Rescue the way up."

"You don't believe me, do you Lieutenant?"

"Sure, why not?" replied Barnett. "Go ahead and wait for Rescue."

Carr headed down the steps and Barnett went back into the room. Saladin was propped up on his side and Walton had placed some bandages over the wound. From what Barnett could see it wasn't serious, but he wasn't a doctor.

"Saladin, what happened?" asked Barnett.

"My old buddy there shot me, that's what happened," replied Saladin. He was smoking a cigarette.

"He said somebody grabbed him from behind,"said Barnett.

"There wasn't nobody here but me and him."

"You didn't hear or see anybody else? And nobody was in the building?" Barnett asked cynically.

"No,"said Saladin. "Don't try to cover for the dude."

"I am not covering for anybody," replied Barnett, testily.

The conversation was ended by the arrival of the Rescue team who put Saladin on a stretcher and whisked him away to Graduate Hospital three blocks away. Wood went with the Rescue vehicle. Saladin was still under arrest. His wound didn't change that. Barnett went outside and found Carr.

"I gotta take your gun, Carr," Barnett said softly. "I also gotta take you down to Internal Affairs Division."

"Yeah, I know," said Carr.

He handed Barnett his gun and went with Barnett to IAD. The investigators there would interrogate Carr and write a report. Carr would be reassigned to the Radio Room while the shooting was being investigated.

Word of the shooting had already reached the district. Leon's squad was working that evening. He talked to his cousin upon his return from IAD.

"You OK?" asked Leon, in a concerned voice.

"I guess. I mean it was tough, but I don't have any problems. Except I'm a more than a little concerned that they're gonna say I shot an unarmed guy in the back," Carr replied, worriedly. "Which is what happened except I didn't want to shoot him. Somebody grabbed me."

"The other thing that bothers me is that I knew this guy in high school. We use to be good friends."

"Really?" Leon asked, curiously.

"Yeah, we were tight. I wouldn't have even had my gun drawn if I knew it was him trying to get out of the building. But it was so fucking dark in there you couldn't see anything."

"IAD will investigate it. Meantime you're going to be reassigned to work in Radio until this thing is resolved. That's just standard procedure, so don't make anything of it," consoled Leon.

"Yeah, I know," Carr responded, gloomily. "I'm just going to finish up what I got here and go home. It's outta my control now."

"Yeah, don't worry about it. Just go home and get some sleep," Leon said. "I gotta get to work."

Carr completed his paperwork and handed it in to the Corporal. It took him only ten minutes to get home after he changed his clothes. When he arrived Stella was highly agitated.

"What happened? I got a call from my mother. Your picture was on TV. They said you shot an unarmed black guy in the back. Some civil rights leader is on TV calling for the FBI to investigate and he's gonna march on City Hall," Stella said in a voice that was two octaves higher than normal. She was near hysterical.

"I did shoot an unarmed guy," Carr said, trying to remain calm. "Funny thing is I know the guy."

"You know him?" interrupted Stella. "Why did you shoot him?"

"I was chasing him in this building. We were trying to arrest him. I chased him up some steps. It was dark. I had my gun drawn, somebody grabbed me from behind. They grabbed my gunhand and squeezed. When that happened my gun fired and he got shot."

"So it was an accident," Stella said.

"Yeah."

"That's not what the TV is saying. The guy on channel 10 is saying you did it on purpose."

"How does he know what the hell I did, or for that matter what happened?"

"I don't know, but he sounds like he does," Stella said, with a trace of foreboding. "You better do something about it before you wind up in jail."

"What the hell can I do about it?" he yelled. "The Department has to do something."

The rest of the day, and into the next, Carr received numerous phone calls from friends and relatives. Some tried to console him. Some were just idly curious. Carr repeated the story ad nauseum. By the time the *News at Eleven* came on, the story was that there were witnesses that Carr had shot Saladin while he was handcuffed and on the ground.

"Witnesses?" Carr yelled at the TV, "You idiot, we were alone in a building. A pitch black building, how could there have been witnesses? Don't you ever check the facts?"

A police department spokesperson said that the matter was under investigation and that is all they would say for the moment. The Commissioner was unavailable for comment. The Mayor issued his usual platitudes about how police brutality would not be tolerated.

The Director of Philadelphians Against Racism Today (PART), Richmond York, was ranting and raving about how the Philadelphia Police had been getting away with this sort of thing for too long and he was going to put a stop to it. He asked for the citizens of the city to help him in his efforts to end racism and brutality in the Police Department. Saladin's lawyer, Beverly Clark was also interviewed.

Carr remembered her. She wasn't nearly as sexy looking now as she was in the courtroom the day she cross-examined him. On TV she looked and sounded like an avenging crusader. She sounded like she was hunting for somebody's scalp--- his scalp.

He turned off the TV and walked down to the corner store to buy a paper. He figured he pretty much knew already how they were going to report it. Sure enough the banner headlines above the fold in the evening edition of the Herald announced:

"Unarmed Man Shot By Police"

The story, written by Neil Foster, related that the victim was an alleged drug dealer. Alleged? Carr thought incredulously.

The story stated how Saladin Christian, a man the police arrested several months ago for drug dealing and murder, was shot by Officer Michael Carr during another arrest attempt.

It went on to recount that the original charges were dropped when it was found that testimony against Saladin was coerced. The reporter speculated that this shooting may have been an act of revenge by police because Saladin eluded prosecution before. Meanwhile city officials have been silent pending an investigation of the incident. The story also related how outraged civil rights leaders are.

Carr folded the paper, tucked it under his arm and walked home. He lit a cigarette and speculated what might happen.

It was obvious that he would be charged, he thought. There is too much political pressure being brought to bear. He wondered when and if the city was going to help him or counteract some of the negative publicity. He wondered what the FOP was going to do. The question is, will they believe the truth?

Joe, or Saladin, knows that there was somebody else in the room. He must have heard and/or seen the door to the roof open. He wasn't unconscious. If he testifies that we were the only two people in the room, then there will definitely be a trial and conviction. It didn't look good. Carr took a long drag on the cigarette and then flicked the butt into the sewer before walking into his house.

Richmond was reveling in the publicity. He had been interviewed more times in the past three hours than he had been in the past three years. His phone was ringing off the hook. NBC, ABC, CBS, and Fox had all called and requested interviews. His biggest concern was to keep out any interlopers like Jesse Jackson and Al Sharpton from trying to come in here and steal the show. This was his city. Let Sharpton stay in New York, and Jackson in Chicago. Richmond York is in charge of Philadelphia.

Not only the media have been knocking on his door, but so have donors. Everybody's calling to offer money. Two people Richmond wanted to contact immediately were Beverly Clark and Neil Foster. York needed to have some pictures taken with Clark and to confer with her about the lawsuits that were certain to be filed.

He would offer her his organization's backing with all its attendant publicity to help her force the city into an out of court settlement. In exchange for his help he wanted a piece of the settlement -- in the form of a large donation of course. York figured the two of them can work out an arrangement.

But before he could bring something to Clark, Richmond wanted to make sure that Neil Foster was quoting him frequently and prominently. Being featured in the paper would increase his profile and he would get more supporters. This would create the image for Clark that he could muster a tremendous group of people--voters-- who could help her in her negotiations with the city. There was an art to all of this, Richmond thought, and he was going to be Picasso.

Neil Foster could smell a Pulitzer Prize in this story. How can the law and order conservatives explain this -- an unarmed man shot in the back by an officer. This kind of thing went out with Frank Rizzo, Foster thought derisively. This cop has got to be a real racist, knuckle dragger.

He had managed to persuade the editor to let him do a series on police shootings, in general. Foster knew the cops were becoming gun happy. Police shootings were on the rise. He felt that his series would raise the consciousness level of the politicians. Only then would the police issue stricter guidelines in use of force. Only then would these cops be in jail where they belong.

Police officers were, after all, recruited from the criminal classes, Neil Foster believed. They came from the low class, white neighborhoods of Kensington, Frankford, South Philadelphia, Tacony, and others. Neighborhoods where they burn down houses when black people move in, Foster thought contemptuously.

He searched his Rolodex for Richmond York's phone number. He checked his watch and determined that he would call York after he finished interviewing Lt. Barnett. Foster had learned that Barnett was with Officer Carr when Saladin was shot. He calculated that he would tell Barnett that he wanted the unofficial police reaction to the incident.

Foster met Barnett at a bar near Aramingo Avenue in the Port Richmond section of the city. Barnett was sitting at a table near the corner facing the door.

The bar had a dartboard to the side where Barnett was, and an electric shuffleboard game to the other. Next to the dartboard was a video machine. Foster took the seat near the video machine. He indicated to the waitress, a good-looking, middle-aged, bleached blonde, that he wanted a drink.

"Bourbon and water, and fill him up," Foster said to the waitress with a smile.

"She is very attractive," Foster remarked to Barnett as he watched her walk back to the bar.

"Yeah," grunted Barnett. "See that big, muscular, handsome guy behind the bar?"

"Yeah," replied Foster.

"That's her husband," Barnett said laconically.

Foster smiled, "I was just admiring, that's all."

"What can I do for you, Foster?" Barnett asked, impatiently.

"Lieutenant, do you mind if I call you Harry?" Foster asked politely.

"No," replied Barnett, tersely.

"Harry, what I want to do is get the police version of what happened. Not the press releases that come out of the Commissioner's office but the real deal. I feel that you guys have been treated unfairly by the media. I want you to have equal time."

Barnett arched an eyebrow and tightened his jaw, "You feel that way, huh? You want us to have equal time, huh?"

"Absolutely, I know that you're taking a big chance talking to me, so I would keep everything confidential."

"You really think the police have been getting a bad deal by the press? You're the guy who has been the lead persecutor."

"I only wrote about the information I had," Foster said. "If I had better information from the police, I could have written it differently."

"You mean the department led you to believe shooting Saladin was an act of revenge? "

"No, I didn't say that. I said that some people speculated on that."

"Oh! Did you happen to question the people who said that? Who said Saladin was shot while he was in handcuffs?" Barnett asked curiously.

"Yes I did. Two people said that," assured Foster

"Did you bother to check out their story?" asked Barnett.

"They corroborated each other. I felt it was credible," replied Foster.

"Credible, huh?" sneered Barnett. "How could it be that a shooting that took place in a room with no lights in a private building no less -- how could that be witnessed?"

"That was an error we corrected," replied Foster, obdurately.

"Yeah, you corrected it on page fifty-nine, Section Z."

"My point is," Barnett continued, "you just accepted that the police would engage in an execution of a suspected drug dealer. I remember a few years ago some black students and some white residents got into a brawl. The story came out in the paper that the white residents were hostile to the students. As it turned out, the black students initiated the confrontation. Did you write that story too?" asked Barnett, acerbically.

"No I didn't. If you remember, the reporter apologized," replied Foster.

"He should have got it correct from the beginning. How is it you people get away with being so irresponsible? Why is it that you believe cops are racist killers?"

"You mean some cops aren't racist?" Foster asked, sarcastically.

"Yeah, just like some journalists aren't," snapped Barnett.

Foster realized he was losing control of this interview. He didn't come here to get into an ideological pissing contest with this cop. He wanted to try to steer the discussion back to what happened. He wasn't sure he could. There was no sense in acting servile. Barnett was too cynical. It would be better to try to make him feel guilty.

"Journalists don't kill people," said Foster, innocuously.

"On no, what about the L.A. riots? The media doesn't have responsibility for fomenting that riot. Inflammatory commentary about racist cops and prejudicial juries. If I remember about 50 people were murdered in that riot," Barnett said, acrimoniously.

"It seems to me that the cause of the riot was that some white police officers were caught on videotape brutalizing a poor, black man," said Foster, even more acrimoniously.

"A poor, black man was violating parole by driving while drunk, which as you probably know, kills people. This was after he led police on a high-speed chase that endangered innocent lives. Why was this poor, black man on parole you may ask?

Because he tried to beat somebody with a club and take that person's money. This poor, black man was beaten because he didn't follow the orders of the police officers after he exited his car," Barnett said.

"But ..." Foster started to say.

"Now even you must admit," Barnett interrupted, "Mr. Foster, clubbing somebody to take their money is not an act of altruism."

"I don't know what precipitated that, but I do know that poverty and racism drive people to criminal acts."

"Oh really," snickered Barnett, "so black criminals are not responsible for their actions because of poverty and racism? Then what about their victims, who for the most part are also poor and black. How is it that they are not criminals? Or is it your contention that all poor, black people are criminals?"

"Of course not. Are you saying poverty doesn't cause crime?"

"Exactly, the proof of that is that most poor black people are not criminals and some rich white people are criminals. Besides are you aware that there have been scientific studies that say poverty reduces crime?"stated Barnett.

"You can't dismiss the fact that some police officers engage in racist acts that result in the arrest of innocent blacks."

"Mr. Foster, did you graduate from journalism school?" asked Barnett.

"Of course, the Columbia School of Journalism," replied Foster, proudly.

"Did you ever learn in journalism school that convicted criminals often maintain their innocence? "

Foster did not reply to the obvious sarcasm.

"Did it ever occur to you that people who are arrested might just be guilty? I'm not saying that innocent people are not falsely accused. I am also not saying that there are not racist cops. There are -- black and white. What I am saying is that a person's skin color does not make them innocent and being black does not give them absolution," asserted Barnett.

"Did it ever occur to you that some people are convicted because of their race? " asked Foster caustically.

"Maybe, but remember, the victims are usually of the same race. Besides there is another study has shown that blacks are acquitted more than whites," Barnett responded, deftly.

"There are plenty of studies that show that police falsely accuse and testify against innocent people, that those people are usually poor and black, and that all the people that are thrown in jail are in there because they are poor and black," Foster said, contemptuously.

"Workers of the world arise, you have nothing to lose but your chains," said Barnett mockingly. "A great Marxist criminogenic theory. It isn't true though."

"Mr. Foster," Barnett continued, "for all of your compassion for the great unwashed, you have somehow forgotten the true victim in all this; the victim who uses the poison sold by Saladin and his ilk; the victim who lies dying in the street from overdoses; the victim who sells her body for Saladin and his friends; the victim who cannot walk the streets at night because the neighborhood is ruled by the thugs, the users and the traffickers; the victim who doesn't have the opportunity to move to the suburbs Mr. Foster, next door to you, because he can't get jobs. He can't get jobs because businesses won't locate in a war zone — which is the best way to describe certain neighborhoods in Philadelphia."

"Business don't...."

"They are war zones," Barnett cut him off, "because the innocent working people can't walk the streets. They can't walk the streets, *Mr. Foster*, because you don't want the criminals in jail. You destroy everything, Mr. Foster. You ruin everything because you think you can pass judgment on people without knowing what their lives are like. Who the hell died and left you boss, Mr. Foster?"

Foster did not reply to Barnett's invective. He did the only thing he could do. He threw some money on the table in the amount he estimated the bill to be, pushed his chair back and left.

"Yo, Foster," called Barnett. "I'll pay for my own drinks. Since you didn't get the information you wanted you probably can't enter this on your expense account."

Barnett took the bills Foster left, rolled them up, and tossed them to him. He then took a sip of his drink got up and left.

He walked out to his car, got behind the wheel and drove to his office. Barnett wasn't sure how much good his meeting with Foster did. He knew from the beginning he would never change Foster's mind. He learned a long time ago that people like Neil Foster were too dogmatic. They believed in something and knew that it had to be the absolute truth, because people like Neil Foster felt that they knew what the absolute truth was.

The Neil Fosters of the world felt it was their purpose in life to tell everyone else the truth. Neil Foster felt no one else was enlightened enough or benevolent enough to know the truth.

While in some ways their self-righteousness was comical, in many ways the Neil Fosters of the world were dangerous, Barnett realized. They would take up any cause and lend their considerable talents to that cause. They were zealots and very often the solutions they advocated damaged society.

They poured money into social programs thinking they would stop crime. All too often, Barnett had learned, not only did their ideas not improve things, they made things worse. Of course, this didn't affect the Neil Fosters of the world because they went home to their white, upper middle-class enclaves, in the suburbs, or their *gentrified* neighborhoods in Center City, or similar affluent sections of the city.

If the Neil Fosters of the world wanted to help the poor, oppressed peoples of the nation, then maybe the Neil Fosters of the world should first live among the poor oppressed peoples of the world. Learn what their life is like instead of acting like the white missionaries in the old Tarzan movies - who are going to bring the truth to the natives who cannot help themselves.

Barnett knew that the Neil Fosters of the world were, in some ways, worse racists than anyone who ever wore a white sheet.

Chapter 19

Hank Fox had been the City Solicitor -- the attorney who represented the city in civil cases -- for two years. During those years, Fox had handled everything from a woman who sued because she twisted her ankle after tripping over a Water Department barricade, to the relatives of a man shot by a police officer. More often than not the city settled out of court. It was cheaper than going to trial.

Before Hank was an open folder that contained typewritten reports from the police department, district attorney's office, and his own office. There were also letters from Beverly Clark of Diamond, Norris, and Pike, and Richmond York of Philadelphians Against Racism Today (PART). There was also a note that Neil Foster of the Philadelphia Herald called.

He searched through the file until he found the statement given by Officer Michael Carr to the Internal Affairs Division (IAD). During the two months since the incident he had seen a steady stream of press releases, interviews, and the like.

This incident, he thought, would be tried twice -- once in criminal court and once in civil court. He would handle the civil case. It was obvious they were going to ask for major damages. Shot in the back, a supposed vendetta by the police, it all added up to major dollars. Why these damn cops act like cowboys is something I'll never understand, Fox thought while reading the summary. Shooting a guy in the back, even a sleaze like Saladin Christian, was a big-time problem.

Through the efforts of "civil rights leader" Richmond York the feds were going to convene a grand jury. More than likely, Carr would be indicted even before the city did anything.

Fox had already determined he was going to settle out of court. There was no way the city was going to win this case. According to the reports, the police had gone to the location of the shooting attempting to arrest Saladin Christian. A chopshop owner had implicated Saladin in a criminal venture. The owner said that Christian and a man named Hannibal Stevens were replating stolen cars with him. The chopshop owner said he could identify both Christian and Stevens. Stevens had denied ever hearing of Christian, and Saladin, of course, never heard of Stevens.

With only the chopshop owner's testimony, the police had a tough case as long as Stevens and Christian denied knowing one another. They needed something to corroborate the testimony of the chopshop owner. If they could somehow link Stevens and Christian together it would damage their credibility and increase the chances of a conviction. Without the link, the police did not have much of case. This would only fuel the speculation in the newspapers that the shooting was a vendetta by the police.

Hank Fox knew that such speculation had been planted by Beverly Clark, a shrewd manipulator of the media. She knew the newspapers, especially the Herald, would be willing accomplices in defaming the police. Fox also knew that Richmond York of PART was willing to do any thing he could to exploit this incident.

What it added up to was a lawyer who was willing to make a name for herself and some money besides, a newspaper that was politically opposed to the police and wanted to make a fast buck, and a civil rights leader who wanted to regain his status in the community and make a buck.

The coalescing of these forces for fame and fortune meant that the young police officer was going to be hung out to dry. There wasn't a damn thing Hank Fox could do about it. He figured to cover himself and offer to settle the suit. He would wait until after Carr was convicted before he did anything.

The photographers and cameramen were mobbing around Carr as he and his attorney came out of the Federal Courthouse Building at Sixth and Market. Carr shoved his way through the crowd and walked towards Sixth Street to where he had parked. His attorney stayed behind and spoke to the bulk of the reporters while some followed him.

Mike ignored them and they returned to his attorney. As he turned the corner to walk up Sixth, he noticed another crowd of reporters assembled around an attractive young woman, and an elderly man. His curiosity compelled him to stop.

253

He recognized the woman as Beverly Clark. She had been in the courtroom and now was holding court herself. Since the shooting, Beverly Clark had become a celebrity. Carr was amused by how much mileage she was getting out of this.

Clark and Richmond York, whom he now recognized as the man standing beside her, were quoted in the media daily. They repeated allegations against the department in general and him specifically. Their accusations were sometimes outrageous, very convincing, and always untrue. If he had not been there, he too would have believed he ruthlessly shot Joe Jobson, aka Saladin Christian.

Carr resumed walking towards his car when he heard his name being called from behind.

"Yo, Mike," called out Leon. He and Tom were walking up the street.

"Hey, were you guys in court?" asked Mike.

"Yeah, we watched the whole sordid affair," replied Tom.

"A real circus," said Leon, nodding towards the crowd around Beverly Clark and York.

"Yeah," said Carr, resignedly. "But you gotta admit that Beverly Clark is cute."

"Who?" asked Tom.

"The woman being interviewed," replied Mike. "She is the attorney for the guy I shot."

"I'm gonna take a walk over there," said Leon. "I want to hear what she's saying."

Leon walked over and in less than a minute returned with his mouth twisted in a frown. "She is filing a law suit asking for one hundred million dollars in damages."

"A hundred million dollar wound," whistled Carr. "If I would have known it was worth that much I woulda made arrangements with him in advance and split the proceeds."

Tom and Leon snickered at the comment.

"You guys want to go get a drink?" asked Mike, changing the subject.

"Yeah sure, where?" asked Tom.

"Xando's," replied Carr. "It's an outdoor cafe; Fourth and Chestnut."

ị

"Excuuuuse me," said Tom mockingly. "You do get around."

"Nah," said Carr, with a smile, "I just like walking around here. It's just down the block from Independence Hall."

"Sounds good," said Leon. "How about if we walk down? Tom and I took the subway here. Where are you parked?"

"I'm across the street," replied Mike. "I could use the walk, but I need to feed the meter first. Otherwise, I'll get a ticket and get towed."

"Yeah, you don't need that."

Mike walked across the street with Tom and Leon. After he put some quarters into the parking meter the trio, strolling leisurely through Independence Mall, walked to the café.

Since it was early afternoon, many of the office workers were on their lunch hours. They did a lot of girl watching and ordered some sandwiches.

As they ate, an attractive woman and a companion walked in and sat at an adjoining table. Carr was stunned. Beverly Clark was sitting next to him. As she took her seat, she glanced over at him, but did not indicate that she knew him.

He leaned over to Leon and Tom and in a low voice whispered, "You see this woman next to me. That's Saladin's attorney."

Tom and Leon both looked over to Beverly. They both snickered.

"We must be moving up in the world Mike," Tom said sarcastically, "we're eating in the same restaurant as a high priced attorney."

"Yeah, Mike," said Leon, in a voice sure to be overheard. "It's not often that two cops eat lunch in the same restaurant as a rich lawyer."

Leon's remark caused Beverly to look at them. She was extremely uncomfortable -- unsure as to what to say. Finally, after a pause, she nodded in greeting.

"Officer Carr," she said. She obviously felt awkward.

"Ms. Clark," Mike said, politely.

"Come Beverly," her companion said, "let's leave."

"No need for that," said Carr, reassuringly. "I'm not armed. I won't shoot you. I promise."

"Oh, well if you promise," mocked Beverly with a slight smile.

Well, whaddaya know, the lady lawyer has a sense of humor, Mike thought. She is very beautiful. She is also arrogant.

"You have my solemn vow," Mike replied with the hint of a grin.

Beverly smiled to herself and returned to her lunch.

"I would like to ask you something though Ms. Clark," Mike said. "Or can I call you Beverly?"

"Beverly will be fine."

"Why is it that you have such a concern about Joe?"

"Joe?"

"Yeah, Joe. You know Saladin."

"Oh,"said Beverly, realizing her error, "I am not use to calling him by that name."

"You should have heard what we use to call him in high school," Mike said, with the trace of a grin.

"In high school?" said Beverly, with a puzzled look.

"Yeah, we were friends at Central High here in Philly. It's near LaSalle University. Very famous alumni like Sam Dash, Noam Chomsky, Bill Cosby, and even Larry of the Three Stooges, Simon Guggenheim."

"I am familiar with the school and its storied history," Beverly remarked curtly. "Very unusual way to renew acquaintances with your former schoolmate."

"More than you'll ever know," Mike said fervidly. "So, why the big concern about Joe?"

"I don't want to discuss the case," Beverly interrupted. She was surprised to learn about Saladin's close relationship with this police officer though.

She was also surprised about how articulate this cop was. He didn't sound at all like a knuckle dragging, beer swigging, loud obnoxious brute. In fact, he looked quite the opposite, thought Beverly. She took particular note of his soft brown eyes. They were intelligent and compassionate.

"Understandable," replied Carr. " How about if I speak in generalities? Let me tell you something about Joe, or Saladin as you call him."

"Joe was the only one out of his working class family that became a criminal," Carr continued. " Why? Because Joe was always looking for the easy way to do things. He always was trying to make more money by hustling people then he could by working. All his brothers and sisters are honest, middle class people. That's why his Dad through him out and he changed his name."

"We went to an academically talented high school," Carr continued. "He could have gone on to college. He *chose* not to."

"What you say may be true," said Beverly defensively. "It still doesn't mean that he should be thrown in jail. People should be rehabilitated."

"Wait a minute. Then you're saying that you don't believe in what the National Organization for Women, and the Anti-Defamation League, or the ACLU or the NAACP believe in?"

"What do you mean?" asked Beverly.

"You say you don't think people should be jailed. Yet all those organizations believe spouse abuse, hate crimes, and police brutality should be punished by severe jail terms. Isn't that inconsistent and hypocritical?" said Carr.

"Yeah, why is it you bleeding heart liberals don't think ax murderers should be punished, but you're the first ones to yell for a cop to go to jail if he shoots somebody. Like right now, you people are trying to nail Mike to the cross. But if he were a drug dealer, who had killed hundreds of people, you'd want him let off?" chimed in Leon.

"That's absurd," sneered Beverly's companion. They still had yet to be introduced but Carr could tell by his thousand-dollar suit he was successful.

"Is it?" asked Mike. "Beverly, did you really believe that Joe was set up by the police last year? Do you really believe he was innocent of the charges?"

Beverly remained silent. Her companion, however, rose to her defense. "An attorney's job is to provide legal representation, not to sit in judgment," he declared.

"That's not what I asked," said Carr, steadfastly. "What I asked was what your beliefs are, not what your job is. It's funny, you lawyers spend a lot of time talking about why everybody else does things, yet somebody questions your motives you hide behind some doctrine or code."

"Beverly let's leave," said her companion. "It is quite obvious they are mean-spirited bigots. I can see how they can shoot innocent people."

"You want to find out how mean-spirited I am?" Leon said, menacingly. He rose from his chair and leaned over to the companion.

"Sit down Leon," Carr said.

"Vern, that was uncalled for," Beverly chided her companion.

"Yeah, Vern," said Carr with a smile, "you see, I don't make millions of dollars doing what I do. When I risk my life chasing after an armed fugitive in a dark room, I don't collect forty percent for capturing him. I get paid the same whether I get him or not. But I do my best, because I know that if I do catch him, other people will benefit. So, you have no reason to feel self-righteous."

"I think we better go," Beverly said to Vern.

"No, you and Vern stay, Ms. Clark," Carr said. "We were just leaving anyway."

Leon signaled for the check and walked to the register to pay. The other two rose from their chairs. Tom threw some money on the table for a tip.

Carr turned to look at Beverly as he walked out. She is beautiful, he thought. He had enjoyed their conversation even though they were polar opposites. He didn't get the chance too often to talk about such things, certainly not with his wife.

"Damn Mike, you put them in their place," said Tom with a grin.

"Those fuckin' liberals are all alike," added Leon, who was feeling his liquor.

"They are the self-righteous, led by the self-serving, for the benefit of the self- interested," said Carr.

After he had dropped off Tom and Leon, Mike walked into his house to find Stella sitting in front of the television munching on some potato chips. All during this ordeal Stella, to her credit, had been the loyal wife. She did everything she could do to make his tribulation as easy as possible on him.

Mike, to his credit, tried to keep her out of the limelight as much as possible. He sure as hell didn't want the talk shows having her as a guest so they could torment her.

Beverly Clark had already appeared on the local morning talk shows. It was obvious that they were gearing up their propaganda campaign so that any potential juror would have to lean towards their side. Unfortunately, neither the police department nor the FOP had planned a counter campaign.

Public relations was something the limited minds in the department and the union knew nothing about. Given the ineptitude of the department and the FOP at courting public opinion, Mike Carr knew that there was a distinct possibility that he would be tried and convicted for the shooting of Saladin Christian. The political climate was such that the there was little doubt that either the Feds, or the City, or both, were going to get him criminally. Then there would be the civil case after that, if things followed a normal progression.

Mike did not want Stella to get involved in all this. She could go on the talk show circuit. She would make a sympathetic and very true picture of the suffering wife whose husband was only doing his duty. It would probably be effective -- but he didn't want any part of it.

The best thing Stella could do for him was just what she was doing -- contending with his manic depressive mood swings and generally taking care of him. He was becoming tougher and tougher to live with as each day passed. The testimony before the Grand Jury was the worst.

"Is there something I can get you honey?" Stella purred. "How about a drink?"

"Nah, I'm not hungry either," Carr said as he sat down next to her on the couch. "I think I'll just sit down and watch TV for a while."

"How was it today?" Stella asked, innocently. "I wanted to go, but you said you didn't want me there."

"Relax, I'm glad you didn't go. The whole thing was a media circus," Mike reassured her.

"Was it that bad?"

"Yeah, these people already got their minds made up. They're just gonna go through the motions."

"Don't say that. You don't know that for a fact," blurted Stella. "In fact just this morning on one of the talk shows a law professor was on defending your right to shoot somebody."

"Really? That's a surprise. What did he say?"

"He said that police officers have the right to use deadly force to save themselves or others. If you felt your life was endangered you legally could shoot him," recited Stella. "He said it would be difficult to say that was the case since this guy was shot in the back."

"Well, that's helpful," replied Mike, sarcastically.

"I was only trying to make you feel better," Stella said.

"I know."

"Why don't you go take a nap. Don't you have to work in the radio room tonight?"

"Yeah, I wonder how much longer that's gonna be."

"Whenever it stops, it stops," Stella said.

She really did not understand what her husband meant. She did not realize that he is reassigned pending the investigation. The investigation will end when the trial starts at which time Carr will be suspended for thirty days with intent to dismiss.

"I gotta go to work too," Stella continued. "So I'm gonna make you some dinner and then go take a shower."

"Okay," Carr replied, simply.

Beverly Clark spent the remainder of the afternoon in her office doing paperwork. However, her mind always returned to Officer Mike Carr. In the few hours that had passed since she met him at the Xando cafe, her thoughts were preoccupied with him. He was not the ignorant dolt she expected.

Before she met him she had already assessed Officer Carr as some functional illiterate - who played ball with the guys on weekends and shot darts while drinking with the boys in the bar at night. A white male who hates blacks and Jews and anyone else who is different from him. The kind of guy that routinely abuses his wife.

Beverly had learned several things about Officer Carr that had surprised her. One was that he had black friends. Another was that he was articulate. Finally, she was surprised that she was attracted to him. His brown hair was soft and wavy. They complemented his brown eyes, which defined the term bedroom eyes. He had a svelte build that was perfectly proportioned to his facial features which looked more Italian than the Anglo-Saxon surname of Carr indicated.

He did not seem to be the kind of person who could shoot someone unprovoked. She mulled over what he had said. It was obvious that ideologically they were opposites. He was wrong about the legal profession. We aren't all money grubbing. Some of us are concerned about helping society.

But Officer Carr didn't seem like your average, white, working class, male. She couldn't figure out what was different about him. But he was different. Maybe it was the way he expressed himself. Maybe it was his sense of humor. She wasn't sure. One thing was for sure, he didn't seem to be a brutal racist.

She wanted to know more about him. She needed to know. But for her to find out would mean taking the unusual step of contacting him directly. She lifted her phone from the cradle and dialed her secretary.

"Give me the address of Officer Michael Carr, and get Vernon Chew on the phone."

Sometime later the firm's investigator, Vernon Chew, was on the phone.

"Vern, I want you to look into Michael Carr's background. I want you to check out his family, neighbors, friends, etc.," Beverly instructed.

"Sure," Vern replied, simply. He was curious as to why she wanted this done, but he knew better than to ask.

"When you're done let me know. And Vern, I want this done within the next two weeks."

" That's asking a lot."

" That's why you're paid well, Mr. Chew."

261

Earlier in the day, the local ABC affiliate had taped an interview with Richmond York for the 6 p.m. national broadcast. NBC scheduled him to appear on their morning show. BET was doing a series with him to be aired in two weeks. CBS was going to do a live interview tomorrow. CNN asked him to be on Crossfire and C-SPAN was going to broadcast his rally and march.

York was more than happy with the publicity he was receiving. He was excited about the march and rally, which was going to be from the spot Saladin was shot, and proceed up Broad Street to City Hall where the rally would be.

York was also happy about Foster's interview with Barnett. The article was a scathing indictment of police procedures. Foster even hinted that the lieutenant may be involved in a cover up.

Just the kind of publicity that will help the cause, Richmond thought. This is terrific, he thought, the leading journalist and largest newspaper in the city are already on side. All that needs to be done is to get them to accept PART as the organization leading the crusade against police abuse.

So far Foster had been very cooperative, indeed zealous, vindictive even.York wondered who or what might have set him off. He called Foster to thank him.

"I read your article. I must say that I thought it was terrific. Just the kind of thing we need to help the movement," York said.

"I don't write investigative articles, Reverend York, to help movements. I write them to expose corruption," Neil said, haughtily.

You write them because they sell newspapers , you holier-than-thou hypocrite, York thought. "Yes, of course. However, you don't have any objection to helping us and our cause do you?" Richmond replied, smoothly.

"Of course not," replied Foster.

"Where were you able to get the information you did?" asked Richmond.

"I have sources in the department," replied Neil. "Reverend York, I have another appointment today. I was wondering if you could get down to business."

"Yes, of course," said York. "As you probably have guessed there will be a civil suit following the criminal trial. Beverly

Clark, Saladin's attorney, will be handling the case. She normally does criminal cases only, but Saladin asked her to handle it and she is."

"Okay, what does that have to do with me?" asked Foster.

"The city will more than likely want to settle out of court. I wanted to know if you wanted to write about the proceedings."

"Possibly."

"I wanted to know also if you concur with me that a commission should be convened to begin an inquiry into this whole business of not only police brutality, but police corruption. I also think we should examine the judicial system and the prisons as well," intoned Richmond.

"That will be quite a big item to accomplish," Foster remarked as he took notes.

"A comprehensive approach is the only way to eliminate the pervasive institutional racism that pervades our legal system," Richmond knew that would make a wonderful quote.

"I will speak to my editor about this," said Foster.

"Excellent," replied York.

Beverly Clark looked at the report that Vernon had compiled. It was fairly inclusive considering the short time he had. The picture it painted was of a man who seemed to be trying to better his lot in life. He was married but no kids. He had graduated from a good high school with average grades, yet did not go on to college immediately. He had taken some courses later on. He had never been known to have any type of drug or alcohol problems. He always paid his bills on time. He lived in an inexpensive row home, in a working class section of the city. There was nothing unusual about him. His neighbors apparently liked him. He was only on the force about six months when the incident occurred.

Could he be telling the truth about the incident? Was there someone else in the room at the time that grabbed his gun? Was the shooting unintentional? Beverly pondered these possibilities as she fingered the pages of the report.

She lifted the phone and dialed the number given as Officer Carr's home. Supposing his wife answered, she thought nervously, what would she say. She couldn't just leave a message, she told herself. This was not only unusual, it could jeopardize this case and her career for that matter. Yet, she needed to know.

"Hell-o!" came the sound of a voice obviously aroused from a sound sleep.

"Mike Carr, please," Beverly said, smoothly.

"Who's calling?" the voice said, suspiciously.

"My name is Beverly Clark," Beverly replied, evenly.

There was a pregnant pause.

"Who?" the voice said with a mixture of surprise and indignation.

"Beverly Clark, Mr. Carr, Saladin's attorney. We met at Xando's a couple of weeks ago."

"How could I forget," said Carr suspiciously. "Why are you calling me?"

"I want to meet with you. Do you mind if I call you Mike?"

"Please do," Mike replied.

"I just ... well after our meeting I just felt that maybe there was more to the shooting incident than I previously thought. I wanted to talk with you once more."

"I don't think I can talk to you about the case. In fact, I don't want to talk to you about the case."

"I can certainly understand that. But that's not why I am calling you. I want to talk about you personally. Sometimes people have preconceived notions about others. It helps if those people can meet and dispel those notions."

"I'm not sure what you mean."

"Simply put, I want to follow up on some of the things we spoke about a couple of weeks ago. You said some things that really resonated with me and I want to get more of an idea about what you think."

Carr took a long time to respond. This whole thing sounded insane – and possibly illegal to him.

Why would the lawyer for a guy he shot want to talk to him? This baloney about wanting to follow up on our last conversation was probably some kind of lawyer's trick, he thought. However, maybe he could use the opportunity to find out what she was up to.

ﬁ

"Okay, but I tell you what, how about if we meet at a bar I know downtown. I go there every once and a while. If there are any snoopy reporters around they won't think it unusual if I go there."

"That will be fine. What's the name of the place?"

"The Avenue Tavern. It's on Second and Oregon. Where are you coming from?"

"My home, Society Hill, Third and Delancey."

Mike let out a long whistle, "High rent district, huh? You're gonna be slumming tonight. How about if we meet some place closer to where you live? You'll feel more comfortable."

"The Avenue Tavern will be fine. I am leaving now," Beverly replied simply.

She hung up the phone before she could get a response. This is insane she thought. Why do this? This could get you in hot water if anybody found out about it.

But what if he is innocent, she said to herself. Don't you have a moral obligation to determine the truth? However, you can't determine the truth can you? All you are really doing is meeting with a man that has piqued your curiosity somehow.

Beverly got behind the wheel, drove down Delancey to Second Street, and drove the twenty-five blocks to Oregon Avenue. She found a spot on Oregon Avenue, pulled in and went into the bar.

Mike was sitting in a corner at the far end of the bar. He was very suspicious about the whole meeting. He felt as if he were being set up. But his curiosity was aroused so he went to meet her.

He spotted Beverly as soon as she walked in.

"Ms. Clark?"

Beverly smiled, "Please call me, Beverly."

"Fine. And my name is Mike. But then you know that."

"Yes."

"Come on, let's sit down over here," Mike said cradling her elbow and directing her to a booth near the corner of the room facing the bar entrance.

His touch shocked her at first. She was a little nervous. More like a high school girl on a first date than a lawyer interviewing a potential witness.

They sat down and Mike signaled the waitress.

"Scotch and soda-- and the lady will have?" Mike said.

"White Zinfadel."

The waitress wrote the orders, then left.

"Why did you want to have this little confab? This is a bit unusual isn't it?"

"After our conversation a couple of weeks ago, I thought about some of the things you said," said Beverly. "About getting out into the real world, about finding out who the real victims are."

"Hmmph. So you want to come down from the Ivy Tower and walk among the proletariat. The patrician who wants to know the plebes. Gracchus in skirts," Mike said, sarcastically.

"Mike, I wanted to make a bona fide effort to learn a perspective about which I feel I don't know enough," Beverly said, poignantly. "I thought that maybe you could enlighten me. If you are going to ridicule me then maybe I should leave."

"No," Mike said, feeling foolish, "don't go. I'm sorry. I was being a wise guy."

Beverly looked at him. He is sensitive although he tries to conceal it, she thought.

"Fine," Beverly said, smiling, "I would really like to find out about your thoughts and feelings."

"Like what?"

"Specifically you mentioned something about the real victims. I think you said something about *bleeding hearts*," Beverly said with a wry smile. "What did you mean by that?"

She has a pretty smile, he thought listening to her. "What I meant was that *certain people* who I would characterize as *liberals* have a tendency to be more concerned about the rights and the well being of violent criminals than they do about the victims."

"I care about the victims."

"I hear all about how criminals should be rehabilitated, and how there shouldn't be capital punishment. That doesn't go along with being sympathetic to the innocent," said Mike. "Beverly, I have only been a cop for six months, but I've learned one thing -- if people knew how easy it was to get away with a crime there would be more of it."

"I don't understand."

"Listen, supposing I walked out of here, went up to the first person I saw, stuck a gun in their face and took their money. What would you think the chances are that I would be caught?"

"Well it's early, well lit , and lots of traffic. I'd say pretty good."

"Nope. Only by accident. First of all, rarely will anybody step in, especially if there is a gun involved. The other thing is, the victim is so terrorized that when it's reported the description is only flimsy at best. I'll give you an example, better yet, get yourself a police scanner and listen for those descriptions."

"I know. That's what I tried to get you to admit when I cross examined you."

"Yeah, I remember. So how are you gonna get somebody who matches the description of a million people?"

"I never quite thought of the difficulties involved," admitted Beverly.

"Most people don't," said Mike, assuredly.

"I'll tell you another thing that most people don't realize. It is what I call the Lone Ranger Syndrome."

"What's that?" asked Beverly.

"It's this belief that a police officer can shoot the gun out of a person's hand and avoid having to kill somebody, like they used to do on the old Lone Ranger TV show. My father bought the DVD's and I watched them with him. They were ridiculous. Have you ever shot a weapon?"

"No."

"I'll tell you what, we'll go shooting at the range one day. You tell me how difficult it is to shoot a small moving target, in broad daylight, while you're perfectly calm. Then you can appreciate what it would be like to do the same thing under more stressful conditions."

"I don't think I would want to do that."

"You said you wanted to learn and familiarize yourself with other things."

"I'll let you know."

"Beverly, I don't know how serious you are about what you said, but I am approaching this as if you are very serious. It has always amazed me how the so-called intelligentsia in our society are so ignorant. You live in a homogeneous part of town. Your only exposure to any other lifestyles or cultures is through books or what somebody else tells you. From that you feel qualified to render opinions and make judgments."

Beverly listened to him with rapt fascination. He was the antithesis of everything she thought he would be, of everything she expected someone like him to be. He was not the ignorant loutish brute she expected. He was intelligent. She was sure of that now. She was certain he was sensitive too.

" There is something else I would like to know. Why did you become a police officer? Why do you think others do?" Beverly asked, curiously.

"The reason I became a police officer is simple. I needed a job. I had been laid off and my wife was getting anxious about us starting a family. She didn't want to work full time, although she has since changed her mind. But she wanted to stay home and be a housewife. Me, I wanted to finish college. But I couldn't get a loan without her co-signing. Since everybody else in my family is a cop, that is my brothers and father and some cousins and friends, they were all telling her I should join. They know I didn't want to. So I became a cop -- under duress," Mike said with a wry grin.

She could see why he and Saladin had been friends. They were very similar. Both were intelligent and ambitious. They were perspicacious. They were independent minded. The difference was that Saladin was selfish, whereas Mike thought of his duty to others.

"I think other people become cops for the same reason. Some do for different reasons. There are some that like the power or the excitement. Some just want to help others," Mike said finishing his drink.

"You think there are some altruistic police officers?" Beverly asked.

"Absolutely. Let me tell you something. I hated the idea of being a cop. I wanted to get a business degree. But I have to admit that I have a feeling of accomplishment, a pride in my work that I never had in any other job before. You do more to help people in this job than any other job I can think of, except maybe a doctor," Mike said, with fervor.

ı

"But don't you feel that a lot of police officers are racist?" Beverly asked.

"No more so than accountants or doctors or *lawyers*," Mike said, simply.

"You know," Carr continued, "there is a tendency to think that because a person has graduated from college that makes them enlightened. You may be educated, but that doesn't necessarily make you enlightened."

"Beverly I grew up among blacks," Mike said, earnestly. " I went to school with blacks, Jews, Cambodians, you name the ethnic group. I've learned one thing - people are people. I don't give a damn what color a person's skin is when I arrest 'em. Most cops don't."

"But you take your average Main Line liberal," Mike said, as the liquor was kicking into gear, "he is more concerned about the criminal's skin color than he is about the victim. He thinks a black person is a victim of a white, racist society. It used to be that poor people were victims of society. That's why we idolize the Mafiosi. They're just reacting to their environment. Bullshit. They're nothing but a bunch of terrorists."

"In fact, the way the liberals think: the cops are the criminals, the criminals are the victims, and the victims are just stupid."

Beverly was amazed by his dissertation. She sipped her drink as she listened.

"I always figured that a white liberal was more dangerous to blacks than the Ku Klux Klan," Mike said.

"Really?" Beverly asked, skeptically.

"Liberals don't like imprisonment and capital punishment. This causes more crime. So, who are the people that bear the brunt of the consequences of that policy? Blacks do! That's why homicide is the leading cause of death among young black males."

Beverly was incredulous, "You think that capital punishment would stop that?"

"Sure. Execution definitely limits the chances of someone repeating a crime does it not? The recidivism rate is very low for someone who was executed."

"What about innocent people being executed?" Beverly declared.

"What about somebody being killed by someone who already was convicted for murder?" Mike replied. "The way it is now there are probably more people who have been murdered by people who should have either been in jail or executed. This leads me to another point."

"Which is?" Beverly smiled.

"When are the judges, probationary officers, parole boards, psychologists, and the rest gonna be held responsible? Every time somebody is let out of prison and kills again, the judge or parole board should be responsible," Mike postulated.

He suddenly realized he had been ranting. "You know, you got me on my soapbox," Mike said, sheepishly.

"Do you do this often?" inquired Beverly.

"Yeah, probably too much," replied Mike, returning her smile.

"Please continue I wanted to hear your position."

"Nah, I'd rather hear more about you," Mike replied.

"I wouldn't know where to start," she replied, coyly.

"How about the beginning," he replied softly.

Beverly Clark began telling her life story to him. There was something extraordinary about him. There was something about him that made her feel she could open up to him. Something that made her feel that she had known him her entire life.

Chapter 20

Stella Carr came home from work and found a note from Mike on the refrigerator. He was meeting the lawyer who represented the guy he shot. They were going to have a drink at the Avenue Tavern.

What is he crazy, she asked herself. Why would he want to meet with him? No, it wasn't a him, it was a her. Whatever, he was stupid. She would only try to trick him. He had enough problems now. Why would he do such a thing? He was always doing strange things, she thought angrily.

When Stella Moore first met Mike Carr they were seniors in high school. They both worked for the same company after school. He asked her for a date and after a courtship that lasted only a year. He asked her to marry him. They were eighteen.

Stella had fallen in love with Mike because she felt he was considerate, intelligent, and compassionate. She felt he would be a good provider and a good husband.

When they were first married, they both worked at clerical jobs for an insurance company. Mike took college courses at night -- majoring in Business Administration.

Mike was laid off soon afterwards. Stella continued to work. Mike landed another job quickly and they bought a house. It was near her mother, which made her happy. This was not unusual. Young wives usually like to live near their mother.

However, he was not crazy about the idea. He wanted a house out in the suburbs.

Where they were going to live was always a source of friction between them. Initially, she had been amenable to moving to the suburbs. However, she had second thoughts, so they settled down in South Philadelphia. They lived in a crowded, narrow, noisy street Mike detested. They lived among the relatives Mike wanted to leave behind.

But as a new bride Stella was frightened at the prospect of moving away from her friends and family. Mike understood that even though, he would routinely point out, where he wanted to live would be only a half an hour drive away.

271

However, that did not matter to Stella. She wanted to stay in her comfort zone. Mike did his duty as a husband to make his wife happy.

Stella's resistance to change was an underlying problem in their marriage. Mike wanted to get away from living in the same places and working at the same jobs everybody else did.

Stella did not. She liked the status quo. Stella Moore was not a risk taker. She did not like to take the road less traveled. Unfortunately, she did not communicate this to Mike before they married. She felt she would change him afterwards.

Stella put the note down and opened the refrigerator. She reached in and took out some leftovers and put them in the toaster oven. Can't even buy a microwave, she thought bitterly, as she turned the dial. He rarely works. When he does get a job, he doesn't like it. All he keeps talking about is finishing college.

"He wants to be a professional student," she said to herself. "He's always talking about long range plans. The hell with long range plans. He was supposed to take care of me. He was supposed to make me happy."

He was going to get a good job. We were going to have nice things, Stella thought. Now we can't even buy a microwave oven. I bet that good-looking guy who flirts with me at the bar can buy a microwave, Stella thought, wistfully. He owns a company. I bet he can buy thousands of them. What was his name, Barry? Barry Keenan. He's good looking. He owns his own company. He's funny. A woman would be lucky to land a guy like that. He's a little older than I am, she thought, about ten years or so. Irma told me he's divorced.

Stella shuddered and tried to get the thought out of her mind. The idea of cheating on her husband was not something she liked to think about, although she thought about it more and more lately. Barry did ask to take her home one night, when she worked until closing. She was tempted, but she told him no.

If only Mike would do what I tell him to do. Damn him, why did he get himself into such a mess, she asked herself. How could he do this to me? He didn't want to be a cop, but did he have to do this? He is going to lose his job. Fortunately the F.O.P. is paying the legal bills, but how will we get the benefits? I don't believe he

﹜

is doing this to me. Stella finished eating her dinner than went over her mother's house.

Mike watched Beverly as she left the bar. That is some woman, Mike thought. She is beautiful, intelligent, and personable. A guy would be very happy with her. Who knows, maybe she'll be my lawyer, he laughed to himself. He finished his drink and walked outside.

Whatever that little chat accomplished is beyond me, he thought as he got behind the wheel. If nothing else, it was a pleasant evening.

When he arrived home Stella was in the kitchen drinking coffee. He closed the door and turned on the television.

"You trying to find out if your chat with the attorney is on the news?" Stella said, sarcastically.

"No," replied Mike.

"Can you tell me what possessed you to meet with her?"

"She called me. I wanted to find out what she had in mind."

"She wants information from you? Why?"

"I don't know."

"Then what did she want?" Stella asked, impatiently.

"She wanted to find out what I thought about race and crime."

"Huh? Race and crime? "

"Yeah, that's what she said."

"It sounds like a trick to me."

"Could be. But she didn't find out anything from me."

"How do you know? Those people are treacherous."

"Because I'm not as stupid as you think I am."

"Yeah, you're so smart. That's why you got into this mess."

"What the hell does that have to do with anything?"

"Because if you had any sense, you wouldn't be in this mess," Stella shouted. "You didn't have to go up there looking for him."

"Yes I did," Mike said. "That's my job."

"Your job! You didn't want this job in the first place."

"No, I didn't. However, I did my duty. Now look what happened," Mike said. "I should never have listened to you."

"You never listen to me—that's your problem," replied Stella.

273

"No, I shoulda done what I wanted to do, which was go to college," said Mike, acrimoniously. "And as soon as I can, I'm going to college, regardless of what you say."

"Is that right?"

"Yeah!"

"Well, maybe I should go somewhere too."

"Whaddayamean by that?"

"I mean that I'm getting' tired of bein' with a loser," Stella hissed.

"Is that right?" Mike replied, angrily.

"Yeah, Ever since we been married you're always out of work. You never work steady. Then, when you finally get a job, you screw it up. Now you're gonna get fired. You may even go to jail. What am I suppose to do? We're gonna lose the house? We'll lose everything."

"I told you I didn't want this job from the beginning. I told you I wanted to go to college at night, get my degree, maybe even an advanced degree. But no -- you knew better. You always know better."

"Yeah, go to school. You want to be a professional student," Stella responded, caustically.

"You know what, I can't talk to you," said Mike, starting to leave.

"Where you going?"

"Out!"

"No, you stay, I'll go," said Stella. She quickly walked past him and went out the door.

Mike walked into the kitchen and opened the door and grabbed a beer. He reached into his pocket, took out a cigarette, lit it, and took a long drag. He leaned against the counter. This was ridiculous, he thought. For months we've been dealing about my life and my career. Obviously, her definition of marriage is for me to work and for her to stay home.

The irony of all this, Carr thought, is that for years men were told that women should go out of the home and work. However, apparently men are not allowed to stay home. Apparently, the enlightenment is only in one direction, he thought bitterly.

The idea of the husband trying to improve his career prospects, while being the homemaker, is completely foreign to her.

If she wants a divorce then fine. The hell with her. This is all bullshit. Let her marry one of those guys she meets at the bar. I'm sure they'll be terrific husbands, he thought resentfully.

Stella was standing at the waitress station at the bar. She had been venting her feelings to one of the other waitresses when Barry Keenan walked in and noticed her standing there.

Barry was captivated by Stella since their first meeting. He was divorced for five years. He owned a moderately successful company that he rebuilt after his divorce. What he wanted was somebody with whom he could have a shallow relationship, based totally on sex. He was not concerned with commitment. An affair with a married woman, especially one in her mid-twenties, would be perfect. There was an old saying that married women never tell.

"Hi, I thought you were off tonight," Barry said, as he stood next to Stella.

"Yeah, I am, but I wanted to relax a little bit. Get away from my husband for a little while," Stella said, flatly.

Barry sensed an opportunity.

"Yeah, I been there. My wife and I use to have those days. When they got to be all the time, we split up," Barry said.

"They seem to be happening more and more. Things are a lot different than they used to be."

"How old were you when you got married?"

"Nineteen. We met when we were high school seniors."

"Let's sit down," Barry suggested, gesturing towards an empty table.

The two sat down side by side. Stella could feel a certain chemistry between them. Inexplicably, she felt very comfortable with this man. She felt like he was a close friend.

"We're going through some difficulty right now. He may get fired from his job," explained Stella. She then went on to recount what had happened to her husband.

"I can understand how such a thing can strain a marriage," Barry said, sympathetically.

"It's more than that though. This has been goin' on for a while," Stella explained.

" It just seems that we don't have anything in common."

" It sounds like you two have grown apart," said Barry, in his best psychobabble.

" I think he hasn't grown up yet!" Stella replied, indignantly.

"Can I get you a drink?" Barry offered.

" Yeah, get me a Scotch."

" Sure thing," said Barry. He went to the bar and returned with two drinks.

" Sometimes getting away helps. When was the last time you went on vacation?" Barry asked, continuing the conversation.

" We haven't gone anywhere in a while," replied Stella.

" Maybe you need to get away for awhile. You sound like you're under a lot of stress. It helps to get away. Just go somewhere and relax. Have a good time," said Barry.

" Yeah, I'd love to, " said Stella, longingly.

" Yeah, I know how it is. My job has a lot of pressure. That's why I keep a place up in Vermont. I go there during the winter to ski. You ever been skiing?"

" No, but I would love to learn," smiled Stella. She placed her knee against his flirtatiously. She was a little surprised at herself for being so brazen.

Barry recognized the flirtation and responded by moving closer. He spoke in a low soft voice. He ordered another drink for the both of them. Why put off until tomorrow what you can do tonight, he thought.

Mike turned off the TV. He looked at his watch. It was four o' clock in the morning and Stella still was not home. He walked over to the door, opened it and walked onto the porch.

There was a stillness in the air. He had called over her mother's earlier and she wasn't there. The only place she could be was the bar where she worked, Mike thought. He wasn't going to go there looking for her. He figured that if he did, it would only cause an argument.

The best thing to do was just to wait for her. But the bar closed at two. Even if she stayed to help out with closing, she would have been home by now. He could walk down and see if their car was there. He realized that would be foolish. If Stella had left, the car wouldn't be there. She would either go over her mother's or a friend's house or stay in a motel.

Or she could be cheating on me, he thought, angrily. The idea of Stella cheating on him had never crossed his mind before. He always trusted her. However, lately she seemed not only distant, but also preoccupied. She seemed to have someone else on her mind. At first, Carr thought it was just the worry associated with the shooting. But it was more than that. She acted like a high school girl who finally was being noticed by the captain of the football team. She was more concerned about her appearance than he had ever known her to be.

He went back inside, grabbed a jacket, took his off-duty gun, and walked down to the bar. The streets were deserted. There was a certain tranquility at this time of night. The silence interrupted only by an occasional bus.

Within ten minutes, he was outside of Ollie's. Parked near the corner was their car. He knocked on the front and side entrance doors. She obviously wasn't inside. She left with somebody, he thought. Male or female, he wondered. What a silly question to ask, he chided himself.

He walked back to his house and sat on the front porch. The sun was beginning to rise. So this is how it goes, he thought. You take a job you didn't want in the first place, get into a jam that isn't your fault, and her first reaction is to bail out on you.

Within a couple of days I'll be fired. My wife will probably leave me. If I don't get sentenced to prison, I'll most definitely be penniless.

Mike reached inside his inner jacket pocket where he kept his gun. He pulled it out and balanced it in his hand. He placed his finger on the trigger. If she pulls up now, he thought.

Why bother, he thought. He turned the gun around and pointed at himself. He deftly placed his index finger on the trigger guard. He then moved the finger to the trigger. He lightly touched it. He moved the gun to his temple. He exerted a little more pressure on the trigger. The hammer of the gun moved slightly. One pull that's all it would take, he thought. One squeeze of the trigger and he could save the taxpayers some money. What a good citizen he would be. He could also save Stella the cost of a divorce. What a good husband he would be.

Why not do it? Everybody would be happy. Stella, the taxpayers, everybody would be better off. Of course, whoever would have to clean off the porch wouldn't be too happy, he thought, wryly.

He held the gun pointed at his temple for what seemed to be an eternity. Why not? You would never live to regret it. Nobody'll miss you. It would solve a lot of problems. Only the person who has to clean up the porch would be upset.

He lowered the gun. He couldn't do that to somebody, he said to himself morbidly. Create all that work. No, it would be too inconsiderate.

He placed the gun back in his jacket. He stood up and leaned on the brick wall of the porch. The sun was dawning casting its illuminating rays over the buildings. He noticed his car turning onto his street from Oregon Avenue.

The prodigal wife returns. I wonder what she'll have to say.

Stella parked the car and walked up onto the porch.

"You still awake?" she asked, simply.

"Yeah, I'm funny like that. When my wife walks out of the house, doesn't tell me where she's going, and doesn't come back until the following morning, I stay awake wondering what might have happened to her," Mike said sarcastically.

"I'm not a little kid. I can take care of myself," Stella replied, pointedly.

"Yeah, or maybe somebody else was taking care of you," Mike said.

"What's that mean?" Stella said, defensively.

"Who were you with until four in the morning?"

"I was with a friend."

"What's his name?"

"It's a girlfriend."

"Who?"

"Are you accusing me of having a boyfriend?"

ı

"I don't know. Do you?"

"Go to sleep."

"Answer my question."

"Leave me alone. I should have stayed out all night!"

"I wished you woulda stayed out all night! In fact, I wish you never came back. In fact, why don't you go the fuck back out. Go ahead, go back over your boyfriend's!" Mike screamed, as he walked into the house.

Stella followed him inside. Quickly, quietly, angrily she went upstairs to the bedroom. She grabbed some clothes closet and threw them into a suitcase. Marching downstairs without a word she walked out the door.

"Good!" Mike muttered. He slammed the door behind her.

"WE DEEMANNDD JUSTICE! WE DEEMANNDD that this police officer be tried, convicted, and sentenced to jail! WE DEEMANND justice! For without justice, there ain't gonna be no peace, nowhere, no time!" Richmond shouted in a sweet street patois.

The crowd was at a fever pitch. Richmond delivered a stirring speech. He enumerated the past injustices committed by the police against blacks. He incited the crowd as they marched from the scene of the shooting, to City Hall, and then to the Police Administration Building, which was a departure from their original plans.

All along the route the TV cameras followed them. The press photographers took pictures. The marchers were interviewed.

Traffic was at a standstill. When they arrived at the Police Administration Building, Richmond stood at the steps and began his stirring speech. He had his best preachers voice. He was interrupted several times by applause. It was an inspiring scene. Flanked by bodyguards, Richmond York knew that he was finally taking his place in the pantheon of the civil rights movement.

"For far too long, we have been oppressed. For far too long, we have had the chains of official repression, even after they removed the chains of steel that bound us to the plantation. TODAY AS WE STAND -- ONLY BLOCKS AWAY FROM

INDEPENDENCE HALL -- AS WE STAND NEAR THE
LIBERTY BELL, SO CALLED BECAUSE IT WAS A SYMBOL
OF LIBERATING SLAVES -- WE WILL REMOVE THESE
CHAINS ONCE AND FOR ALL!"

The crowd let out a tumultuous cheer. The applause lingered.
The crowd sang. Other speakers joined Richmond. Finally they
marched around the Police Administration Building.

The rally ended only after Richmond told them that he was
going to meet with the mayor and ensure this police officer was
prosecuted and sentenced to the maximum allowable.

Neil Foster had been with the marchers the entire rally. The
crowd had been much larger than had been expected. He
interviewed some marchers, some speakers, and did an exclusive
interview with Richmond York. The demonstration would be the
headline story above the fold for the morning paper.

Richmond York sat in the leather chair of the mayor's office.
The mayor was completing a telephone conversation with the
District Attorney. He hung up the phone and said, "Reverend
York, you will be pleased to know that the District Attorney will
prosecute the officer involved in shooting Saladin Christian. They
are notifying Internal Affairs today. Officer Carr will be
suspended for thirty days with intent to dismiss."

"Now I can go to my people and tell them that we have taken
the first step towards justice being done, Mr. Mayor," said
Richmond. "I want the DA to know that we will be following this
closely."

"I am sure they are aware of that," the Mayor said. "Let me
assure you that others will be following this too."

"Good day, Mr. Mayor," Richmond said, abruptly. He left the
office quickly.

The Mayor did not like Richmond York. Richmond had
actively campaigned against the Mayor. Richmond wanted the city
to have a black mayor.

Michael Carr received the phone call from his captain. He was to meet him at the office of Internal Affairs. There he would turn in his gun and badge. He would then go to Personnel and complete the requisite paperwork.

In less than a year since graduating the Academy, Michael Carr was fired. Fired from a job that he never intended to take. Not only fired, but charged with a crime for which he will more than likely be convicted.

As he drove to meet the captain, Carr thought about what it will be like to go to jail. NOW this was something that never entered his career plans before!

He laughed to himself despondently. He wondered what jail would be like. How long would he be there? He knew there was no way he was *not* going to jail. The case had been too politicized by now.

He pulled into the yard next to the old brick building that housed Internal Affairs. He walked up the deteriorating steps and opened an old creaky door. He told the person at the front desk who he was. A few moments later he was told to go to the second office on the left. He walked slowly over to the office. His captain and an investigator from IAD were in the room.

"Carr," said the Captain, "this is Lt. Smith. He'll take a statement from you. I have to take your badge and your gun."

Carr took his badge out of the holder he had received as a graduation present, and tossed it on the desk. He then took his gun from his holster, removed the clip, cleared the chamber, and placed it next to the badge along with the clip. He then sat down and listened to Spencer read the official statement from the Commissioner.

"Carr," said Spencer, softly, "this is unofficial, but, I want you to know that we are going to do everything we can to find that guy you said was in the room. I can't say everybody here believes you. Most think you were just a nervous rookie who shot too soon. But your captain and some others think you are telling the truth. Among those who think you're innocent are Lt. Barnett, Officers Grant, Walton, and Walker, and Sergeant Beck."

"That's good to know," Carr said, simply.

281

"But I'm not going to kid you," cautioned Spencer. "The only guy that can get you off is Saladin -- and we can't get to him."

"Thanks for the kind words, Lieutenant," said Carr, simply. "But we both know this is too political now. Even if you could pressure Saladin, it wouldn't do much good."

Spencer didn't reply. He shuffled the paper on his desk and said, "Go over to Personnel and complete the termination papers."

"OK Lieutenant. Thanks Captain," Carr said simply as he left the office.

Saladin Christian watched the rally on TV in his bedroom. He had been released from the hospital days before. His wound was not serious. But it could have been, he reminded himself. It was difficult for him to believe that Mike Carr would have shot him. He and Mike went back a long way.

They were high school buddies who were born on the same day. They use to celebrate their birthdays drinking in the alley across the street from the school. He was no racist, at least not then. Of course, people do change.

He did recall hearing someone in the room. Hannibal was supposed to be in the stockroom. It probably was Hannibal. The only question was, was he trying to help me escape or was he trying to get me killed.

Malcolm was suspicious about the manner in which Washington Paxon had made excuses not to bring him to the speakeasy that day. The warrant had to do with a replating operation. Malcolm found out that the replating was Hannibal's operation. Hannibal must have known about the warrant. Why didn't he say something about it?

Could Hannibal have used the serving of the warrant to stage a coup, Saladin wondered.

The warrant was issued on the basis of the testimony by this body shop owner -- who really worked for Hannibal. He apparently identified the both of us, Saladin calculated. If Hannibal were there when Carr came to serve the warrant, they could have arrested both of us. So to the extent that Hannibal wasn't there, that was good. If they can't tie us together then I can't get arrested -- or at least, they would have a tough time convicting me.

But if the police came to serve the warrant, and Hannibal knew it, but doesn't tell me, it's because Hannibal figures to take over the whole operation – with me, permanently, out of the way.

That's why Paxon was with Malcolm. Paxon didn't want Malcolm over the speakeasy. Hannibal goes to Washington and figures that the two of them will take over when I go to jail. But there is one problem with that, Saladin corrected himself, if I go to jail so does Hannibal.

Hannibal doesn't want me to go to jail. Hannibal wants me killed. When that happens, Hannibal can take over because the police will probably not worry about him. Hannibal has to eliminate Malcolm before he could take over. Malcolm would lead an opposing faction. That would explain why Paxon kept Malcolm home. He was probably waiting for Hannibal to come over and give him the okay and they would kill Malcolm.

If what I am thinking is true than Carr is telling the truth, Saladin thought.

Chapter 21

The Herald has gotten a lot of mileage from this case so far, thought Foster. He sat down on the sofa in his Fitler Square house and turned on the TV news. The lead story was the trial of Officer Michael Carr. Good, thought Foster, my efforts have paid off.

At least once a week for the past two months Foster wrote about police brutality. He featured the case of Officer Michael Carr, but he also dug up some other incidents. His stories were used by the networks.

Neil Foster had once again distinguished himself and brought credit to his paper. His reports on police brutality were sensational. Indeed, they were more sensational than accurate.

More importantly the stories were selling papers and he was being considered for the next vacancy on the editorial board. It had been a long time coming as far as he was concerned.

But as his career was nearing its zenith at the Herald, Foster felt that he had outgrown the paper. It was time to move on. Maybe to the New York Times or the Washington Post. Maybe Newsweek, or U.S. News and World Report. Who knows? The Mike Carr case, and the police brutality and racism in the Philadelphia Police Department, would make a great book. He could appear on all the talk shows. Maybe have his own talk show.

Foster remembered that he was suppose to call Richmond York. He reached over, grabbed the phone and dialed York's number. Richmond answered on the second ring.

"Hello," Richmond said.

"Richmond? Neil," said Foster.

"Neil, good to hear from you," Richmond said.

"I wanted to know if you heard the news. I presume the DA's office already contacted you?" Neil asked.

"No, they didn't, but I did hear the news. But that is only part of the job. We still have to make sure that he gets convicted. None of this bullshit where he gets a white jury. I want blacks on that jury."

"We've already written an editorial stating that."

"Yes, I intend to contact the District Attorney and explain to him the feelings of the African-American community. I am also contacting the U.S. Attorney to ask him how he is proceeding with his investigation," Richmond said.

"I understand that they are going to wait until the criminal procedure is completed -- which is what they normally do," said Neil.

"In the meantime," Richmond said, "I plan to make a speech tomorrow night at the African-American Workers Party meeting in Nicetown. I will say that the African-American community is satisfied with the investigation thus far, but we intend to ensure that this officer is prosecuted to the fullest extent of the law."

"Hello," Saladin answered the phone on the first ring.

"Saladin, it's Beverly."

"Yeah, what can I do for you?" Saladin asked. He recognized the distressed tone in her voice.

"Saladin, I have been thinking about your case. I don't think I can represent you," Beverly said, abruptly.

"Why is that, Beverly?" Saladin asked, calmly.

"I just can't .. I mean I don't believe... I don't think Officer Carr intentionally, or accidentally, shot you. If I don't believe in the case, then I won't take it."

"Would you care to tell me why?"

"I've spoken to Mike personally. He doesn't seem to be the type of person that would do that. I think this warrants additional investigation. Pending that, I will not represent you."

Saladin smiled to himself. *She refers to him as Mike huh? Woman's intuition or is she in love. Whatever it was, she seemed adamant. She was a good attorney. An ethical attorney. I want to keep her as my attorney. Besides, he thought, I was already coming to that conclusion.*

"Beverly, to be candid with you, I have already considered that possibility," Saladin responded. "But before you move forward on this let me call you back. I want to think about some things."

"Okay," replied Beverly, "I think I should sleep on it anyway."

"I will get back to you as soon as possible."

Saladin Christian read Richmond York's speech in the Herald. It was replete with the usual platitudes. The reporter, Neil Foster, demanded that another Simi Valley trial not take place in Philadelphia. The Herald would not allow such a thing.

I guess not, Saladin thought, between PART and the Herald, the political pressure was really on the DA. Even the FOP was not opposing the trial. That boy is going to jail, Saladin thought.

Saladin dialed the number of Malcolm Hadfield.

"Malcolm, come over here, as soon as you can," Saladin said.

"Anything wrong Saladin?" replied Hadfield, in a concerned voice.

"Yeah, I talked to my attorney yesterday. She has told me that the cop who shot me is going to jail," Saladin said. "She is not happy about the idea. If she's unhappy, I'm unhappy."

"Why wouldn't she be happy?" Malcolm asked, puzzled. "She becoming one of those people who side with the cops?"

"She isn't becoming anything, Malcolm, except in love." Saladin replied, smiling to himself. "She just doesn't think he shot me on purpose. I also think she is right. I think I was setup by Washington and Hannibal."

"Besides Mike and I go back to high school together. One Central alumnus would never shoot another," Saladin added, dryly.

"Yeah, you think those two wanted you out of the way?"

"Yup, and I think you and I should have a talk with them."

" Okay I'll have them meet us," replied Malcolm. Saladin knew what that meant. Hannibal and Washington would be taken, unexpectedly and involuntarily, to an abandoned warehouse Saladin owned. There they would be questioned and, quite possibly, cut into tiny pieces.

Beverly dialed Mike from her office. She urgently wanted to speak to him. She was now convinced of his innocence. Her conversation with Saladin had convinced her. Saladin almost expressed regret about Mike's dilemma.

"Hello," Mike answered.

286

"Mike I want to see you. I have to talk to you about something."

"Why, what's wrong?" Mike asked, bewildered.

"I don't want to say over the phone. Meet me at Xando's."

"I don't have a car. Taking a bus will take a while," Mike said.

"Okay, that'll be fine. Does your wife have the car?"

"Yeah, sort of. We split up," Mike said.

"Oh, I'm sorry to hear that," Beverly said, insincerely.

"Yeah, well it's better this way," said Mike flatly.

"Was this because of your problems?"

"Yeah, but it would have happened anyway," Mike said. "How about if we talk about it at Xando's."

"Okay, do you want me to come and get you?" Beverly asked.

"No, I'll either hop the bus or the subway. It'll give me time to think," Mike said. Maybe instead of hopping on the train I'll hop in front of it, Mike thought despondently.

Sometime later Mike sat down next to Beverly at a table at the cafe. She looked beautiful, Mike thought. She was wearing a very alluring business suit that tastefully accentuated her sensual, yet athletic, figure. Not that that mattered, she would look stunning in anything. Her hair sort of cascaded onto her shoulders. Her smile lit up a room.

How different his life would have been had he met someone like her. How different things would be had he married someone like her.

"What can I get you?" Beverly asked.

"I'll order," Mike said, signaling the waitress.

"Scotch and soda," Mike said, "and the lady will have...?"

"Vodka and tonic," Beverly informed the waitress.

"So what do you want to talk about?" Mike asked.

"I am thinking of calling a press conference and announcing that I am not going to represent Saladin Christian," Beverly said fervidly. "I am also going to say that I intend to represent you."

Mike was amazed. He could not believe what he was hearing. Why would the high-priced attorney do this? His cynical side took over. Was this a publicity move on her part? Was she using him to further her career?

No, if anything this would have a deleterious effect on her career, he thought. The politicians are intent on sending me to jail. For Beverly to announce what she intends will adversely affect her politically. She will have a lot of pressure placed on her.

"Why would you do such a thing? You're gonna jeopardize your own career," Mike said.

"Because I believe you're innocent. I can't participate in this persecution. I know you couldn't do what you've been accused of doing. What's more, I don't think Saladin thinks you did either."

"Saladin?" Mike said, surprised.

"Yes, I spoke with him. He mentioned that he has been thinking the same thing."

The waitress returned with their drinks. Beverly took out her purse to pay for the drinks. Mike grabbed the check off the tray and replaced it with some dollar bills.

"Mike, I asked you to meet me. I'll pay," Beverly protested.

"Don't worry about it," Mike said, dismissively.

"You don't have the money," Beverly insisted.

"I can pay my own way."

"What is this some kind of macho thing?"

"Do you want to talk or argue? I can argue with my wife, I don't need to come here," Mike said, angrily.

"I'm sorry. I just feel guilty that you are spending money on me. I know that there are better ways for you to spend your money," Beverly said, contritely.

"Don't worry about it," Mike replied. "Besides if you do what you say you're gonna do, you're gonna be collectin' unemployment yourself."

"I won't be unemployed."

"You're sure as hell swimming upstream on this one. A lot of powerful people already had me in Graterford prison."

"I know," replied Beverly, "that is one of the reasons I am doing what I am doing. The politics behind what is going on leads me to believe that this whole affair is sordid."

"I don't know, a sordid affair doesn't sound bad to me," Carr said with a smile.

Beverly returned his smile.

"What did you have in mind?" she asked, flirtatiously.

"Is the lady lawyer propositioning me? Is this the price I have to pay for your help. You mean I have to sell my body?" Mike said, with mock indignation.

"I didn't mean that. If that's what you think," Beverly said, her feelings obviously hurt.

" I was teasing, Beverly," Mike said, moving closer to her. " I know you're not that type of person."

" What type of person do you think I am?" she asked softly.

" A compassionate person. A sensitive person. An intelligent person. An' you ain't bad lookin' either!" Mike said with a smile.

"You think you can charm me into defending you, do you?" Beverly said. Now she was teasing.

It's funny, Carr thought, how they can joke about something this serious when Stella and he would be screaming at one another. Yet, he felt that at this point in time, if he went to jail tomorrow, meeting her made it worthwhile.

" I'll do whatever is necessary," said Mike, sensuously. He moved closer to her and placed his lips on hers. She slowly pulled away. A warm sensation of arousal sweeping over her.

"I'm sorry," Mike said.

"Don't be, I'm glad you did. I just didn't expect you to do so here and now. If the Herald had a photographer here, we would be front page," Beverly said.

"This is true," said Mike.

"I guess you'll have to marry me now," Beverly said. Immediately she knew it was the wrong thing to say. "Now, I am the one to apologize."

" No, don't. It's just that you're right . Things are moving quickly. A few months ago I'm a cop who's married. Now, I'm effectively divorced, headed for jail, and close to having an affair. This is insane."

"Come on let's leave, " Beverly said. She placed some money on the table over Mike's objections. The two of them walked to a cab stand nearby. She placed him in a cab.

"He'll tell you where to go," Beverly said to the driver and handed him some money based on what she thought the fare would be. She leaned over the window of the cab.

"Beverly, what the hell do you think you're doing?" Mike protested.

"Be quiet," Beverly said and quickly kissed him. "Wait for me to give you a call."

The cab drove off. Beverly turned and began to walk to her house a few blocks away. She was going to get in touch with the District Attorney tomorrow, but first she wanted to call Percy Norris and tell him what she planned to do. He wasn't going to be a happy camper that's for sure, she thought.

In the basement of an abandoned warehouse Hannibal Stevens and Washington Paxon sat bound and gagged in metal folding chairs. The room was dark and musty. The only illumination was from a bare, low watt bulb, in the middle of the room. There were eight other men in the room.

They had been sitting there for over two hours when Saladin arrived. He looked at them and walked over to where Malcolm was standing.

"They say anything?" asked Saladin coldly.

"No," Malcolm replied.

"They will," Saladin said. He walked over to a tool bench on the other side of the room turned on the light and sorted through the tools. They were left over from a construction crew had started to renovate the warehouse but the developer couldn't fund the job so Saladin took over.

Saladin found the old rusty saw he knew was there. He walked over to the men. He figured he would start with Paxon. Saladin suspected that Hannibal had planned to have him killed. Paxon was too stupid to come up with the scheme.

"I want to know what you were planning. All the details," Saladin said sternly. He walked in front of them with the saw. He cradled it in his arms.

"Paxon?"

"Hannibal?"

Hannibal mumbled something. Saladin motioned to have his gagged pulled down.

"We didn't plan anything Saladin," Hannibal said.

Saladin walked over to Hannibal with the saw. He gestured for two of the men to grab Hannibal's arms. Another one replaced the gag. Saladin quickly placed the saw on Hannibal's arm and in one stroke sliced the arm half off. Hannibal's muffled scream echoed in the cellar. He quickly passed out.

When he was done with Hannibal, Saladin turned to Paxon, who mumbled desperately. Saladin had his gag removed.

"Hannibal had planned for you to get arrested on the replating charge. He figured while you were in jail he was gonna take over the operation. He was gonna have me keep Malcolm in his house until you went to jail. Then we were gonna talk to Malcolm and explain the new set up," said Paxon, hoarsely.

"What was the new setup?"

"Hannibal never told me that much," Paxon said.

"He didn't?"

"No, he said that he was goin' to talk to me after you were in jail. He din't say nuthin' about killin' you. I woulda never done nuthin' like that."

"You wouldn't?"

"No Saladin, I wouldn't go along with that."

"So, you don't remember nuthin about what you two were gonna do? Nuthin at all?"

"All he said was that he was operatin' a stolen car operation for you. The owner of the shop was gonna testify against you because he saw y'all together. He would testify against you because the cops wanted you and not him anyway. He figured you was gonna get the maximum sentence and when you was in jail he was gonna take over. But nobody wuz s'pose to git kilt. Malcolm was either gonna join up or retire. That's all," Paxon pleaded.

Saladin thought about it. The story Paxon related made sense. Knowing how ambitious Hannibal is, and how cautious he is, Hannibal wouldn't tell anybody his actual plans. The idea of making the police take responsibility for the shooting was genius, Saladin thought admiringly.

Now the problem was what to do about Hannibal. If he killed him now, Saladin would surely be tried for the murder. If he let him live, Hannibal would try to kill him at a later date.

Another possibility, Saladin determined, was to turn himself in. He would admit to the replating operation and testify against Hannibal. He could arrange for Hannibal to be eliminated in prison.

The other benefit to this was to let Carr off the hook. He could testify that Hannibal was in the room and that Hannibal was trying to assassinate him. He will probably be tried for attempted murder as well. But if he did that then he would dime him out, Saladin thought. This is too convoluted. It would be easier just to get them out of town.

"Untie him," Saladin ordered, gesturing to have Paxon released. Paxon was untied and stood up.

"Get your clothes on," Saladin said. "Get your friend straightened up. Get him to the hospital."

"Sure thing Saladin," Paxon said, not quite sure what to make of it.

"You take what you have and get out of town before morning. You go to the cops, you try to take over, you won't live another sunset."

"Sure thing Saladin," Paxon said.

"Just leave town as soon as you can. You're not getting any money from me."

"Sure," Paxon couldn't believe it. This was all? Saladin's reputation of a merciful personality was well deserved. Paxon gathered up Stevens and left.

"Help him out," Saladin ordered two of the men.

They bandaged Hannibal's arm with some rags and helped him to car waiting outside, which would take him and Paxon to the hospital and leave them there.

Paxon wasn't the only one mystified by Saladin's act of benevolence. Malcolm Hadfield was dumbfounded. As soon as Paxon and Stevens were gone Malcolm expressed his astonishment.

"Of all the damn fool things I have ever seen in my life that has to be the dumbest. Don't you realize that they are going to attempt another assassination? This time they gonna be smarter about it. Next time they ain't gonna let the cops waste you they gonna do it themselves," Malcolm wailed.

"Malcolm I'm surprised at you bro'," Saladin said, soothingly. "You don't think I'm that stupid do you?"

Malcolm looked at Saladin and grinned, "You sly devil. You got sumthin planned don't you?"

"Let's just say I have examined all the options," Saladin replied. "How about you and I go back to my place. I've got some phone calls to make."

Saladin walked out of the warehouse and into his car. He was joined by Malcolm a few moments later.

"So watcha got planned?" Malcolm said as he got in the car.

"If I kill them now, the cops are gonna be on me like white on rice. Plus I got an attorney who I think is not gonna take too kindly to me executing someone. I need her on my side. Beverly is not like other attorneys. The lady is not a hired gun. She only does what she believes in, and when she does, you can keep F. Lee Bailey. On the other hand, if they disappear, then the cops can't tie me to Stevens. We'll get to the shop owner, so he won't be a problem."

"Okay, so now Stevens and Paxon are gone and you is outta jail," Hadfield said, mulling it over. "What about the white cop?"

"I don't know yet," Saladin said, pondering his possibilities. "I'll say that there might have been somebody else in the room and ask them to drop the charges. That'll get my old high school buddy and my attorney's beloved off."

"What's that to you?" asked Malcolm.

"I told you I need to keep the lady happy. She is one great attorney and I want her on my side. Besides I don't want to see the boy go to jail. He didn't do nuthin wrong."

"What's the difference? He's a white cop."

"Yeah, an old drinking buddy a mine who was doin' his job. Ain't no reason to go to jail. Us Central High boys stick together."

"If you say so Saladin," Malcolm muttered shaking his head in disbelief.

"Turn on the radio Malcolm. You're frettin' like an old lady," Saladin laughed.

Malcolm reached over turned the radio on and found the news station.

"Can't you put on some music. You must be getting' old turnin' on a news station," Saladin teased.

"Wait listen up," chided Malcolm.

"Repeating our top story," the announcer said, "KYW has just learned that tomorrow, Beverly Clark, attorney for Saladin Christian, victim of a police shooting, will announce that she will no longer represent Saladin Christian. In an unusual turn she will represent the police officer accused of the shooting, Michael Carr. This story comes from a source inside the district attorney's office. No reason has been given for this incredible change."

Saladin laughed when he heard the news.

"You think this is funny?" Malcolm asked. "That's your attorney and she doesn't even call you to let you know that she's changing sides on you. Can she do that? That ain't legal is it?"

"Be cool bro'," Saladin said calmly, "I figured she was gonna do something like this. I told you the lady ain't no hired gun. If she believes the dude is innocent she ain't gonna help jail him. In fact she's gonna try to get him off."

"You must know what you're doin', " Malcolm said. "But she shoulda told you first."

"Chill, she already told me she was thinking about it," Saladin said, "she probably tried to call me, but I haven't had my cell phone on. I haven't been home for twenty four hours. She probably left messages on my phone and machine. This story was probably leaked by some shithead in the DA's office."

When they arrived back at Saladin's house he checked his voice mail. Sure enough there was a message from Beverly asking him to give her a call. She left her pager number, as she would be in a late night meeting with Percy Norris.

"What'd I tell you," Saladin said, smugly. "I knew she would call me."

"You gonna call her?" asked Malcolm.

"I think I'll wait awhile," Saladin laughed a deep throaty laugh, "let her work up those feelings of guilt. This way she'll feel she'll owe me."

"Saladin, you are evil," Malcolm snickered.

"That's what makes me so charming," Saladin said with a smile.

ا

Beverly sat in the office of Percy Norris across the mahogany desk from Percy. He was very upset with her. He felt, very strongly, that she should have at least discussed her feelings with him before taking such a controversial move.

"Mr. Norris," Beverly said, contritely, "you have every reason to be upset with me. I should have spoken with you before I called the DA. However, Saladin Christian is my client. I have represented him in criminal cases, and he specifically requested that I represent him in this possible civil suit. Saladin and I have a very good relationship that I believe is different than the normal relationship."

"I wonder if your *special* relationship will continue given that the DA's office has leaked your recusal to the media. No doubt the subject has been broadcast in the electronic media and will appear in the late editions of the print media," Norris speculated. "Conceivably, he will hear about it from the press before he hears it from you."

"I've left him messages to call me. If he hears about it before we talk, I will explain it to him," Beverly said.

"Regardless of the specific matter," Percy continued, "the fact is that you cannot be so feckless. We cannot have such a person in this firm."

"I understand Mr. Norris," Beverly said. "If you would like, I will have my resignation on your desk in the morning."

"That's not what I want, Ms. Clark," Percy said. "What I want is for you to refrain from this type of procedure in the future. I feel that it is only proper to discuss with the partners any action on your part that will affect this firm."

"I understand, Mr. Norris," said Beverly.

"I don't think that I am requesting anything inappropriate, do you?"

"No, sir," Beverly replied.

The tone of her pager interrupted them.

"That must be Saladin now," Beverly said. "May I take this in my office?"

"Actually I would like to hear this," Percy replied. "If you get Mr. Saladin's permission."

"I'll ask him," Beverly said.

Percy Norris offered the phone to her. Beverly dialed the number. In a few moments Saladin answered.

"Ms. Clark?" Saladin said, pleasantly

"Yes, Saladin," Beverly said.

"I have heard that you do not want to represent me anymore."

"If I could, I would like to explain," Beverly said. "Also, if I could, I would like to place you on speakerphone. I am in the office of Mr. Percy Norris, the head of the firm. He would like to join our conversation."

"That'll be fine," Saladin said.

Beverly pressed the button allowing the call to be on the speaker.

"Saladin Christian, meet Percy Norris," Beverly said when Saladin was on the speaker.

"Good evening, Mr. Christian. Please call me Percy."

"Please, call me Saladin."

"So Ms. Beverly, why have I fallen out of favor with you?"

"It's not that Saladin, but after our last conversation I was convinced that you were as certain of Mike Carr's innocence as I was. I do not think that he intentionally shot you."

"Yes, go on."

"I could not, in good conscience, assist in a lawsuit against him. That is why I withdrew from the case. I also feel that there has been an orchestrated effort to have him convicted of criminal charges in the court of public opinion. I will not only *not* be a party to such a thing, but I will do everything I can to oppose it," Beverly said.

"Ms. Beverly, I can appreciate your position," Saladin interrupted. "You might like to know that I not only appreciate your position, but, I would concur with it."

Beverly was amazed. So was Percy Norris, who leaned back in his chair with a wry smile.

"Ms. Beverly, I have come by some knowledge that an associate of mine, who apparently is wanted by the police for a stolen car operation, was in the room at the time. Officer Carr was telling the truth. I was going to request that the charges be dropped."

Percy Norris shook his head and smiled at his young employee who was sitting, stunned, with her head being supported by her hand.

Beverly smiled to herself. Not only was Michael Carr off the hook, but she was as well. The only thing that remained was to reply to the media inquiries and requests for interviews that would be inundating her office.

Saladin would also have his problems. A lot of politicians were joining the chorus to have Mike convicted. They will not be too happy about his dropping the charges.

"I am pleased that you are willing to do this. I would not like to have an innocent man sent to prison," Beverly said, earnestly.

"Especially one as handsome and charming as Officer Carr, eh Ms. Beverly," Saladin said, smoothly.

Beverly blushed in front of her boss. "That is not relevant to this matter," Beverly said, unconvincingly.

"Huh, uh," replied Saladin. "Mike was quite the ladies' man at Central High."

"You know you will have to stand trial on the stolen car operation," Beverly said, changing the subject.

"I don't think that will be a problem," Saladin replied.

"They do have a witness against you," said Beverly.

"That operation was being handled by an associate of mine. It was not something I was involved with," Saladin said.

"But the owner said he could identify you. That he dealt with you directly," Beverly insisted.

"I'm not sure that's true," Saladin said. "Well Ms. Beverly, I have to go now. You will make arrangements for me and do what is necessary to have the charges dropped?"

"Yes, I will be notifying you."

"Good, and give Officer Carr my regards. Tell him we have to get together someday, drink some Thunderbird and talk about chemistry class."

"Thunderbird?" asked Beverly.

"Wine – Thunderbird wine. He'll know what I mean," laughed Saladin.

"I'll make sure I pass it on to him," said Beverly, blushing.

"Good-bye, Ms. Beverly and thanks again," said Saladin.

"Good-bye Saladin, thanks for returning my call," said Beverly, as she pressed the button turning off the speaker.

"He is quite a character, isn't he?" Percy remarked.

"Yes, they both are," said Beverly. wistfully.

"Both?"asked Percy, curiously.

"Saladin and Mike, they're very similar," said Beverly.

"Understandable," responded Percy. "They come from similar socioeconomic classes. The reason working class whites are such racists is precisely because they are similar to the blacks. Sort of a family squabble as it were."

"Is that what you believe?" asked Beverly incredulously. "You know what? Saladin is not his real name?"

"I didn't know that," replied Norris.

"Yes, Mike told me that," she continued, "it seems the father threw Saladin, or Joe, out because he did not want a criminal living in his house. Saladin's father told him to change his name because he did not want a criminal for a son, nor did he want his brothers and sisters to be associated with him. Saladin's mother and sisters would send back the money he sent them because they were the wages of crime."

" It seems everything turned out well," Percy said changing the subject. "You must have a lot of work to do now."

"Yes, I guess I better get started," sighed Beverly.

"Just remembered what I said about this type of thing in the future," admonished Norris.

"Yes, sir," Beverly replied. "Good evening Mr. Norris, thanks for your help and for being so understanding. I am very grateful."

As she walked back to her office Beverly Clark had a revelation. For the first time Beverly realized how much of an egotistical ass she has been all her life. Listening to Percy Norris pontificating, Beverly could hear herself.

She used to share his beliefs. But since she has gotten to know Mike and Saladin, her preconceived notions about black people, poor people and working class whites have changed. She no longer thought of blacks as being helpless victims. They are human beings -- no better nor worse than anyone else. The same about the working class whites. The type of people who worked for her, yet, people she never really got to know.

She laughed at her gullibility when she recalled how Saladin had sensed her prejudice and told her the tale of changing his name because of his slave past. Mike was almost hysterical laughing when she recounted the story to him.

Mike said Saladin was very creative. He told her some of the more inventive excuses Saladin used in high school to get out of class or to avoid suspension.

She also thought differently about police officers. They are not predatory beasts. They are not bullies. Neither are they heroes. They are not knights in shining in armor. They are just human beings. Some are good. Some are bad. Some abuse their power. Some do more than is expected of them. Most just do their job the best they can and go home.

Beverly lifted the phone from the cradle and dialed Mike. The phone rang several times before he answered.

"Hello," Mike answered, sleepily. She wondered if he had been drinking.

"Good morning,"Beverly said sarcastically.

"Bev?"

"Awake, awake, sweet prince,"sang Beverly.

"What's up?"

"I was just having this wonderful dream about how terribly I miss you," Beverly teased.

"Yeah, I miss you terribly, now what's up?"

"What have you been drinking?"

"Tequila."

"Saladin says you and he have to get together and drink some Thunderbird."

"Thunderbird, huh, I can't believe we use to drink that stuff," Mike said. "How did he take you droppin' the case?"

"Quite well, actually," Beverly said. "He's dropping the charges."

"He's droppin' the charges?" Mike replied in disbelief. "Why?"

"Although he didn't come out and say it, I think there was an attempted coup and you were the instrument of that coup."

"So I'm not going to trial?"

"I doubt it," Beverly said.

"I don't believe it,"Mike said coming out of his stupor.

"It's true," said Beverly.

"I gotta go out and get a drink."

"Haven't you done that already?"

"Yeah, but now I'm sobered up. I gotta start all over again," Mike said. "Care to join an incorrigible alcoholic?"

"I thought you would never ask," Beverly cooed.

"Well come on down," Mike said..

"I'll be right there," Beverly said.

Mike got up from the couch and turned on the television. He found a news broadcast. Sure enough the talking head was excitedly announcing the *exclusive* news that Saladin Christian's attorney was going to stop representing him. Mike laughed to himself. Maybe he should call a competing station and inform them that the charges are going to be dropped altogether. The hell with them, Mike thought, as he turned off the TV and went upstairs to take a shower.

By the time he was done the doorbell rang. Mike opened it thinking it was Beverly. He was surprised to find Stella there.

"I need to get a few things," Stella said tersely. She walked quickly past Mike.

"Yeah, sure," Mike said softly. He had not seen her since she left. Once he went to where she works. He started to walk in, but when he noticed that she was engaged in an intimate conversation with a handsome, older guy. He left.

He was certain that night their marriage was done. He was also certain that he wasn't the cause of their marital problems. Whatever guilt he felt about their marriage dissolving vanished that night.

Stella went through the house taking various items. There was a stillness that you could feel. Two people who had nothing to say to one another and didn't have any desire to do so. There was nothing left to say. The marriage was over. They both knew that. The only thing left to do was to divide up the property.

Maybe Beverly can recommend a good divorce lawyer.

When she finished she walked slowly towards the door where he was still standing. She held a bag with the things she was taking.

"I'll be back for the rest of the stuff later," she said bitterly.

"Yeah, sure," Mike replied.

"I hear that woman lawyer for the guy you shot is not gonna be his lawyer no more," Stella said.

"I don't know," Mike said.

"Yeah, right, you don't know," said Stella. " Has she got the hots for you?"

Mike grabbed the doorknob and slammed the door in his wife's face.

Chapter 22

He walked across the subway platform to the newsstand. The trip was going to be a long one and he wanted something to read while enroute. From the subway, he would catch the underground trolley to 22nd Street and go to his lawyer's office.

After he was done with his lawyer, he would again catch the underground trolley to 30th Street Station and take the R5 train to the Radnor station. Beverly was going to meet him there and they were going to her parent's house for dinner. This was not something he was looking forward to doing.

He promised himself that this was the last Herald he would ever buy. Considering their enthusiasm to have him in jail he wasn't going to contribute to their profitability.

The story was in banner type above the fold, "Charges Against Brutal Officer Dropped."

The writer was Neil Foster. Carr recognized that Foster's byline appeared on nearly every article about the shooting, as well as a series on police misconduct. The article recounted how Saladin changed his mind after consulting with his attorney Beverly Clark, who was recusing herself from the case.

Foster quoted civil rights leader Richmond York as being outraged and called for an investigation by the U.S. Attorney. Foster speculated that Saladin made a deal with the District Attorney's office to drop the charges against him in exchange for him dropping the charges against Carr.

The subway train pulled into the station, Carr folded the paper and tucked it under his arm as he boarded the train. He would read the sports section and leave the rest of the paper on the seat. That way someone else could use it.

Carr got off the subway, transferred to the underground trolley, and exited at 22d Street. He walked the two blocks to his lawyer's office, filled out some paperwork and left for the 30th Street Station, where he caught the next train to Radnor.

When Beverly suggested to Mike that he come to dinner at her parent's he immediately refused. She insisted and eventually made him feel guilty enough to accept.

ｉ

There were two reasons why he objected. The first was that he did not want to start playing house with another woman just yet. He wasn't even divorced - just separated. Stella was living over her mother's and he was living at the house.

The other reason was the same one that had been bothering him ever since they began dating. Beverly Clark came from a world about which he knew nothing. She was privilege and wealth. He was working class. They had little in common. Although their romance would make a good TV show - sort of a *Dharma and Greg* and *Who's the Boss* combined - it would be problematical.

This was all complicated by his personal problems of divorce and unemployment. This was not a recipe for a stable relationship. He was absolutely sure her parents would not approve.

So Mike Carr was not expecting a warm reception from Mr. and Mrs. Lee Clark III when he arrived at the Clark estate. Beverly met him at the Radnor train station driving her father's silver Rolls-Royce (one of his two cars, her mother had two more). The ride took only five minutes. Mike would have preferred it would have taken longer -- a week perhaps. He would have had more time to prepare. However, when Beverly pulled onto the grounds Carr realized that no amount of preparation would have helped him cope.

The Clark estate was a ten-bedroom French Normandy mansion, in the middle of the most beautiful five acres of ground Michael Carr had ever seen in his life. He knew that places like this existed, but he never thought he would be having dinner in a house like this.

"Geez Beverly," Mike said, flabbergasted, "I can't believe you're takin' me to dinner here."

"Oh, stop," Beverly chided," this is my house and these are my parents and I wanted you to meet them -- and I want them to meet you."

"Normally, I would need a green card to come out here," Mike said.

"Oh hush," Beverly scolded. "You're here, now be quiet."

"Yes, Miss Beverly," Mike said, obsequiously.

Beverly smiled and got out of the car. Mike walked with Beverly to the front door. He surveyed the house and the grounds around him.

" Whaddaya call this place -- South Fork?" Mike asked. "How much land do you have?"

"I think it's only about five acres," Beverly replied.

"You know, where I come from," Mike said, "you could put about a thousand houses on a lot this size."

"You tell my father that," Beverly replied, grinning. "I'm sure he will be more than happy to subdivide for you."

Carr smiled at her and together they walked into the house. Mike was even more impressed when they entered the mansion. The anteroom was all marble. There were sculptures and paintings in the hall. Mike was expecting a butler to meet them and was disappointed when one did not appear.

Who did appear was a very attractive woman. Mike estimated her to be in her mid-fifties. She walked gracefully into the entranceway. Her presence brightened up the room.

Mrs. Lee Clark III, the former Cordelia Grange, was a debutante who graced many charity balls before she met her husband. It was at an annual charity function, she was introduced to the young attorney with whom she immediately fell in love. The Grange's and the Clark's both approved of the courtship of Cordelia and Lee. Both families were descendants of men who ventured to Philadelphia with William Penn. Both families were beneficiaries of commercial and industrial fortunes created by their ancestors.

Cordelia Grange and Lee Clark married in St. Mark's Episcopal Church in Bryn Mawr. They lived with Cordelia's family in the beginning. Beverly was born there. The family moved into the Clark estate while Beverly was in high school.

"I see he didn't get lost," Cordelia Clark said with a grin. "Beverly thought you might get off at the wrong station."

"Is that right?" Mike said. "I guess she thinks I'm absent-minded. I'll have to prove to her how good I am."

"You've already done that dear," purred Beverly.
Mike blushed and Cordelia smiled.

"Don't let your father hear you say that," Cordelia cautioned.

"Yes, mother," Beverly said. "Where is Daddy?"

"In the parlor," Cordelia said. She took Carr and escorted him into the parlor. She sensed Carr's unease and gave him a little hug.

Carr smiled at this gesture. She does have a way of making someone feel welcome, doesn't she, Mike thought. It was obvious where Beverly got her charm.

They entered the parlor and Lee Clark III rose from his chair to greet them. Now Carr knew where she got her looks. Lee Clark was a tall, svelte, distinguished looking man in his mid-fifties. He had dark hair with a slight tinge of gray that just enhanced his urbane image.

"Mike, glad you could make it," said Lee, suavely.

"Thanks for inviting me," Mike replied.

"Not at all," Lee said. "Come, let's go to the bar and have a drink."

The four of them walked into a room that functioned something as a family room would. Lee went behind the bar.

"I'll have a vodka and tonic," Beverly said.

"I will as well dear," Cordelia said.

"What about you Mike, or is it Michael?"

"Either way, Mr. Clark. Whatever you feel comfortable with."

"Okay, we'll make it Mike. But you must call me Lee."

"Okay Lee, I'll have a scotch and soda."

"Good choice, will Dewar's be okay?"

"Yeah, sure."

Lee made the drinks and Mike distributed them. He took a seat next to Beverly and Lee sat down next to Cordelia.

"To just verdicts," Lee proposed.

"Yeah," Mike muttered.

"I understand you've had quite an ordeal Mike," Cordelia said.

"Ordeal is a good word to describe it," Mike said.

"I would think so," Lee said. "Being falsely accused of a crime must be a horrible experience. It is the sole reason I am against capital punishment."

"If it's not one of the worst things in the world," Mike said, "it's right up in the top ten that's for sure. Although I wouldn't want to eliminate capital punishment because of it."

"Really?" Lee asked, curiously.

305

"Yeah, I think the greater danger is letting the guilty go free. Things are just out of control right now."

"Mike, you promised you wouldn't talk politics," Beverly said.

"Beverly, please, I would like to hear what he has to say," said Lee. "He has a perspective that I do not have. At one time Mike, I was a prosecutor, and for a while a criminal defense attorney. But that was some time ago and even then I never dealt with the type of cases that you have in the inner city."

"I don't know what it was like before Lee, and I'm not a veteran cop either. But what I do know comes from what I've been told by my relatives, who are veteran cops, from growing up in the inner city, and from being a cop. That's why I say, the way things are now, the biggest concern is to protect the innocent. Do you remember the story of Saint George and the Dragon?"

"Not really, no."

"Saint George was a knight who defended those who couldn't defend themselves. In his town, he got rid of all the evil people so he went looking for other people to protect. He comes across this castle that is all charred, the land around it hasn't been farmed, there are no people in the fields, no kids running around and playing. Just a desolate place."

"The only person is this beautiful princess who tells him she is being sacrificed to this dragon. This dragon has terrified the community and steals from it. Saint George kills the dragon and pretty soon there are people in the fields, kids are playing around the castle and there is prosperity."

"I do seem to recall that now," said Lee. "So what you're saying that if you impose law and order there will be affluence."

"I just gave you the truncated version," said Mike. "But my point is there are neighborhoods in Philadelphia that are just like that castle was before the dragon was slain. In this case the dragons are the criminals. Get rid of them and those neighborhoods will be comfortable again."

"I think everybody would want that Michael, but the question is how?" said Lee. "Do you throw everybody in jail? What do you do when there are no more jails?"

"Build new ones," Mike replied simply.

"We imprison more people now than any other industrialized country in the world. Do you propose to keep throwing people into prison until everybody is in jail?"

"The only people who are going to go to jail are the people who are criminals," Carr replied. " I don't know what the other industrialized countries are doing. It would seem to me that it's not that we're locking up more people; it's that we keep letting the same people go. They're the ones who are committing the crimes. You know, one out of twelve murderers has already been convicted of a prior murder and four out of six already been convicted of a felony."

"Dinner's ready," announced Cordelia. She and Beverly had left the room when the men started talking.

"I wish you two would talk about something other than politics," complained Beverly.

"Actually Beverly, Michael was rather articulate in presenting his views on the state of the criminal justice system."

"Good, now let's present your stomach some food."

The four took their seats in the dining room. The table was set with china and silverware that Mike estimated to cost more than his house.

The dinner setting made him uncomfortable. Mike was used to eating with a spoon, fork, and knife. He did not know what to do with two spoons and two forks. Beverly noted his confusion. She discreetly helped him by indicating which utensil was to be used.

" How is everything, Michael?" Cordelia asked.

"I feel just like Julia Roberts in *Pretty Woman*," Mike said with a wink and smile to Beverly.

Cordelia's reply was a puzzled look.

"I'll explain later mother," Beverly said with a grin.

Mike had no idea what he was eating. He listened as Beverly mentioned the name of every item. He committed each item to memory for future reference.

"So Michael, what is your status with the police?" Cordelia asked.

"I should be reinstated. Hopefully I can start work in the next week or so," Mike replied between bites.

"Initially there were some protests against his reinstatement," Beverly interjected.

"Protests? From whom?" Cordelia asked, in amazement.

"The Herald, some civil rights leaders, and community groups," Beverly replied.

"Why would anybody object? There is no question of his innocence," Lee said, echoing his wife's amazement.

"The Herald and Philadelphians Against Racism Today still want to get some mileage out of this issue," Beverly said, cynically.

"You're starting to sound like me," Mike snickered. Beverly nudged him with her knee.

After dinner Beverly drove Mike back to the train station over the protests of his hosts and Beverly who wanted to drive him home.

"I don't understand why you won't let me drive you. It'll only take me a half an hour," Beverly said, as the train pulled into the station.

"Truthfully, I just feel like riding the train. I need to think," said Mike before giving her a good night kiss.

She waited until he boarded the train before leaving. She waved to him as the train departed.

It had been a long day, he thought, as he waved to her from the window. It was also a strange day. People like Mike Carr from South Philadelphia normally do not dine with the Clarks of the Mainline. He started whistling Billy Joel's " Uptown Girl."

Where was this relationship going? Beverly seemed very interested in him. What did she want from this relationship? What did her parents think about it? Sure they were nice and polite at dinner. Who knows what they said when Beverly was not around. Were they already in the process of hatching plans to break them up?

I would probably do that if I were in their shoes. I sure as hell would want my daughter to date someone she had something in common with. Somebody she can relate to instead of someone who does not know the proper silverware to use at dinner.

Not only do I need to know where this relationship is going, I need to know, perhaps more importantly, why was it going? Was

)

Beverly just feeling sorry for him? Was this some kind of Cary Grant in *Mr. Lucky* scenario? Was she just going through her 'bad boy' phase?

Then again maybe she was in love with me. I ain't that bad you know, he thought, looking at his reflection in the window of the train. She could do worse. Just because I don't have an Ivy League degree or some numbers after my name doesn't mean that I couldn't or I shouldn't. Isn't it possible that someone like her could fall in love with a guy like me? This is America, isn't it?

So many questions, so few answers, he thought wearily. Yeah, it has been one long and one very strange day.

By the time the train pulled into Mike's stop he was sound asleep.

Beverly Clark drove back to her parent's estate. She thought about Mike the entire drive.

He was different from anybody she ever knew. Some of those differences were positive. He had a set of values that she was not sure others she knew possessed. She wasn't even sure she possessed them.

He thought of others sometimes. He did not always think of himself or his career. He was not calculating like most of her peers. She did not have to guess where he was coming from. What you saw was what you got with Mike Carr.

Mr. and Mrs. Lee Clark III watched their only daughter pull into the estate after she returned from taking her new friend to the train station.

"Do you think she is serious about this – this *police officer*?" Cordelia asked her husband.

"You know as well as I do, dear, that when it comes to Beverly anything is possible. She has always been a little strange," replied Lee as he relit his pipe. "You do remember how she looked when she brought home that stray kitten?"

"What stray kitten? " Cordelia responded. "Ohh, I remember now. She stayed with it for days. Kept it in her room. Nursed it."

309

"Yes, that is the one. Do you remember how she looked whenever she was near it? That is the same way she looks when she is around Officer Carr."

"No, you can't be serious Lee."

"Quite serious."

"He is not a kitten. He is a human being."

"A human being who needs help. Our Beverly is a very nurturing person."

"This Michael is so -- so bourgeoisie, He is not even that -- he is petite bourgeoisie."

"He is someone who has suffered a grave injustice."

"Not only is he petite bourgeoisie," Cordelia continued, "he is still married - albeit separated – from his wife. He could return to her at any time."

"I'm sure that Beverly knows this, Cordelia."

"Then why is she seeing him?"

"Remember the kitten Cordelia. You keep forgetting about how your daughter feels about those who are unfortunate souls. Besides if you recall, she dated one of her peers many years ago. That did not have so fortunate an ending, now did it?"

"Not everyone she meets will be like he was. There are plenty of available men, attractive men, from good families she can meet."

"Do you have anyone in mind Cordelia?" Lee asked with a devious tone.

"Yes, I do as a matter of fact," Cordelia replied.

"Someone I know?" Lee asked

"Yes you know him - or at least you know his father. Digby Sheridan, you know his father, Corlies."

"Of course, Corlies. Investment banker. Digby is a broker of some sort."

"Yes and he is doing quite well. He has his own jet, a place in Bermuda, and a chalet in Utah. Quite handsome too."

"You know this how?"

"His mother is a member of the DAR. I see her at the meetings. She is always talking about him. One day he stopped by."

"How do you propose for them to meet?"

"I was thinking. The next time you and Beverly go golfing, ask Digby and his father to meet you there."

"Absolutely not. I have not spoken with the man in years. I will not now - just to introduce his son to my daughter. You know his mother - arrange something."

"I'll just have to have his mother to tea and tell her what I would like to do. I'm sure she will not have any objections. She thinks Beverly is darling. I am sure she would appreciate Digby meeting such a fine woman as Beverly."

"Yes and you would appreciate Beverly meeting such a fine young man as Digby."

"Yes and why not. He is the type of person Beverly should be dating. Not some policeman from a poor section of Philadelphia. Whoever heard of such a thing? They have nothing in common."

"If she rejects Digby, or Digby her, what are your plans then?"

"She won't reject him nor he her. They are very compatible."

"It is not always a question of compatibility. It is a question of availability. Currently our Beverly is not available. She is preoccupied with her – bourgeoisie - isn't that what you called him - friend. She will not be interested in anyone else right now."

"She'll be interested. I know my own daughter."

York read Foster's story about Mike Carr's reinstatement. He had tried to keep him suspended, but the Commissioner and the Mayor no longer wanted to discuss it. As far as they were concerned, Saladin's statement proved Carr's innocence and that was it.

Richmond did not want to damage his relationship with the Mayor. PART was a highly regarded organization now and contributions were flowing into the treasury. It was best not to be perceived as too far out of the mainstream. If he made too many outrageous demands, he would alienate certain people. People who were powerful.

Politicians, journalists, business leaders, and community activists were all part of his constituency. Keeping them all happy required him to do a balancing act. A very dangerous balancing act. One slip he would be consigned to history's dustbin.

"If it weren't for Saladin, this story would have been in the news for months. We could have used this incident at every fund raising function. People would be digging in their pockets every time the name Saladin would be mentioned. Damn him," Richmond muttered to no one in particular.

Saladin will get his. Guys like him always do. They think they're so tough and so smart that they can do what they want to do. There will be a time when Mr. Saladin Christian will need him. He will need Richmond York because Richmond York can open doors for Saladin and he can close doors for Saladin.

He will get jammed up for some reason and he will need him for help. Guys like him always do. Then that is when he will repay Saladin Christian. He will not return his phone calls. He will refuse to meet with him.

Let him get his white cop buddy to help him or his fancy, white bread woman attorney. Wonder how much good they will do for him. Let him get one of his girlfriends to help him.

No sir, when Saladin Christian comes with his hat in his hand Richmond York is not going to be there. Saladin will learn that he needs to cooperate with people if he is going to advance in life.

York closed the paper after reading Foster's article about Carr. Still, he pondered, it is good that an innocent man did not go to jail – even if it were a white cop. There are plenty of them out there who ain't innocent and there will be plenty of other opportunities to protest, he thought as he folded the paper and placed it in the wastepaper basket next to his desk.

He next turned to his appointment calendar that served as a desk pad. There were several this week including the Mayor, Police Commissioner, the Democratic City Committee Chairman – always fun meeting with him - and four community activist groups.

One wanted more housing funds for the black community. One wanted more funding for art murals in the black community. One wanted more city contracts for black firms. One wanted him to judge an essay contest.

An essay contest, Richmond said to himself. Now that would be fun. He recalled he used to participate quite a bit in those things in college.

He wanted to meet with the School Board president. There were some ideas he wanted to share about increasing attendance in some high schools in black neighborhoods. He also was getting some complaints from some black teachers who were being transferred.

He had a busy week scheduled. It felt good for him to be busy again. For a long time he was in the civil rights equivalent of Siberia. Now he mattered once more. Now people took his phone calls instead of a avoiding him, he thought smugly.

He started to buzz his secretary when she buzzed him instead. York answered using the speaker phone.

"Reverend York, the Chairman of the Board of Manayunk Containers is on line one,"she said.

"Fine," replied York, as he lifted the receiver from the cradle, "Howard, I'm glad you called. I wanted to find out what time we tee off at Whitemarsh."

Malcolm Hadfield entered Saladin's office in the rear of the Bainbridge speakeasy. Saladin rose from his behind his desk and walked over to an industrial size vacuum cleaner in the middle of the room. Saladin turned on the vacuum and motioned for Malcolm to join him near it.

"Just in case the cops got bugs planted in the room," Saladin said to Malcolm.

Malcolm nodded his head.

"You take care of our associates?" Saladin asked.

"Yeah," replied Malcolm with a grin, "they collected their reward."

" Good, there is no doubt about it. They wanted me dead. They just didn't want me arrested. Some cops I know said they spread the word that I would never be taken alive. That I would shoot it out with the cops."

" It don't matter what they said anymore 'cause they don't matter and never will. I figure after they find the bodies it will take a few weeks for the cops to identify them."

"Good," replied Saladin. " What about the guy who did the replating? The guy who was gonna testify against me."

"We showed him some photos of his buddies after we got done with them. Then we gave him a plane ticket outta town. He took it – fast. I don't think the sucka bothered to pack."

"Alright then," Saladin said. "Now let's go back to Germantown. I need to check on the recipts."

"You know Richmond York is mad at you," cautioned Malcolm.

"Yeah, so what," Saladin replied laconically. "He just a little fish in a small pond right now, who thinks he is the Kingfish. He makes any trouble for me I'll disabuse him of that notion right quick."

Neil Foster finished clearing out his desk. He labeled the cartons and waited for Otto to help carry them to his car.

His recent series about corruption in the Philadelphia city govenment earned him accolades from his peers. It also earned him some national notice.

Time and Newsweek both used his pieces. They were part of a general series about municipal corruption that Time was doing and about corruption in the Democratic Party machines that ran big city politics in the United States that Newsweek was doing.

TV also came calling. His interviews with MSNBC were well received. So much so that MSNBC made him a proposal.

He was already considering a counterproposal by the paper to the Time and Newsweek offers. He might have stayed. Then came the call from the network.

The NBC offer was lucrative. The money, the perks, and the opportunity for media exposure was everything he could ask for in an assignment.

The owner of the paper was gracious about it. "Obviously we cannot compete with a network like NBC, Neil. I guess in a way we are a victim of our own success," he said.

" Well sir, I have enjoyed my years here and - yes, you were very much a part of the reason for my success," he replied just as graciously.

The two parted company amicably. Foster remembering the maxim about never burning your bridges. NBC would be precarious. The highway making the transition from print to electronic media was littered with more than one journalist's career.

Otto walked in the office, "Is that every thing?" he asked.

"That's it," replied Foster. Each grabbed one of the remaining cartons and carried them to the elevator.

"You know Neil, you got a great face for radio," said Otto with a smile. "You should go far in New York."

Neil just smiled. They got off the elevator and walked to his car and loaded the cartons in the trunk.

"Stay in touch, Neil," Otto said.

"Sure thing," Neil said.

Mike Carr found his old locker and began placing his gear into it. The Civil Service Commission had approved his return with full back pay two weeks earlier. Today would be his first day back to work. His first tour was daywork, which was fine by him. He would need to get used to the rotating shift schedule.

"Yo, rookie, you back to stay this time?" Darnell Walton yelled across the locker room.

"I didn't plan to leave the first time," Mike replied. "And I'm not a rookie anymore."

"You're always gonna be a rookie to me Carr," Walton replied. "Beck got us working together today on 1705."

"Fine with me," Carr replied. "You drive."

During roll call Mike received the acknowledgments of the rest of his squad. Nearly everybody welcomed him back. They even had a little cake for him in the squadroom. Afterwards, Beck called over to Walton and Carr.

"There's a couple of 5292's in the subway at the end of the Ellsworth-Federal Streets subway station. Homicide's already been there. It looks like it's mob related. I need you to transport them to the coroner's office," Beck said.

"Great way to start the morning," Carr said, smiling.

"Welcome back, Carr," Beck said, with a grin.

As Walton and Carr walked to the van and prepared to begin duty, Grant drove passed and yelled, "Good have to you back Carr."

Carr waved at him and yelled, "It's good to be back.".

The following day, on the fifth page of the City section of the Herald, was a one column story about two men found dead near the platform of the Broad and Ellsworth subway station. The police said that they believed the men to be homicide victims.

The Herald published the names of the two victims. They were identified as Hannibal Stevens, 30 years old and Washington Paxon, 25 years old. Both were from the West Oak Lane section of Philadelphia. Both were known to have extensive criminal records.

There were no suspects in the slayings.

Michael P. Tremoglie is currently a writer for The (Philadelphia) Evening Bulletin and a columnist for FrontPage magazine. His work has regularly appeared in publications such as the Philadelphia Inquirer, Philadelphia Daily News, Human Events, Pittsburgh Tribune-Review, the Lansdale Reporter, Delaware County Daily Times, and Insight magazine, among others.

A former Philadelphia cop and managed care executive, he has a Bachelor's degree in Accounting, and a Master's degree in Criminal Justice, both from Saint Joseph's University, Philadelphia. His writing reveals his direct experience in many of the important issues of the day - whether it is law enforcement, managed care, single parenting, or welfare reform.

He has been invited to appear on TV and radio programs like the Donahue Show, Fox News Channel's Special Report, the Chris Core Show (WMAL 630 AM Washington DC), Philadelphia's Dom G. (WPHT 1210 AM), and Sam Greenfield and Felipe Luciano Show (WWRL 1600 AM New York City).

Mike has also contributed articles to Men's News Daily, Intellectualconservative.com, Accuracy in Academia, and Accuracy in Media. Websites such as Rush Limbaugh.com, Michelle Malkin.com, Free Republic.com, John Jay Ray.com, Sean Hannity.com, Howard Stern.com, Glenn Sacks, KKLA-AM (Los Angeles), KSKY -AM (Dallas), Townhall.com, the History News Network, Second Amendment Police Department, Jewish World Review, the Club for Growth, Swift Boat Veterans for Truth, and LaShawn Barber have all reprinted his articles.